GERARD ST. GEORGE

THE RED WATERS OF LIFE

The Hidden Chronicles of Gorra Bois

WORKBOOK PRESS LLC
187 E Warm Springs Rd,
Suite B285, Las Vegas, NV 89119, USA

Website: https://workbookpress.com/
Hotline: 1-888-818-4856
Email: admin@workbookpress.com

Ordering Information:
Quantity sales. Special discounts are available on quantity purchases by corporations, associations, and others.
For details, contact the publisher at the address above.

Library of Congress Control Number:
ISBN-13:   000-0-000000-00-0 (Paperback Version)
               000-0-000000-00-0 (Digital Version)

REV. DATE: 24/11/2020

In all my life, never would I have thought the day would come, when I would fear the embrace of the sun. My mystical life giving sun, it seems just like yesterday, walking in her grace. I, the one who walked confidently in the sun's rays of hope and love knowing it would never harm me. Needless to say, now it takes great comfort in being my death. Yes, the one whom once waited for her beams of love in total peace and commitment, but that would be suicide for me now.

As if death would have any real meaning, I have come only to know the experience of the shadows and tender shades, walking on the currents of night's breath. (Damn, I want some crackling bread. I long for that bread my gram' once made on every Sunday noon.) Instead of feeding on the endless sorrow of the victim's blood, that through me death has claimed. It is true that all creatures living and undead must hunt for their survival. This lesson I had to learn the hard way and was cheated by fate from teaching the ones I had made. What you are hearing may seem crazy, but have no doubt that this truly is a prison without walls. A hell of everyone's making. Such a logical end to all this madness… Is this not the normal way of all living things? I will never forget when I became cursed by death's kiss and life's embrace.... If only I knew then what life has shown me now! If only death was as kind on me as it has been to those whom through me were brought over. A life no human really is prepared for, but must learn to cope with never the less.

You know, like the Devil telling souls they are damned after they have already arrived into Hell... Ha, ha, ha… Let me stop wilding and tell this story for which brought you here today

I am a Master Vampire, Xavier. My birth name holds no real importance to this story. Besides, I would rather have you wonder if this story may be true or just the madness of one man's mind. I am blind to the eyes of your kind and even those, whom have seen me, have no real idea what they are looking at. I attract them to me just as I did you. We all receive this gift from what I call the black kiss. For some time I found it hard to believe, so much has happened to me. I once believed that the greatest thing that would happen to me was graduating from college. I must admit, that going to college was just as great. I loved the dorms, classes, study hall and the parties. Boy, did I love those days. I was a handsome young black man, if I do say so myself. Most women love my brown, deep-set eyes. They loved my long, black curly hair even more. My curly hair, however, made me seem to be a god in their eyes. The bad thing about all of it was that my hair was wild, because I really didn't comb it. I would like to say that my body was one to die for, but the fact is... I was and still am a tall thin frame male with a light-skinned complexion. To be six foot only seemed to add to my beauty and grace. I was truly a "Mack daddy"! Ha! Ha, the things I would say! The way women would lose themselves in my beauty was just sinful. Girls would live on my words as if I was giving them drugs. They would even try to get guilt or jealousy from me when I would end our relationships. I remember how women who take me back to their spots under the excuse that we were going to talk. We spoke for some time and usually we would end up kissing, O' how I loved their soft moist lips. We started to lose ourselves in each other's lust and in time, I would be making love to them for hours, trying to carry them to a higher level of ecstasy or until I climaxed first. I would try to continue but then it would occur to me that what we were doing was so wrong, George called me a prick for my behavior but the truth is they would have only blamed me for their actions as if I tricked them.   Anyway, I second-guessed myself all through school... I tried to figure out the meaning to everything around me. In some ways, I felt blessed because of all the people I came to know, in fact, came to depend on!

I look back now and realize that I was lucky to have the friends I had back then. The way we debated about almost every human behavior. George made it a point to bring events before us and watch us argue about it. Most of the time, we would figure it out the behavior of that person and the outcome of their actions. I truly miss my friends. I would give anything to have them here right now. To see the world through their eyes, I wish I could hear the rage in their voices as I used too when we fought with one another. Even to hear the voice of the one who held us together. I will call him George so to protect his family and know this… I will do the same for all of my friends. Whom I long to hear their voices right now, for they had always given my twisted soul peace. Now, Landis (I called him the great mind of minds) always forced me to find peace in myself. He always was the one who felt he had to look out for everyone's well-being. Landis never really wanted to depend on George and felt neither should the rest of us. Then there is Marco and Drew... They both shared the title of best friend and my roommate. They seemed to fill in the role of my father, whether I wanted them to or not. Drew was the laid-back type of guy. He would not read too deep into anything. He pretty much would just deal with a problem as soon as it would arrive. Marco, however, was the type of dude that would just laugh off things that he felt was not too deep, but if you pushed him, he would come out full force. Marco was truly a cold dude when he had to be. OK, now! Next to George, I would have to say Garrett is the wisest out of the rest of us. Then there is George's other children, who I got to know through him. Though he has taken too many, the only two I came to bond with were Zack and Vinnie. George often told us that people fell into one out of three human nature types. They were light, dark or chaos. Zack and I debated often rather Garrett or George was the smartest. They both seemed to understand these three levels and both was very good at figuring out people's intent. Vinnie, however, was never in our debates, because he was loyal to George to a fault. I still recall the fights we had over his blind trust in George. Not everyone else besides Casper, Marco, Drew and even Landis really gave a shit rather George really looked out for us or not. I guess I would have to say that I would not want to change anything I have lived through, but boy I wish I could change everything that happened after we died.

Now Peter was a very good friend of mine who went to our school as well. Though he had very little interaction with the rest of the guys; he and George had a strange bond. I would have never known they even knew each other. However, to my surprise he too was one of George children. I eventually betrayed his friendship as well, by loving Elizabeth. Peter will not forgive me for what I did to him and our friendship, which had nothing to do with everyone else's. He usually tried to understand my situation before making judgment, but this time he allowed his rage to blind him and cut me out of his life. His hatred towards Elizabeth out weighted everyone else's. He was very closed-minded when it came to her and me. He would have killed her if given the chance. I just could not get him or the others to see her the way I did. To understand what she did for me. It is true that she betrayed me in the end just like the others but her love for me cannot be questioned. I still can picture her as if it was just yesterday. Elizabeth has the most perfectly shaped lips and reddish long soft curly hair. Though she stood about 5 foot six she had the frame of a dancer. Her grace drew attention towards her whenever she entered a room. I did love my friends and respect their opinions, but I also loved Elizabeth. To this day, I am forced to ask, "Why I could not have them both!" Perhaps only God knows....(smiling) or prehaps maybe George! The choice between the two was really too much, as time came to show me. A bond I come to miss. George must have decided this to be my fate. A world without my love or my surport. Forcing me to accept a new degrees of awareness I had to find within myself. I learned to love the freedom of my mind. The behavior of many natures trapped in one ideal place. I am still unable to control the different levels of my mind's growth. (I am wilding.) The truth is I am not the man I once was and really have no idea how to return to my former self. I guess in a way, if I did find a way to return to that former state of being, I would not take it. I would never allow fate to destroy Elizabeth's memories and my love. Because of her, I see the world through colder eyes now. The innocence I once had is truly dead... If I could still cry, this would be a reason for such an event. Is there any other death in life that could take so much and allow you to live within its effects...? Maybe it is true that in death everyone will be alone until the day that God pulls us all before Him. Many years have passed since the last time we all spoke. Who was the reason for us not speaking...? It would not be fair for me to guess, so I really will not say. All I will say is that I have lost so much in these past few years. Their absence falls so heavy on my mind and soul. I guess I am writing now in hopes that one of them will read this and decide to search me out. I fear deep within my heart that this will not come to be, but I have to try before I give into this fate. I have tried to reach them through my mind and discovered nothing; it is as if the world has swallowed them all. I fear George has demanded them to abandon me. Since he refuses to overlook the love I feel for Elizabeth. George was blinded with rage since I chose Elizabeth over them. You would think that he out of anyone would understand what love would make a man do. If only I knew then that the last night I saw Elizabeth would be the last night I would see them all. I would have done things so differently... I have to admit. I forced their hands. I gave no one a choice in what had to be done.

On the evening I arose from my long sleep, I awoke in a dark, cold and damp chamber or prehaps a tomb. Never the less i felt something in my mouth so I spit it out and tried to study my surroundings as my eyes became adjusted to the darkness around me. It wasn't long before I picked up the smell of death around me. I was unable to remember much at that moment. I couldn't remember how I got here or what happened to cause this. As I layed their my eyes began to see the walls of my prison. It appeared that I was in a prison of stone. I looked around and realized I was in a basement of some kind. As I sat up I discovered that i was sitting on a table of some kind along the sides of the table their were many dead rats. As I thought about it I asumed that the poor things must have tried to feed on me and in turn gave their lives towards my resurrection. I rose from the table and made my way upstairs to see where I was. Once I exited the basement I realized I was in Elizabeth's home. Elizabeth was not to be found. I was so lost and confused. I walked from the basement into a very close and empty house. No one was there. It was as if she decided to move on without me for some reason. I retreated to Landis's apartment, but it became obvious that he no longer resided there. It looked as if the whole building was remodeled. As my anxiety attempted to claim my heart. I decided to rushed home, for surely Marco and Drew would be capable to explain what was happening. I was lost and truly confused. I decided to wait until the next night and see if anyone from the school seen or heard from George or Garrett, but to no comfort. My mind started to race and only bad thoughts took control. I feared that maybe Elizabeth had planned their demise before she meant her fate. Perhaps she feared I would not forgive her. One thing this new life has shown me is to choose my battles carefully and to learn to forgive even faster. I walked the street for endless nights and could not find anyone, neither my friends nor my sweet Elizabeth. I miss her most of all. I realize that they would not then and maybe even now understand the power she and I shared. I truly loved her and wished they would have the compassion to try to understand that. I have searched the city and the state for them, but I fear they are alive and have seen me. I fear that I cannot find them for they wish not to be found. I cannot really blame them… I guess I have to leave it up to you, the reader. Maybe someone out there is hiding them and if so, then I have to pray that you will read this book. I hope that I will gain your compassion and your help. Then after you read this and see things my way, maybe you will try to help me find them or force them to read it. Here is my story and I hope it will move you enough to allow you to help me find my friends if they are still alive. I know you are thinking that I have showed no signs of an immortal and you are right. However, then you would have to ask yourself... When was the last time you seen a human that looked like me. Read on!

Chapter 1
The Immortal Sin...

It began in the Old City part of Philadelphia! It was Monday, June 09, 1997. It was a warm breezy night, the kind of night one would not mind staying in its embrace as long as possible. The sky was full of stars and the moon was shining like never before, at least in my mind. I was returning home from a movie at the old theater house on the corner of Second and Walnut. (I do not recall the movie.) Well, I was walking along Walnut Street noticing the buildings in the Old City area. I loved the way those buildings were constructed and the way they looked. It would seem as if I was carried away through the realms of time. I would become a part of that forgotten era that we all need to remember. Well, maybe I should not say everyone... I mean; I can understand why some of my people have a problem with the slave thing. I myself never thought about that when I looked upon the buildings. All I saw was the great artwork done on these buildings. I am sure I am not the only person that loves the feeling of that old era, but I would like to believe I am the only one willing to watch it for hours. Did you know that many of the buildings of that time were constructed with all kinds of unique forms in their structure! I would study the buildings and its hidden artworks that many of the bricks once held and time stole from them. The gargoyles that once were believed to run evil away from the hidden walls of their time. Back in a time, when people believed witches and demons walked the streets of Philadelphia. I would study these buildings until I would scare myself. Until I could see the gargoyles in the building start to move. I would look onto the lion heads and the pit bull faced gargoyles that would sit on the side of the building and wish I could see them moving in the streets. I know this isn't unusual, but it was odd.

Usually at this point, I realized I needed to pay attention to where I was going. Then again, I never really watched where I went. The problem had always been that I never really was a time-based person, so I usually just traveled without really worrying about time or my surroundings. I guess you could say I always walked in a dream state... Well, anyway! As I walked up Walnut Street on this day, the sky seemed to become dry and the air refused to give me comfort from what then became a hot summer night. I walked towards Fifth Street and was studying all the building of a more recent past. Just then, a strange feeling came over me and I felt as if someone was following me. I stopped and looked around, but saw no one. I continued to walk, but the feeling got stronger and the desire to run entered my mind, so I decided to reach Fifth St. and turn onto it. I turned the corner and continued to walk down Fifth Street towards Spruce St.

Then I had seen this man standing in front of me. He stood about halfway up the block. I heard him calling to me, but I ignored him. I continued to walk towards him, but with caution. Something in me told me to pay attention, because I really did not feel like being bothered with this homeless dude. I realized that the block was longer than usual. I stopped and looked towards the man in front of me for a second. The dude was standing in front of what looked like the back wall of a graveyard. He stood there in such dirty clothes and yet he seemed to stand with such pride that it was intimidating. He had such long hair and the mud only hid it from my sight. I could not fully take my eyes off him at first, but decided to continue. I looked around the street to see what my options were. The only choice I saw that I had was a street that looked like an alley, but I think it was really Locust St. So I quickly decided to cross the street and go up this alley. Even though I walked across the street, I was still uneasy at what I saw. Since I still was not at the alley of my escape, I turned my eyes towards him to study his behavior. His eyes seemed too turned red. I mean red like a bulb. They seemed to glow in the darkness that surrounded his face. He was so dirty and nasty looking with his hair caked up with mud. There was dirt all over his face and hands that I could not tell what color he was. I could not really see what he was wearing, because all the dirt hid his clothes, their color and style. They looked worse than anything I could have imagined or had ever seen, but there he stood in them and with pride. They looked as if they rotted on his body and he was too lazy to remove them.

He decided to speak once more saying something like, "Xavier!" (He actually said my real name, but that does not matter). Life is the key, but death is the house which life has locked everyone out of, but do not fear! My young Xavier, I shall open the door for you." Fear filled my heart like water into an empty bucket. I had no idea how he knew my name, or what he was going to do. My heart started beating so fast that I became lost and confused. All I did know was I had no idea who he was or what he wanted, but at that moment, I suspected my death. I was so confused that I really forgot where I was or where I was going. My fear took over and reason left my mind, I turned to my opponent who looked so calm and yet ready for whatever would come next.

Looking at him with as much aggression that I could project, I stated that the dude was 'tripping'. Locking my eyes to his and allowing myself to show as much anger as I could, I told him he needed help and if he tried something I would fuck him up. He seemed not bothered by my statement and in fact, he slowly made a half-curved smile. I stood there for just a second and then I turned into the alley of my escape and started running towards Sixth Street. Before I could fully enter the alley, I felt something grab hold of my neck and waist. Its nails gripped the skin of my neck and dug into the base of my throat muscles. Its other hand wrapped around my waist like a lover embracing its mate from behind. I could feel the blood running down my neck as his nails cut into me. He pulled me close to him as he lifted me up and carried me through the small street that I thought to be my escape. It seemed to walk at first and then it must have started to run. Nothing human could have been doing this, I thought. When it first grabbed me, I thought it had to be the dirty man, but when it started to move faster, I became lost and confused in its grip. I moved through this well-lit street like a child being carried on wings. There were two or three light poles in the middle of this street. They stood at least ten feet apart with a tree planted in between each pole. I remember trying to grab for one of them and then the other as I passed them, but failed every time. This street was too small to even be a street and it did not have a driveway for cars. It looked as if there was a building there at one time, but it was taken down and redesigned into a street. The creature carried me through this street and into a small park where the famous statue of the Unknown Soldier resided.

It threw me against one of the benches and I looked up to see that it was him, the man..! He looked even more insane than the first time I laid eyes on him. His speed loosened up the dirt on his head and body. He shook the dirt from his hair and then looked down at me. He stood perfectly still and patted his hair and body as if he realized how dirty he looked. My heart raced with fear and I kept repeating, "Who are you?" I pleaded for answers, but he just looked at me with his dark, strong eyes. They glowed like two spheres of light that could take the soul of the Devil himself. This man must have been about six feet tall or taller. His frame was so... so powerful that I felt weak by just looking at him, with arms that seemed to be powerful enough to rip my body apart if he wished. His hair was a dark color and very long. It flowed with some grace once the cakes of dirt were removed from it. I seemed to be seduced by its movement. He almost did not look human... He then smiled at me. He smiled as if I was to know who or what he was. He allowed his chest to expand and his head to tilt downward so I could see his full face. As I looked at him, I mean looked, I could see he was nothing I ever seen or imagined. His smile seemed to grip a hold of his face muscles with such force that it caused the darkness around him to sit deep in his face like nothing I ever seen before! As tears rolled across my face and my nerves caused me to shake uncontrollably in the bench that he threw me upon, I felt something give way and I knew I was sensing something I could not ever understand. I sat there and watched him for what felt like forever. Then I realized he was not smiling. He was allowing me to see his teeth. He was letting me figure it all out in my own time, something I came to figure out much later that night. As I watched closer, I realized that his teeth had grown. Well, not all of them, but the two that people call fangs and they seemed to thicken.

I yelled, "Lord Mary mother of Christ help me get the hell away from this dude!" I jumped from the bench and started to back away, slowly at first, then quickly. I turned and tried to run before he could grab me again. I heard him laugh as I ran down the path towards Sixth Street. He stated how good it was going to feel to walk amongst the living again. "Run if you think that will cheat me of what I need and will have. For if I were you, I would do no less," he said. I wanted to look back, but did not. I knew I had to get away, but had no idea where to run. He moved like the wind, without me ever hearing him. He picked me up and carried me out of the park. He ran through the streets with such force, I had no idea where I was! The streets were just a blur. He carried me with such force and speed that all I could see was the parked cars moving away from me.

In seconds, they soon became nothing but color spots before my eyes. Even the city blocks seemed to form a tunnel that vibrated faster than my eyes could follow. I was not even sure if I was still on Walnut Street anymore. In fact, I was not sure, if I was still awake or if this was nothing more than a dream. He wasted no time. I had felt him penetrate my neck. Breaking through my skin like needles... I was mere prey! I was so afraid... threatened! Yet, my mind shut down and I became very detached. All of this became too much for me to believe and I took it to be a dream. A dream that appeared to be very real... He sucked from me like a newborn child drinking from its mother breast. My neck felt like it would break at any second. All I heard was the gulping sound. I listened to him swallow my blood and I felt such pain in my neck! Yes, pain... It felt as if my pain only gave him pleasure... I could not do anything but scream. Only, it was a voiceless scream. On the empty street that held my dying body. My heart betrayed me as it pumped my life giving juices into this beast's mouth like a never-ending river. Soon my hands grew cold and stiff, my heart started beating harder and louder. My legs began to shake; I knew that this thing had claimed my body and soul. The more he drank, the worse my body began to feel. I felt a chill that was unlike anything I ever felt. If death wanted my soul, then it was truly going to take it. It did not matter how much I wanted to live, my body was betraying me.

It was at this point, my body went limp and almost lifeless. So lifeless that in my mind I began to see visions. I saw people and places, but none of it made any sense to me. They looked as if they were from the past and yet, it felt like the present. I began to see my life replay itself in my mind. Images of George and my other friends ran through my mind and then I saw deeper images of my parents and my sister. So many images and then they just stopped. Believing I heard him say something about not the one!! How many are there. I felt my body being lowered and believed that he laid me on the ground. I felt him dig deeper into my neck with his fangs going at least another inch or so. Then he continued to suck. I no longer cared if death was to claim me or not. The fact was, at this point, I welcomed it! The cold hard ground seemed to punish my still body like millions of sharp pins had pushed into my skin, even through my clothes. For some reason my body felt everything. The ground pushed up against me, the wind cut through me. Even the pain he gave to me was broken down into parts. His body felt like a heavy weight upon mine. His nails dug into my chest and the back of my head. He had cut me slowly and very painfully. His tongue felt like sandpaper against my neck, that lapped up the blood his teeth released as they penetrated my neck. He made sure I was able to live through it all. It was as if he wanted me to know what animals feel, when one overtakes another and eats it, while it is still alive. Nevertheless, someone must have surprised him, because he stopped and pulled his teeth from my neck. He slowly rose from my body and then ran away. I have no doubt that he left me to die, but I did not, and I owe that to the one who saved me. Their presence caused him to release his teeth's grip on my neck. I felt his teeth as they left my throat. My blood quickly filled their place and overflowed the holes he left, causing a stream to run down my neck to my shoulder where my shirt collar drank the remaining life-juice of my body. I was too weak to survive, or so I thought. However, I was to survive against my greatest wish.

As I closed my eyes to await death, a voice came to me from what seemed to be a dream. Clouds formed in my mind and it turned into a beautiful skyline. I appeared to be standing on the edge of something like a mountain. I am not sure because in my dream, I did not look down, just outwards toward the sky. Then a woman appeared behind me. I turned to face her, but was not sure what to expect. My heart seemed to leave me as I turned and looked upon this woman who stood about six foot-five. She was very pretty, with eyes that seemed to shine like crystals. She smiled and welcomed me. She called my name and then called me her child. She told me much will change for me now and I must seek her out for only she can help me now. She told me she was the light and I was to follow her light and trust her with blind faith. I was not sure why I was dreaming this, but I knew it was a dream. She reached out and hugged me. Even in this dream, she was very strong and I could not break from her grip. She told me to trust no one but her and when I was strong enough to seek her out, I was to do just that! She had the longest red hair I had ever seen. She said some more stuff, but I just could not remember it.

When I awoke, I was under what looked like a bridge. My eyes could not adjust well in the darkness of where I laid, nor was I dealing with the sounds I was hearing. I just stayed there, confused and weak. When I felt that some of my strength had returned, I started to move my arms and hands. I blinked my eyes and I was able to focus a little better. At least to the point of me knowing where I was. The strength I thought I had gained was lost again. I could hear cars and voices, but was not aware of what direction they were coming from. The question of where was I entered my mind. I decided to do something, but what..? I had gotten a little nervous again, I knew I had to focus! I just had to... I used all my neck muscles to make my head turn in the direction I was hearing sounds. I breathed as if every breath was my last. I focused on the street sign, but was not able to see it too clearly. My vision was not clear enough. The sign seemed to blend with its background. I focused again and looked a little harder. I was able to read it; the sign said 'Christian Street'. I watched it for some time and then blacked out for a bit. I was able to feel the breeze of the wind. It cooled my face and gave me peace. Sweat started to run down my face. I grew a little confused. The idea that I was sweating and feeling cold at the same time appeared to be crazy to me. When my mind cleared, I heard a man speaking. It took some time for me to realize he had been speaking to me. I felt a lot stronger, so I tried to move my head. It moved for me and I tried to see the image before me. Focusing on my eyes once again, I opened them. I was able to gather something of an image. The image was of colors and forms but nothing to clear.

The colors began to take shapes and one of the shapes became a man. The man was the one whose voice caused me to open my eyes. Behind the man were many more colors and I could only assume that they were people too.

The shapes were people, homeless people I believed, as they looked at me. The man that had spoke acted a little strange. He had yelled for me to 'leave this firkin' area'. He acted as if he was insane, as he jumped around and waved his hands about. At one point, he called me a homeless bum. Then I heard other people ask him if I was dead. I believe a woman out of the crowd called him Joe. Another person spoke as if it was normal to find a black man dead in this area. I looked at the white man who was drunk and dirty. He looked liked he had not taken a bath in about two weeks and smelled just as bad. I was tired and very weak, but knew I had to get the hell out of there. As I turned over onto my stomach and rose to my knees, it came to my attention that the night was passing quickly. I wasn't sure how many hours had passed. With the fact that I was gone for so long, I was sure that my roommates would be looking for me. Marco and Drew usually did not look for me but they did look out for me. They are the type of boys that mind their own, but when I do something too out of the way they usually notice and call me on it. I knew if I was able to get up and walk to Front Street, then I would be able to take a cab home. I stood, but with great effort and waited for the dizziness to pass. The people started to laugh at me. They thought I was drunk and maybe somebody had robbed me. The man called Joe yelled, "You're a dumb motherfucker to be walking around here." I stood there and looked at him with pure pity. Then I turned slowly and started my way down towards Front St. I pushed past the people that gathered around me. A few of the women was telling me to stay there because they called the police. One woman told me I needed to get to a hospital.

At this point, I did not want a doctor or them to bother me.

As I walked through the people around me, I noticed there was a cab on the corner of Water Street. I moved towards the cab as fast as I could. The driver was too busy sleeping to notice me approaching the cab. When I got to the cab and pulled the back door handle, I entered the cab and I told him where I lived. I made eye contact with him shortly before I passed out in the back seat. The look on his face was of complete confusion. I could see he did not want to do this, but was not left with much of a choice. Just imagine how he must have felt waking up to me pulling on his cab door and the driver seeing the group of people behind me. Joe still yelling out I do not belong around here. My clothes were all ripped up and blood stained. Those stains were so big that it would have been safer to believe it was the color of the shirt. He had to see the illness of my fever in my face. He must have thought those people were going to kill me. As much as this man may have hated having to help me, he was left with no real choice. I, as a young black man in South Philadelphia, was at his mercy, was completely helpless. And if he threw me out of his cab, I believe it would have been on his conscience. He tried to talk to me but I was not really listening. He was asking me something about a hospital. He drove as fast as he could and I knew he was a little scared that I might die in his cab. So, I spoke.... I told him that I was fine and that all I need was rest. He told me that I really needed to pay attention to where I hang out at this time in the morning. When we arrived in front of my house the fare came up to three dollars and forty-something cents. I reached into my pocket and realized I did not have my wallet. My wallet was gone and my money was in my wallet. Someone must have robbed me while I was passed out. It was around five-thirty in the morning and I came to realize I was broke. The cab driver just repeated the fare to me.

There was no way I was going to tell this dude that I had no money. I just looked at him and he knew. He began to curse and punch the top of his seat. He then went silent for a moment or two and gathered himself. He asked if I had any money in the house, I did not answer. He got out of the cab and walked around the back of the cab. He must have been about six -foot three and looked all of two hundred and ten pounds of pure muscles. This dude could rip out my heart with very little effort. He was not bad on the eyes for being a cab driver. I do not know why, but most cab drivers in Philadelphia do not seem to care about how they look or how they make their passengers feel. He was different; he seemed to be a pretty decent white guy. I would have cried if I were not so weak. As he stopped in front of the back door on the side where I was sitting, I thought, 'This was it'…I just bit my bottom lip and closed my eyes. I thought he was going to pull me from the cab and kick the living shit out of me! Then, I heard him knock on my front door. I opened my eyes to see that after the third knock, Drew answered the door. They talked for some time and then I heard Drew laughing; I knew the driver must have told him I did not have money. I was still tired so I closed my eyes again. Drew paid him very well and the cab driver returned to the cab. He opened the cab door and must have stood there for some time. I mean, I heard the guy open the cab door, so I tried to pull myself together to stand, but it was not happening. He finally decided to help me out of the cab. He looked like he was Italian with black wavy hair and green eyes. I was right earlier; he was six-foot two and strong as an ox.

I stared at him for some time. I grew sick as I stood there. I pulled away from him, grabbed hold of the cab, and released everything in my stomach. I vomited heavily at first, then dry heaves onto the curb beside the cab. He grabbed me again. I wrapped my arm around his neck and started to walk again. I grew weaker as we walked towards the house. When I felt my stomach begin to shake, I stopped and gripped the driver's neck even harder. It seemed like forever, but I finally got to my front steps. Drew was at the front door as I looked up to him. He looked at me as if to say, 'What the fuck happened to you?' Totally forgetting that my clothes told a story in itself, I climbed the steps as he came down to meet me and I began to tell him what happened. Drew thanked the driver again, wrapped his arm around my waist and helped me into the house. We walked over to the first sofa that faced the living room windows. There he helped me to sit. I must have blacked out again because when I awoke, he was sitting on the sofa that was next to mine. I asked him if I was really home. He looked at me as if I was crazy, a fact that I questioned myself at that moment! I told him the whole chain of events that took place. Even how the strange dude bit into my neck and started drinking my blood. Drew shook his head as if I was lying to him. I turned my head to the side to show him the bite marks, but they were almost healed. He may have wanted to disbelieve in what I was telling him, if not for my spoiled clothes and the two puncture wounds on my neck. As well as my blank expression forced him to believe that, something happened...Not the fact that what I said was true! Drew rose and walked past me towards the front door. He said nothing. He just looked over at me and started to sit on the sofa that was directly in front of him. He picked up some weed off the table and placed it into his pipe. He looked at me again and shook his head. Drew then reached for his lighter and held it in his hand as he put more of the weed into his pipe. He returned to the other sofa that was across from me. He looked at me for some time, while he was stuffing his pipe. He gave me that smile (you know the one), that smile of disbelief while shaking his head from side to side. Then he accepted that no more weed was going to fit in his small little pipe. So, he lit his pipe and took a good long drag, then stared at me again.

He leaned back into the sofa. Resting his hand on his leg and said, "Xavier, Xavier, Xavier... Dude! You got to stop bugging, man. You be wilding... Damn!" My head rested on the back of the sofa I was sitting on. I could still see him talking but I was tired. "Only you would get into fucked up shit like this. Look at you... Man, you're fucked up!" he said as he took another hit on the pipe. I wondered what he was thinking as he looked upon my person. It crossed my mind that he thought I was high but I knew he was smarter than that. Drew then took another hit off his pipe and then passed it to me. "Go ahead, Xavier, take a hit. Man! You look like you really need It.," Drew said. He seemed so calm like this was just another one of the things I gotten myself into. I really had no choice but to listen to him. My heart was racing and I was still weak. It just did not make sense to me what was happening. I raised my arm to reach for it. I could smell the weed so clear and it was such a strong odor. Stronger than usual, but I thought maybe that was because I was tired. I knew that I was lost right then and maybe the weed would calm me down enough to think. So I took the weed into my hand and without moving my head I put the pipe into my mouth. I took a good drag off of it. I held the smoke in my mouth for some time before exhaling it. The first hit always did it for me, but this time I wanted more. After we finished smoking the weed, Drew said that he felt I needed to get some rest. On my way upstairs, my stomach had other plans, so I went into the bathroom first. I must have emptied my entire body into the toilet, because when I was finished, my ass felt raw. Dizzy and tired, I went to my room. I was still weak and confused. Undressing was difficult, but the blood stained clothes sickened me even more than I already felt. I lay on my bed and went to sleep. Luckily I never usually open my curtains, because if I had, I might not be here today. Well, when I awoke, it was already night, I guess around seven p.m. I was not able to remember my dream. So I thought that maybe I better go see Peter, my best friend. Peter is from Europe and has seen a lot of deep shit. I rose from my bed and went to my closet to get out something to wear. I noticed that the closet door seemed different, I mean, it was the same door, but seemed different in some way. The wood seemed to have more detail and texture. Even my clothes seemed more alive than usual. I thought that I must still be high, or something. After grabbing a pair of pants and a shirt, I threw them on my bed and headed out of my room. I went towards the bathroom. The hall was dark, but I could see just fine. Everything was in such detail that I ignored the fact that the hall lights were out. I walked into the bathroom and shut the door behind me. It sounded as if I slammed the door, but I barely touched it. Not that our bathroom is usually big or anything. But it seemed even smaller than usual.

In the shower, I was able to hear everything going on in the house. Not even the water running over my body was able to block out the sounds I was hearing. I tried to calm myself by resting my hands on the shower wall; still I was able to hear Marco and his girl in his room enjoying each other's company. I could tell that they were really into each other, because of how loud they were breathing. It sounded like we were the only ones home. I listened closer and soon I could hear the dripping water in the kitchen sink. I was able to hear a flicking sound like something was burning. The sound was faint, but I was able to hear the burned ashes fall as the object continued to burn. The water started to feel like pins against my skin, so I began to lather up my body, working the soap over my arms and legs. The lather was thick and made my body respond a lot different than it ever had before. As I started to wash my chest and stomach, I realized that I moaned. I moaned in response to my own touch. My body started reacting with every touch from my hands bathing it. Passion grew within me as I continued to bathe myself. The stimulation overtook me for some reason and I felt too weak to stand. I dropped the soap and grabbed hold of the wall. I knew that I had to get out of the tub, but before I could, my legs started to shake, my head began to spin. A strong pain ran through my lower stomach and I fell to the tub floor. It felt as if my knees where broken. My body began to shake and my legs went numb as the water ran over me. Tears filled my… My eyes as I yelled out, "O' God! Please help me." The pain subsided and I reached hold of the toilet which was only two feet away from the tub and pulled myself out of the tub. I knew I was going mad, but I could not stop myself. I wanted to yell for George, but he wouldn't have heard me. I laid there truly scared until my strength returned. I pulled myself completely out of the tub and realized that a smell overtook me. It was the worst smell I'd ever smelled before. Then I noticed that the smell was coming from the tub. I relieved myself in the tub without even knowing it. It was so much that I was amazed that it all came out of me. I vomit as I stood there. Even though I was shaken, I turned the shower on and cleaned it up. Then I showered again before returning to my bedroom. I sat on the bed and was still confused about what was going on. I looked at the bite marks on my neck in my bedroom mirror, but they pretty much had healed. They looked more like older wounds than those from the last night's attack. I went into the bathroom again to look at them in that mirror, but it was the same. I laid my hands on to the sink and lowered my head feeling like I wanted to cry, but could not. I turned to leave the bathroom and a smell crossed my nose. I walked into the hall and the smell overtook me. It was such a strong smell of incense. I went towards Drew's room and the smell of the incense was very strong. I grew sick from it and ran back to my room. I shut my door and quickly got dressed.

Now, our home isn't really anything to talk about. I mean, it is a three-story house with all white walls. It has mainly two nice size rooms on the first floor. The living room itself is long enough to be two rooms. The kitchen has cabinets along the two walls facing the south side of the house and a large four foot by eight foot window that allows us to see the yard. The house has two bedrooms and a nice size bathroom on the second floor. The third floor duplicates the second floor. As I reached the bottom step into the living room, I was amazed by the brightness of the living room walls. I mean, it still had the three old sofas wrapped in front of the television, which was sitting in front of the windows, but for some reason they seemed very clean. Not the kind of clean you get when someone cleans up, but more like the kind after someone paints their house. The walls seemed to glow with brightness. I went into the kitchen and it was pretty much the same way as the living room. I just thought maybe the whiteness on the walls were bright because of the weed I smoked. I grabbed some chicken out of the refrigerator, but could not eat it. For some reason I lost my appetite, so I put it back and left the house.

As I walked into the street, I felt as if I walked through the Looking Glass. I was able to hear every sound around me, from rats running around the dark street looking for food, to the cars driving by a few blocks away. I could even hear the men hanging around on the corner of our block. I could not believe I heard my neighbors' voices as I stood on the steps. It continued as I passed by their houses. My mind raced like a madman as I walked on. My sight was just as amazing as my hearing and smell. I could see everything in the street with clear distinction, from the rats that hide in the grass of the empty lots and houses around the neighborhood, to the birds sleeping in the nearby trees and the people who was looking out of their windows, but for some reason did not want to be seen. I was seeing everything with new eyes. It was great! The long blue skies seemed to glow with such colors like purple, Greenish blue, red and orange. Even with all these colors in the night sky, it still appeared to me to be on fire. I was able to smell every rat, every person, and everything I passed. There scents seem to define itself to each creature and object. Until then, I really never paid much attention to all these different scents. The cars that passed me seem to move slower to my eyes, so slow that I was able to see every clear detail on and in it. Even the street seemed to change. The pavement seemed to also have the same fire in it. I began to study this fire that bared no heat, but was clearly vibrant. The more I watched these vibrant waves, the more I tried to make sense out of all this. Then, it came to me that this was my eyes seeing the moving vibrations in everything. The vibrations were pitches like music and sound. This pitch had to be that in which life is controlled by. I know music, because I love to play the drums and guitar. They release a pitch that pulls my soul to its sound. So, if music is vibrations and those vibrations have power… Then, the power has to be energy. Energy is patterns. Everything is fused sound! I could now, for some reason, see the vibrating pitches or patterns that everything worked on. I began to listen to the wind that was around me, and as I walked I seemed to be floating through the street forgetting about all the stress I was going through just a few minutes ago. I was walking, but it was so fast and with very little to no effort at all. I had reached Peter's apartment nearly three times faster than normal. The bricks, windows and even the front door were vibrating to my presence. I was now not sure what was happening to me and grew a little scared. As I entered and walked towards the elevator, I took comfort in knowing that Peter would be able to help me figure this out. The hall was just as bright as my living room. His door seemed to come to life too, not that I was surprised. As I reached the door, I knew he was home, because I could hear him and smelled his scent as well. The smell that was coming from Peter was very different from the way I smelled Marco or the other people. As I knocked on the door, I was able to smell this new scent stronger as Peter came closer towards the door. My body began to tense up and my hands began to shake but his blood. The smell became stronger as he came closer and closer to the door. I seemed to lust for him or it, I just wasn't sure I became so scared, because my passion for Peter grew and I wanted him. I wanted him more than anything I ever wanted before. I never had a feeling like this towards anybody before, but this was different. My body was beginning to shake as I felt him reach for the doorknob. My heart was pounding so loud, I knew he had to be able to hear it. The fear of what I was going to do claim my soul. At this point I just ran away. I ran from Peter's apartment! I turned the corner at the end of the hall and gathered myself as I heard Peter open his door and then close it.

Confused and lost in my thoughts, I ran through the streets in a frantic rage, until I appeared before the college that I had just graduated from. In about ninty four seconds, I was standing in front of the school. Can you picture running a great distant in seconds and not minutes? As I sat upon the school's front steps, I noticed that everything around me took on a form of life. The walls seemed as if they were breathing with me and the wind appeared to laugh off the walls, and seemed to not even care if I could see all this madness. Knowing something was wrong, I had to admit that my body was going through some kind of change and I knew it had to do with my attacker. For some reason my mind was racing and whatever attacked me was the cause of it. Whatever was injected into my system was running its course and causing this nightmare called my life. I was not sure when he did it, but I knew he had to have been the one to have done it. Then I thought that maybe it happened when he bit my neck. Maybe he was infected with something and that would explain why he bit me. Could it be that the disease he was infected with was in his saliva? When he bit me, it entered my body and now was taking an effect on me? I started to become aware of my surroundings again.

Chapter 2
My Angel of the night

I realized that I had sat there for a long time, hours actually. So I rose and started to walk around again. My mind raced over the many different possibilities that could have happened that night, but none stood out. It was not long before the night air hit me and I realized that it did not seem warm or cold. I really did not feel different at all. It was as if all that I just experienced a few hours ago meant nothing. My senses had gone out of control at times and then they became numb. I had gone on as if I was no different from any other person on the street. It did not take long after this thought that my body began to shake for some reason. I tried to continue walking, but then it happened. My hands started to shake as my legs grew weak, seeming to be falling asleep. I could not comprehend why all this was happening. Like most confused and frighten children... I started crying, praying to God that it would stop, but it did not! The reason was not clear to me why my body was doing this, but deep down in my heart. I knew it was something I would live to regret. I was so scared and confused that I forced myself to continue to walk. It was trying to take over my body the way my lust had back at Peter's place. This time I was not going to allow it to consume me. I closed my mind and focused on continuing to walk and the more I walked, the easier it became for me to fight these new feeling. I started thinking about the guy who attacked me. What could have happened to him and now me? Could he have been trying some new drugs, but then what kind of drug would do this, for that matter, what could I do to stop it? It must have surely been more different than any drug I had ever tried before. My mind raced over this again and again, but came to the same answer. I needed to go to the hospital and get checked out.

I started towards the hospital to get answers. As I walked, I tried to recall the events of the night before, remembering if my attacker did anything else other than grabbing me and running down the street with me in his arms. I just could not remember the full details of everything that happened. I walked through the streets like a madman, pushing my way past people and then out of nowhere, my mind seemed to open and images started to run wild. I tried to force the images to take form and show me what happened, but got nothing. Of course I started to talk out loud like most people. I started repeating the events that took place. But my mind raced, my thoughts, unclear. It was as if I made things up as I went along the streets, in hopes that I would remember something that I did not. I really wanted to understand why my body was betraying me and my mind was aiding it. As I walked in my own world and thoughts towards nothing more than my own peace, a voice came to me...no, entered my mind. The voice was so soft and beautiful it replaced the images. It was as if I had listened to a child who spoke to me and my whole body gave way to it. It was such a sweet madness that I had to follow it. Like a flower growing through the emptiness of space, did she too amaze me? As I drew closer to her sweet voice, I looked around to see if the people around me could hear this angel of the night too. They walked as if nothing was happening. I realized that they were unable to hear this high pitched song of madness. What sweet madness...! I looked around the streets to see if I could see her. The dim lights and darkened streets only aided her in remaining concealed. I was amazed that no one else could hear it. The sound started getting a little softer, so I decided to move quickly and follow this mad sweet voice that played only for my ears. The more I ran, the further the voice seemed to move from me. I was not sure if this voice was leading me somewhere, perhaps to the man that did this to me...As much as I wanted to stop, I could not give up this chance to get answers.

Hours passed and by this time, the trance from this sweet voice was broken. Anger filled me as I realized this person had played me for a fool, so I stopped running. This had become a game that I no longer desired to play. I looked around the street and saw nothing, nothing out of the norm. I turned around and headed back in the direction of the hospital. At first everything was normal or very close to what I could perceive as normal. After a while, I started to feel something out of the way. For some wild reason, I could feel that this girl who wished to play did not stop at the same point I did and had decided to follow me. I made my favorite statement, "Word!" and looked over my shoulder. I had to smile at her behavior then I ran away with such great speed, I thought I was flying. Even more speed than I used earlier. I believed that there was no way she would be able to keep up. But the more I ran, the closer this one from the shadows came upon me. I moved with more speed than any man could follow. Moving like the wind I leaped over cars like they where nothing at all. Crossing streets and moving through cars and people, it was truly amazing. Then I cut through an alley not too far from the school, around 18th Street I believe. I began to grow dizzy and it was not long after that point I fell to the ground in pain. Pain like what I felt earlier in the bathtub, but now greater. It started in my stomach and quickly took over my body. I tried to stand up but the pain claimed me. The pain was so much greater than before, even greater than I could ever imagine. I tried to crawl, but my body was not very helpful. The night shadows of the street grew over me and the sweet voice of madness chose to give me comfort. Her voice filled my mind as she got closer to me. As she stood over me, I realized this was it. She was to end this. She was so beautiful and I hated the idea that he sent her to destroy me and that I was in some forsaken alley somewhere in Center City. The alley was no different from any other, with the smells of rotten food, rats and sour water, water that poured into it from the restaurants along this street. Nothing was any different in this alley than any other...well, except I was to die in this one. She was to finish the job that the mad man started.

I was repeating, "Please no" over and over again. Then she spoke to me...This voice told me that she was here to aid me. She looked down at me and smiled as if someone had told her a joke that had amused her and then she spoke to me again. She told me she could tell me what was wrong with me...what I was craving...what I was becoming...why I was going through all these different things. She told me she could stop my pain. She could make it all better and could save me. She said, "Yes, you are being consumed by the waters of the darkened realm, but you can still be saved. You must say you wish to live. Say this and shall I save your soul. Cleanse the demon-like nature that will claim your body and soul at the end. Yes, there will be an end to all of this! This was written in the lost books of Gores Blocs! It is not pain you are feeling, but death." I looked at her with such fear, but I just did not know what to do or say. She continued to speak. She said, "Yes, you are dead, for you died a mortal's death last eve and now you are becoming one of the damned souls of Joseph. You are damned, by that which once fed on you. Now, you crave the need to feed on others as innocent as you were. It may seem to be unfair, that one can be damned without a choice. It really is a shame you know? But now you are being given one! The choice is yours. You can choose to be his slave when this is done or I can free your mind and soul. Say you wish to be cleansed of this darkness that is stealing your soul and I will aid you. Do not and I will allow it to run its course, but when it is done...I will kill you, for I would rather damn your soul than let you damn another as his slave."

As the pain grew, I began to regret more for what I was about to say. I was weak, my mind was unclear, and the pain was more than I could bear, but I did not wish death, so I did as she told me. I pleaded for my life with all the strength I could muster.

Whatever was to come from this life, I was willing to accept it. She bent down to sit before me. Her dress opened like wings of an angel. She lifted my head up to her breast with one hand while wrapping her other hand around my waist. Pulling in close to her as if I was a child, she held me to her breast like a mother breast-feeding her young… She removed her hand from around my waist. She reached into her dress and pulled a sack from between her breasts. She took her fingers and wrapped them around this sack that looked as if was made of human skin. The bag was about four inches wide and six inches long. She then took my head and guided me to her breast. She placed the bag to my lips and told me to bite into it and drink. I began to smell the blood through the skin bag and I felt pain in my mouth as my teeth grew! One could say I lost my virginity again upon that night. The pain was so great that I grabbed her arm and held on tight in hope that the pain would subside. I could feel my gums bleed as my teeth pushed their way out. My hunger forced my fangs to protrude from my gums. Elizabeth remained calm and just kept telling me to feed on the immortal blood that damned me and to join her battle. "Together, we shall save all the souls of the living and the damned." she said.

I closed my eyes and bit with all my strength. As my teeth broke the skin of the bag and the blood filled my mouth, I began to drink. The pain was gone and I was left to accept that the pain really was me craving blood. I was craving to drink the blood of the living. The blood of that, which fills all living creatures, now was to be my meal. (It's funny in a way. That we were always told that vampires drink only human blood and the truth is that any blood would do.) A peace of mind came from this truth...It made sense! It all made sense...I laid there and took peace in that it was not Peter that I desired. Peter's blood was what overtook my mind and body. I never saw myself making love to a man...So I realized that the images I saw were me watching myself feed on

Peter. Everything was connecting to one another. Even this thing I became, this vampire. As I continued to drink from the bag, peace filled my mind and my heart seemed to grow stronger, for some reason (The oddest thought just came to me. It felt like I was making love when I thought about feeding on Peter...sorry... anyway...). I listened to my heart beat stronger and stronger as I drank from her bag, but I could sense her grip around my head growing weaker as I fed. The fire of life seemed to fill me and this forced me to continue to feed on this empty bag. I sucked and sucked like a child nursing on his mother's dry breasts. I sucked and sucked, pulling the bag harder and harder until she pulled it away from me. I hit the ground and without thought, I flung back toward her to continue to feed some more, but the bag was empty and we both knew it. She jumped back and landed on top of a large trash dumpster. She made sure to stay out of my reach. I saw fear in her eyes as she watched me go mad for more of the blood. The more I tried to reach her, the more she moved out of the way, until..! Yes, the blood took full effect. The new blood that was driving me insane with greed caused me to fall to the ground in convulsions. I could fill the blood warming my body and my cold heart, at the same time causing my body to make new changes.

She watched as I became possessed by the blood. My eyes became clouded and then blind. My first fangs that grew, fell out! I felt my hairs as they fell to the ground. As I could hear and feel my body contract and stretch I started to scream as my body went into convulsions and I laid their begging for help. She did nothing but watch as I tried to fight what was happening. This must have lasted for about a half of an hour. Then my sight returned and was sharper than before. Now they were able to clearly distinguish the different vibration levels of each living and non-living entity. I laid there for some time and watched her move her lips, but could not hear anything she was saying. I focused hard to listen to her speak, but I could not make out what she was saying. I felt my body grow stronger and my hair firm up even more than normal. I could truly feel my body responding to this blood in ways that I just can't explain to you without giving you the gift of death. Then it stopped and my hearing returned. I finally rose from the ground and looked around with my new sight. As I looked around the alley, she told me that this was just the beginning. She could help me find myself and get control of all the things that had just happened. She told me that I was lucky that she found me first. Because if Joseph, the one who made me came upon me before her. He would have given me the blood I needed. Then waited for me to change. He would have then killed me, for he would have drank me to death. If for no other reason than to take my new found power. She spoke with such passion that I had to believe her.

She told me that she was going to help me control the powers I gained from what he did to me. She asked me of a favor, that once I learned to control these gifts, then would I help her hunt and destroy Joseph. I saw enough movies to know that only in killing Joseph could my soul be free. She did not lie to me by saying I was going to become human again after his death. She told that I would become something better than human and greater than a vampire. She was going to help me to become a Vaingel, a creature of noble blood. That meant that we will not need to feed ever again. A Vaingels is a creature that is created to hunt the damned ones of the world. I wanted to ask so many questions about this thing called a Vaingels, but she said, "Concern yourself not about your end, but focus on what is happening now. For you have been through much this night and now you have drank from the blood of our master. Return home, my young Xavier for you need your rest. Tomorrow I shall wait for you in the Rittenhouse Park after the sun sets. I smiled as I rose and took her hand. She rose as well and turned to walk out of the alley. I followed. We shared not a word until she turned and kissed me good-night. She called me her love and rubbed my face with her right hand. I closed my eyes at her touch and like a gust of wind she was gone. After she was gone, I decided to walk around for a while. I must admit I did take comfort in the fact that now I knew what I had become. As I walked the streets I thought about all the movies I had seen in the past years on vampires. I thought about what was believed that these creatures where suppose to be capable of doing. I wonder if I could do any of those things. I decided to try, but failed the entire test I set for myself. Becoming frustrated and the time was late I decide to return home. I started to walk back to the house, but could not help but to think of her and remember her smell. I felt such sweet joy that I wanted to yell or jump or something, but nothing came to mind. I walked home renewed in some kind of twisted inner peace. As I approached the house, I realized that the lights were off and that meant that I would be in the house alone. I entered the house to discover I was correct. I knew things had changed. I just could not see the world the same any more. I thought about George and realized I would have to deal with him tomorrow as well. I started up the stairs. Since I really could not be certain who would come home with Drew or Marco, I decided it would be safer for me to sleep in the basement. I went up to my bedroom to get a blanket and pillow. A part of me wanted the basement to be cold and damp, but was pleased to find it wasn't. I knew I would sleep like a log for some reason. I went to the basement and cleared a corner of the cellar out for me to make a bed. I took some boxes we had down there and made myself a bed out of them. . I fell asleep almost instantly and slept very well…

My dream was a little weird, but I could not really remember much about it, except that there was a guy and he was alone. He was sitting in this chair that looked like a throne chair or something. He looked as if he had a great deal of wealth. What made him stand out were his eyes they were so clear and so blue. I mean the kind of blue that water looks like on a tropical island. He seemed to be talking to a woman. The woman was not that much older than the one who saved except that she seemed to act much older. He seemed to be telling her something about me and she was just looking at me. She looked so wild. She was definitely a woman of great power of some kind. She wore her long black hair up in a beehive and had two large diamonds in her ears. Her necklace was like one of the old chokers one might see in an old movie. Her dress, or should I say, gown was a soft green unlike any kind I had seen. It seemed to be of some kind of silk. The lace on the gown looked to be hand sewed. Her lips were so long and thick like a model's or actresses. I remember her eyes as well. They were a soft tan with very black pupils. Her lashes only made them set out more beautifully. She was truly the woman of my dreams. I could not believe it but she looked like my savior in some ways. Even in my dreams, this angel shows herself to me.

I slept through most of the day; I started to hear talking at some point. At first, I thought it was them, but soon realized it was Marco talking to Drew. I tried to awake to talk to them, but could not. It seemed to me that it must have been morning and they were getting ready for work. I guessed I was really tired and just listened to them talk. I listened to Drew' repeat everything I told him. Marco laughed and they said that I was crazy! (Back then, we called it wilding.) They laughed, but continued to talk and share their concerns about my behavior. I so wanted to rise and confront them in my defense, but the fact was I could not. It was as if I was dead to the world. No matter how hard I tried to awake, I just could not. Soon my sleep reclaimed my mind completely again. I found myself chasing something through some trees. What I was chasing was not certain to me, but I felt I needed to see it with my own eyes. I ran after it for hours it seemed, running into caves and across open fields. It was as if I was not even in America anymore. At times, it felt so real that I forgot that I was dreaming. I felt that I could smell the flowers and touch the buildings that I seen. I was being pulled to this place that I knew not. Soon I stood in front of some old ruin and some lost tribe of some kind. I could not tell anyone how to get there; I did not even understand what took me there in the first place. I walked up to the building, or what was left of it. And as soon as I touched the wall of this old weak structure, I awoke! I rose from my bed of boxes and could tell it was dark outside as I left the basement. I headed up the steps to the kitchen and stood in the kitchen for some time. I went to the refrigerator for something to eat out of habit. I smiled when I realized what I was doing. I found it funny that I still felt the need to eat and headed upstairs to get dressed and meet my savior. I went to my room and pulled out a pair of black jeans and a black pullover shirt. I decided if I was to meet her, then I needed to look good. I placed my clothes on the bed and head to the bathroom. I jumped in the shower; boy did I fall in love with the feel of the cold water slowly becoming warm. As it ran down my newly reborn body, I stood there as thoughts of that sweet voice entered my head and soon followed by that beautiful face. Her face was of an angel... I felt like a teenager in love. I thought about how sweet her voice was and how soft her hand felt against my face. As the water ran across my body, I pictured her face again. I slowly lathered my body with soap, imagining it was her hands. The more I rubbed the better it felt. My senses were going crazy at my touch, but I could not stop. I pictured her soft red curls slowly falling to the side of her face as her lips curved to kiss me. I felt a stir in my loins and before I knew it, I was slowly stroking my stiff penis and pictured only her. My hand worked my penis and I began to do what most guys do in the shower. I just kept picturing her green eyes and her soft lips, her sweet firm breasts softly rubbing against my chest. Our eyes looking into each other's every time we kissed. We lock our lips in a passionate kiss. I could picture her grabbing my penis and rubbing it so softly that I would lose myself in her touch. My mind raced with the wild thoughts of her kissing me grabbing me and finally having sex with me. I was really getting into my fantasy and lost control of my loins and shot one long stream against my chest followed by three smaller shots that hit the shower wall. I released the largest load of my life. My spent load stole my strength from me, causing me to grab hold of the shower door and the wall at the same time to keep from falling. With what was left in me as far as my strength I sat down in the tub and allowed the water to calm my body and mind. I sat in the tub for about twenty minutes before I was able to wash the remaining sperm off my chest. I was really lost for words, for I had never experienced anything like that in all my life. It was so intense, but over very quickly.

I got out of the shower and returned to my room to dress. I really felt like I needed to wear all black at that moment. I ran out of the house around ten at night with a new found energy. I ran to Broad Street. and then decided to walk the rest of the way. I found joy in the world through my newfound eyes. I felt like I was in love but did not really understand why. I wasted no time and went straight there. The park was very crowded as I entered. I was a little lost because I realized we never picked where in the park to meet at, so I walked over to the fountain and waited... A part of me feared that I may have missed her, but prayed that I did not. I had such a warm feeling from the thought of seeing her again. After about ten minutes, I hear her voice in my mind. She was saying that she feared I wouldn't come. I looked around to see if I could see her. I could not as a group of people passed in front of me. Then, there she stood, looking so graceful and refined. I smile at the sight of her. She came over to me and I rose to greet her. I knew she could see the peace I had in this new life. I smiled at her presence as I reached to wrap my arms around her... We hugged for a brief moment as she began to speak. "I must teach you all I can because he will soon come for you and want to finish what he started. I must have looked at her like she was mad because she rested her soft hands against my face. He will try to kill you! Know this to be true...yes! Have no fear of him, for he is not capable of finding you. He is still too weak to attack you since you have drunk of his blood and completed your change. We have very little time, for when the time is right. He will search for you through the eyes of many. For he is capably of searching through the eyes of most people to look for us but that is not as easy as I make it sound."

She pulled away from me and turned her back to me. She continued to say, "I have very little time to teach you all you will need to know, because when he grows strong enough to destroy me, he will start his hunt." She wanted to make sure I understood that he hunted her as well, so we did need each other. "Now... Gather your composure and stay with me. Xavier, be careful to whom you speak because he can read the minds of mortals and hear their thoughts. Time is against us and you must learn all you can. It is important that you do not feed on the blood of the living, for it will not give you the power you will need to grow stronger. If the time comes that you may need to feed on man, then accept this fact and move on. It is important that you do not allow such setbacks to stop you, for the blood will force you to feed. Now... follow me and I shall give you what you will need to live on for now." she said. She headed out of the Park and I followed. When she walked out onto 18th Street. she waited for me. We walked towards Chestnut Street. without saying a word. She looked at me and told me not to be afraid for she was not going to leave me. We turned the corner onto Chestnut Street. She told me to try and follow her. With that she started running. We must have run for some time.

I was moving so fast that I did not pay attention to where she was taking me. We ended up on Twenty-third and Market. She stopped at the corner and smiled at me like an angel. I stood beside her and felt like the man. This sweet woman… was standing beside me and totally into me. She told to me follow her to the train tracks and I did. We crossed Market Street and walked down Twenty-Third Street. I thought we were going into the building on the north side corner, but we ran down Twenty-third Street towards Arch Street. She stopped and pointed to the parking lot that was behind the building on the corner of Twenty-third and Market. She took my hand and we entered the parking lot. We walked through the lot and reached the gate at the end of the lot. The gate separated the lot from some railroad tracks. She leaped into the air and time seemed to stand still. As her arms stretched out in both directions and her legs bent so graceful, I stood in amazement, No wonder I fell in love with her. She landed like an angel and turned back towards me. Her green eyes were so beautiful I lost myself in them. I never realized how nice they looked until then. She yelled for me to quickly jump the fence. Her voice broke my trance, so I regained focus. The fence was not very high, maybe about five feet but I was not too sure if I would be able to make it. I backed up a little and took a few steps and leaped into the air, I cleared the fence with at least two or three feet to boot. My landing was not as graceful as hers, but I landed ok. She smiled and took my arm. We walked over the tracks back towards Market. We reached an entrance under the bridge of Market Street. The entrance had a hill of dirt that opened to some kind of old cave or what was left of one. Then I realized it was the underside of the bridge that ran to Thirty Street Station. We walked into the area and my vampire sight allowed me to see my savior, whom I later discovered that her name was Elizabeth, clearly. She walked over to a corner where a large pile of trash sat. She dug through the pile of trash and threw some of the trash around. She then pulled free a bag and in the bag was a huge glass bottle of red liquid. The bottle looked like one of those large bottles you might find a snake sitting in at

Harry's occult shop, or someplace like that. She told me that this was the master's blood. She said, "I feel like I am responsible for you being in this mess, so I am giving you this. Be careful for every time you drink from it you will grow stronger, but do not drink too much at one time for then the blood may consume you and then you will risk becoming insane. Though I do not feel this is the right time, I must ask you for help. I want you to help me find him and kill him."

I asked, "Who? Joseph?"

"Yes! You must say you will and mean it, or I am going to need to drink all of this blood myself and risk going insane If you do not agree then it will be the only way I will be able to defeat him. If only I could have stopped him the other night. Though the blood will make me stronger, I will risk too much and beside that you will need it more than I. It may make you even stronger than me. I am not sure, but then again, no one can ever really be sure of anything. The more blood you drink the stronger you will become and soon we will be powerful enough together to defeat the Master." she said. She gave me a kiss on the cheek and handed me the bottle. As I took the bottle as well as the kiss, I remembered what she said. But I still wanted to learn about the Vaingels and their creation. She laughed and said, "Vaingels come in many forms for they are born from the ones that survive the attacks of the un-dead. It is believed that a Vaingel is a vampire's salvation. It is when a vampire has destroyed its own bloodline. See, if I had destroyed Joseph and then drank his blood. The blood of the dead master would break the spell of the dead. I wouldn't have to fear the Sun nor other weapons that vampires must be concerned with. We could live as true immortals. Walking with mortal man and never having to allow them to know us as being something different. When the bloodsucker drank from you, I was in pursuit of him and he lost me. When I discovered his location, he had already attacked you. I saved you that night, and may God forgive me. For it would have been kinder to allow him to kill you. I wish I could at least tell you that I was able to catch him, but he got away."

She seemed so ashamed that she was not able to stop this Joseph, She started to cry some and then I just held her. I could see how sorry she felt but she knew she could not do anything to change it. I wanted to ask her so many things, but with her crying and us talking I did not know that so much time had passed... The sun began to rise and I felt its heat fill this lost cave of dirt. The caved filled with such a powerful morning glow. Its soft rays began to cook me... I covered my eyes and ran as she was saying something, but I was too afraid to hear her or focus, so I kept running. I knew I wouldn't be able to make it home, so I decided to go back to the school. I could smell my own flesh as it cooked in the sun soft rays. As I crossed Market Street, I began to smoke so I thought quickly and ran to the underground trolley system. I reached the underground tunnel on Market Street. There was no way the sun could kill me if I avoided its powerful rays. I remained there until the pain from the sun left me unharmed. Its marks remained with me but I know I had to get going. When I was sure there were no trains on the tracks I ran with my vampire speed. I knew if there was a train coming, it would be behind me and it would have to stop at every platform. I was running straight to City Hall, so the chance of me getting stopped by the train was impossible. As I passed every platform, I could see that the sun was growing stronger and its rays were becoming more deadly. I did not expect the westbound El train to make so much noise, but it did. It made so much noise that I could not continue to run. I dropped to my knees and covered my ears as the El train ran past my awaiting body. I had to really focus after the train passed to get up and continue running. I knew that one of the trolley trains would be coming soon so I picked up speed so not to get caught by it. Once I reached City Hall Station, I rose from the tracks to the platform and went towards the free exchange to the Broad Street Line. I was lucky, because the southbound train was just pulling up when I reached the platform. So I got on it and went to the Lombard & South Station. I was afraid to leave the station and enter the sunlight. I realized that if I waited too long, the sun would have completely arisen and that would be my death... So I ran with God in my heart and the sun's rays on my back. I pulled my shirt over my head for some protection, but not much. I took in a deep breath and ran up the steps. I ran as fast as I could and in seconds, I was on Broad Street and Pine. I came up the north side stairs so I was on the right side of the street. I ran down the block, crossed Pine and ran until I entered the building of my school.

As my skin began to burn, I entered the school and since the front entrance of the school was all glass, I ran past the guard. It was George who was on duty at the time. I ran to the back of the building and took the steps into the basement. Scared and in great pain I ran and hid in the men's room. I ran over to the mirror to see how badly my skin was burned. My skin was like flakes of paint peeling from a wall. It looked sickening. The flakes of skin was curling up and falling off my face as I just watched. I could still smell the burned skin as it fell to the sink. I know I would be fine but the fear in my eyes and the pain in my face will stay with me. I can still remember the way I looked that day. When I calmed down, and my body began to heal itself, I was amazed the way my skin had healed itself and the pain departed. I washed my face and looked up in the mirror again. For the first time I was able to see myself with my new eyes. My skin was so beautiful it turned into some bronze-like color. It was soft and graceful. No signs of age showed. It was as if time stopped and painted me a perfect face. To look at it gave me peace and then I fell under a spell. I touched it with blind amazement. My eyes seemed to shine like two crystal spheres. The lashes were long and had the most beautiful black curl. They looked as if they belonged on some kind of doll. I wondered if they were always that long and I just never realized it. My hair was to die for... It was long black curls, really no different than before but seems to be blacker for some reason. I reach for it slowly. I kind of felt pulled to touch it. I could not fight the feeling of its seductive wave. As I played in my hair I felt a strange presence. I was so caught up in myself that I did not notice George standing behind me. I quickly bent down and splashed my face with water. George said, "Xavier, what has happened to you?" I saw him looking at me in the mirror. The look in his eyes told a story of their own. I wasn't sure if he seen my whole trans formation but the horror quickly left him. His face went completely blank as if he know more than he wanted me to know. I realized he was looking at my new skin... Man, was he surprised. He asked, "What have you walked yourself into...now?" He took a small step back as he rested his hand on his chest, as if death stood before him. He tilted his head just a little, slit his eyes and spoke again, "Look at your skin! Are... You OK?"

For some reason his reaction pissed me off... I spun around and asked, "Why are you looking at me like that!? (I ran in front of him and stood there.) Are you afraid?" (For a brief moment, I wanted to feel his fear.) But, George being George, just continue looking at me as if he was sure of whatever he knew. "Or are you here to find a way to blame me for the events that took place three days ago?" (He seemed surprised that I knew.) "Yes, I know that Drew spoke to you. Everyone speaks to you when I do something. Why do they feel the need to always search you out and you try to blame me for everything that goes wrong? Maybe... I haven't done anything! But you still need it to be my fault. You really hate the idea that something happened to me and I did not run to you. I came into this school and said nothing to you for a reason. I do not want your pity or your help. I can fix this on my own." (I really did not know why he enraged me, but he did. I knew I had to get him the hell away from me. I just could not handle his shit. I was not ready for how I get myself into things and never think about how I am going to get out. I wanted to tell him that I was the victim, but telling George that was like telling a priest I can't believe in God.) He always believed that we create our own hell on Earth and after death. When I stood there and looked at him. Fear never entered his heart. He knew I was upset and I guess felt I had to work things out for myself. So he closed his eyes and turned away, deciding to leave and told me if I wanted to talk, then he would be in that following night. When he left the bathroom, I believed he was pissed off, but no one could never really be sure when it come to George. Especially when he gives in so easily... I knew I had to stand my ground. It was neither his life nor his problem. George could never deal with not being able to control someone else's life. You could easily see it in his eyes and his mannerism. He always wanted to be right. I could not really tell you a time that George did not get upset when he was not having his way. He really was an aggressive person, but this was not a time for me to stroke his ego. I had to decide what to do next...

I walked around the basement for a while and talked with some of the students but realized that this was going to be hard. There was no way I was going to be able to stay in the basement all day. Then I remembered that there were no windows on one of the upper floors. On my way to the elevator, I realized that the one who did this to me was still alive. This Joseph was still walking the streets and feeding on others. I felt ill at the thought that he was claiming the souls of the helpless, only to grow strong enough to seek out the one who had become my savior. I had no doubt of whether or not I would have to help her stop Joseph, but to destroy him!? I mean, God has created everyone and he is nothing different. I had no right to decide to take the life of this guy, no matter what she says he did. For all I knew, she could be lying and I would be helping her to kill an innocent man. I mean, it is one thing to teach a person a lesson, but to kill them is something different all together. I mean even if he did this to me I could not say he was evil. I really wanted to help her, but to kill was just not me. I wondered if she had already realized that and thought that she could change my belief. I wanted to believe that she had all good intentions, but the fact was that I did not know much about her. If I was to believe that this guy was a nut of some kind. Then I needed her to prove it to me. As I stepped on the elevator, I felt a strange feeling come over me. It was as if I sensed another being in my mind. As if! Someone was trying to talk to me but I thought that I was just bug' in. As I got off the elevator, I walked to the eating area and decided to hang out there for a while. Watching everyone eating throughout the morning was very boring. I kept falling off to sleep and waking back up. You know, a bunch of cat naps. Sometimes I could hear people talking and later realized I was hearing their thoughts. I really heard them when they looked upon me and was thinking, "What's wrong with him?", "He seems so strange", or they would find me "beyond attractive." They seemed to draw to me like a drug. I mean, it was unnatural, the way they watched me and some lusted for me with unbelievable passion. Many of the girls would start a conversation with me in hope to kiss me or do a lot more. It was strange the way I was able to hear their thoughts. It even appeared that I could control many of their minds. I decided to try a little test. I concentrated on this girl who was sitting down at the table next to me eating. At first she was able to fight my thoughts but then it happened. She rose from the table and walked over to some guy who was trying to decide on what he wanted to snack on from the machines in front of him. She walked up from behind him and wrapped her arms around him. As he turned around to see who she was, I made her kiss him on the lips. She kissed him like they were lovers and as she pulled away, I released her mind. He was at a loss for words, but seemed intrigued over what she did. He stood there and just smiled as she looked into his blue eyes. It was really cool, the way he slowly reached for her waist. She pulled away from him and he just stood there unsure what to say or do. She was so confused and was not sure if she should run away and just returned to her seat with the most lost look in her eyes. He told her his name and she told him hers. Actually they started to talk and soon her action was pushed aside and they hit it off pretty good. I was happy that they were cool with it, but I was still bored so I just looked around to see who else I could bother.

Then some guys came into the area and I decided to play with them as well. One of them was about six foot tall and the other two were about five foot ten or eleven inches. The tall one was a red hair and the other two were blondes. I laughed as one of the blondes was talking 'bout the other one being gay. The other one was a little passive, so I decided to have fun with the more aggressive one. I took control of his mind quickly. I was not sure if it was because he was not focused on anything important. He grew quiet and just looked at the taller one, who was also picking with the other blonde too. Then I made him grab the red hair friend's crotch area. The red hair friend was pissed and knocked his hand away. Then the red haired pushed him away from his side. I released the guy's mind. The guy was confused at what was happening, but the red haired kid was so pissed that he called the guy all kinds of assholes. I was laughing so loud that it grabbed their attention. The quiet blonde just laughed to himself and looked at me as if he understood why I was really laughing... He was a very attractive young guy. I even had to admit to myself that he was going to be ok, even though he was hanging out with two dickheads for friends. I realized the red hair guy needed to do something now. So I made him grab the aggressive blonde headed boy into a headlock and caused him to go down to the floor. After he had the guy who grabbed his crotch were on the floor, I made him sit on the guy's chest and rub his friend's face into his crotch and demanded his friend to beg for it. It took some time before the guy did it, but when his friend finally did it. I released the redhead's mind. He knew what he did, just not why he did it. When he released his friend from under him the aggressive blonde ran off and the second blonde looked at the redhead as if to call him an asshole. Then, he ran after the first blonde begging him to wait. The redhead just stood there confused. This went on for some time. After a while I decided to stop playing my game on the people nearby. I sat there in peace for some time until I realized that someone called the guard on me. The only thing that bothered me about the fact that security would walk by and look at me as if I was not supposed to be there. It wasn't that they ever said anything to me but the fact they grow nervous at my presence. This game grew boring fast so I decide to cause the guards not to register my presence. Around seven of clock, I headed down stairs. As I reached the first floor, I could feel the heat of the passing sun burning my body as it escaped my sight, being tortured by its power, but being forbidden to see its face. Just a day ago, this sun that teased my eyes and embraced my body in it's love, was about to cook me. I knew then that I was a vampire and that I should find this one who saved me. I was able to sense her in my mind's eye, but was not able to see where she was. I thought about finding her right then, but my friends came to mind. I realized they had to be worried about me, because I never returned home. I knew I was going to have to go home sooner or later. I thought it would be best to go now. On my way home, I began to think: What was I going to tell my friends!? What questions could I answer and what facts would they believe?

There was no way I was going to tell them that I was a vampire, let alone ask them to believe I am going to try to become this

Vaingel... That is, if I myself was to really believe what she said was true. As I walked down the darkening streets of Philly, I realized I really did not know much about my savior. All I remember was that she was my savior with the most beautiful eyes. Moreover, why? I am not sure! Perhaps that was because when the blood took control of my body, her eyes where the first things I took notice of. As I approached my house, I began to anticipate what Mark and Drewwere going to say. I stopped at the front door. I knew George must had called and told them what happened, so I just took a second to gather myself before grabbing the doorknob. As I opened the door, my ears awaited those famous words I always hear: 'Xavier, dude, where in the hell were you?' But I heard nothing. There I was, standing in the open doorway, listening to nothing but the wind, echoing through my empty home. I heard no one. I sensed no one. Here I stood... In my hour of need and my friends has left me alone. Those who I have sought for aid have fuck' in abandoned me. I'm left the fuck alone. I grew pissed. I decided at this point to just change my clothes and go eat. I could not believe that with all this madness going on that they would just pull up and roll like that. I quickly became focused as hunger for blood grew and my pain grew more intense. I ran to the refrigerator, as if the sustenance that I craved was actually there. I gripped the door handle of the refrigerator and it occurred to me that I no longer was human. What I needed, I left at Thirtieth Street., under the bridge. If the bottle of blood was still there, it was still early; I thought that maybe I could make it there and back OK... If the girl did not take it, I would be okay.

It crossed my mind that I left her there. I mean, she could be near death, because the sun did rise. Maybe I thought of her because she needed me. Maybe, I was to go to her when I first sensed her. I decided to return to the bridge for the blood and whatever was left of my savior. I ran out the door, not even thinking to check if it was locked or not. All I knew was that I needed to get there as fast as I could. I ran up Lombard Street to 22nd Street and took 22nd Street straight to Market Street. When I got there, I was able to see the parking lot that she took me to and I ran across it and jumped over its fence. I landed like I was made to fly. I ran back towards Lombard Street, following the train tracks until I reached the spot where she gave me the blood. I went to the trash pile and there it was the large jug of blood. I looked for her remains, but there was not anything there. All I saw was a hole in the earth. The hole looked like it could have housed rats, or maybe something larger. I took the jug and started back home. I continued to walk towards Lombard St. until the train tracks passed a park. The opening in the gate led me to 24th and Locust. This was crazy... I decided to take a drink and then go home. As I sat there, I drank the blood of my attacker and worried about my savior. Surely, she was dead... I knew I had to hide the blood and return home. While closing the bottle back, I felt a strange feeling in my stomach and I fell to one knee. I placed the bottle down and braced myself for the blood effects to take place just as it did last night. I felt my arms thicken and my legs. They hurt with such pain I just screamed out loud. My body started to shake and I tried to claw into the street. My eyes went blind for a moment and then my teeth seemed to thicken. My face started to cramp up. This went on for about ten minutes and then passed. I rose again and grabbed the bottle of blood. As I walked up the street, I accepted that this was going to happen every time I drank from this blood. I hid the bottle and wasted no time getting back home. I opened the door and without thinking about the fact that the door was unlocked, I walked in.

I was greeted by Drew, Marco and Landis. They seemed a little bothered by my behavior. Marco stood looking at me through his light-brown eyes that seemed to reflect the light of the room. Marco was not a big man, but was able to scare me easily. He was about five-foot and nine inches tall. He had to weigh about a hundred and twenty pounds. I think it was the way his hair seemed to wave when he got upset with me. Marco spoke first and pretty much talked about my comings and goings. He said, "Yo!' Xavier men, what's wrong with you, dude? You been gone for two days, man... Yo', what the fuck? You had us looking all over for you and nobody saw you. Then you come home and leave the front door unlocked. Damn, man! Why are you bugging like this? 'Drew is like telling us about that weird shit you laid on him 'a shit... what the fuck! Xavier, man, you got to get yourself together." I watched as his body began to tense up as the veins in his arms began to show themselves. Landis was standing there with his hands on his hips. He was just a few inches shorter that Marco, but with his shaved head he was even more intimidating than Marco. His eyes locked with mine. He had so much anger in them. He took a deep breath and then raised one hand to his mouth and pulled down on his face in frustration. He looked at Marco, then back to me. Landis said, "What the fuck are you doing, Xavier? I spoke to George and he told me what happened between you two. Drew explained what you told him the other night. Now you leave for two days and then when you finally come home, you leave and do not even lock the door. They're all running around worried about you and about your behavior... not to mention that crazy ass story you told Drew." At this point, I looked at Drew, then Marco and finally back at Landis. I apologized to them for my actions, but I had to tell them...that the story was true.

'Drew looked at me again with his disappointment stare. Landis and Marco started to talk again. I waited until they were finished speaking their minds. I told them to calm down and be seated. I walked across the room thinking about the best way to start my story. I repeated the part that I told Drew and then I started to tell them about the woman and everything she told me. Drew told me that he felt the woman's story was about as crazy as the vampire story. The time came where I was forced to show them everything I could do. First, I told them what they were eating before I came home, for I was able to smell everything that they ate. I then told them I could hear Marco's girlfriend upstairs in his room. I was able to hear her on the phone even though she was on the third floor. Marco picked up the phone, only to find out that I was right. As they turned to look at me, I used my speed to move to the other side of the room. I laughed and then ran again. Drew jumped up and turned with fear in his eyes. I then sat down beside Landis and started to laugh. Once I showed them that there was something different about me and that I must be a vampire. Drew said, "I think that we need to find out what you are... Even if you are correct, or should I say if the lady is correct, then we need to find out what you can and cannot do. This is not some normal shit! We have to be sure that what you are saying is true. Marco said, "I think we need to go see George. He should be able to help!" As we walked towards the school Drew asked, "Do you really believe that happened? Come on man, what happened to you that night?" I told him that I was not too sure what happened when I awoke, nor when I tried to remember it yesterday, but for some reason can I not remember every detail of that evening now. Landis stopped us from discussing it until we got to the school.

George was working in his usual building but to our surprize so was Garrett. So when we got there Landis said, "What's up, George?" George rose, like a father waiting for his children. He hugged and shook hands with George. George and Garrett started greeting each of us with handshakes. I walked over to George who was standing there, allowing his arrogance to exude from every pore. I looked at him, and then asked George for his forgiveness about the other morning. He hugged me and told me that he was not angry with me, just disappointed in my childish behavior. He said that he felt that I just needed time to myself. He turned towards everyone else and asked why they were here. Drew demanded me to tell George everything that I told them. I really was not sure where to start, so I started from the beginning. Everyone sat around the lobby as George's eyes grew sharp and focused directly on me. I started with the fact that I went to the movies that Monday and it was late when I headed home. I told him that I was walking up Walnut Street and then turned on Fifth Street... George interrupted...

"What made you decide to go out that night and why would you turn on Fifth Street? For that matter, why would you even walk up Walnut Street?" George asked.

"I do not know I just wanted to...." I answered.

I grew a little nervous about answering George's questions. They always lead conversations to places I never felt comfortable with, but I knew he was going to ask them. He looked at me as if he already gathered something. I continued and told him that I then turned onto Locust Street... George interrupted again.

"Why did you turn onto Locust? There's nothing there..." George asked.

"I just did..." I said.

"Really..."

"Yes, but there was a man on the corner and after I passed him, he then appeared in the middle of the block."

"How did he appear in front of you?"

"Well-"

"Did he run in front of you?"

"I am-"

"Or did he appear in a cloud of smoke?" (At this point Marco and Drew laughed)

With every statement I made, George had a question. This only confused me even more. Garrett demanded that I be allowed to finish and then they would question everything to find out what was important and what wasn't. George turned towards Garrett and started vamping:

"It is all important! How else are we to know what happened?" George asked, almost frantically.

"Xavier will tell us everything we need to know." Garrett said.

"And how is Xavier going to tell us anything, when it is clear to me that he isn't aware of anything?"

"George!!"

"What will Xavier leave out? Maybe the fact that there isn't anything there of concern, but that apartment building and maybe the graveyard we used to drink in.", George said.

"George, it is Xavier' story: We need to let him tell it."

"Garrett, we are far from children. Are you trying to tell me that you do not know where this is going?"

"George. The point isn't what I know or do not know. The fact is that it is Xavier' story let him tell it."

"Fine..."

Garrett gave George a stern look, something he only did when he had enough of George's bitching or being a drama queen. I gathered myself and started again. George looked at me while I spoke, but showed no form of interest and went into his aloof state. I felt a little intimidated, but I kept on explaining the events as they happened, even up to the point of when I met the woman and continued to where she gave me the blood. I was a little concerned about telling them anything about this woman. Or what she said about the Vaingels. Therefore, I did not tell them, I figured that if they could help me figure out most of this, then I would be able to deal with the rest of it on my own. Once I was finished, they commented. George commented first.

"Xavier, I believe you."

"George! Why are you playing with Xavier's head?" Landis said.

"I am not playing. I do believe him."

"George, stop this bullshit. You do not believe him any more than the rest of us."

"Well, then what the hell do you think happened!!?"

"Everyone calm down... Now, I do believe Xavier believes what he had experienced was real and George is forced to take Xavier' word just like he would take any of yours." Garrett responded.

Well, at this point George went crazy and started yelling. George usually does this whenever he doesn't get his way in our debates. I guess in some way, I should be grateful that he was on my side... Or was he!? I listened as George sarcastically pointed out what was obvious about me.

"First of all, we should not play as if any of us are surprised at this because if Xavier had bothered to attend the meeting I requested a week ago we would not be having this conversation. Now! Maybe I am blind, but it seems obvious to me from the door that his skin has gone through some form of abnormal change." George said.

"Maybe so, but that doesn't make him a vampire. At most, it tells me that Xavier is tripping again. For all we know Xavier could have been wilding on something more than weed!" Landis answered.

"Oh please, Landis! You mean to tell me that you do not see all the changes in Xavier's behavior as well? Even the way that he sits there and studies our actions? His vampire nature is taking control of him as we speak. Now, I knew Xavier was becoming something more than human. So, Garrett and I went to study up on the history of vampires in the city library. Not that the shit they have is real, but it is something."

"So, you believe that he is a vampire and that the woman saved him?"

"I never said that... I said I believe what he said, but the fact is, Xavier needs to tell us everything about what happened that night and about this woman whom I have no doubt he has labeled his savior. I do mean everything, because for all Garrett and I know, he can be something totally different."

Well, Landis was still demanding that George stop treating me like a child. He looked at George with such stern eyes and everyone else just sat there. I could feel the fear of his rage moving throughout the room, but George did not bend. Garrett seemed to have been intrigued for a moment, and then Landis began to explain. They sat there and listened to Landis talk about my careless behavior. Landis said, "Look George! You have to stop doing this. I mean, every time Xavier decides to do something dumb, you try to make sense out of it. The fact is there is no truth to Xavier's story."

"Then Xavier's imagination is so wild, that we are all being affected by it. Come on, Landis, It is clear, clear enough for anyone to see that something attacked Xavier." George responded.

"I am not saying that something did not happen."

"Then what are you saying?"

"If we are going to help him, then we need to be honest and look at the facts... Really look at all of them."

"The facts... are being?"

"Xavier always does this. He disappears and returns with some new kind of madness, it isn't Xavier's first time vanishing for days..."

"Yes." George said, raising his right hand from the desk. "But it is his first time to return with such evidence of his experience. Even you cannot deny this or explain the things Xavier told us he did back at the house."

Everyone started to debate against George about me as if I was not there. I even wished I wasn't. Landis's raged at everything going on around him and anger took focus on George. "How in the hell can~ are you doing this? You're playing with his mind and ours. You have no more of an idea on what happened than the rest of us. You're sitting here and acting as if you dealt with things like this before." Landis said.

"Those who seek advice from a fool are either fools themselves... Or in denial..." George said...

"What are you talking about, George!?"

"And to be in denial of this fact, is to avoid truth..."

"Avoid truth!?"

"And where are you without truth?"

"George...You're not listening..."

"For that matter, WHAT are we without truth??"

"Enough!" Garrett said. "Look-, If George is right, and then...

we have problems. One is the fact that the one who made Xavier may be looking for him."

"What!" Landis said.

"This master vampire was able to read Xavier's mind. He had to be able to see his memories. If he did do this,

Then he knows who we are and where to find all of us. For all we know, he may be listening to us right now." Garrett said.

"Garrett, you're getting as crazy as George!"

"Remember, he called Xavier by his name... Say Xavier isn't lying.

Then we have big problems."

I remembered what the woman said about the blood of the Master and assured them that the Master could not read my mind, since I drank the blood. George looked at me as rage filled his eyes and demanded that I tell them everything! Stop leaving things out. Even if I did not think it was important, they wanted to know it. Therefore, of course, I told him all I could 'remember'. George asked me to tell him more about this woman that saved me. There really was not much I could tell him, except that she was a woman who was so beautiful and graceful that she would cause any man to fall in love with her. George spoke again,

"No... Xavier...!!" George said, shaking his head, "Do not tell me... You're in love with her, right?!?"

"No..." I answered.

"Do not lie."

"I am not~"

"Of course, you are..."

"But George, Man... It isn't~"

"Of course, it is! And you and I know it. You're falling for this bitch. For all you know, she is lying to you and you're repeating her lies..."

"Dude, I am only telling you what I know... That's it!"

"Yes, you always tell us what you know... The problem is that there is still even more going on that you do not know. Can't you see that, or is it too late for me to reach you?"

"That's not fair and you know it, George! Man..., I am dealing with a lot."

"Yeah, you are! I guess! I should take comfort in the fact that you can see that."

"Why are you getting upset?"

I regretted the question as it left my lips. Now you must first understand that George is a very powerful force of will for one to have to deal with by himself. So picture what I must have been feeling since all the others were there as well. George rose, allowing his flamboyant nature to take the floor. He walked across the lobby like the diva he claims to be. Allowing his five foot eleven inch frame to master the area like an actor on stage, he raised his left hand in the air as if to mock me. He looked at everyone as if they were all challenging him.

"Why? Because you are standing here and telling me that you think you might be a vampire. But, I shouldn't be pissed! Perhaps I should feel sorry for you. Xavier! Would that please you? Is that the George you want to talk with? Well, that's too bad; because the fact is that you are no more surprised by my behavior than you are at the fact that you are a vampire."

"But, I am not sure..."

"Stop lying!"

"George, Man..."

"The facts are the facts. You were taken advantage of by this mad man, but if you are trying to make me believe that you can't see the changes in your appearance as well as all these things I am sensing to be coming from you, then now I am even more pissed. It is clear that I have been wasting time and knowledge on teaching you to look outside of yourself for clues that everyone gives freely when they seek to use someone."

"George, man, it's~"

"Xavier!"

"No, George you don't~"

"Xavier!! Listen to me, this woman is using you. Perhaps the master can't read your mind, but what about her? Can she really be trusted!?"

"No, George, she isn't~"

"Then you are a fool." Everyone tries to interrupt, but Garrett stops them and allows George to finish chastising me. There is no way in Hell, I am going to believe that she saved you out of the goodness in her heart, that is, if she even has a heart. That bitch did something to this master and used you to do it. Or is responsible for what happened to you. Then, on top of all of that,

You are showing me that you might be in love with this creature that bears no name. Who no doubt, is old enough to be your mother and for that matter, she is probably old enough to be your mother's mother! Damn it!"

"That's not fair! Man, you do not even know her."

"Xavier! Look at the big picture... You're running around this forsaken city pretending like the world owes you something. Well, wake the hell up. Your parents: I have no doubt haven't seen or heard from you and are worried sick. Now, as for your friends and their twisted views on you're fucked up life. I have a few words on that. I may not be that much older than you, but I am older and I will not allow any of you and your backwards views to blind me from what I see and know to be facts! Xavier is in trouble and whether he brought it upon himself or not, we have to do something and fighting over something we can't change is not the answer." George said.

George did upset me, but I must admit, even now, I still desired her. This woman whom: is old enough to be my mother. This creature, which for some reason has become closer to me than anyone I knew. I have to admit that he did make me realize that I had a lot to think about. George wouldn't stop being a smart-ass, so I decided I was going to just leave. I told them that I was going to think about what all of them said, but I needed some air. I walked out of the door and used my vampire speed to move, so I knew they were not able to follow me. I went to Rittenhouse Square and sat on the bench across from the water fountain. I watched the people who were entering the park from Walnut Street I started to think about everything, I mean..., so much has happened and so quickly. In no time at all, my life has changed completely. Nothing is as it was meant to be and my savior is the only thing that came to mind. She really was a beautiful woman and so graceful that any man would love her.Only thing I had to deal with was the fact that this woman was old enough to be my mother.

I thought back at how I looked at her and asked why the blood of the master was so important. Why could I not have just drunk from her? She just laughed and told me that the blood you drink must come from your maker for if a vampire drinks the blood of another vampire then there is no telling what gifts the blood will give them. With every vampire you drink from a new gift could be born or you could grow stronger in the gifts you already possessed. See, that is why you can't drink the blood of the living. It is true that it does ease the hunger. But it doesn't give us anything else of val~. Then she stopped herself and said, "That is not true it does allow one to connect to their emotions for a short time. Making one feel as if they were still alive. It would be unfair of me to say that the blood of many beings didn't have an affect on us." There are many kinds of creatures in the world. It is just that humans believe they are the only ones. I guess they take comfort in knowing or believing that there is nothing stronger or more intelligent than them. Never the less, for me to pretend that if you did not have some reservation about helping me. Then I would be foolish. You should be afraid for so much has happened for a short time. And the more comfortable you become with who you are the more you'll learn of the real world. You will see the world through new eyes. You will come to understand that humans are not alone.

Chapter 3
The First Lesson

I sat there just thinking about everything, especially this Vaingels stuff. It really was too much for me to accept, let alone to try to get someone else to believe. My mind raced at the thought that this was not real. I began to wonder if this was a dream. You know, the kind that seemed real, but then you awake to only find out it was a dream. I sat there in silence, when I heard a voice that was sweeter than any candy one could taste. "You seem lost, my hero. Why are you so confused?" the voice said. I turned and stated that she was the problem. I told her that I did not even know her name. She looked at me with her big green eyes. Her long reddish curly hair falling over her shoulders, as one piece hung over her right eye. Her lips parted with such grace that I was forced to watch the words release themselves from their captivity. She said, "My name is Elizabeth. Lady Elizabeth, Mistress of the Red Waters of Zarasgale."

"The Red Waters of Zarasgale", I thought. What a strange name, I asked her what it meant, but Elizabeth did not answer. She looked at me and smiled. She reached around me and rested her arm on my shoulder. I took comfort in her touch. As we watched the crowd of people passed us, I knew that she was telling me the truth. The fates had crossed our paths for a reason and to love her was only one of those reasons. I rose, she joined me and we walked arm in arm towards Locust Street... I asked her if we were evil beings or were we beings of darkness. She laughed and told me that, "We are nothing but beings. It does not matter whether you see us as beings of light or darkness. We are just everyday people. I have lived for two hundred years and I have not seen any great sign that makes us any more or less than that. We are different, yes, but better? No, just different... We have a great deal of problems connected with what we are, such as being hunted like any other creature and killed just the same. Yet, we are more than any one could imagine. That is why we are able to exist." She stopped and stood in front of me and placed both hands on my arms and said, "Xavier, you must understand that we are amongst the last few survivors of our kind. We must grow stronger and then create new ones to aid us in our cause. We will be able to destroy the Master and free ourselves from his curse. The undead are damned souls, but Vaingels are saviors and their jobs are to give others salvation or death. The fact is that Van Gels have been around as long as every other creature of nature's realm. It was said that Vaingels are God's tools to help the damned ones to find salvation." We started walking some more as she continued telling me of many rules that I was to follow and that the most important was never to drink the blood of the living. For once one does become a Vaingels and if that Vaingels drinks the blood of the living, then that Vaingels has chosen to become offspring of either darkness or light. When this happens, we then will be forced to destroy that Vaingels."

To destroy a Vaingels told me that we can die. I asked her this in hope to discover some way to end this fate that I have damned myself into. She said, "Concern you not of this, and just know that it can be undone... You are immortal and like a phoenix, you shall rise from your ashes to be anew. Know that a new Vaingels is too young to walk in the sun and usually is for the first hundred years." With that, she stopped speaking and started to smile. She looked at me and then started to run. I followed her. She started to use her vampire speed and so did I. We ran over to 15th & Samson St. She jumped into the air and grabbed hold to the third level gate of the parking garage on the corner and so did I. She started to climb up the fence and then leaped into the air and landed on the roof of the photocopy store on Samson St. I was almost too afraid to follow, but I did it anyway. I realized I would follow her to Death's gate if she asked me to. I was in love and that was the fact that I accepted right then. I understood what it all was about... I loved her! I love Elizabeth. She was the one of my dreams. She had waited on me for over two hundred years so we would be together.

When I landed on the roof trying to catch my breath, she kissed me and started to run to the back of the roof. I followed, running up on her like a child playing with his friend. I grabbed her from behind and wrapped my arms around her waist and we fell to the floor of the roof. She looked back towards me and smiled. I was a little lost for words but I looked in her eyes. I felt like she knew what I wanted to say, so she said it for me. She told me that she was falling in love with me as well. I leaned towards her and we kissed. We kissed with such passion that I knew she was the one. I started to kiss her lower and upper lips separately. Then I felt the fire between us break and I bit her lower lip as she moaned, passion filled her eyes. I sucked the blood from its soft tissue as I caress her body. She responded by returning the bite and sucking my blood, our blood mixed as we kissed. She turns over on top of me and we grind against each other. She rose while still on top of me and tore open my shirt as she leaned over and bit my left nipple. She started sucking on it and this drove me wild. I grabbed the back of her head and gripped a hand full of her hair as I forced more of my chest into her mouth. My heart was racing and I loved the feeling she was giving me. I pulled her off me and forced her onto the other breast. I started to grow weak as she drank but did not care. She was causing me to have wild passion attacks. First I got the shakes, my legs locked and my eyes rolled up into my head. Then I started to rave with passion as she caressed my waist and slowly undid my pants. I was unable to control the feelings that were surfacing. She kissed down my stomach toward my mid area. Her hands rubbed across my inner thighs, and then she raised her head, smiled and bit into my upper thigh, right next to my penis. It drove me crazy! I felt her teeth enter my thigh and the pain was replaced with passion. I started telling her, "Suck me, yes... Suck me, baby... Please do not stop... I love you... Please... Please...", and with that, she rose and kissed me on the lips again.

Blinded by passion I was acting without thinking. I started kissing her back. Our lips separated slowly as I moved onto her neck and lowered myself to her shoulders. I place small bites on her neck and shoulders. I kissed and sucked on her neck, then her shoulders. My hands caressed her breast as we rolled over and I was on top. I rose to my knees and straddled her stomach. I bit into her neck and she clawed my back. I knew she loved it, so I started to suck on her even harder relishing in the pleasure I felt as her blood entered me. My mind raced with thoughts that I never could have imagined without this night happening. We were truly connecting! As I drank from her I listened to her heart beat with fire as I no doubt believed she did when she bit me. I was possessed by the blood and went wild. I grabbed her breasts and bit into them and sucked as hard as I could without ripping them off. I could hear her heart slowing down but she told me to continue. She forced my head even harder against her breast. She encouraged me to continue and I did. Her blood warmed me and blessed me with even greater strength than I already possessed. As our bodies recovered from this experience, we just laid there, lost in each other's thoughts. She started to pat the back of my head. It felt like my penis became erect, but I guess that it isn't capable anymore.

We gathered ourselves and I lit up a cigarette. We sat there for more than twenty minutes not saying a word. I turned to her and told her that my friends know about her and the Master. She said that she already knew. She said that she knew I would tell them. She became interested in what they thought. I told her that George thinks that she is evil, or at least, lying to me. He believes that you are using me. She turned and place one hand on the roof and the other she rested on her shoulder. Elizabeth said, "Tell me, my little Xavier! Do you trust me, my love?" I told her of course I did! She smiled and then kissed me. I told her that I needed to go home and get new clothes. She laughed and told me that she would join me in my walk home. We gathered our things and then got up and walked to the edge of the roof. I told her that I do not think I could jump off the roof. Elizabeth said, "You can do anything you want to do, if you really want to do it bad enough." With that, she jumped off the roof and landed on the ground. I started to jump, but a man turned the corner, so I stopped and waited for him to leave the block. When I jumped, she laughed and told me that I should have seen my face. We both started to laugh as we walked down the street. We walked past the school and I was able to see that the guys were still at the school with George and Garrett. She looked and said, "Is that them, your friends? Do not worry! They can't see us. I closed their eyes to our presence." I looked at her and then said, "Word!!" What a dumb thing for me to say, but I said it anyway. I quickly thought back to when I did the same thing to the guards in the school earlier.

We turned and walked down Pine St. and I asked her what else can we do? She told me that we could do many things like run at great speed, control humans beings minds. We have great strength and our eyes can see clearly in the dark. I told her about the things I had seen and did after the virus entered my body. I told her how I awoke and heard wild shit and seen crazy things. She laughed and said that we all go through that kind of transformation. That is how we become what we become. I laughed and thought that this is some wild, God-fearing shit going on! We continued to walk the streets and I ran into people I knew or they knew one of my friends. She told me that back in the old days, many of them would have made great meals. I asked her to not speak like that;

after all, they were my friends. She laughed and told me that she was sorry and wouldn't make jokes like that again. I told her, "Cool.", and we continued to walk. We reached my spot and one of my neighbors was sitting on his steps, so I asked her to make him not see us too. She looked at me and said, "No, Xavier... You can do it too. Just close your mind to everything around you and focus on him..." As I did it, she said, "That's it! Just tell him that we are not here and that he is looking straight through us. That he is still seeing what was here when we weren't." It worked and he continued to act like nothing was happening. He really did not see us or hear us. This gave me an idea. After I changed my clothes, I told her that I wanted to go back to the school and to sit with my friends. She looked as if she really did not want to even bother, but decided to follow me anyway.

When we got there, everyone was still talking; in fact, even Zack, Vinnie and Casper were there. I stood outside at the door until Tayguya came by and opened the door. We entered the building with him. I told her everyone's names and who they were to me. I decided to sit on top of a trash can and she stood beside me. I was not really sure if any one saw the can move, but since they continued to talk, I believed they did not. We listened as they all were talking. Drew and Landis took turns explaining my story to everybody in the lobby. Mark would input his opinions as they talked. They were very hard on my whole behavior and really showed no sorrow for my dilemma. I was a little hurt by their actions, but the truth was that this was who my friends were. Elizabeth was shocked at everything they were saying. She believed that I had no idea that they felt the way they did towards me, but I ensured her that they spoke that way in my presence. Tayguya started to laugh and commented on the fact that this is just like me. I was not sure if I should have been upset, but I wasn't... I figured that he would say that. So it was cool. As we sat there, I started to think about how George always says he can sense his children and usually he does, but I am never sure if he does, or does he see you and makes you think he is sensing? He is such a bull shitter that we never really can tell, or at least, I can't. Landis and Casper started to debate whether if what George said is right and what if I was a Vampire. Garrett, being his usually protective self, said,

"Then we have a problem! See, it isn't the master we need to fear. It's the ~

"Quiet..." George said.

"Xavier is wild and that is true, but he is one of us and we~" Casper said.

"Quiet..." George replied.

Everyone grew quiet and looked at George. The fact of the matter was that even I grew nervous at George's response to what was happening. I sensed this was the moment of truth, for at that second, I would know how much of a bull shitter George really was. I wanted to warn Elizabeth, but chose not to, for I wanted to make sure there were no clues for him to see or hear. He looked around the room, and then looked in my direction. He waited there for a second, then looked away and then looked in my direction again. I grew even more nervous. Landis asked what was wrong and George responded that he was able to sense me. He insisted that he felt that I was there with them. Everyone began to laugh at George's madness, but Garrett did not and told them to be quiet. What really got me was he asked George where I was standing. As if he really believed that George was telling the truth. They watched as George looked around the room. He looked at me, but I was not sure if he saw me or not. Then he looked away and I did take comfort in that. Zack and the others started to look around the lobby, studying the walls and floors for some kind of clue. I then felt that George was guessing and relaxed, but he looked at me again and this time he did not turn away. Zack stood in front of me and studied the trash can that I was standing on. George told them that he was not sure, but he felt I was not alone. Marco told George that I wouldn't be dumb enough to bring someone here to see what they looked like. George told them that he felt the presence of another with me. Zack told everyone to look at the trash can. They all watched the can bend as if someone was on top of it. I got scared that George could feel our presence and there was no denying that the others did see my weight bending the can. I was so scared that I jumped off the trash can and knocked Zack out of my way. I ran out the door. Elizabeth seemed confused by my actions. She chose to followed me as I ran away, I looked back to see Garrett, Zack and Landis standing outside the door looking for us. I could not believe that George was able to sense me. George knew I was there and now so does everybody else. I wanted to just die. She looked at me while we were running, but I was too ashamed of myself to look back. I hated everything I was doing to them and now to myself. I made them my toys. I know I could not go home now, not after this. I then thought about the danger I put them in. I mean, if Marco was right, then they could be in great danger. What if she does kill them? What if she uses them to make me kill the Master? I grew ill and tripped over my own feet. I fell to the ground and ripped up my face and arm against the ground. I sat up on my bended knees. I released a bloody pool of vomit in front of myself. I did not realize how badly I hurt myself, because the wounds began to heal themselves rather quickly. She stopped and leaned over me to see if I was OK. Through my bloody tear-filled eyes, I looked into her eyes and then I knew I was worried about nothing. She was the one who saved me and wouldn't dare turn against me... No, not my Elizabeth!

I stood and decided that the time had come. I turned to her and told her that tomorrow night we would train for the hunt of the

Master. I figured the sooner I did this, the faster it would be over. I mean, if I killed the Master, then George would be wrong and everyone would be fine. She nodded her head and kissed me. She told me until tomorrow, then turned and ran off. I decided I had to find somewhere to sleep since I was not going to go home. I walked the streets for a while before I went to Peter's house. Apparently, he was not home, so I waited. He turned the corner on his block and approached me. I asked if I could chill out at his spot for a while. Of course, he did not have a problem with it, so I spent the day there. We talked about a lot of shit then he asked about my skin and eyes. Peter has always been direct and would freely put someone on the spot. After I told him my story, he laughed and repeated the same thing everyone else said, "Only you, Xavier, dude! Only you..." I sat there for some time before falling off to sleep. He stayed there with me for some time and rubbed my head like the big brother he always was to me.

My dreams were of more crazy shit. There were many faces appearing in my mind. I had talked to some of them, but fear kept me from hearing what they were saying. Some became beings that I fought with and others just watched as I worked my way past them. These images seemed so real, but I knew they could not be. I started running around and trying to fly. No sooner I would take to the air, I would drop back down to the ground. I knew I was dreaming, but I still was not able to control the images. Perhaps they too knew I was dreaming. Anyway, I saw this temple. It looked like a church or something close to it. I just thought my mind was playing tricks on me. I saw dirt roads and old buildings. I saw images of old people and great fires with a lot of death. I saw many people being burned alive. I thought this had to stop, but had no way of stopping it. I got vicious pictures of people dying heartless deaths. Blood was running out of one person's hands and ankles. Another was hanging from a ceiling or something and their head was removed. There were vampires there and they all drank from a large bowl that lay beneath this dead body. I was losing control and trying to wake up, but could not. My mind seemed to be trapped in this movie of madness and could not leave. Just when I thought I could not take anymore, Elizabeth's face appeared and overtook the dream. I awake in a bloody, sweaty mess. Thank God that Peter's floor was tile. I was able clean up my mess and decided to leave. I headed out to find Elizabeth so we could begin my lessons as a vampire. I knew I had to learn all I could if I meant to fight this Master.

As I walked down Walnut St., I was able to sense Elizabeth's presence and I followed my senses to Arco Park. She looked at me and then spoke to me inside my mind.

"This is how we speak, we the children of the Master Joseph."

"Word" I answered through my mouth.

"No one can hear our thoughts, but us."

"How do I do that?"

"Speak through your thoughts, feel what you want to say and allow your senses to find me and then I will hear your thoughts."

We sat there for about an hour before I was able to do it well enough to the point she was no longer concerned about her reaching me or I reaching her. We then started implanting thoughts into normal people's minds as they passed by. I did not have the heart to tell her that I already learned that, so I pretended not to know how to do it. Besides, I felt that I may have been doing it wrong and she would teach me the correct way it should be done. She explained that mind control was easy for us to master and usually it is one of the powers we learn to master first. The more she spoke the more I realized how important it was to her that I learned to use these powers. She pointed out that mind control isn't as easy as I may think. We only can get people to do things that are in there nature. Elizabeth explained that if we ever tried to force someone to act against their own nature, it could drive them insane or cause their minds to burn out. Sometimes they go into a coma and other times, they just lose their grasp on reality. For my next lesson, she took me to the Gallery shopping mall. She told me that the next lesson was to track people. We sat there and she chooses this man who was passing us by. I followed him in his mind using his eyes to see things around him, but I lost him when he entered a crowd of people. This happened a few more times, but it was very difficult to follow humans when their minds are grouped together in one place. All of their thoughts and feelings would become one, as they grouped together. I would lose them almost instantly the moment that a large group of people would come in play.

I did this for almost five hours and then realized I was too frustrated to continue, so we stopped and we headed back to Peter's apartment. I was tired, but I knew this was going to get harder. Elizabeth told me not to be worried. She placed her hand on the side of my face and rubbed me so gently. I grabbed her hand and kissed the back of it as she turned and tried to walk away. I held onto her hand and told her until tomorrow. I ran up the steps like a child with a new toy. These gifts were so wonderful to me. Only if I knew then what I know now. I lay down on Peter's floor and in no time, I was asleep. My dream took hold of me again and this time it was more orderly. First, I fell in a tunnel of light with some form of stone. It reminded me of a tower or something like that. I looked around and came before a man with deep features. He looked like a statue of marble. His skin was very cold looking and his hair seemed to grab hold of his neck like water running over a rock. He started to grow inside and he raised his arm while waving his hand. I flung across the room and hit the ivory stone wall. After hitting the floor, I looked to see him still standing there with his arm still in the air. His brown eyes scared the hell out of me. I tried to stand, but fell again. I fell and this time I appeared in the temple I was in during my first dream. As I looked around the temple room, I saw nine statues and they were in clothes. I thought "How odd!", as I looked even closer. I then realized that they were alive, they were people and not statues. As I looked closer, I could tell that they all weren't completely white like ivory stone, but some were more like cooked clay as if they're skin was too dark when they were alive to turn completely white. They looked at me with such hatred that I rose from my knees and flung back away from them. I began to hear cries from every direction. They were yelling, "Traitor, traitor, traitor ..." I covered my ears, but still heard their cries. I told them to stop, but they wouldn't. Then I saw Elizabeth, my sweet Elizabeth appears at the door of the temple and she showed her fangs to them all and they showed her theirs. The tension grew thick in the room and my own fear kept me from moving. She ran across the room and struck one of them. She struck another and then another. They were in the heat of a bloody battle, and then he showed himself.

Yes! The man that I kept seeing in these dreams... He looked at Elizabeth and she flew against a wall, then another. When she hit the floor, I took her to be dead. But then she spoke to me in my mind and told me to listen to her thoughts, but say nothing back, just obey her. We locked eyes and thought about him burning and the more we thought of this, the more he grew enraged. He caused both of us to hit the wall and I thought for sure that she was dead. Something snapped in me and I attacked him. I rose to my feet and without thought, I caused him to fly back and then I caused the table and chairs to turn over. The others began to move, so I ran around the room striking everyone of them. I seemed to have been moving too fast for them to see. When I stopped on the other side of the room, they all locked their eyes on me and I started to bleed from the sides of my eyes. I grew angry and time seemed to have stopped. Everyone was just standing there. They were all like living statues.

I remembered that this was a dream, so I caused smoke to bleed from the wall and created wood stakes from the arms of their chairs. I grabbed as many as I could to run through their hearts, but I blew up in flames. I smelled my own flesh as it cooked before me. The pain was so unbearable that I screamed out for help, but they all watched as I Zackced around the room. The thought of this was too much for my mind and I awoke, again in a pool of bloody sweat.

My body was very weak; I was barely able to move. This dream seemed more real than I ever could imagine. When I rose I felt the pain of being on fire, but my skin was fine. I went through Peter's drawers and found some clothes. I jumped into the shower and then got dressed. I knew that the dream was real. Somehow, it was real. I knew that Elizabeth was going to have to explain what was going on. I focused on where she was at and followed her vibe there. I located her on the bridge on Walnut and Twenty-fifth St. When she saw me, she started to laugh and ran towards me. She wrapped her arms around me and yelled, "You have survived their mind attack. You are even stronger than I imagined. Janus will think twice before coming after you again." I was confused and wanted answers, but without asking her anything, she told me that they were trying to destroy my mind. They were the second generation of the Master. They were the children of Janus. Yes! Janus was the one who I kept seeing in my dreams. He was allowing me to see him. "He was just testing your strength to see if you were stronger enough to defeat him, but he will not attempt that mistake again. He will find another way to control you. He will try to make you become his just like the others who do not seek to be a Vaingels." she said. It began to make sense to me and I realized that he was the reason that she kept running. He was the one hunting her just as she hunts the Master, or was Janus this 'Master' that she speaks of? I was not sure, for that matter, I realized I did not really remember what this 'Master' looked like. As we walked towards the train station on Thirtieth St., I realized I was in great Danger and if these dreams were not dreams then I have to do this quickly or George would be right and I will have enDangered their lives. I would be their death. I could not let that happen, I could not risk their lives anymore. I was a man and not a boy. I had to take control of this matter like George said and put an end to all this.

Chapter 4
My first hunt

I turned to her and asked what we were to do tonight. She told me that my powers were greater than she believed them to be, so I was to hunt with her and she was to teach me control. She told me, "Now we shall hunt and remember, allow my thoughts to become yours. Just like last night. Do as I do and you will get the idea." She reminded me that this was just an exercise. We stood in front of the Station for about an hour, then she chooses a woman that was passing us as we spoke through our minds. We started to follow her. Elizabeth walked in front of her while telling me not to pull in too close behind her. She was walking across the long road towards Seventeenth and JFK Blvd. Elizabeth allowed the woman to catch up with her and turned to speak to the woman. As they acknowledged each others' presence, I remained behind them at a good distance. The street was getting darker, accept for Elizabeth and me, the woman realized she was alone. We reached the first cross road and Elizabeth told me to close in on them. As I did, I could see that she was getting nervous. The woman tried to seek comfort in Elizabeth's presence. Elizabeth turned the corner at Sixteenth St. and the woman followed. I could smell her fear and feel my body growing stronger as I approached her. I began to lose myself in the lust for her body. I was beginning to taste the kill and desire her blood. I was lost in a passion of desire, my contact with Elizabeth grew weak, and then I heard her yell at me not to get attached to the kill. I regained focus on the task at hand and felt my madness pass. My senses grew sharper as I closed in on her. She then crossed Sixteenth St. and Market, but I turned onto Market St. This game had become more of a challenge than I thought it would be. Elizabeth was reading the woman's mind as the woman, who had seemed calmer, turned onto Chestnut

St. towards Broad St. I followed them in my mind's eye. When the moment of attack came, I moved quickly to Fifteenth St. and turned towards Chestnut and crossed them at the exact moment the woman approached the corner. Elizabeth and I were so in contact with each other, that there wouldn't have been any way the woman could have escaped. Elizabeth turned back around to see me. She ran to me and gave me a kiss while wrapping her arms around my neck. She was really pleased with how I did. The woman was confused with what we were doing, but chose to continue to walk on. Elizabeth told me that I was perfect. She said she was able to sense my skills were sharpening as we followed the woman. She said the time was close, but now I had to go feed and she would find me tomorrow.

Elizabeth told me that the following night's lesson will be even tougher than that night's was. This worried me, because I was not even confident about my actions that night. Elizabeth stopped me before I could say a word. She covered my lips with two of her fingers, gently telling me to hush. She then caressed my face and smiled. She said, "My love, there is no need to worry. We will destroy the Master and we will rule the night together... forever." She then walked away from me and I decided to feed before returning to Peter's apartment. Once I was there, I wondered what the guys were doing, since I haven't seen them for about two days. I walked over to the school and saw Garrett, George's cousin. I asked Garrett how was everybody was doing. He told me that they were worried about the other night. When I brought Elizabeth back to the school with me and choose to hide her from us. I mean, he spoke as if he had no doubt that what George said that night was true. I asked, "How do you know it was me?"

He said, "Because, even though George is a little wild at times, he doesn't lie. If he said he sensed you, then I must believe it was you. It was you he sensed, was it not?"

"Yes... It was me", I said.

"The vampire who attacked you… Your master! You do know he's not finished with you.
If he was, he would have killed you."

Garrett paused and his eyes grew very glassy after saying this, as if he was trying to go easy on me. Maybe he thought I needed some time to think this over.

"I know what I am doing... Why can't George and the guys believe that?"

Garrett looked to the floor, then to the ceiling as if his answers were coming from either place. "I hear you, Xavier. But quite frankly, Xavier, your master is a God-damned vampire. He doesn't care whether you know what you are doing or not. He doesn't care whether George and the guys believe you or not. He doesn't care about how you feel about this mysterious woman-"

"Elizabeth."

"Elizabeth... Umm-hmm... all right... How old do you think she is?"

"I... I do not know, but... word, she saved me. I trust her. It's like I'm learning so much from her. I could not tell George that, you know he'd freak. So I do not even care how old she is."

"Well, Xavier, maybe you should. I mean, from what you're telling me, she and your master share a history, probably going back many decades, or even centuries."

"I do not know...I do not care, Garrett, I don't. When I look into her eyes, man, and see the passion and fire in them, I just know that we are meant to be."

Garrett looked as if he was about to say something, but looked to the floor and shook his head a little. He then smiled slightly and spoke again.

"Xavier. Try to understand. I'm not down playing your feelings for Elizabeth, but really, what do you know about her? She's probably seen more things in life and death than any normal person will ever see. God knows what she's really up to! Now my other concern, Xavier...my other concern is that your friends could become this master's..., or even Elizabeth's latest victims... All because we got in the way.

"Elizabeth's not like that. And he's not my master, okay??"

"Yeah… How can you be sure? You're in love. Something to think about, huh..?"

"Yeah, but... You're not going to help me, are you?? I should have expected it. You would agree with George. Everyone agrees with George! Word..."

At this point, I decided to leave the school and Garrett. I walked about twenty feet away from the school and my vampire senses took in the sensations of the busy city around me. But then I heard Garrett back at the school muttering, "Hope I got you thinking, Xavier. If not, we're fucked." I heard him mutter this even through the noise of the traffic, I heard him. Did he know I could hear this? "Why was he being so hard on me? Why was everyone playing with my mind? First, this master Joseph… then George and now this Janus. Even Garrett is driving me mad!" I thought. I walked towards City Hall and just thought about how fucked-up all this was and the fact that when I needed my friends the most, they turned against me… (To live in fire is to die in the cold...) Ha, ha, ha...Word! I mean, the idea that my friends were behind me was taking on a meaning I did not like. They were abandoning me and blaming me for it. What a crazy idea. As if I wanted all this to happen. George, of course, will always find fault in me. He seems to make it his life to find me the blame for everything that happens in our lives, well... in my life anyway. Not that I do not bring things upon myself, but this was different. I was the victim and still I was to blame... Fuck! This was not fair and no one besides Elizabeth even cared. Some friends I was cursed to have! As if they live such perfect lives. The more I walked, the clearer I thought and the angrier I became. I really was getting pissed and felt that I had a right to give them all a piece of my mind. I stopped at Broad and Walnut and turned around to head back to my house and in route, I thought about the fact that I was bringing a lot of madness in these guys' lives. The more I thought about it, the worse I felt, so I stopped again and just headed back to Peter's house and chilled. And at least Peter never judged me. I kept thinking about how fucked up my friends really were and the fact that I cannot even talk to them so to make sense out of all the hell I been placed in. Somehow deep in my soul I blame George. Damn it that fuck'n George. What if this was his entire fault. What if he brought all this upon me? The more I thought about it the more humorous it became. Mr. self-righteous himself, the Master turned me just to get to his self-righteous ass. Ha, ha, ha, ha. As crazy as the idea seemed, the funnier I found it, how I would love to be able to wash his face in it and see if he would take responsibility. I guess in away George is right on the process of how things go on in my head. At this point I decided to stop acting crazy and start focusing on where I was going. As I walked down the streets, they seem to become emptier but somehow I felt like I was being watched. I looked around to see if anyone was there but saw nothing. I used my gifts to see if I could see anyone but all I saw was large dogs but they seem to be hiding in the darkness. So I wrote it off as me just wilding again.

Chapter 5

The Fallen

After getting inside, I sat down in the living room. Since I gained my vampire sight I have become accustomed to sitting in the dark. I lit up a cigarette even though I was trying to quit, (you know all that talk about cigarette smoke will kill you...). I allowed myself to relax from my busy day and watched the night slowly pass into the day. The city noise took hold of my ears. It truly played on my vampirism gifts. The sounds of people walking by the house, the cars moving through the streets and the thousands of other sounds that people just endure every day. As I became more relaxed, I heard the breathing of another. I did not move or changed my attitude in anyway. I wanted this person to believe that I did not know someone was in the room with me. "You are better than what the Master believed", the person said. It was a man's voice and it was so deep that it seemed to have a power of seduction. I slowly looked to the corner of the room and there he stood. "I could have killed you, you know." he said.

"Word and what should death mean to me now?!?" I replied.

"The Master wants you to come before him. I have come to take you."

"Where is Elizabeth? "

"Elizabeth? Who is this Elizabeth?"

"Dude, do not play with my mind."

"There is no Elizabeth that exists amongst us. The Master will explain, come...

"Word..."

"Yes!"

"Hum… No dude, I think I want to stay here and ask Elizabeth about all of this."

"Oh, I am sorry if I led you to believe that you have a choice."

He moved across the floor with such speed. I was not really able to see him, but luckily I was able to get out of his way before he struck the chair I was in. I moved with my own speed and stood on the other side of the room. I turned to see him destroy the chair. He broke the chair as if it was nothing but a piece of paper. I warned him that I would fight back if he did not just leave. (The dude was tripping) He charged me again. This time he hit me with such force I thought my head was going to fly off, but of course, it did not. I fell against the wall and returned with a blow just as strong or even stronger. This did not go on for long, a few seconds before he yielded to the idea that I was not going with him, nor was he strong enough to change my mind. He quickly jumped from the window and by the time I got to the window, he was gone. This dude really pissed me off. You know what really got to me was the idea that he came to Peter's home and attacked me as if I did something to him. He was the one who invaded my life and fucked up my world. This dude really was working my nerves. It was really too late to leave Peter's home, so I believed I would be safe here for now, but that I would have to rise early and leave here before he returned, maybe with others.

As I lay there, I realized that I haven't seen Peter since the night I came to stay with him. Yes, it was true that I slept through the day, but still Peter usually checks in on me. I was a little concerned, but soon sleep claimed my mind. I started to dream again and much was the same as before, but this time something new happened. I saw all my friends fall in a pit of darkness and blood was flowing from them but Peter who apparently was chained to a black pole in some kind of dark room. Peter was being tortured by Janus. I saw the temple again and this time I saw it from the outside. I realized it was no temple I was seeing, but a church. The church that was located on Broad St. and Pine. I could not believe that I was seeing this place. I started running in my dream towards Broad St. from somewhere that seemed like it was eighth and Locust Street. As I reached the Doubletree Hotel, there stood the three ladies of my childhood dreams. There they stood like three angels looking at me. I never really understood what they represented in my life, but there they were again. They wore the dresses they always wore. One was in white, the other was in red and the last one was in black. Their hair even went with the gowns; the one in white had blond hair and so on. I watched as the ones in white and red turned away and the one in black walked towards me. She said not a word, but turned to her right and behind her stood nine crows and they were eating from something that died. As I continued to look, I saw another form and that form was me sitting alone. The three women were gone and I was standing over a body of water and the water was running into many rivers, but I could see that the waters changed as it entered the different rivers. In one river the water seemed not to move at all. In another river, the water became strong and forceful. Then this continued in the other three rivers. I did not understand what this meant, but I was very afraid. I turned from the waters and started to walk away. Then the yells of horror started and I knew it was Peter. My dear friend Peter was in great pain and I had to save him. I could not stay in tune with my surroundings and lost the dream.

Again I awoke in a sweaty pool of blood and was starving to feed. I arose from the floor and looked around the room. I realized it was not too bright of me to stay here knowing this madman was to return and now fearing that Peter may have become one of their captives. I knew I was not a match for all these guys and Peter was going to need help. There was no way I could ask my other friends becuase they just wouldn't be strong enough. I knew Elizabeth was my only hope. I tried to reach her through her mind, but I was too upset to focus. I wanted to go out and find her. As I walked to the window, my skin began to burn. Even through the thick curtains that Peter had over his windows, I was able to feel the power of the great life giving sun.

So badly I wanted to open those curtains and end this madness for once and for all, but then Peter would surely die and I could not let that happen. It was a long shot but I called Marco and 'Drew. Even though they were going to flip, when they discover I involed him but I needed some kind of lead to find Peter. I focused on Marco and then Drew's mind, but grew tired and used the phone. After four rings, 'Drew picked up the phone. I explained my dream to him and questioned if anyone had seen Peter at the school or around the way. Drew and Pete never really partied together, so I really was not expecting Drew to find out much, but the fact was that I needed to find him. I guess I was blaming myself for his safety. It really was because of me that he was now in danger and I knew I was going to have to save him. As the night approached, I grew more impatient to move through the door of my prison. I could not help but think that this could have been anyone of my own family. I knew I had to stop this madman and that was final.

The last ray of death passed and I ran towards the door, and then stopped. I remembered how Elizabeth showed me to take to the rooftops. I went out the window and leaped for the large tree outside of Peter's apartment building and from the tree I went to the roof. I ran and leaped and ran some more. I must have covered the Center City area in about twenty minutes. I finally appeared at the waterfront of Penn's Landing. I was looking at the water and was truly lost for words. The guilt of what had happened to Peter was eating me alive. Then I felt it again. The same feeling I received in the apartment. I turned and there stood the man I seen the night past. I looked at him with my usual passive stare and waited for him to speak. Of course, I was already expecting him to tell me that they had Peter. I mean, I'm no rocket scientist but, I can put two and two together. He looked me over and then smiled with the most perfect teeth and tipped his head a little as if to greet me. I froze up and made sure not to show any form of emotion. I figured that as long as he did not know what to expect he would move with caution. I felt him trying to read my mind so I closed it to him. He then yielded to the fact that I have grown stronger in such a few attacks. Then he smiled and turned towards my side, and from behind, I was attacked.

It came at me with such speed that I barely was able to see it. I hit the ground, but before I could see who it was, it moved across the ground like a ribbon in the wind. I could not believe what I was seeing. I thought that it would be wiser for me to run from him, I believed I knew who this being was. I turned and took off... The streets seemed to pass me like blazing waves of colors. I did not stop until I hit Broad and Lombard. To my surprise the young man, well, maybe it would be truly better to say the 'man from the docks', because young he was not. Anyway! He stood on the corner across from me and this time I was able to see my attacker. My heart fell from me when I looked upon that ghostly face and saw Peter! I felt the tears form in my eyes and felt my knees give way. As I fell to the ground, they surrounded me and began to strike me over and over again. I must have passed out because when I awoke, I was laying in a bed surrounded with beautiful covers and pillows. The silk design took comfort on my face and nude body. I rose when I realized that I was nude and gathered the covers over my naked body. As I looked around the room I was amazed at the design and good taste this host had. The windows were like large balcony doors and had a very old style to them. I could easily escape through them, but there was no way I was going outside that building without my clothes or

Peter, my friend.

I went to the door and grabbed hold of the doorknob. I turned it and the lock in the latch released. I was not too sure what to think. I mean, could they have left the door unlocked for a reason. Surely, this master must had realized that I wouldn't dare leave without any clothes on my body. I mean, not that I could not have ran fast enough that no human eye could see me, but still just the idea that these freaks took me, ripped off my clothes and left me bare assed for their own sick pleasure. Now, what really got me was the fact that Peter was one of them and that he would help them attack me. Then again, I feared that he aided them out of anger towards me. I feared that he too blamed me for all of this. For if any bored the right to hate me, than it would be Peter. I mean, Peter truly was worthy of giving me such hatred. I wronged him and I knew it. I was the reason for his madness.

I started down the hall and studied all the beautiful paintings on the wall. Many of which seemed to be copies of early century art. I was surprised that they were just copies and not the real thing. I guess I was too used to the movies. You know, where you see many rich and rare works of art throughout the master's lair, but this was not the case. I walked across the wall to wall rug that seemed to have some form of French or Asian design on the edge of it and was a beautiful red and deep blue color. There was not really many works of arts in the hallway, but the stairwell was a work of art itself. The wooden rail was curved with all forms of designs and had such a feel of mystical warmth that I really felt as if the house was haunted or something like that... I walked through the hall and started trying doors to see if any were open. I tried the doorknobs lightly in case there are was anyone in the rooms. The doors were locked so I headed down the steps, unsure what I was going to encounter, and even the steps themselves scared the hell out of me. I walked slowly through the first floor, kind of afraid of what I was going to see.

I turned the corner to what appeared to be the living room. Then out of nowhere, I was struck to the floor and I rolled backwards unto my feet and ran backwards to the wall. I was afraid, but I knew I must face the one whose power was equal or even more than mine. I ran through the doorway to the center of the room. I ran so quickly that everything was a blur until I stopped and had seen that my attacker was Peter, well at least it looked like Peter, but he did not act as Peter would. Then it hit me that the master must not have given Peter the blood he would need to think freely. So, Peter was his slave by force. I regretted what I was to do, but did it. I struck Peter with all the strength I could muster and knocked him out cold. I picked him up and carried him towards the door. At this point, I no longer cared that I was nude, so I walked towards the front door.

As I reached the door, I realized that this was getting too far out of my control. If Peter did survive all this, I knew I was going to have to get everyone together. We were going to have to kill this bastard. As much as I hated to admit it, Elizabeth was right and this man's death was our only way to freedom. As I walked outside, I realized that I was not in Center City anymore. They took me and carried me into Mount Airy. I found it hard to believe that they carried me this far. I looked around the street and knew I was not going to be able to carry Peter from rooftop to rooftop. I walked for some time, and then I was lucky enough to see a cab. I walked over to the cab driver

And before he could speak I looked him straight into his eyes. He wanted to run but could not. He tried to focus on my nudeness, but I demanded his attention and told him that I wanted to go to 15th and Locust. I could tell by his behavior that he did not want to do it, but my mind was stronger and he obeyed.

I quickly put Peter into the cab and we were off. I knew I had to keep Peter out cold or the Master would see us through Peter's eyes. As the cab was driving, I could not help, but think upon what was to be the next thing I was to do. After a few minutes, it came to me. I would take Peter to Landis's and turn him into a full- blooded drinking vampire. My mind wandered throughout endless ideas that really added up to nothing. The cold breeze hit my body like tiny pins running across my skin. I tried to endure it, but I commanded the driver to roll up his window. We were there in no time and I took Peter out of the cab. The street was kind of empty except for the people who were inside the restaurant on the corner next to Landis's apartment building. I walked over to Landis's apartment building and tried to reach him from the intercom. There was no answer...

I grew upset for a second and decided to go home. I laid Peter on the floor of the apartment building and walked over to the glass doors that divided us from the street. I looked out the glass only to see this homeless man lying next to the dumpster outside of the fancy restaurant across the street from where Landis lived. He had a very dirty Grayish looking coat laying over him and it looked as if it would cover me, so I ran out the door with my vampire speed and grabbed the coat and returned to the apartment before he was able to realize what happened. I picked Peter up again and turn towards the front door. I knew I would have to make myself invisible to the homeless guy as I left, so I did. Well at least I thought I did, but when I stepped out the door he saw me and started to yell that I took his coat. I started to walk faster in hopes that he wouldn't follow, but he did. As he continued to yell, Peter was awakening.

Fear took control of me and I turned towards the man and allowed him to see what he was truly following. I let him see the pale skin, the deep blue veins that showed themselves under my eyes and around my ears. My illuminating eyes, that looked at him. He froze with fear, as he should have. I continued to walk and then run, faster and faster. I ran and was not sure if I was going to get home fast enough before Peter truly awoke. I realized that I was not even sure how long I was out and that time was important. The one thing that truly decides whether we live or die as a vampire was time. It's kind of a sick joke by God... Living forever but never forgetting how important time is. And I did not have any idea of the time. The sky did not really seem to be too light, but the point was, I needed to know the time. I reached the front door of my house and realized that I did not have a key and that meant that I was not going to get in. I sat there for a minute and then remembered that if I went around back, then I would be able to break into the house. I would jump on the brick fence out back and from there I would leap to my window and raise the glass window pane that I never locked.

Sitting Peter on the steps, I set out to do just that. I got into the house easy enough and decided to put some clothes on, then returned to Peter. When I opened the door, Peter was sitting there and looking around the area as if he never been here before. I grabbed him into the house and sat upon his chest. He was trying to get free, but I begged for his forgiveness then took my nail and cut the backside of my arm. I allowed the blood to hit his lips and then run into his hungry mouth. His eyes went completely black, then completely white. He locked his hands around my arm and started to drink from me with force and lust. He moaned with such passion that I was reminded of the feeling I was given when I first drank from Elizabeth and from the pouch that made me what I have become. I started to grow dizzy and felt my own strength give way to my sure death.

I tried to push him away, but he continued to drink. I grew afraid that I was going to die. That Peter was drinking too much and I was to be a sacrifice to Peter's birth. I was thrown from his body as he started to go wild, for the blood had taken hold of him. He fell back and curled up in a ball. I just watched as the blood took over his newly made body and freed his mind. He started to shake at first, and then he clawed at the floor as if he was pulling himself out of something. I was worried about what I had done, because my transformation was not this bad, nor was it ripping me apart, but I was too weak to help him in any way. He rolled over onto his back. Then he arched his body so that only his head and ass was on the floor. His lips opened and the screams started as if his whole body was in pain. I felt guilty as I watched what pain my blood released in him. I grew afraid that the neighbors could hear him and would call the police. He went silent as his hair laid perfectly over the floor and his eyes became perfect green gems. His skin was even lighter than mine and had even more of a pasty look about itself. He looked like a man who died and was cleaned up for his funeral. He laid there and I realized why I loved him so much.

I went to him and sat beside him waiting for him to re-open his eyes and look upon me the one who has given him a new hope, a new life. I knew he would blame me for all his torture, but hoped he would find peace in his new freedom. I sat on bended knees as I felt my love towards him grow even stronger. I had to love him, for why else would I go through all this? I guess I was forced to love him in a way. He has always been my eyes in things around my life that I could not see. I looked at him as his body and face became even more beautiful than normal. For some reason I wanted to touch him, to... to... take him in my arms and kiss him the way I kissed Elizabeth. I ran my fingers across his lips and up to his closed eyes. I ran my fingers over the contours of his face and then leaned in to brush my hair across his face. I felt my teeth start to grow as my lips came close to Peter's. I felt the passion, the pain he released and knew only that I wished to have him the way I wished to have Elizabeth.

As my lips came closer to Peter's he slowly opened his eyes and quickly pushed me away from him. He rolled away from me and sat up with his knees bent out in front of him. He looked over at me and then rested his arms across the top of his knees and laughed. "You're one wild mother fucker Xavier," Peter said. I wanted to explain, but the truth was I was not sure what to say. It seeemed that the power of his allure was very strong. Perhaps that is a defence we all get when where first bitten. I mean think about it. If their allure is triggered then you will fall under their spell and never attack them. "First this crazy mother fucker gets me and then you save me from him. Now you get me from the bastard and now you feed on Me.", Peter said. I looked at him and felt kind of bad, but the truth was I was going to feed on him. The difference from vampires and humans is that we both have an attraction towards each other, but vampires want the blood of one another most of all, for that is where our power lies and our attractions are towards. I watched him for a while and then we both laughed. I had to admit, I was fucked up. We got up and started to move around the room. Peter seemed to have a better grip on being a vampire than I ever had. He did not seem bothered by the way things looked through his new eyes. I wondered how he was able to adjust to his new life so easily. I asked him if he remembered what happened while the Master Janus was controlling his mind and he told me 'yes'.

Peter stood up and walked around the house and I followed. He started to explain that he was able to remember everything he did and that he was sorry about what happened at the waterfront. He told me, even though he was able to remember, he had no control over his actions and that the Master Janus knew it. Janus would talk to him for hours, he said. Peter turned and looked at me with a very hard stare. He told me that he did not trust Elizabeth and wanted me to stay away from her. He started to tell me that his Master Janus told him, "Elizabeth took the blood of a renegade Grand master vampire. How she awoke him, they are not sure, but now he had to be stopped. He was forced to feed once he awoke and escaped his prison. He attacked you because he was starving and she caused this." I tried to explain to Peter that she told me all of that, but what his Master Janus did not tell him was that all the Grand Master's children helped her. Peter looked at me as if I was making this up. As I was going along explaining, for some reason, I grew enraged and allowed this to be seen by Peter, who, for some reason, refused to fold under my aggression. He just looked at me, and then looked through me; I felt my anger grow even stronger as we locked eyes.

Then something happened that I never felt before. Peter was locking eyes with me and returning aggression equally towards my own. His will was very strong. He was stronger than the guy I fought at his place two nights ago. I actually felt my body being pushed back and only my own will was keeping me planted where I stood. It did not matter how strong Peter was. I refused to betray Elizabeth again. I was doing what I should have done with George and the guys when they attacked her. Peter's force began to grow weaker, but we continued to look at one another until Peter threw his hands up in the air. He declared that I was right and that he was too weak to fight on this point. If I trusted her, then he too was to trust her. I felt that he was lying, but something in me wanted to believe him. He came over to me and wrapped his arms around me. "It is over for now, my Xavier, and I will never speak of her to you again." Peter said. He asked me to go back to his place with him so he could rest. I was reluctant, but even I had to admit that it would be the last place the Master would look, especially since it would be the first place we would fear him to go. As wild as that seemed, it did make sense, so we went back to Peter's apartment for the night.

As we walked the streets, I could not look at him. I kept thinking about how he and the others were always questioning me and my decisions. I was kind of pleased that Peter was nothing like George and did give me the benefit of the doubt. He was saying something to me, but I really was not listening. As we walked,

I was able to sense Elizabeth following us. I told her to stay away for now and that I would join her tomorrow night at 30th Street Station. Peter did not seem to notice Elizabeth's presence, so I assumed that this was because he could not. He was just brought over and still was not used to his new gifts. Then for some reason, I found strength in that fact. I started to smile and it caught Peter's attention. He looked at me from the corner of his eye. He said nothing, but continued to walk. I tried to hold in my pride over his shortcomings, but it was hard. I never looked at myself being better or worse than Peter, but for some reason, I loved having the upper hand on him this time.

As we entered his apartment, I felt bad for him in a way. Here he has gone through so much in such a short time and still he concerns himself with my safety. I helped him undress and laid him in his bed. I knew his strength was leaving his body as we walked down the street, and by this time, he was really weak and tired. It would take some time for his body to adjust to its new freedom. He fell asleep just as soon as his head hit the pillow. As he slept, I watched over him and realized a few things. See, unlike me, Peter in a way has two masters: the one who bit him and me, the one who brought him over. Peter was different from me. I was not sure how the venom of his first master and my own was reacting to one another in his body. I knew I was going to have to ask Elizabeth about this. I needed to know what effects would this have on what Peter was to become. As he lay there, I felt for him again. I longed to taste his sweet, graceful neck and drink from him as I once drank from Elizabeth. His hair fell over him like a stream of water falling over a graceful waterfall. The lightest breeze lifted his hair and caused it to fall upon his neck again. Even his closed eyes added towards his beauty. I sat there and watched him until sleep claimed my soul and I too was gone to its mystical place. My dream that night was no different from the night before. More faces and places that did not make sense to me.

I awoke before Peter and waited for the sun to set. I knew that this would be the best time to go to see Elizabeth. I went to the bathroom and washed myself. I came back to Peter's room and grabbed some of his clothes from his closet. I looked at him through the mirror as I dressed. And since he was still sleep, I walked out the door. I thought it would be wiser to walk normally through the streets and not try to grab attention towards myself. I walked to 30th Street Station and waited in front of the McDonald's restaurant until Elizabeth arrived. The wait was not long, because she showed herself shortly after I arrived. I told her about Peter and about the place they took me to. She seemed to know of the place and its location. She started to tell me what she believed Janus was up to when Peter appeared behind me.

"Yes, Christina..." (We both turned towards him) "Tell Xavier all about Janus and why he is really after you." said Peter. Before I could speak Peter said, "You are a fool. To hold such strength in the words of one who did not even trust you with her real name. She hasn't told you anything other than the fact that she wants the Masters death. Look at her... you!! She has been lying to you from the beginning, Xavier. She is not going to help you but use you to provoke a war and in the end, she will have everything including you. For her to want this Masters death after so long means that there are other things happening that you are not aware of. "

Elizabeth snapped back saying, "No, you are wrong. Janus is using you to protect the Master. He doesn't want this to end. He wants to remain a vampire and live forever. He longs to create death. Whereas I only want to welcome it and know that my soul is saved from Hell's reach."

"You are a lying bitch." Peter said.

"No, it is you who doesn't know what Janus is about." Elizabeth said.

"True, Janus may be lying, but I know you are."

"How can you be so sure? Janus has used people before."

"Yes, and so have you, or have you forgotten?"

"Janus lied to you. I have never used people for any reason. All I wish is to find peace."

"Then I will give it to you... through your death." With that, Peter hit me and went for Elizabeth or 'Christina'. Which one was her real name I did not know and really did not care, so I continued to call her Elizabeth? As I fell to the ground, Peter hit her as well. She moved with the hit, rolled across the ground, and turned to shoot a burst of energy at Peter. He closed his eyes and seemed to focus the energy elsewhere. He did not burst into flames like the others did in my dream. This surprised Elizabeth and me, I yelled for her to run as I leaped from the ground and wrapped my arms around Peter trying to hold him from reaching her. She took my advice and moved like light through the station. Peter seemed to grow even more pissed as he broke free from my grip and was on her trail. They moved so quickly, I was the only one who could see what actually happened. I tried to follow them, but for some reason, Peter appeared to be stronger than me. He seemed to have a strength that was nothing like what I had expected. I ran behind them and was able to follow them only through Elizabeth's senses, but even that was hard. They ran down JFK Blvd. with such speed that it looked as if they were flying and I was unable to keep up. I reached Nineteenth Street and gave up. I knew I was not going to be able to follow them. Looking back now, I must admit, it probably was best that I could not.

Oddly enough, I decided to go back to Peter's apartment to

wait his return. As I walked across Nineteenth Street towards Walnut, I realized that Peter was kind of like my nephew as well as my son. Janus, Elizabeth and I are all that are left of the Master's first children. Because of this, I knew Peter would never catch Elizabeth. She was older and faster. Peter just was not old enough in his new life to do something as powerful as to take Elizabeth's blood to her death.

Peter however, was something new in this puzzle. Why was Janus turning him against Elizabeth!? What was the real reason that he took Peter!? Was he trying to use Peter against Elizabeth in order to stop me from hunting him!? And if Peter was to turn me against Elizabeth, then why wouldn't he just come to me and explain his half of this madness!? I was going crazy thinking about the fact that he was behind this. I knew he was trying to push me in some way, but what? What in the Hell was he trying to get from me? For that matter, did I even have it?? It... Yes, that is was this must had been about!! The blood! How dumb of me to overlook the one thing that made sense. He did not want to turn Peter against Elizabeth, because of me. NO, it was the blood he wanted. He must want Peter to find Elizabeth and force her to lead him to the blood.

That is why I was allowed to leave with Peter so easily. He wanted me to take Peter and convert him to a full-blooded vampire. Then, in return, Peter would kill Elizabeth and take back the blood, but I had the blood. I knew that when Peter realized that I had the blood and not Elizabeth, he would have to return here to me. I figured that all this was a setup and that I needed to have a surprise for Peter and his master. When I got back to Peter's apartment, I turned off all the lights and focused on trying to reach Elizabeth. I tried for hours, but got nothing. I then tried to reach Peter, but still with no luck.

Chapter 6

The Sleepers Awake

I decided to block out all the sounds around me and focus my heart, using my passion for the two I love to help me locate them. Everything went dead at first and then I heard very little sounds, then nothing. This went on for some time, until I started to hear vibrations. The vibrations turned into howling winds. I had to focus my thoughts and then I heard it. I heard the cries of another. It was very faint at first, but grew stronger as I focused on it. The more I concentrated on it the louder it became. I was confused at first. I was not sure if it was Elizabeth or Peter. My heart jumped for I know it had to be Peter. As I listened, I discover that it was not Peter, No, not at all. The feeling I was sensing was different. The emotions that I was responding to were not the same... It was Marco or Drew. One of them was crying out as if they were in pain or needed help... My help! They did and I had to go to them as quickly as I could.

I ran to the window and opened it. I looked down onto the street to see if anyone would see me. Then I jumped to the tree and then to the roof. I took off like the wind. I ran across the rooftops like an angel in flight. I never thought I could move so quickly before. The wind whipped across my face like a thousand needles. Fear took my soul and I knew nothing more than the fact that I had to get to my friend or friends for that matter. I leaped and ran, then leaped some more. I moved in ways that I never thought was possible. Before I know it I was standing outside of our home. It truly surprised me that I had no real feelings about what I was going to find. I mean I realized what I was supposed to feel right about now but the fact was I did not feel anything. My heart continued to beat fast then I came to terms with the fact that this game was getting bigger than I thought about before. Now I know this was more than what Elizabeth or Peter told me. The Master wanted something from me. For some reason He was trying to push my hand, but to do what!? That I still did not know, but I began to understand how he was going to do it. Now that I was there I was able to better sense my friend, No! My friends... The reason I was not sure who needed me was because they both were calling me for help. I smiled for a moment at the thought that George was not there. He is always saying how he can sense when things are going to happen, but he did not sense this. I guess he is not as good as he led us to believe. I knew now that I surpassed him and the fact that I was there and he failed them, told a story in its self.

The door was cracked open and the lights were out. I opened the door and walked in. I stopped in the door way and with my sight I was able to see in the room as if it was well lit. The room was a mess everything was thrown about and turned over. My emotions were running wild. I was a little confused who would do this. Everyone was turning against me and there for I could not trust anyone. I first thought maybe Peter but then for what reason would he do it. I walked past the over turned sofa towards the kitchen. I stopped in the doorway of the kicthen and realized that my emotions was getting out of control. So I calmed myself. Then I heard it, breathing coming from behind me. It was to light for a human to pick up but it sounded as clear as day to me. As I turned around I saw someone under the over turned sofa. His legs were slowly trying to pull him free but they could not. In fact he was barely alive and trying desperately to get out from under the sofa. I walked over to him and with one hand I lifted the sofa from his person and saw that the weak struggling man I was helping was Drew. He looked as if he saw death's face and cursed the world to have seen it. There was blood all over his body. He looked a mess, his clothes were torn and stained from his body fluid the holes in his neck and the smell of his person told me that this happened some time ago. With so much of his blood gone, I was surprised that he was alive at all. I could see that the Vampire virus was taking over Drew's body and that was the only reason he lived, but he was so weak and that I could not explain. I thought that maybe it was due to the fact that he lost so much blood and that his body needed more blood than what was left. Without thought I bit my arm and fed him. He gripped my arm and drained it as Peter did but I was much too strong for him. I pushed him off me after giving him enough blood. I did not stay to watch him completely change over. I rose and ran upstairs to find Marco. I listened for his breathing as I walked throughout the house until I heard a sound in the yard. I looked out the window of Marco's room and there he was... in the yard pulling himself back to the house. He must have been trying to reach Drew but his body was too messed up for him to walk. I leaped from the window and landed by his side. He looked at me with such fear and rage, I felt ill. He started to yell some wild shit at me. I turned him onto his back and looked his body over. His legs were broken with large cuts all over his body, as if he was thrown through something. It was easily to see that the virus was healing his body as it was doing for Drew but it was not working fast enough. I cut my arm again to fed him my blood as well. But to my surprize he refused to drink from me. I demanded that he had very little choice now. For either he drink or become his attacker's slave. It took him some time to decide but he in the end. He reached for my arm to drink. To my surprise he pushed me away after drinking very little of the blood. I stood there waiting for him to begin to complete his change when all of a sudden I heard the voice of Drew.

"Well, Xavier! Are you happy now?"

"NO!" I said as I turned to face him.

"Come on now! Xavier don't tell me that you did not think this was going to happen."

"Dude what are you talking about?"

"You know what I am talking about!"

"Drew... I had no idea this was going to happen!"

Drew stood there for a second and then walked passed me. He was so attractive, the way his hair fell back over his head and down to his shoulders. He always wore braids but now they looked like thin ropes in his hair. They were all prefect in shape and form. Not one looked out of place. His eyes looked as if they could see straight through a man's soul. They were a nice dark brown and the pupils where as black as ebony. They way his six feet, two inch frame moved across the ground were as if he was floating on air. He looked as if his body was no longer normal. I could see something had changed in him but was not sure what it was. He walked over to Marco's side and watched as Marco began to change. Marco curled up on the floor like a child in pain. He fell onto his back again and dug his nails into the ground. The veins in his arms where so thick and his arm muscles became so defined. He started moving his head from side to side. The cuts on his body began to vanish and his hair to pull itself closer to his body and then fell to the ground. Marco has always worn dreadlocks and now they were truly locked. He rose into the air about a foot and then fell back to the ground. I was scared as fuck. Man. I did not expect to see that. In some ways, I regretted not seeing Drew change over. Marco laid there shaking and then he passed out. I guessed he had to go through some more changes in his mind and need to sleep in order to do it. Drew bent down and lifted him up into his arms. I was surprised at how easy he carried Marco inside. He walked pass me as if I was not even there. He was completely relaxed; it did not even faze him that all this was happening. I said not a word as they came into the back door. Drew just walked through the door as if there really was not anything else to say. He said nothing, but just walked over to the sofa, which landed on its back from when I removed it from his person. He used his foot to flip it back up right and laid Mark on it. He looked at Mark for a second and then spoke.

"Only you could have stopped this."

"How could I?" I said.

"Fuck'n… Look at us Xavier. Just look. This is fucked up!"

"I am sorry. Man, but I did not know this would happen."

"Dude, that chick knew. She knew from the beginning."

I wanted to say something, but I knew I better not. Drew started to tell me of the events that took place. He told how it all happened and about the one who attacked them. He said, "The guy knew who we were and called us by name. What was really strange is what he said before he attacked us. I mean he grabbed me up into the air and called me the mist walker. Then he bit my neck, at first I thought this guy was crazy but strong as fuck. He held me like I was nothing but a rag doll. He showed no sign of fear. He drank from me for some time before Marco came down stairs. Man! When he heard Marco, he pulled his teeth free from my neck and looked at him. I was about to tell him to run but before I could…, Marco was flying across the room and hit the dining room wall. He landed on the pool table, but it was not strong enough to take the impact. The table turned over, he hit the floor and the table hit him. Man, I tried everything I could think of to get free but neither my hits nor Marco's hits had any effect. He just kept looking at me. He would feed off of me for a little while and then look over at Marco. When he was sure I was done, he dropped me on the floor and walked over to Marco. Marco was really messed up but he was like me. He was trying to fight back, but just was not a match. Man, He grabbed Marco up and tossed him into the kitchen. He watched as Marco hit the floor and then walked over to him. As he walked towards Marco, I tried to fuck him up with the knife I found on the floor next to me. Dude, I went through that motherfucker right into his back. He was fucked up for a moment. He turned towards me and all of a sudden, the sofa turned over on top of me. I heard some more noises and then a window broke and Marco yelled. It was so quick, man. He was not playing games with us by this point. We were to make some kind of point he was trying to get you to understand."

This made me nervous for everyone I knew. Marco was coming around by then, but all he said was call Landis. Drew just turned from Marco and walked over to the phone. He started dialing Landis's number. He said nothing, but turned back to face us. It never dawned on me that if this guy knew them, then he knew all of my friends and family. That meant that everyone I knew was in danger. As Drew spoke on the phone with Landis, he seemed very calm and they spoke for some time. I could tell from Drew's statements that something happened. Drew hung up the phone, turn towards me and Marco, His look was a little troubled but he told us that Landis was attacked too. Marco rose from the sofa and stood as straight as Drew and Myself. It seemed to me that they were ready to go to Landis's. I felt it was very dumb of us to travel so close to dawn but they wouldn't listen. I walked to the door as if there really was not anything left to say. As we walked down the street, Drew repeated what Landis told him. Even with their new found power I could still sense that Drew was hiding something. I felt that Drew left something out of the story and that is why we were truly going to Landis's. As I got off the elevator onto Landis's floor I could sense the essence of the master in the hall. As I got closer, I could smell the blood of Landis and two others. I sensed they were all attacked and I knew what Drew was hiding. I was correct for no sooner we entered the apartment of Landis's, there sitting in Landis's wooden chair was George and standing by the window was Garrett. They seemed too have been as worn as Drew and Marco was. The difference was that George seemed to have changed more than any of us had from the virus alone. Garrett too seemed different. His skin looked as if the melanin was being removed from Garrett's body. He looked like a ghost or someone who seen one. Neither seemed to show any real concerns of what was happening. I was annoyed that they were attacked as well and I did not sense it. Now, I knew why George was not at my house because he too was a victim. I knew he wouldn't see himself as such, but more so as a fool for not expecting me to get them mixed up in all of this.

I followed Marco and Drew inside and said nothing. I know I was being set up but was not sure what angle they were going to use. George looked at us as we entered the apartment and Garrett stared out the window. This seemed odd since the only view it showed was the side of the neighboring building. They were just as quiet as I. Then Landis spoke, "I guess we do not have to tell you that we were attacked. Drew told me what happened at your house. I think we need to figure out what to do now. Xavier, I know you think we are blaming you. I just want you to understand this could've been avoided, if you would have listened to us earlier, but now we have to listen to you. We need to know everything you know and everything she told you whether you believed it or not. This is now our fight and no longer just yours. There was a reason why this master allowed us to live and we need to figure it out. Now, we remember you saying the woman explained the rules to you... So now tell them to us!"

I stood there for some time and then decided it was time for me to be truthful with them. So I told them, "It works like this... One must first choose a victim or a spawn. Once this is done, you drink from them. After twenty-four hours, they will become a mind slave to you. They will hunt others and drink from them, but can't pass the trait to their victims. Only after they receive the blood of another vampire, will they themselves be free from this curse. The master is trying to make me do something, but I do not know. I should have known he would have attacked you, since... he took Peter and made him into a slave. Pretty much the same way he made you guys one. He drank the blood from all of you and allowed you to live. It's really simple. By doing this, the virus lives in your bodies and your minds are going to become blank. Well, maybe not blank... Peter said that, while he was being controlled by the master, he could still hear and understand everything that was happening around him. He just could not control his body. I am not sure how many days it takes before this happens, but I do know you three will need to drink from me if you do not want to be his slaves. Because once you become his slave, he will use you against me. I think he plays on the fact that you're my friends and I won't hurt you and you can't fight the emotions to hurt me."

I was amazed when George looked back towards Garrett. George the one with all the answers was quiet, lost for words. Even though he wanted to convince us that he was in control, I could see he was scared. I could not believe George was scared. Garrett however, wasn't. I could not sense any form of fear. Garrett was so weak from the attack, yet I could not read his emotions. Here I stood a full powered vampire and I could not read the emotions or mind of a soon to be slave. I felt something coming from him, but what it was I was not sure. He stood as if he was not ever attacked. As if he was still just a bystander looking over George's children. I tried harder to read his mind, but got nothing. Then Garrett spoke, "We already figured that out Xavier, and we called Casper and the others to come here as soon as they could. The master, if that is what you want to call him, attacked all of us, not just to get to you, but to also force us into this as well. This master is no fool and he is not trying to get you to do anything. Can't you see or maybe you can't. He doesn't give a shit about you. He has attacked us to give you something other to deal with other than hunting him. You have been playing games with this girl who is trying to use you to defeat him. Any one of us can see that if he wished you dead, then you would be dead. This thing or person is growing tired of your games and so are we. Now, you have a choice: convert us to be one of you or watch us become his slave. But either way, know this is all because you would not listen to what George and the others tried to tell you." He came towards me with such force I finally felt his rage and it was focused towards me. His dark eyes cut through me like a hot knife into butter. The fact that he was weak had no effect on his will to destroy me if given the chance and power. I looked at him and then back at George. I knew George would never let that happen and besides that, I could rip him into two if I wished. George tried to get in between the two of us, but was too weak to rise. I smiled a little and then told them that I am sorry that this happened to them and that I wouldn't allow the master to enslave them just as he already done Peter. I thought for a second and then came to understand Garrett's rage and fears. So I decided to turn him first.

I walked past the chair in which George was sitting and walked over to Garrett. He locked his eyes with mine and did not look away. I could tell he did not trust me and was not going to allow me to win his trust from my words. I moved very slowly so not to alarm him as I cut my nail into my wrist again. As the blood began to pour from my arm, Garrett's eyes began to glow, unlike anything I have ever seen before. He grabbed my arm and attacked my wrist like a man starved for food. I was not sure if I could take this form of abuse for long. He was causing me such pain in my arm and it slowly began to affect my chest. I could hear my heart slowing down and for some time, it felt as if it stopped. I tried to pull away but he held on. As I felt him growing stronger, I knew I was dying. He was drinking my life forces out of my body as well as my blood. Then I felt and heard it, he crushed my wrist. I must have lost control for a second, for I threw him into the bedroom and fell to the floor grabbing my arm. I looked over to Landis, who just sat there. I little amazed, but too weak to care.

I felt his fear as he watched what I did to Garrett and realized from the look on my face that I was growing too weak to be doing this. He started to speak. I told him to say nothing, come, and drink while I was able to give him the blood he needed to be free from this master's control. He looked at me for some time and then he looked over at Marco and Drew. They both said nothing, but looked back to me, as to say you must drink. Landis sat there for some time and then rose. You could see it was taking every bit of his strength to stand, but he did it and approached me. I sat there and looked up at him. I told him I was weak, so he needed to drink only what he needed. I told him that I was not sure if he could control himself, but I was asking him to try. He bent on one knee and placed his hands on my arm. I looked at him and then reopened my wrist for him to drink, since the first cut I made for Garrett had healed. I knew that the pain I felt would be gone and my arm would be healed too. Landis licked my first drop of blood. He seemed to have full control of his emotions. He licked a few more time and then slowly sucked the cut. I could feel his tongue as it moved over my cut. I felt it enter the cut for a few seconds and then it returned to the outer walls of the cut. He was drinking my blood as if he was making love to my arm. I was feeling a wild vibration as he fed from me. I knew it was time for me to stop him. I knew I was going to have to pull away, but as soon as my body leaned to one side. Landis stopped and placed his right hand on my shoulder. I was very surprised to see him change over so quickly. It was as if it was painless.

His eyes turned from its light brown shade to a bronze yellow and shined as if they where flames. His smile showed the most beautiful white teeth I have ever seen. Landis's hair had completely vanished. His skin was a pasty shade of brown. I thought it may have been because he was half Puerto Rican, half Black. His skin oddly glowed and I felt drawn to it as well as to him. He rose in front of me and looked as if he was six feet tall. It was hard to believe that he was only five foot six inches. He smiled at me for a second and then told me to rest. It was as if he could see the toll it would take to change all of the others. He walked over to George and told him, "Xavier is too weak to change you. He needs to rest and maybe even eat before he will be strong enough to convert you. I think we better wait for the others and then we will deal with you." Oddly, George agreed and just sat there. I rose and made my way back to the bedroom, in hope that I would be able to rest from the sun and rest of the world.

Garrett came out of the room as I entered, but I did not get a good look at him. Maybe it was because of how tired I was. He said nothing, but let me past him and he joined the others in the living room. I must have fallen to sleep the moment I hit Landis's bed, or was it Casper's. I can't remember, anyway, I fell on one of their beds and slept like a baby. I slept through most of the afternoon but was awaken by some voices I was hearing in the living room. I awoke and walked into the living room to see that Zack, Vinnie and Casper were sitting there speaking to the others. It was not really a surprise that Casper was there, since he lived with Landis as roommates. However, Zack and Vinnie threw me for a loop. I looked around the room and saw that everyone was still there, not like they could have gone anywhere. Anyway, George was still sitting there, but something was different. They all looked different to me for some reason. I asked what happened and then Landis told me that he and Garrett gave George some blood. Then they all gave him some. At first, the change was very slow, but the more blood they gave him, the more he changed. I grew so upset that I pushed Landis across the room with my will alone. Everyone was surprised at this, but I felt it was time I took control here.

After all, I was the first one to be changed and I understood what was happening. I told them that the reason he kept changing was that every time he drank from one of them he gained their strength and their gift. He was going to be stronger than the rest of them now. I could tell they really did not care. I did not understand how the blood truly worked, but I knew a little. I was not sure if he would be stronger than them or weaker because of the level they were to him. One thing I did know was that this was not going to be good. I told them that I could not let him or them drink from me again. Not until I spoke to Elizabeth. George looked at me as if to be studying my movements and then it looked like he was doing something more, but I could not figure out which. If he was stronger than I was, I would have believed he was trying to read my mind, but he being the third generation of the blood, I knew he was not strong enough.

"Zack and Vinnie had decided to be vampires as well", Garrett said.

I turned to them and said, "No! Are you two crazy?"

"They are not crazy, just smarter than us."

"Garrett, what are you talking about?"

"They realized that if we were attacked, then it is a matter of time before they are."

Oddly enough this made sense, so I agreed. But Casper however, did not want to join this fate. He felt he would aid us better as being our eyes in the daytime while we protected him at night. We all knew he would need to protect us during the day, especially since we did not know who our true enemy was. I granted them both their wishes and Vinnie and Zack would become vampires. I knew the blood I drank from them would be more than enough to restore my strength and more than enough to turn them over. I told them that it will be a few hours before they would be able to go outside and see the world with their new sight, but I knew they would love it.

I walked over to Vinnie first and he rose. I looked him in his eyes and for a second he was afraid, but it went away. He looked away from me as I leaned over to his neck. He looked at George, and then stopped me. He looked back at me and said he decided he wanted George to turn him over. He walked over to George and bent down onto one knee and presented his neck to George. I watched as George's teeth penetrated Vinnie's neck and his blood ran over George's lips. His blood must have been so warm! George held onto him even harder. He had to feel so good in George's arms. I wondered if it was different from the others. George's chest seemed to broaden and his back straighten the more he drank. Vinnie began to close his eyes and his body grew weak. He started to fall from George's grip. I knew it was time, so I pulled him away from George. I knew George truly had to fight the craving, so not to continue feeding on him. I knew if I did not stop him, then he would kill Vinnie and not even the virus would save him from death's grip. Vinnie dropped to the floor as we all watched.

Then I turned to Zack and motioned him to approach me. He was not afraid at all; in fact he walked over to me baring his neck for my kiss of immortality. I leaned down to him since he was much shorter than I was. I placed my hands on his shoulder and slowly moved in for the bite when he grabbed my head and pushed my mouth to his neck. I bit him too hard and he tried to pull away, but something in me took over and I grabbed him in a vise grip and held him still as I fed. The more he tried to pull away, the more I wanted to drink. It felt as good as sex to the living and I did not want it to end. He was now off the floor and I held him in my arms like a lover. I felt the fear of death rise in him and knew he was my prey. I was not going to stop! No, not this time... I could not stop if I wanted to. I kept on feeding until he was not moving anymore and then I heard a voice, a voice was so strong that it made me release him and grab my ears. The voice demanded that I release him and when I did not, it released images of the worst fears I held within me. I dropped him and grabbed my ears. I fell to the floor and knew one of them had attacked me. I was not sure who it was but I knew it was one of them. As I tried to get myself together, everyone gathered around Zack to make sure he was still alive and at first Zack did not respond. George rose from his chair with such speed that I was amazed. He stopped at Zack and bend down to feed Zack, his blood. It was crazy the way he bit into his own wrist. He opened Zack's mouth and allowed his blood to pour inside. Zack did not respond for a few minutes so George went on to feed Vinnie. Then he began to change... Somehow Zack cheated death and the virus restored him.

Vinnie's skin turned to a pasty, dark-brown, wax-like surface. He looked as if he was a doll in a museum. His braids were thinner than Drew's, but just a beautiful. They were as black as his mustache and eyebrows. His teeth turned as white as a sheet of paper. I fell for the beauty in his eye; it offered death to any who was willing to welcome it. They glowed as if the sun shined through them. I could not get over how his body remained lean, but looked as if it was stiff. His fingers looked more like claws. He looked over to Zack who was now changing himself. Zack lay on the floor for a bit and then he started to turn his head from side to side. He grabbed for the floor like an animal clawing the dirt. He was in pain but seemed to love it. I was able to hear his heart beat and pick up its beat pattern. His body looked the same, but something did change and at the time, I was not sure what it was. I kept looking as his hair took shape and his eyes turn to their new lively color and his teeth too turned white, but looked longer than the rest of ours. I looked as his fingers turned to claws as well. It struck me odd that he and Vinnie's nails became claws and the rest of us remained fingers.

I looked over at Casper who seemed as if he shit his pants at what he was seeing. He just stood there and watched. His body was motionless and his face frozen in terror. I could not help but to read his thoughts of how crazy this all was. He wanted to run away, but feared what would happen if he did. He was scared of what was happening and he feared us as well as the master. I think that was the first time he ever really considered what we had become. I smiled as he came to terms with the reality of what he was seeing. His huge body frozen like a statue and nothing under God was going to move it at that moment. Then to my surprise, his love for the group took over and the fear subsided. He looked at Vinnie and then Zack... He wanted to do something, but he knew not what. I knew he would turn on us in time. For most humans grow to fear what they can not control. They're need to survive always bring the darkness out of the most pure of souls. Even priest can justifie murder if it threatens their way of life. But Casper always was a strong person of character, so I wouldn't be surprised if I turned out to be wrong. At that moment, I had to trust he would aid me in this, just as the others were. Vinnie rose from the floor and walked over to the bathroom to him of what was left in him from being human. He was in there for some time. I could see in Zack's face that he was not able to hold it for long and we teased him about it. It was not long before Vinnie returned and Zack was off. We just laughed as he pushed his way past Vinnie. This brought a question to my mind and I asked what did George and Garrett do once the virus kicked in. And Landis smiled and said, "I gave them some of my pants".

It was odd that through all of this George did not speak. He just looked and smiled a lot. I tried many times that day to read his mind, but could not. Somehow the mixture off all their blood gave him the gift to block me out. I knew that this would be a problem, especially if he could read my mind. I decided to put up my guard and close my mind. I could not prove it, but I knew it was him that attacked me earlier. We sat there and talked as well as laughed until we made our way into the bedroom. I was not sure how strong the sun rays were, so we all slept in the bedroom where there were no windows.

Chapter 7
Blood for Blood

At some point threw the night, we heard a loud noise in the hall. So we jumped up and ran from the bedroom. We ran into the living room and Landis opened the door. Everyone ran behind Landis to see what was happening. Casper was lying on the floor and Elizabeth was feeding on him. She had her teeth so deep into his neck, I thought him to be dead. His blood was all over his clothes and the floor. His clothes were torn and there was very little left of his shirt. I am sure, that where I stood, she was not able to see me. She released Casper and threw him at Landis. As Landis caught him, she charged the door and everyone who was standing in it. She knocked Landis back against the window where I was standing. Before they could do anything, she ran into the apartment and grabbed Landis. She picked him up and threw him towards the bedroom. Garrett jumped in Landis's way and stopped him from entering the bedroom. I was still standing beside the window where Landis landed, but to afraid to speak. Elizabeth was so full of rage that she was not registering me. Marco showed his fangs and jumped on her back and tried to feed upon her, but she quickly through him across the room. He landed on his feet and was about to charge her again. Then it happened! George locked eyes with her and then it was like she went mad. She fell back grabbing her head and all I could hear was George speaking, "NO!! You foolish woman. You have no idea who your playing with!" His mouth never opened, but I could hear his words. I am very sure everyone in the room could hear it, but for some reason it affected Elizabeth a lot worse than it did us. He locked his eyes with her for only a few seconds and she closed her eyes and shook her head screaming. She was turning in circles yelling like an insane woman. George turned his eyes towards me for a split second before returning his attention towards Elizabeth. Garrett jumped into the air over Landis, who was on the floor in front of him. He was about to strike her and something snapped inside me... I used my speed to move across the room. I grabbed her out of the way. It was like the room just froze I watched as Garrett was in the air and George was just standing there. They were more than she could have dealt with. I wrapped my arms around her waist and moved her back by the window where I was standing. Then everything started moving normal again. Garrett landed on the floor and caused the floor the crack in every direction. Then before I could do anything, she attacked George. She knocked him off the floor and he flew into the wall. He looked at her for a second and passed out. She then turned towards Garrett and did something to make him freeze in his steps. I thought Landis was passed out, but out of nowhere, he punched Elizabeth into the wall next to the sofa. Marco, who was standing there, did not even move. He just turned towards her after she landed beside him and kicked her into her ribs. I could hear her ribs crack from the pressure of his foot. Elizabeth fell to the floor grabbing her side. Before I could reach her, Drew attacked her. She was already striking Drew back with an upper kick and he fell on the sofa. Vinnie leaped to George's side and made a face as if he was an animal protecting its master. Zack, however, showed me that I was not the only one the venom gave a gift too. For his body became like a chameleon and turned to the colors around him. In seconds, he went into the wall. I could not believe it. He was there and then gone. She rose from the floor to kick Drew's ass, but just when she went to strike Drew, Zack fell out of the ceiling on top of her. He ripped into her back, cutting her with his claws like an animal digging into its prey. She screamed and whipped her hand behind her back and knocked him off. She used her speeded and kicked Zack in the neck and I was able to hear it crack. I yelled for her to stop but she was out of control. With blood flying everywhere she ran over to Marco and backed handed him with such force that it broke his neck as well. Drew ran behind her and forced his hands into the cuts Zack made on her back. Screaming, she tossed Drew away from her and into Landis who had the same idea. She turned to Garrett, who still could not move. Elizabeth tried to do the same thing to him that Drew did to her. She tried to stab Garrett in the chest, but could not break his skin, much less crack his bones. Landis went to hit her from the back again, but this time, she was ready and turned to him. She ran her fingers through his chest and pulled out his heart. I froze for one second, and then fell to the ground, feeling ill. She was making easy work of all of them. She threw his heart to the floor and Elizabeth turned towards Vinnie who was looking at her all this time with a vindictive smile. She grabbed for him, but something happened. The room turned black and the floor began to spin. He looked at her with hell in his eyes and a wave of heat overtook the room. Elizabeth Felt the power and tried to fight it. George awoke and rose behind Vinnie with hatred in his eyes… In our minds you could hear him scream so loud that Elizabeth couldn't focus. Elizabeth knew she was no match for both of them so she pulled back.

She turned to me and told me to follow her quickly. I could sense she did not want to deal with Vinnie and George together. I knew I had to do something and since I was in love with her, I followed. I prayed they understood, but I had to explain to her what had happened and who all of them were. I knew once I told her everything, it would be fine and she would aid them just as she helped me. She jumped out of the window and I followed her as she climbed her way to the roof. After we reached the roof, we sensed Zack was following us. So we ran towards South Street. When she reached Spruce Street, she jumped from the rooftop to the roof on the other side of the street and I followed. She could no longer sense them so she stopped and turned to me. She asked if I was ok. I told her I was fine, but I needed to explain all this to her. I wanted to know where Peter was. She grew quiet for a moment and then told me, "He chased me to the river and the more I tried to lose him the faster he moved. So I decide to return to the station on Thirtieth Street. He followed and almost had me, but then I remembered the place where I hide the blood so I ran there. He followed and once we were under the bridge I took an iron rail and rammed it through his chest." I looked at her with such shock that she knew what I was thinking and then she told me he would be fine. "It will slow him down a little but he will live", she said. She looked so sorry for what she did and I could tell she really believed she did not have any other choice. I asked her why she attacked my friends. I knew she knew who they were, but I did not understand why she acted that way. She said, "Xavier, My Love. They are not trying to help you, but stop you. Can't you see! Janus already knew what their feelings on this matter would be and how else to stop you, but to use your friends. Yeah, look at them. They believe it is a blessing to be immortal right now but wait for a hundred years or so."

"Then they will change their minds and all this understanding they have towards the master of the damned will be changed. Then it will be too late. He will be too powerful for any of us to stop. We will all be damned through all time." She walked away from me and I could feel her sadness. As she walked away, I started thinking about everyone back at Landis's and Even if Landis was still alive. I could feel her pity for my friends. They were cursing her and she was feeling pity for their souls. I told her, "I have to help them and you have to help to do this." I knew I was not ready to tell or show them all they needed to know in order to be a vampire. She smiled and placed one of her hands on the side of my face. I knew she was going to help me. Even if they did not think they wanted it. She told me to return to them and she will think of something. I kissed her and began to walk to the back of the building we were on and climbed down to the street.

As I headed back to Landis's, I realized I was still a little weak. See, human blood does aid vampires in surviving, but another vampire's blood restores our strength and powers. Sometimes, it even gives us new gifts and that is what I feared for when it came to George. I was not then or now sure what powers all their blood gave him and I knew he would never let me know it either. It was very plain to me that we did not trust each other anymore. Since George seemed to live for power, now to have it really made him dangerous. Isn't that crazy... Two people forced to depend on each other but neither trusts the other. I guess I was wise not to trust him for I knew he would try to rule over us. We once again will be his children and it isn't a role I wished to play.

I decided it was time for me to put a stop to all this by first getting control of the group and then find Peter. I knew I had to pull them all together and then I could decide how to stop the master. I Headed to the grave yard on Eighth Street, where I hid the blood I had left. Once I got the blood and drank of it, my powers were restored and I could feel its power growing in me. I so wanted to drink it all, but knew I had to control how much I drank. I placed it back in my hiding place and headed to Landis's place. It was around nine o'clock at night and I knew they were going to want to go out to see the streets and the people on them. For with everything that had happened this evening, I knew it would be wise for me to take leadership as soon as I returned to Landis's place. It did not take much time for me to get to Landis's but to my surprise they weren't there and I had no idea where they might have gone. I knew that it would be best for me to check out the school and my place in case Marco and Drew went to get changed. I traveled to the school and then home, but found nothing. I was confused. I knew Landis was hurt a lot worse than the others, so they could not have taken him too far.

I sat in my room and tried to find them in my mind. I kept getting images, but was not sure if it was them. The images were of the waterfront, so I decided to go there and see if they need me. I traveled the streets in the shadows mostly to avoid any other vampires that might have been following me. The riverfront was cold and empty. It was odd but no one was out, it was as if the waterfront was close for some reason, then out of the trees my hunters showed themselves. It was the guy who I fought with a few days earlier. He seemed prepared this time and brought friends with him. They circled me quickly and attacked me all at once. I must have fought with them for more than twenty minutes before they finally won. One struck me with an open palm and the other clawed my back. They started beating on me so much that I did not know what to do. As I lay on the ground, covering my head, I thought about what Elizabeth did to Peter. Even though she failed to hurt him, maybe I wouldn't be so lucky. I focused my vampire speed to the level of my gift. And like I did earlier, they seemed to freeze and I leaped into the air. I landed on the left side of them. I charged up my energy and released it at one of the new guys.

He fell back and was screaming in such pain. And then it happened; he burst into flames. I was amazed I did it, but I knew I could not stop there, so I continued to do it to the other two, who also aided my enemy. They too went up in flames and all three ran towards the water to jump in, but the first one did not make it. I laughed and turned towards the man from the dock and said, "I guess this time I had the upper hand." He pulled out a stake and charged towards me. Something happened I did not expect. As he ran towards me the street seemed to spin and he was forced to drop the stake. It was like the harder I looked at him, the more the ground spun. I was amazed that I was doing this, but glad that I could do it. As I walked towards him, I could see the fear in his eyes. For it was clear to me he never seen anyone use this power before. I smiled and then told him if I ever see him again, I would kill him too. I then turned and walked off.

The faster I walked, the more overwhelmed I became. I had just taken another person's life. I... am a killer! It became evident to me that I was newly made and freshly taught. These powers I was given was too much for one person to have. I wonder why I surprised everyone that I came across. Then it hit me... That the blood I drank must be very old and powerful. The master vampire must have lived a long time as well as the fact that I have Elizabeth's blood in my veins as well. I needed to sit down. I had to get my head together. I sat on some steps or something. I'm not too sure. But there I stayed. I must have sat there for over an hour when I heard the voice of my sweet love. "What is troubling you my beloved?" she said. I looked up at her and snapped. I jumped to my feet and pointed to her. "You're what is wrong! I have lost everything that I am or was, and for what? Lies and games. I have too much power to be new at this shit. I am doing things to people that I never meant to. My friends hate me because of you , Peter doesn't believe anything I say because you lied to me about your name.(I looked her straight in her eyes) Either you tell me everything or I am out of here and for good. She seemed confused at first, but knew I meant what I said so she walked past me and asked me to follow.

In no time, we were at the Unknown Soldier's Park. She said, "I think this is the place to tell you everything. (She looked to the ground and started.) I was born and raised in New York City. It was the year 1867 when my brother and I were sent to live with our Aunt in London. Our uncle died and my father felt that my brother could aid her in the affairs of her husband's death. I being a young lady at that time, my parents felt that the trip would do me good as well. Back in those days, a lady so young did not have many rights. When we were refined enough, we may have met an older and settled man to take us as his wife. So, to my parents it was important that I learned to become a perfect lady and bring our family great honor. (Tears ran down her face and its red color left its presence behind. she looked at me and continued.) It took a great deal of time for me and my brother Janus to reach the London port. As the months passed, we got to know each other very well... Or at least I believed it. Anyway, as we arrived to my aunt's estate, we were treated like royalty. I could not believe it. She was wealthier than either of us thought, No wonder my father sent my brother. Back then, a woman without a man holding so much wealth was unheard of, but when my uncle died he left a good friend of his as overseer of his estate until the time came when my brother would come of age to take over the estate.

David C. Smith was the man's name. He and my brother soon became good friends. My aunt seemed not concerned at first. For her life did not change much after we arrived. She seemed to have parties every night. What was odd was that we never really met her once, since we got there. I mean, we got to see her in passing, but never really spoke to her. Even through those parties, she seemed to keep her distance from us. Janus and I spoke about that many times and after a while, it did not bother him anymore. He told me that we had to come to terms with the fact that she was used to being treated like a queen and we weren't important in her life, but he promised me that would change. And change it did. After about three years had passed, my brother was pretty much running everything and I became the lady of the house. My Aunt just seemed to disappear. One night as I sat in the dining room a woman entered and walked over to me. She demanded that I rise and as I did she introduced herself to me. "I am your Aunt Lady Constance and you're little Elizabeth, named after your mother. Well, I will not call you that! I will call you Lady Christina. One should always have a name of their own. That way they are able to write their own destiny." she said. There she stood, so tall and so graceful. I remembered stories my mother told of our aunt when I was a little girl. How my father and her never really seemed to get along. He used to get upset at her lifestyle and her way of wasting wealth on parties and swore she would go poor. But she wasn't, she was a strong, wealthy woman who knew how to maintain her wealth even if it was with the help of my brother. There was talk back then that she really ran everything and my brother was just her puppet.

Xavier, she stood there with her long black hair. Usually it was always up high but this time she allowed me to see her with it hanging by her sides. Her eyes glowed like to bulbs of green lights. Her skin was so white and milky. Not a mark could be seen on her skin. It was as if she had never had bug bites, a fall or anything. I mean, her skin was so beautiful, I grew jealous deep inside myself. She smiled as if she knew a joke that no one else knew. I took comfort from that night, because since then I would see her every night after. In time, she taught me how to address people of the state and people of blue blood. We would laugh so much behind their backs. She would teach me all I needed to know in order to fit in. Months went by like days and soon she started to travel. She would leave me for days at a time. After a while, days became months and then years.

Everyone who served under Janus became very distant towards me. It was as if something happened and I was not included in the secret. Even Janus shut me out... then I started to notice things like the fact that Janus would only show himself at night. I would be alone throughout the day and around the eve of every day he would appear. Even his skin became as beautiful as Lady Constance did. He seemed to have changed overnight. Janus avoided me like a plague. He wouldn't talk with me and soon I was not even allowed to have audience with him. This went on for about six months, I started hearing rumors about him and Mr. David, and it seemed that they had taken company with each other. It was talk that they would go off together every night and would not be seen until early the next morn, I pretended to be blind to their goings on, but our family name and honor was being challenged. So I demanded an audience with Janus or I was to leave London that very night. I really would have left that night... And he knew it. He came to my quarters and we spoke, more like argued. I yelled at him and him at me. So much anger was released that night, but like you, I wanted to know the truth. He told me that our family was cursed. We were to give birth to a child and then leave this way of life to claim another. I did not understand at first, but the more he talked. I got the picture and understood we were plagued with the kiss of death upon our family.

He told me that when he discovered this curse, He asked our aunt to keep it from me for I had not married nor gave birth to a child. I laughed and told him that he did not either. To my surprise, I was wrong for he had mated with a woman who lived in Paris. She knew who he was to become, but did not care, for he gave her great wealth. Then he told me that our Aunt was missing. The last time she went to travel abroad, something happened and she did not return. He and Mr. David have gone out every night in search of her, but failed to find her.

Then he told me the nightmare that was to haunt me for years. See, my Uncle was a vampire as well as my Aunt and was killed by a drinker. See, drinkers are evil beings. They rape vampires of their blood and drink them to their death. The vampire grows stronger every time he drinks of a different vampire. The older the blood, the stronger its affects will be. See, Joseph was that drinker and he drank from my Uncle and later we discovered from my Aunt as well. My Aunt chased him around the world for twenty-five years. We received word of the hundreds of vampires he murdered. He killed in Suzack, Chad, Asia, Brazil, Paris, Rome, and finally Finland. My Aunt found him in Norway before he killed her. I had grown so upset that I was not thinking clear and demanded that my brother cross me over, so I could aid him in defeating this monster, with great remorse he prepared to change me.

Mr. David's contacts told us that he was on the move towards Algeria. Mr. David told us that there was one there who was believed to be older than all of us. If Joseph had got to taste him, he would have been unstoppable. It took us some time to get there, but we sent word that we were coming. Mr. David, being far older than us at this new life, was able to fly, so at night he would take to the air and made safe heavens for us as we followed him. Of course, word got out that he was killing complete dens and drinking from them. Janus knew he was going to be hard to kill, so he decided I needed to learn to fight. Not fight as a woman in our day might, but as a man would. Every night before we took to the road, he would fight me and have me learn from my mistakes. He was very good to me and his love for me seemed to show. It was the winter of 1892 when we got to Algeria. The great Master was not so easy to find. Many did not hear of him and most of the savages did not understand our language. After about three months, we came upon a tribe that knew the name of a vampire and worshiped him as the wind spirit. His name was Mo'lym and he traveled with the four winds. We stayed in their village for several days until one of Mo'lym's women came to Mr. David. She told us her name was Tessie and Mo'lym would see us back at his cave. I did not like her for some reason; it was like she would read my mind whenever she looked at me. I took it as their way of keeping their god safe. I did not know then that they protected him because he protected all the secrets of what we were. He had the records of our history deep in his cave. I thought he and his friends were savages. The thought of them living in caves like cave dwellers of some sort left me with something less to desire.

We stayed with them for several months and the four women that protected him took to me and me to them. I can't tell you their names, for it would only make matters worse for you. But I can tell you I got to read their books of our history. I took to the books so well that they called me Lady Christine, the Keeper of The Red Waters of Zarasgale. In the book, I came across a passage that wrote about how if one's bloodline was destroyed so is all of one's kin. This confused me, so I asked question about this passage. Mo'lym told me that it meant that if Joseph was defeated and his body burned, then a great fire would sweep throughout my family tree and destroy our entire vampire heritage. I thought he was saying we all would die. So I got upset and then he told me that he meant we would not be vampires anymore, but Vaingels. Roaming spirits on the earth, like him. One who doesn't feed to live, but lives to protect what is meant to be. I stayed there in his cave for weeks and learned all that I could, especially after finding out I was from Joseph's bloodline. I went to my brother and told him my thoughts about if we drank Joseph's blood and destroyed his body, then we would be free. I told him how I came across a spell in the books I read that could make us human again. The spell would only work if the master was dead and his blood was cleansed in holy water. He told me to forget it.

He told me that Mr. David and the four women located Joseph just outside of the village and defeated him and that Mo'lym stripped him of his power and his blood. I could not believe it; they defeat him and never told me anything. David and one of the women took Joseph and his blood to the New World to bury him for all time. That way, he would never harm another, nor would his death destroy any other generations. So much time has passed and now I had the chance and failed. Janus now wants to return to London and let him come for us, but that is too Dangerous. He will only attack us after he regain all his power and strength. There is a chance that if he regains his powers and strength that he could defeat us all. So, now you know everything. (She looked at me with such sadness in her eyes.) I only pray you will still help me destroy him before he does to me what he did so many years ago to my Aunt and Uncle."

I was at a loss for words. Here stood a woman who has lost everything, even her brother's love, to a monster's fear. I decided then and there not only was I going to help her, but I was going to get the guys to help her as well. I told her I was sorry for what I said to her. I then told her that I was not going to just abandon her. I could now see that she really needed me and that I would be there for her like she was there for me. She turned to me and we kissed. It was with such passion and fire that I knew once again how much I loved her. My arms found comfort around her waist and she took safety upon my chest. It felt as if time stood still. We broke our kiss and I looked into her eyes. I told her that I must leave her and find my friends. I ensured her that I would convince them to help her. That's if Landis did survive. I knew they would be enraged with her for attacking them and even trying to kill them. I believed I could fix all of this. Her story was all I needed to get them to understand her and me.

I turned from her and took off. I ran up Walnut Street to fifteen. I started to walk, as I turned onto Fifteenth Street and walked up to Locust. I was not sure what I was going to say, but I realized it was late and they probably were as tired as I was. So, I was going to have to explain things quickly. I got into Landis's apartment building rather easy and went up to his floor. As the elevator doors opened, my ears could pick up the talking form inside the apartment. Marco was saying, "Look man I do not care what George is going through, we need to watch him too. Now more than anything." then I heard Vinnie respond, "O, look George is going through just as much as we are and if you want to consider something, then it should be what are we going to do with the girl and Xavier?" Drew quickly said, "Hey, Dudes you all need to back off Xavier. So he fucked up, but so did we. He really isn't any more at fault than he is at fault for anything else he does. We all knew what Xavier was going to do and did nothing to stop him." Vinnie said, "And how were we going to stop Xavier from being him?" Landis spoke saying, "Look, I say kill Elizabeth!! Fuck it. She is the reason all this shit is happening. If we kill her then the master wouldn't have any reason to continue this madness." Zack laughed and said, "I think we need to wait for George and get his point of view on all of this." Then I heard Marco's Voice again, "What the fuck, Man... George is out of it. George fuck'n thinks he is Elizabeth; I do not trust him either right now." Casper said, "Look, I think we all need to think out all of this first and foremost. Ok, I mean, even Xavier needs to be heard before we decide what we should do. But, for the record, I want the bitch dead." Then they all started asking Garrett what he thought. Garrett never responded. Fear entered my heart as I touched the door knob and heard Garrett say," Come in Xavier, we were just discussing you." I opened the door and walked in. I was not very sure what to expect. It was wild how Garrett knew I was there listening. So, I walked in and sat on the sofa. I sat there with my legs wide open as if I wanted them to know I was a bigger man than the last time they saw me. I rested my elbows on my knees and looked down towards the ground before I spoke.

I said, "Look! Guys, I had been through a lot in the last few days and maybe if it was not for me, you all wouldn't be in the position that you're all in. And for that, I am sorry. Even Elizabeth is sorry for what she did... She just did not know what was going on and thought that you all where holding me captive. When she ripped Landis's heart out of his chest, it was only to stop him long enough for us to get away. She wouldn't never hurt someone, let alone kill them. She is not that type of person (I ran my hands through my hair as I continued to talk). She has as much to lose from all of this. We all need each other and I came here to ask for you guys to help. I realized that you may all have questions and I want to answer them all. I want to put this all behind us guys. So we can be friends again. I know once you guys get to meet her and know her, you'll come to love her just as I do."

Marco looked at me and then towards everyone else. I was not too sure who would speak first. I looked around the room in hopes to pick up any of their feeling on what I said. Landis spoke first. He said, "Do I look as if I am stupid to you, Xavier? Is jackass written on my forehead...? Damn. You have balls of steel to come here and ask us to overlook... that fuck'n bitch tried to kill me and let's not overlook the fact that she bit the shit out of Casper! Thanks to George, she did not get the chance to kill him." Casper next saying, "Xavier man, you're one fucked up dude. Man you're going to sit here and justify this bitch biting me." "And let's not forget the fact that you fuck'n ran off with her, after she tried to kill Landis." Vinnie commented as he rose and walked around Landis, who was sitting in front of the window. I knew Vinnie would protect George no matter what, but this sense of protection he was now showing towards Landis was something new to me. He stood so bold and looked at me with such defiance. I could not imagine him ever helping Elizabeth. Drew started to laugh a little and then commented, "Look dudes... I can't imagine us helping Xavier, when we can't even trust each other. I mean, look around... We no longer have faith in our own friendships. We have only been vampires for a short time and in that time, we have gone through great changes. "Landis looked at Drew as if he was crazy and then spoke, "What the hell are you talking about!? We trust each other... We just do not trust Elizabeth." Drew looked around the room and just nodded his head." Look! Man! I do not care what any of you say. The fact is that we just became vampires. We can't even trust our selves, let alone trust each other. (Waving hand in the sky just above his head) Hey, all I am saying is that we need time to understand what has happened to our selves before we even think about what is happening to us as a group." Drew said. Landis placed his hand on his chest and said, "I think you're wrong! I mean, I know what happened to me and I am sure so does everybody else. Now, if you do not understand what is happening to you, then I feel sorry for you man, but there isn't any time to play catch up." Drew looked at Landis for some time as if he was considering something. Drew turned towards Garrett and asked, "Do you feel I am tripping here or what? Garrett! I think the best thing we can do right now is make a pact that we will work together for now. Only then will we have some form of trust between us. If we do not ensure some form of loyalty with each other, how are we ever going to form it with Elizabeth? I think we need to make a pact first." Zack spoke next saying," We do not have time for this ego shit!" Vinnie looked over to me and then towards Garrett and asked, "What time is it!? George still isn't back yet." Every one began to trip at the thought that George did not return yet. It amazed me that even in his absence George could steal the floor. We looked at the clock and realized that it was five thirty in the morning and the sun would soon be out in full glory.

Garrett calmed every one down rather quickly and told us it would be best for us to get rest and finish this when we awoke. Everyone listened to him and some (Vinnie) questioned his reasoning. Vinnie seemed never to trust anyone when it came to George safety, but he followed everyone else into the bedroom. I stayed in the living room after everyone else left the room. I turned towards Garrett who now was heading towards the door. I asked if he was going to find George. He turned and looked at me in a way he never looked before and told me to trust him. He wanted me to keep it to myself. He insured me he would be back and with George. I looked towards the bedroom door and then back to him. He had already walked out the door and when I walked over to the hall, he was gone. I returned to the sofa and did as he asked. I guess in a way I was a little foolish to give him so much trust after everything that happened. I fell asleep in no time and again I was over taken by a dream.

I was surrounded in a pool of clouds and then as it cleared I seen six black ravens flying over my head. I followed the ravens as they flew across the sky. Then I seen Elizabeth wrapped in cloth and blood running from her body. The blood ran in seven streams and into one lager pool. Then from the pool of blood, a white dove flew into the sky and the six ravens ate the dove. The dream was so crazy that I could not awake. I was forced to sleep through the whole dream. When I finally awoke I so wanted to talk to everyone about it, but they were already awake.

Landis said, "Where could he have gone?"

As I opened my eyes, I asked if he was talking about Garrett. He told me yes, so I told him what Garrett told me. Landis snapped and started yelling at me. Everyone got crazy as if I sent Garrett out there. As if I told him to do something so insane. I knew I did not agree with his choice, but it was his to make. They must have been flipping like this for about a half an hour when Casper just lost it. He leaped for me. He was yelling how he was going to rip my fuck'n head off. I did not know what to do. He was twice my size and equally as powerful. Before he was able to reach me, the others grabbed him. It took some time, but they managed to get him into one of the chairs and hold him there. Landis just stood there... Looking! He did nothing to stop Casper or to help him. It was as if he really did not care if Casper killed me. He just watched as the rest of the guys were holding him and trying to make him calm down. The front door opened and everyone stopped. We watched as if death entered the room.

It was George! Man, something changed about him. He was thinner and younger or so it seemed. His body seemed to have no fat, but all muscle. He looked at Casper and then at me and

Landis. Then he said, "What are you doing? Have you boys all gone insane?" Garrett pushed the door open even farther and walked around George and entered the room. Garrett seemed to have been smiling as he spoke, "I told Xavier I would be back." We all were at a loss for words. Garrett had changed as well. His skin seemed to make him look more like a wax figure or something. His body had changed, too. He was not like George. His body had thickened up and all his fat seemed to have turned into muscle. He looked as if he could destroy all of us with no problem at all. Vinnie walked over to George and touched his face. George looked as if he was a little frightened by Vinnie's behavior, but he stood his ground as Vinnie rubbed his hand across George's face. Vinnie slowly caresses George's face as if he loved him. As jealous as I was even I was attracted to him. It was as if he was blessed by Aphrodite herself. Vinnie just looked at him so gentle, Then said, "Your skin! Your fuck'n body! George man (starting to smile), you got to tell us what happened to you." George leaned in and hugged Vinnie as the rest of the guys got up from the chair and allowed George to sit down. He looked so weak, but yet I could sense that he was actually much stronger. His eyes were as if they seen the world just as different as I did, or perhaps even more so. There was no doubt in my mind that he and Garrett had grown a lot since the last time I had seen them.

Garrett shut the door and stood beside George as he started to tell their story. "When I left this morning it was raining, so I figured that if there was no sun, then I could not get burned. So I walked over to the school and got one of the raincoats out of the guards' office. I decided if I was to find George, then I would need to cover him and myself or we both might die. I walked around for a while and then it happened. I felt an urge to walk toward Front Street and then over to Spring Garden. When I reached Spring Garden, I knew I had walked too far, so I walked back up to around Sixth Street and then back south one block. Oddly enough, there was a graveyard there. I never knew one was there, but there is. When I went in, I felt him. I walked around for a while, but by this time, the heat from the sun was penetrating the clouds and was starting to burn my skin. As my skin started to burn, I knew I had to find George so we could get the hell out of there. But when I located him and opened the hiding place he chose, his body burst into flames as if someone placed him on fire. I quickly closed the lid to protect him, but grew scared for what I did. I knew if the sun would continue to grow stronger, then I would be cooked too. I looked around and then realized I could take the heat of the sun better than George could. And maybe it wouldn't affect me the same way it does the rest of you. So, I made a pile from the wet leaves on the ground and pulled them over me, to protect me from the sun. It must have been enough protection because no sooner then I was done, I fell asleep. I awoke fully healed and ran to retrieve George. As I helped him to get out of his crypt, he told me about the blood he took from Elizabeth. She hid it and he found it. He drank it and that's how his body changed. I drank it after him and this is what it did to me." Landis felt that if this was the case, if drinking the blood that Elizabeth took from the master was able to make Garrett and George more powerful than it had to be able to do the same to the rest of the guys. I did not like the idea that George stole Elizabeth's blood and drank it. Nor did I want to deal with what might happen if they all drank from the blood too. I quickly told them that if George found the blood and they drank from it then there is no more left. For the blood consumes all who drink from it. It would make pigs out of its drinkers and may even cause one to go insane. Garrett agreed with me, but then told us that George did not turn into a pig. He had given Garrett the blood. And then Garrett drank all the rest. "I might have drunk from George if the blood did not take over and cause me to fall back to the ground and made me this", Garrett said with a laugh. As we came to terms of what was happening to us.

I felt it was time for us to return here. Then Landis spoke again saying, "Then we will drink from you and George."

Garrett said, "Sure that will work."

"With yours and George's blood in us, we will become stronger too," Landis said.

I spoke once more, refusing to allow this. I realized that they wanted to get stronger and needed to feel more secure about being safe, but Elizabeth would give us this safety. I told them it was too dangerous for them to keep drinking the virus. For every time you drink, something will happen and in Vinnie and Zack's case, it may turn them completely into animal-like creatures. Even Drew and Marco needed to think about this. I mean, they changed some from drinking mine. I looked at them and then I turned to George and looked at George's body. It was as if he had no fat at all. He looked inhuman and Garrett looked as if he was something that you would find in a wax museum. I told them that I felt we needed to find Elizabeth and get her point of view before we continue this madness. I informed them they were tripping. (Man, they were so lost and confused about all that was happening...) But to spite me, George made the group choose between him and me. He raised his thin arms in the air, offering them to the group and saying, "Those who wish to follow Xavier go and with my blessing, but those who wish to feed and feel the power the blood has given me.... Then drink!!"

The room went silent for a moment and then everyone turned against me and chose to drink from George. Of course, the first two to sink their fangs into George's wrist were Vinnie and Zack. The others grew restless and pulled them from George's wrist. As Vinnie and Zack fell to the floor, Landis and Marco took their place. They seemed to pull on George's arm as if the blood was not flowing out of him fast enough. Garrett grew alarmed and pulled them off of George as well. Casper and Drew walked over and looked at each other and they drank George's unholy blood. George blood seemed to flow quicker and he slowly closed his eyes as if their drinking was causing him to pass out. A part of me feared this would be George's death, but another part of me welcomed it. Garrett pulled them away from George, too. Then it happened... Casper went mad and leaped for George. The blood was driving him insane and all he knew was that he wanted to feed more. Garrett jumped in between them and Casper, not being able to get through Garrett, decided to feed on him. I was surprised for when Casper bit down on to Garrett's neck; his fangs could not break Garrett's skin. Garrett was unable to be fed upon. Unlike George's, Garrett's skin was unbreakable. Then the blood took over and Casper was just like the others, on the floor yelling and fighting to keep control. Thinking quickly, I turned on the radio and had the music blazing to drown out everyone's voices.

The yelling went on for some time before everyone went quiet. I was amazed to see how everyone changed.

Vinnie caught my attention first. He stood up and looked directly at me. His skin was smooth like wax. His eyes seemed to shine because his facial hair became a very deep black. Against his dark chocolate skin, he looked so attractive. His teeth were like white pearls. They seemed to glow because they were so white. His hair became as dark as his facial hair. His hair seemed to carry the wind, even when there was none. It was hard to remember he was only six-foot one. He seemed so much taller now. I felt as if I had to look up at him. His body seemed to become thinner. Where there was once fat, now only muscle. His fingers were so long and yet his finger tips remained the same. His hands were so strong and defined. Their veins looked like spaghetti string running up his arms. His chest sat out like he was arching his back to create this effect, but he wasn't.

Zack was the second to rise and he changed as well. I feared that the blood would change him and Vinnie into some kind of animals, but it did not. Zack stood on too much defined legs and his ass muscles seemed to fill out his pants and his waist was not only thicker but it was truly defined. The virus this time made him completely defined and even his face was defined. It looked a little scary at first, then his facial muscles released and I was able to see his beautiful fangs. They were as thick as Vinnie's... They looked as if they were about two inches long and a half an inch thick. His teeth were white and seem to reflect light. Zack looked as if he was a lightweight fighter or something. Hands that looked no different from Vinnie's, but hair that looked very different. To look at Zack, one would easily believe he came from one of the Hawaiian Islands. Standing all of five-foot seven and looking onto the room with his yellowish eyes that had a very deep Green strip running through them, kind of like a tiger or some kind of cat. His skin was great; it turned into a golden brown tint. I grew a little jealous as I looked upon him, but did nothing to let it show. He turned to Vinnie, as they looked each other over. It was not long after Zack turned to Vinnie that Landis and Marco stood up. They looked at each other and smiled. Their fangs were as thick as Zack's and Vinnie's. What was odd, their fangs were longer at least by a half inch.

Landis's head was still bald and his eyes were still the same. At first, I did not think it changed him at all, but then I saw it. His five-foot six body was completely muscular just like the others... His eyes seem to catch the light every so often. He looked at everyone in the room as if he was studying them. He seemed to imitate movement more than usual. Normally he was pretending to act like just one of the guys but it was like his body was trying to remain in our presence. I feared what gifts the blood had just given him.

Now, Marco however, his light-skinned complexion truly

looked like caramel chocolate. Against his skin, his beautiful yellowish green eyes made him so attractive. He looked like he could be Brazilian. I had to smile as they all looked onto each other. I am not sure how long it was before Casper and Drew came around because they sat on the floor and were smiling at each other just like I was doing. Drew said, "Damn man, that shit was fuck'n wild." He rose and I got a good view of his well-defined body. He looked as if he was from Africa itself. Drew deep-set eyes and his dark complexion made me think of him like a model. His eyes were brown with a thin black ring around them. The white in his eyes seem to glow. He stood to be six-foot one inch. He seemed to have the body of a biker very strong arms and legs with a much defined chest. His braids seemed to weave tighter and looked as if they were long ropes of hair.

Casper just laid there on the floor and smiled. He turned towards Garrett and told him, "No hard feelings". He explained that the blood took over him and he went mad for a moment. He looked so massive laying there. His body was as built as Garrett's, if not even bigger. He finally rose and I could see the power in his hands and arms. He was truly as strong as Garrett. His arms had veins running through them just like the others just a little thicker. He looked like a mannequin; his skin seemed to be painted on his body. His skin seemed a rich chocolate color, but it seemed different in some way. As they all looked each other over, I realized that no one paid attention to George... that he had passed out in the chair.

All the blood they drained from him must had taken its toll and now he was helpless. I started to laugh, the great George could not take it, and he could not handle turning them all over to their next level. My laughter grabbed the others attention and they turned to see George passed out. They did not find it as funny; in fact they did not find it funny at all. Landis could not help but point out the fact George turned six of them over before he passed out, where

I could not turn four of them other before needing sleep. They did not go out that night. They all stayed in Landis's apartment to watch over George as if he needed it. No one spoke a word; they all just keep looking at each other as if they did not trust one another. The way they acted, it was as if they were all strangers to each other. They all had changed and I was not too sure if it was for the better. It must have been around three in the morning when George awoke. The moment they heard him moan, they all ran to his side. They took to him as if he was their girlfriend or someone. The way Landis held his hand and Marco took hold of his other. Vinnie came to stand beside the chair he sat in and leaned over to softly ask him if he was ok. I just shook my head... Drew cut his eye over at me as if he was going to attack if I even acted like I would do something to George. George nodded his head in response to Vinnie's questions. Garrett demanded that they give George room to breathe. I laughed again (As if air would restore the blood he lost.) I told them that George would be weak for some time, until his blood is replaced. I turned their attention back to my question I asked earlier. They all looked at me and then Landis said. "Look I told you no..." Raising one of his hands in the air, Garrett said, "Wait a minute. I think that Xavier is right."

"What! Are you kidding? Garrett! There is no way you could feel that Elizabeth can be trusted."

"Look, I am far more powerful than all of you. I feel that I may even have the power to destroy Elizabeth, but what none of us has is the skill! We need to understand what we are and what it means to be what we have become. Elizabeth is offering to give us those answers... and whether you think you need her or not I am telling you all that you do."

"What? Elizabeth!! I will not." George said, pulling himself upright in the chair. For a moment, I thought his strength had returned.

Garrett turned to him and said, "George, We have no choice. We need her to defeat the master and we need to know all the things we can do. We can't keep running around blind and hope that it will work out ok."

"I am not hoping a damn thing. I know it...," George said. His words just stopped in mid sentence, but it looked as if he and Garrett were still talking. After a minute I realized that not only he and Garrett were talking to George, but they were talking to everyone in the room except me. I guess this too was another one of his new tricks. At some point the conversation continued until it was only him and Garrett speaking alone. They must have been talking for about ten minutes then it happened; George seemed to get upset. The room started to spin and then we all started to bleed from of eyes and ears. It was so painful that all we could do was to close our eyes and grab our ears. Garrett must have realized what was happening, so he grabbed George and ran in the bedroom. The door seemed to close on its own. I was not sure if the others seen it, but I knew what I seen. The room was very quiet for some time. We all waited for the door to open again. Then it did and out came Garrett followed by George. Garrett started to speak immediately, "Even with the blood you all have drunken from George, you are not powerful enough to take on Elizabeth. If you do, you'll be defeated if not killed. Please do not allow your feelings towards Xavier alter what we must do." Everyone just looked at him for some time but said nothing. Landis spoke first saying, "And do you agree with this, George? Huh? Do you? Well, answer me, or does Garrett have your tongue as, well? George remained speechless. I could not believe it, but what was harder to believe was that Garrett was agreeing with me. I was finally winning and thought George put up a good fight. I was finally gaining control of my children. My spawn... Landis stood there for some time and then refused to come with us. The group seemed to be pulled in two directions. George looked up at Landis and said, "And you do not have to. If what Xavier says about Elizabeth is true, then your choice to join her or not should not matter. She should not want you to do something that is against your nature. This goes for all of you. Xavier claims that all Elizabeth wants is to put a stop to all of this, then I have to agree with Garrett. You all need to meet this woman that Xavier praises so highly. I myself am going not because I trust her or because I believe anything Xavier has said, but because you all do believe him and I have to ensure that she does not harm any of you. I am the only one who has seen her soul; I know what she is capable of doing to you. Landis, I must ask you to understand that we all are on the same path, but everyone has to take their own route." With that said, Landis told us all that he was going to leave and we wouldn't be able to find him.

Chapter 8
The Great Gathering

I felt bad for him; I wanted him to be a part of what we were doing. I knew George was up to something, but as their new leader, I knew I could not allow him to stop me. I told them that I felt I needed to take over things from here and Garrett could aid me when needed.

The first thing I did was put us up in the Hershey Hotel the next night. I felt that Landis's apartment held to many bad memories and with all that had been happening to us I felt it would be wiser for us to start everything off on a new foot. I got the room number and told them all to meet me there that night. I left them at the break of the evening to find Elizabeth and to convince her to come with me to meet my friends. Finding her was not very hard, since she was sitting at Rittenhouse Square. She was at the little fountain pool watching the people walk by and amusing her. I walked up on her so quietly that she did not hear me. I told her that I did it; I got them to listen. She seemed amazed at first. But when I explained it to her, she was very impressed. She hugged me and we kissed. I wrapped my arms around her soft, sweet smelling body and vowed never to leave her side. I knew that now we all could be together. We walked for some time and I told her of the events that had unfolded. She grew concerned about Landis and asked if it was wise to let him just go off on his own. What if the master found him? I did not think about that. She thought that maybe it would be wiser to let them knew what the master was like. I felt she feared that if Landis was attacked by a vampire, then the group may feel she had something to do with it. I understood her point, but felt that once they got to know her they would know she wouldn't do anything like that. Once we got to the hotel, I discovered that Garrett took care of the bill and I was left a key at the front desk. I took that as a sign that everything was working out fine. Once we got to the room, I walked in first holding onto Elizabeth's hand. I could not believe this was really happening. The room was so beautiful, with its sofa and two chairs. The place was packed. George was sitting in between Vinnie and Zack on the sofa. Casper and Marco were sitting in the chairs. But my heart stopped when I seen Landis and Garrett looking out at the night sky. I walked in a little confused at first because though Landis was there I did not see Drew. After we entered the apartment, Drew came out of the bathroom. Elizabeth looked them over and then smiled. I felt the tension leave the room once she did that. They all introduced themselves to her and a chair was brought out for her from the bedroom area.

She sat there for some time answering their questions. She knew if they where to help us, then they had to come and trust her. Everyone asked her questions but George. He just sat there for most of the evening and just when I thought it was over he spoke. "You know I drank your blood." George said.

"I know... You got its location from my mind the night I attacked you guys." Elizabeth said.

"Yes, along with other things as well and in time I may come to unravel those things to get a better understanding of what I had seen."

Perhaps you will, or you could just ask me."

"Very well, what are these images of Peter that I am seeing?"

Elizabeth looked at me before she answered George. She realized I did not tell them about Peter and in all truth, I did not want them to know, not until I had the chance to find him. I know if they heard about him before I had a chance to make right everything that it might have changed their minds. I grew nervous as she started to speak.

Elizabeth said, "Those are images of Peter being stabbed in the chest by me. He was also made into a vampire by Janus, my brother. Just like you all where. Peter decided to help my brother and destroy me. I had to slow him down and that was the only way. Peter is very strong and quick. My brother must have fed on him for some time. He must have turned Peter over slowly. See, Xavier saved Peter from my brother and when Xavier gave him his blood, the blood reacted to the virus my brother had already put in Peter's body. Because the virus was older than the vampire's blood that made him, the virus took a stronger hold of him and the gifts he received from my brother over powered the gifts he may have received from Xavier. Peter seemed as strong as or even stronger than Xavier and me. He would have killed me if I did not use that iron rail to slow him down. Please, believe me. He is still alive.... He may need time to regain his strength, since he lost so much blood. Xavier and I wanted to give him a chance to calm down and then we will find him and explain everything to him as well."

"Ok! I will accept that for now, but you both will find Peter as soon as possible or I will be forced to find your story and reasons to be both lies."

"I do not understand?"

"Of course you do... I am not going to allow Xavier's blinding love for you blind me from all I see and know. If what you are saying is true, then you will find Peter and return him to us. You will replace his blood with your own or Xavier's. At this point, I really do not care. Xavier caused all of this and it is time he cleaned it up. But since you choose to be by his side, then you too are being held responsible. I know in my heart that Xavier is blinding himself to a lot that he has seen and I know he is leaving a lot of things out of our conversations, but now it is your responsibility to tell us what Xavier is to afraid to tell us."

"I take great offense to you calling Xavier a coward. Nor do I take kindly to you calling him a liar."

"Oh please... I can safely bet that since I took memories from your mind when I attacked you, so you were also flooded with memories of my life and my feelings. Plus, by now you are very aware of who and what I am."

"What are you saying?"

"You are playing a dangerous game. We both know I am the lost unicorn, and your saying things you believe I want to hear. But, you're wrong! I mean what I am saying and Xavier knows it. No more lies, or I and the others will walk and if that means our death by this Janus person, then so be it. Let me say this as well; I am also aware that it will mean your two deaths' as well."

"Do not be too sure of that."

"Oh please... I do not need Xavier to tell me anything to see that without us, you're both sitting ducks. Perhaps Xavier is dumb to the world, but I have no doubt that if it is important for Xavier to bring us all together then Xavier has met someone who is capable of destroying him. See, unlike you, Xavier isn't strong enough to block me out of his mind. So, for the record, I have Xavier's blood too."

Everyone said, "What!"

"That's right. I took Xavier's blood and hid it from all of you. And I think Garrett knows me well enough to know that if you do not find and help Peter, then I will find him and allow him to finish the bottle of the master's blood. The choice is yours."

It appeared that no one was expecting George's traitorous nature to take part in this. The room remained quiet for some time and no one moved. Then Garrett walked over to the chair where Marco sat and placed his hand on top of it. He started talking about all of us going out to find Peter. I was truly amazed that he was willing to help us find Peter. Soon everyone was agreeing. George, however, did not say a word. It was very clear he was not leaving us choices. Garrett took out the map of Center City from the Yellow Pages and started giving us all areas to search. He asked George if he knew where Peter was at, but George did not respond. He just sat there and looked at us like we were all complete fools. He rose from the sofa and shook his head as he turned away to leave the room. Vinnie gave us a smirk and followed George out of the room. We all expected him to do no less.

Elizabeth explained how we could sense another vampire. She explained how when a vampire is near another you get an ill-like feeling in your stomach. It's not the kind of feeling that makes you want to throw up, but the kind of nervous feeling you get when something is about to happen. She made sure we understood that even if we can't see him or her, trust that feeling for it is never wrong. Then she added if you start to feel the same kind of feeling you get from me, then get out of there because that means there is a vampire much older than you in the area. That is usually how a newborn is able to find its maker. "Though the feeling is a little different when it is your maker, just as your feelings from my vibe is different from Xavier's", she said. I had to admit I was just as impressed as everybody else. Now, I knew how to detect another vampire. I did not forget about George, but knew I had to deal with him later. I knew I could not risk losing the guys to him so I had to win at his game and once I received the blood back, then I would decide what to do with him. George was painting a line and I knew I would be forced to confront it eventually.

We all paired off: Casper with me, Drew with Marco, Zack with Landis, Garrett with Elizabeth. I was not sure why Garrett chooses to partner with Elizabeth, but I knew I was not in a position to protest. We all decided that it would be best if we met up first at the Clothes Pin in three and a half hours. Then together we would bring Peter to George. This way it would force George to keep his word and return my blood back to me. I knew George was losing his control over the group and this was going to be the last straw. We all walked out of the hotel together as if nothing was wrong. Casper and I went to Peter's apartment in hopes that he was there. He was not there, so we headed to one of his girlfriend's place. It looked empty from the outside, but I knew I had to make sure. I ran up to the house and leaped onto a small ledge that stood about four inches out from the rest of the building. I looked into her window and saw that it was empty. I forced the window open and stepped in. Her apartment was very dark, but my vampire sight allowed me to see everything very clearly. I walked into the bathroom. There it was, the proof I needed; his blood-stained clothes. I just stood there in pure amazement when I heard Casper from behind me. "It's hard to believe he would be still alive after losing so much blood. I wanted to feel bad for what Peter was going through, but the truth was it was no longer in me to really have the same feelings I did when I was alive. I think it was because everything had changed, life and death had taken on new meanings. I did not really understand what those meanings were, but I now knew they existed.

I turned to Casper and told him I had an idea where Peter had gone to. We walked out the front door of her apartment and down the street as if nothing was out of the way. We walked over to the school and up to Peter's studio but he was not there either. We decided to walk around the city and try to pick up his scent. We must have walked for over three hours before we decided to head over to the Clothes Pin. I wanted to believe someone found Peter, but feared no one located him. We sat in front of the Clothes Pin for about twenty minutes. Landis and Zack came from around the corner of Chestnut St. We started talking about how none of us could find him. Then Elizabeth and Garrett showed up. They had no better luck than we did. I wanted to really be the one that found him. In a way, I felt I owed him that much, if not anything else. We continued to talk, when out of nowhere Marco and Drew showed up. To my surprise, Peter was with them. He looked so tired, but yet still strong for someone who had lost so much blood. He told us that George spoke to him in his mind and told him that we were coming to find him. He told me to go to the love park and wait there for Marco and Drew. I did not know if everyone else got upset, but I was pissed. That fuck'n bastard, George, was playing fuck'n mind games with us and I had enough of his shit. Peter and Elizabeth just looked at each other and then Elizabeth went to him and told him to feed on her. She knew in her heart that she owned him that much. He looked at the others and then me. We all stood in a circle around them for him to kiss her neck and drank the life fluids from her. People looked at us at first, and then just went on with their own business.

As she reached around his waist and he leaned into her ear and whispered that he would rather die first. He turned to Garrett and told Garrett to take him back to George. We all were a little confused but did as he wished. He got to the apartment and Vinnie walked him into the other room where George was closing the door behind him. I was so pissed… George played this simple game, when he could've simply told Peter to come to him. After about 20 minutes the door open and they joined us in the outer room.

Peter turned towards us; I was lost in my own lust. His eyes were two green crystal spheres, outlined with the most ebony eyelashes and brows. His light brown hair fell with the softest waves around his face. His skin looked liked a soft wax or plastic pinkest flesh color. His body was like a roller bladers. His body was not very muscular but it was toned with very strong legs.

I just looked at him and grew angry at the fact that George was playing these sick games. I turned to the group for their view on George's actions. Elizabeth pointed out that George may have been testing her and me to see if we were really going to help Peter. In case we did not, he was going to make sure Marco and Drew did. As we all walked around in the hotel room, we were quiet for the most part. Once I got control of my emotions, I walked over to George who was sitting on the sofa and demanded my blood back.

George looked at me with the calmest demeanor and said, "My Xavier, I never told you I was going to give the blood back to you. I told you if you did not find Peter, I would give it to him. Your greed to have more power than the rest of us is what led you to believe I was going to return it to you. The fact is that the blood is important to all of us, for it can restore our bodies and powers if any of us get hurt in this battle to come. Now, your past record has shown that I cannot trust that you will remain loyal to the group. There is nothing in your behavior or Elizabeth's that assures me that either of you would save any of us if something goes wrong."

"What? You are my friend, which is what assures this to be true." I said.

"I think Peter would tell us different!"

"What the hell are you talking about, we just saved him."

"No, I just saved him and used you to do it. If you were truly going to do it, then it would have been done before now."

"George I want my blood, now."

"Sorry, but that is not going to happen."

"Who the hell do you think you are?"

I am George! And I need no woman to stand beside me in order to have a backbone. You have done nothing, but damned this entire group; and the outcome is for what!? A woman!! You may have fooled the others in believing that you know what you're doing, but I know different. Based on that fact... I am keeping the blood and through it, the control of this group."

"Do you all hear Him? Do you all hear our new God?"

"Yes, Xavier! I'm a god and so are all of you! We are immortal. That means we live longer than any other. I am sure there will be times that we will welcome death, but not be blessed with it. There may be or may not be any other so like us. I understand this and now it is time that I make the rest of you understand it. (Turning his sight to Elizabeth and locking eyes with her.) You are no longer strong enough to take control of my mind. My thoughts are mine to keep, but you are not so lucky. For soon the time will come where I will know your thoughts just as I know the thoughts of the others."

"Too hell with you, I am not going to allow you to make us nor Elizabeth your slaves."

"And I am not going to allow you to make us her victims." George said as he looked back towards me.

With that being said, Vinnie brought in glasses of the blood. I looked at him, as if hate wouldn't do justice to my feelings towards him. He gave everyone a glass and told them to drink the blood of the master's, for there will be much more in time, that he and George broke into a blood bank van and took several bags of blood. They took the blood and mixed it with the master's blood. I never thought about it before, but it did make sense. If the virus reacts to vampires' blood, then it would only grow stronger by taking over human blood. Elizabeth and the others drank without a though so I decided to drink as well. I wondered how much of what George said was true and how much of it was just spite. I knew from that moment on, I would have to watch George and his lackey, Vinnie. If there was going to be a way to retrieve my blood back, then I needed to watch them to do it.

For the next few weeks, we floated from hotel to hotel. Every night the group stayed somewhere different so not to be court by any other vampires. Elizabeth would go off with a different one of us, except for George. He wouldn't allow himself to be alone with her. Neither would Vinnie for that matter. Vinnie seemed to become George's mate, in a way. He wouldn't leave George's side. I guess in away, the rest of us sought Elizabeth's company. I had grown jealous of all the attention the other guys were giving Elizabeth. She seemed to love our little fights over who would spend the night with her. A part of me knew she was only training them to control their powers, but I still feared that one of them may take her heart from me. Landis and Garrett, I did not need to fear. For they still took to George and would see to it he knew their loyalty was towards him. (I must allow you to understand that as vampires, your standards of normal relationships can change. Though we can mate like humans, we could never reproduce. This however, changes your reasons for mating. As vampires, we seek to find one who brings comfort to the torment of loneliness.) I guess in some way, I grew angry at the ways George took to Vinnie. Every eve, they would rise and leave the rest of us alone. Garrett questioned what they did every night, but George wouldn't answer or if he did it was through their minds. Garrett always seemed to grow angry at George's behavior. I grew tired of all interactions between me and the group, so I decided to leave them for a while and try to make sense of how we were to kill this being that has lived maybe over ten thousand years.

As I walked the streets, I kept thinking about how hard it was going to be against someone so old. I mean the fact was that even after what Elizabeth did to Peter, he turned out to be fine. Though he was weak, in time his body would have forced him to feed and he would have been as good as new. My mind was racing for some time before I realized that I was being followed. I decided it had to be the dick head that I fought at Penn's Landing. I decided it was time to end this, once and for all. I started to run towards Market Street. Then I heard George in my mind; he was asking what was wrong. I did not respond because I was not sure how to, nor was I thinking about it when the guy was so close to catching me. Somehow, George pieced it together and told me to take the guy up to the park right off of JFK Blvd. and he was coming with the others. I followed his directions and located the park. Once inside the park, I ran to the middle of what looked like a baseball field. I stopped and turned around.

There he was, standing there, looking as if he was ready for me. I reminded him of my warning I gave him the last time we fought. He just smiled and said, "Are you really that dumb? Do you think the master would send someone incapable of dealing with you? I have been playing with you and now I am tired. Your act against my two sons was unforgivable and I am going to make you pay. Now since the master no longer wishes to try and save your twisted soul. I can destroy you without fear of punishment." With that said he leaped in the air and kicked the shit out of me. He seemed to move much quicker than before and he truly was much stronger. I flew across the field and landed on my back. He flipped and leaped around like a gymnast hitting me on every pass. I could not maintain balance long enough to hit back. It was like fighting an animal. He was clawing my skin and knocking me around like a child. It all happened so quickly that before I knew what was happening to me, he was sinking his teeth into my neck and drank from me like there was to be no tomorrow. I was sure I was dead.

Then he dropped me and grabbed his head, just like Elizabeth did when she attacked Casper. I think he tried to fight back, but before he could, I heard George speak saying, "Hear the voices of all you have damned and all the souls you have cursed. Listen to all the victims you have fed on. Yes, you blood-sucking bastard from hell, hear the pleas of those who you closed your black heart to. Hear the children of your two hundred year reign in darkness... (I watched, helpless, as he went mad grabbing his head and screeching at the top of his lungs for the voices to stop. I laid there and watch as blood tears flooded down his face and he struggled to get away from the voices or George, I could not really tell) Yes, that's it run, away from my child. Return to the one who has damned you and tell him of me." I Remember George walking over to me and smiling down at me, but then I blacked out and when I awoke, I was back at the hotel suite. Elizabeth was trying to get me to drink the blood. As I drank, she explained that the guy George described was called Darvis. He was made around the same time Elizabeth was made and he may be just as strong as her, or stronger. She told us that George mind attack only worked because like her, George caught him off guard. She believed that if Darvis would have sensed George, then he would have killed us both. Garrett was pissed that George would come for me without them, but he assured them that Vinnie and him could have dealt with Darvis. Maybe alone this Darvis was Dangerous, but the odds were in our favor.

Elizabeth laughed at the thought that Janus would be insane with anger over all of this. George did not care one way or the other, he just kept yelling at me for acting so foolish. We all stayed together from that moment on. We believed that Janus wouldn't try to attack us if we weren't all together because of the Danger factor it would put his own guys. I guess we were right, because everything was fine until Peter disappeared and I knew in the deepest part of my heart where he went. Even after all this we went through, he still chose to serve Janus. He still did not trust Elizabeth. I warned the others, but they did not seem to care. Their attitudes were that everyone has a right to make a choice to what side they would fall on and so does Peter. Garrett felt if in the future we crossed roads with Peter and find him to be an enemy then we will destroy him, but if we find him to still be a friend, then we will welcome him. Garrett was not sure if I was right or wrong, but did agree that we were not safe at the Bellevue so we had to move on. As much as we loved their beautiful rooms and their accommodating staff, Garrett was not hearing it from any of us. We left that following night. We knew that Peter would expect us to return to the Hershey, since we lived up there too. But Garrett felt it was time we left Center City and went more to the north of the city.

We knew we could not take the Twenty-three bus, because of all the attention we would have attracted. So we walked the streets until around midnight and took the train to Erie Ave. Erie was very much a wonderful place to get lost in. It was so chaotic that no one paid us any attention. As we came out of the subway, we were hit with sound and colored lights. The lights came from cars and store signs. The bar on one corner had some guys out there, yelling obscenities in front of it. While on another corner there were hacks trying to give people rides around the city for wild prices. The street was truly fascinating. We walked to one of George's brother's homes. George did not seem to really want to go there, but we were low on money and had nowhere left to go. His brother had a very small home and it was well off the beaten path. I knew there was no way Peter or the master would find us here. His brother greeted us at the door and greeted Garrett with open arms. He and George did not seem to have the same level of regard for each other. He invited us in to his home in and offered us a seat. He led George and Garrett upstairs to speak alone. A part of me knew it was rude but I had to hear what they were talking about. Believe it or not he was just like George, he asked them what they did to themselves and what kind of mess have they gotten into. He would not accept it being anyone else's fault but George. I could hear George again ranting to his brother just like I would against him. He went as far as to tell his brother that he failed us all. Had he had the skill to train us better this would not have ever happened. I could hear Garrett telling them it was not his fault and that I'm the one who caused it all. With a slight laughter and staying true to his cold nature said, "Xavier will always be the wondering fool and he should have seen this coming." Landis must have realized what I was doing because he interrupted my concentration and made it quite clear that whatever George and his brother were talking about it was their business so stay out of it. It was very quiet upstairs for a while before we heard the door open and they all headed back down the steps. George's brother was a very light-natured type of guy who opened his home and his wisdom to us. It wasn't long before they joined us again. Unlike George, his brother and Elizabeth hit it off very well and in fact they did most of the talking all night. As the dawn approached, he opened the basement door and asked us to retire there for the day. Garrett, being able to withstand the daylight, stayed upstairs and the rest of us retired to the basement. There were several chairs in the basement and Garrett brought us pillows and covers. As Garrett went back upstairs, I realized that our lives would never be normal again.

The next night, we all awoke a little drained, but knew how refreshing it felt not to have to fear anyone finding us. As we exited the basement, we were greeted by Garrett and George's brother who informed us his name was Keith. They had glasses of blood sitting there on the table for us. Keith explained that he worked in a hospital and had a friend of his gather up some of the blood that came into the blood bank that day. Of course it could not be a lot or else it might be missed. His friend wanted money for services. Garrett didn't seem to have a problem with it but

George did. George did always make things bigger than what they really were. After Keith and George spoke for some time George finally agreed. Garrett looked at Elizabeth and asked her if she agreed with his decision. She nodded and started to drink her glass of blood. He told his brother that he would repay him for giving the guy the money but would fix things so that they didn't need him again. With that, he walked out of the house. His brother asked Elizabeth to forgive George behavior because he has always been this way. "George is a pain in the ass at times. He acts from the heart, not the brain." he said. Elizabeth decided that maybe she should teach Keith how George's gift should work, but I decided to follow George and left as well.

I cloaked myself and follow him. I had to admit, I was happy Elizabeth showed me how to do that. Anyway, I followed him for some time, when he stopped in front of a guy. He looked directly into the guys eyes and asked him something. I walked over to the curb and then I lost any concept of reality. He caused the guy to take off his jewelry and give it to him. In fact he begged George to take it. George caressed his face so flirtatiously as if they were lovers. Somehow he made this guy seem as if he was in love with him. I was truly at a loss for words. He placed the jewels into his pocket and walked away as if nothing was wrong. I was amazed, but continued to follow him. He walked for a few blocks and stood on the corner for a moment, then out of nowhere he took off. He ran for several blocks until I could hear guns shooting. I believed that they were drug dealers fighting, but it did not matter to George. He stayed in the darkness and allowed the fight to play out. When it was all said and done he stood over the loser. He looked into the guys eyes with no emotion at all; then got up and ran up the alley. As if he read the guy's mind he walked over to where the guy hid his money and stuff. I was at a loss for words. I mean, I was not sure who really the monster...was! To me, George was far more evil than Elizabeth could ever be. I watched as he leaped from the alley to the back roof of someone's home then to the second roof as if it was nothing. He watched as the police arrive and did their thing. I could not see any type of remorse in his eyes for what he was witnessing. I mean idea of watching these young guys kill each other for nothing. I couldn't believe that he was able to read their minds and he knew what was going to happen when he could have stopped it… For that matter he should've stopped it. I was so enraged with the idea that he allowed these two kids to try and kill each other, just for their loot. I was so enraged that I wanted to do something but I couldn't risk the chance of lowering my cloak. This was not the George I knew. For once I was not sure what George would do if I allowed him to know I had seen everything he done.

After he left the roof top, he headed over toward a park and waited. It was as if he was waiting for someone, out of nowhere a woman appeared beside him and they started to talk. For that matter kind of arguing, now I really was lost. I could understand why George would be talking with this woman or that he would have known she would be there. It became quite clear to me that it was not only Elizabeth who was keeping secrets. I tried to listen in on what they were arguing about, but couldn't. Then out of nowhere a guy appeared about 20 feet away from George, who acted as if he was expected. Even the young woman seemed as if she knew he was there. Then it happened, the dude turned into some kind of doglike creature and attack George. Now, I know Elizabeth said that George is very young in his powers and was no match for her or Darvis. But it is something I never would've imagined. He raised his hand and closed his eyes as the woman was telling him what to do. Like a puppet this animal starting clawing his own body until it was barely standing. I watched the woman walk over to the creature and cause it to bleed out through its eyes. She returned to George's side and gave him a kiss on the cheek. Then I saw a blinding light and she was gone. I felt as if I was doing drugs I have never seen any shit like this before. He looked in my direction as if he may have known I was there, and then used his hands to brush his hair back. I watch him gathering himself and he returned to his brother's home.

Once inside I un-cloaked myself and struck him across the room. With tears running down my face, everyone pulled us apart and demanded I tell them what was wrong. George did not even try to defend himself. He told them the truth and then gave the jewelry and money to his brother. He told his brother to do whatever he needed to keep their secret safe. Everyone looked at him and some of them were just as disgusted with his behavior as I was. George rose from the floor and sat in the chair that was close to him. He looked around the room and said, "Yes, I killed them!! I allowed them to do to themselves what they were going to do anyway. Could I change their minds and make them play nice, yes I could but that would not have served our purpose. Look, I am no holier than thou person, nor shall I pretend to be. They did what they had to do to and so did I. And as far as for the guy with the jewelry that is personal and none of your business. Remember that we all have personal lives and don't tell me you haven't done everything to bring closure to your past. Somewhere deep inside of all of you, there is a story to be told or simply kept as your own secret. So the next time you decide to take Xavier side in judgment. Judge yourselves first… This is our new life… people! Rather you want to look at it as a dream that will end or with a happy ending. The truth is that it will end, but it will not be happy nor will any of us walk away innocent. So yes, I allowed evil to destroy evil or maybe to only replace it with a greater evil. But the point is I can control my evil, without guilt. Can YOU!? Now, before you decide to answer me or judge my behavior, remember that we plan to destroy one that we do not know. We plan to destroy someone for what!? Our survival! Now, I did not want you to come not out of shame, but out of concern that none of you are ready to do what must be done for us to survive and by the way we both knew you were there that's why you was not able to hear our conversation. Some things are not meant for you to understand. I unlike Elizabeth my life truly am an open book, but tread carefully because there may be chapters you're not prepared to read."

I told him he was full of shit. He only did what suited him and if he was really thinking about us then he would've stopped those guys from shooting at each other and I reinforced that they were innocent because they did nothing to us. His brother sat there and just watched as the others held me from going after George again.

George looked at me and said, "Xavier, you are the last one to speak about protecting the innocent because if you did what you so bravely preach upon right now... then none of us would be vampires, now would we? Just like those guys did with their lives. You chose to do with yours. Now, everyone must play out the consequences of their actions as we now have to play out the consequences for yours."

I stopped and looked at him as the reminder of my own sin stood in front of me. I lowered my head in shame and again asked for their forgiveness. As tears ran down my already blood stained face, Elizabeth came and wrapped her arms around me. George shown no sorrow for the words he spoke and turned to his brother and asked if he would continue to help us. His brother smiled and said of course, but he did not understand what the money was for or that the jewels were for him to sell at Jewel's Row. Garrett was to go with Keith and make sure that the guy did not cheat Keith out of its true value or Keith them... Once he had the money, he was to save it for them to use later. Keith looked as if he didn't understand what George was talking about, but neither did we. We stayed there for a week before Garrett felt it was time for us to move on. George had attacked different people every night in different parts of the city. He always made sure that he did not feed on any. As they counted the money, I had grown sick at what I had released on the world. In no time, they have gathered up seventy thousand dollars. Garrett told Keith that we were to leave the next night and from now on, he would send money to Keith to watch over for them, because the day would come that they will need it to disappear. I believed that would be the last time I seen Keith and I thought it was meant to be that way. The next night when we awoke, Keith was gone. Garrett told everyone to call their families as if nothing was wrong. This was to make sure that no one was looking for us. I called my mother and what a mistake that was. My father got on the phone and did just what I thought he would do. He started yelling about how heartless I was to have my mother worried about me. How I could have called her and let her know I was ok. Being grown-up means to take on responsibility. I did not fight the point, but just gave in and promised I wouldn't do it again. I told them that I had got a job in New York and went there a few weeks ago. I promised them that I would call more often. I told him that I loved him and mom with all my heart and that I would make the proud of me. After we finished our calls, we headed back to Center City.

We decided to stay at the hotel on 13th and Walnut. It's a new Holiday Inn and it did not seem too high-profile, so we were able to come and go without being bothered by other guests. We all decided to take a little time to our selves. Garrett gave us all money so we can get into clubs or whatever. I decided to go to the coffee house on the corner of 12th and Walnut. I sat outside for some time when a man came and asked if he could sit with me. I did not seem to be bothered by his presence, so I told him he could. As he sat there, I could not help but to notice how beautiful his skin was. He had a very creamy complexion. His smile seemed to only add to his perfectly white teeth. He asked me my name I told him Xavier and he told me his was James. He told me he was new to this country and that he had only been here for a few days. I told him that he would love it in America. He smiled and agreed. I just seemed to fall in love with his eyes. They were a beautiful, crystal blue with very black pupils. His eyes were like the guy in my dream the night I first drank the blood. His hair was a beautiful-looking brown and he wore it in a ponytail. He started to ask me questions about how long I lived here and if I liked the neighborhood. He wanted to know my likes and dislikes about this city. Then it hit me that this guy was trying to pick me up. He was gay and was hoping we could hook up. I smiled at him and told him that I was not interested in dating guys. I was just trying to enjoy a nice cup of coffee. He smiled and said his good-byes, but not before mentioning that he found it odd that I never took a drink from the cup. Especially since I claimed that was the reason I was there. I just smiled and continued to look down into the cup. For some reason the warmth of the coffee seemed to feel so good against my face. I must have sat there for about an hour before I decided to walk around some more. I was not ready to join the others, so I just walked around the city for a bit more. I could not get this James out of my head. He was one of the most attractive white men I have ever seen. He stood about six-foot two and must have weighted around two hundred and twenty pounds. He was really built, but not thick. Only then did it cross my mind that his nails were perfectly clean. Not clean like bathed well, but clean like never been damaged. Not by labor or even cracked. They looked as if they were taken care of very well. His hands were very smooth as well. He must have money. I thought at first, that maybe he was one of us. But I did not get the weird feeling that Elizabeth spoke of. So I dismissed that concept and continued to walk. It just puzzled me that maybe it was not nothing odd at all but just that now since I am a vampire all my senses had been so heightened that I am able to pay attention to things that I would have been blind to before. My wondering led me somewhere around Tenth and Callow hill. I was walking towards north Philly, when this guy who was walking past me from the other direction quickly turned and knocked me into the wall of the bridge. As I fell back, he kicked me in the balls. I was so amazed at how bad the pain still was. One would think since I can't reproduce, they would have less of an effect. Anyway, I fell to my knees as he continued to kick the shit out of me. He was yelling for me to give him my fuck'n wallet. He grabbed my head, slammed it into the wall and pulled a gun out of nowhere. As he pressed that cold hard steel against my over-sensitive skin, he started to taunt me about being afraid and begging for my life.

Chapter 9
The Face of Freedom

Then I awoke looking at a water fountain; it was so pretty. I thought that perhaps I was dreaming. I thought the guy seemed real. He was gone and I was sitting at the Love Park with some guys skate boarding around me. They were very talented. I sat there and watched as these guys entertained me. They soon took notice of my amusement and started talking to me, asking me what I thought of what they were doing. They started to do some tricks for me and I had to give them their props. They were very good and must have practice on it for some time. After awhile, they all took a break and we all chilled together. I thought they quickly took notice of my skin and how different I looked from them, but then I noticed that they weren't looking at my skin. They were looking at my clothes. They were looking at the blood that was drying on my shirt and pants. They started to ask me if I was all right, but I looked at them and then a lie came to me. I nodded my head very slowly and told them that I watched a guy get hit by a truck. They started to ask what happened to the guy. I told them I did not know after the rescue and everyone came. I told them that when the truck hit the guy, I ran over to see if he was all right. He was still moving, so I held him still and kept repeating for him not to move. Blood was pouring out of the back of his head or neck. I told them I was not really sure where the blood was coming from, but he promised he wouldn't move if I held his head on my lap so I did. The cop told me I might have saved his life, because I kept him calm. They took care of him there and then they took him to the hospital. They started telling about how cool I was and everything. As they talked, I took off my shirt and washed it in the fountain. The blood did not stain the shirt too bad. I knew I needed to deal with what just happened. At this point, I knew I was not dreaming and I had done something to the guy who tried to rob me. I told the guys to take care and I walked off. The time had come for me to deal with what I did.

I walked back towards Tenth St., when I saw the flashing lights of the police. They stayed there for some time. So I decided it would be best for me to return to the hotel and tell the others. It was very late, so I knew they would all be back at the hotel. When I walked into the suite, I was greeted by Garrett, who was smiling. He told me that everyone was in the other room down the hall. It seemed that they were having their own party. I changed my clothes and tried to remember what happened between this guy and me but could not. Nothing about that event came to mind. It was as if I was not even there. I remembered his face as if it was a dream and nothing more. Some part of me felt as if I should feel sorry for what I may have done, but I could not. I was so detached that it just did not matter. No matter how hard I tried to make it matter, it just did not. I realized that this was going to be something that I told the other guys. So I went back into the room where they were sitting and informed them about the events that took place. George stood up and looked at Landis and they both walked toward the door. Landis turned to the rest of us and told us that they were going to check it out and let us know what happened. They must've been gone for about a half hour to 45 minutes. When they returned Landis told us that we didn't have much to worry about. It seems that someone beat the hell out of a guy and broke his arms. Then beat him unconscious and in the struggle it appeared that he shot himself in one of his shoulders. George read some of the police men minds and came to discover that he had warrants out. Landis was so pissed that I was so careless that he must've yelled at for about an hour. Landis always had a way of making me feel less than nothing. I got so upset that I went into the other room and slammed the door. I looked at myself in the mirror and saw nothing. I fell out of the chair I was setting in and landed on my ass. I hit the floor and clawed away backwards from the mirror, so quickly that one would think I seen death itself. My heart raced with fear. I could not fathom that I did not have a reflection. I was truly at a loss for words. Elizabeth never mentioned that this would happen. I was gone! I was nothing more than a ghost. A fuck'n' goddamn ghost! I was never more lost than at that moment. Nothing was the same. It no longer was all right. I was not any longer this understanding kid. I was this fuck'n' ghost… How the fuck was I going to fix this? How was I going to get my damn life back? I turned onto my hands and knees and started punching the floor. I stopped when I saw my tears fall to the floor. I was taken away as the blood filled tears dropped from my face and I watched as it stained the rug beneath me. All I could think of was that I was dead and I also killed my friends. How could I take the life of those I love…? I sat there truly lost in what I did and I really was not sure if I could fix it. I finally had to except this was beyond me. I was being pulled into something that I had no control of.

It took some time for me to pull myself together, but when I did, I rose from the floor and finished dressing. I combed my hair as if it mattered and Marcohed down the hall of the hotel to the other room we were staying in. I knocked on the door as Landis opened it. I walked in as if nothing was bothering, but the truth was, I was going insane. I said nothing as I walk into the room and saw everyone laughing about something or another. I looked at them until no one was speaking any longer. I told them that is was getting crazy. We are running around in circles and I feared we have waited too long. I told them that I wanted out of all this. All I wanted to do is finish living what was left of this fucked up existence. Elizabeth told everyone to forgive me and she came over to where I was standing. I looked her in her eyes and I really was not sure what I was feeling. She asked me to come with her back to our other room where we could talk. I looked around the room and decided to follow her. She wrapped her arm around my waist and I hers. We walked out the room and back down the hall. After we were in our room, she shut the door and kissed me. Her cold lips compressed to mine and soon warmth came between us. As we kissed, she told me that she understood what I was going through. She wanted me to understand that what was happening to me was normal. I was just coming to terms with what really happened that night the master gave me his dark kiss. I wanted to get away from all of this; I wanted to have her to myself once again. I bent to her and wrapped my arms around her like a vise grip. I started to kiss her again.

My hands slowly moved across her body and I felt her sweet anticipation of what was to come. As we kissed, I felt her giving herself to me just as she did in the past. As we kissed, I knew nothing had changed between us. I was her one love as she was mine. I locked my lips to hers and felt her hands slowly rub my chest. I felt her hands move into my shirt and felt her soft skin touch mine. I felt the passion take control and my penis became aroused. The more we continued, the harder my penis became. We started to undress each other and as we did, we made our way over to the bed. As the back of my legs hit the bed, I lifted her up and turned her around without breaking neither our deep embrace. Nor our passionate kiss. We lay across the bed like lovers of so long ago. I grabbed parts of her that felt so new to me and I am sure she felt the same it was as if we were getting to know each other's bodies again. My hands rubbed up and down her waist. As I grind my pelvis into hers, I was lost in the passion of what was happening. We kissed and kissed, locking our hands into each other's. I raped her and she me. What was passion quickly became lust. I bit into her breast and licked up the blood as it ran across the soft white flesh of her tit until I ran my hot tongue over the moist nipple of the other breast. O' yes, it felt so good against my lips and on my tongue. I used it as if it was lotion and I massaged it into her skin. I felt as if I never wanted to move it from its new home. I grind harder against her breasts, knowing I wouldn't be able to wait any longer. I licked over her breast working one then the other. This went on for some time only to drive me even more insane to be inside of her. I began to kiss down her soft, milky skin and played with my tongue inside her navel. I continued until I got lower and the lower I went, the slower I moved. I stopped just above that tunnel that gives women so much pleasure and rose to kiss her once more. She was lost in her passion and wrapped her arms and legs around me. I came down in her the only way I could and as I felt my penis enter her warm, tight tunnel, I knew she was my love and my mate forever. I lost all reason as each inch of me was consumed with in her sweet grip. Her hot sweet walls wrapped around by tool as if it was never to leave. I held onto her and whispered, 'I love you' into her ears. It felt so good, so right, I knew she was mine.

If I wanted to leave all of this, then I would have to take her with me. For tonight, I came to know we were one. As we made love for hours, we felt the warmth that many mortals take for granted. Even the burst of the Sun's rays added to our lovemaking and its death passing over us as my penis gave her something not even death could destroy. We took comfort in the fact that if we were to die, then it would be while we made love. The thick curtains that hung in the window ensured that would not happen. We finished and fell asleep, still embraced in each other arms. It felt like a dream, making love to Elizabeth in the heat of the passing sun. I guess that was God's way of letting me know he was still with me. I mean, it is easy to say the thick lining of the curtains saved our lives, but I rather believe God made sure those curtains was in the room we had. I awoke before her and I looked at the clock on the table next to the bed. How odd that after we had been through up to that point, I still was concerned with the time. I noticed that it was a little after six p.m. in the evening. I rose from the bed and looked back at my dark angel. I sat back down as I watched her sleep. I rubbed my hand across her hair and leaned over to kiss her forehead. She smiled at my kiss and opened her eyes. She reached over and grabbed my hand that rested nearest to her. She told me how much she loved me and I confessed the same to her. I rose from our bed and walked into the bathroom. I needed time to myself. I needed to understand what I was about to do. After shutting the bathroom door behind me, I realized that if I was to put an end to this, then I did not need to talk to everyone. I knew I was the reason they all was in this mess. I accepted that if I was not acting like a child now and then that I would have been able to stop Janus from changing my friends over. I looked out the bathroom window and wondered what would happen if Elizabeth and I just left. I knew that George would deal with Janus and take care of the others. I had no doubt that when the time came to stop this Darvis guy and the others, they would find a way to win. George was always good at reading people. I knew he would find a way to stop all of this and help the others with this new life they were given. I turned the shower on and waited for the water to become very warm. For some reason, I liked the warm water against my skin. As the steam filled the room, I stepped into the shower. As the water ran down my hair and over my sex scented body, I thought of the happiness my absence would bring the other guys. I wouldn't have to try and keep control over them, nor would Elizabeth have to be a mother to them. George would definitely love the fact that he was the queen bee again. I knew how much he hated sharing the others' attention with Elizabeth. As I stood under the water thinking of how to do this, I heard the bathroom door open and seen a figure walk in. It looked as if it was Elizabeth. She opened the shower door and stepped in behind me. She wrapped her arms around my waist as if to say everything will be ok. She said, "Fear not my Xavier, for together we stand, but divide, we fall." I turned to her without breaking her grip. For now I knew what I had to do. After we made love in the shower and joined the others in the other apartment, everyone was talking and joking except for Vinnie and George. They sat on the other side of the room and were talking to each other. A part of me may have been wrong, but never the less, I felt they were having an affair. It was just the way they kept to themselves. I walked over to George to ask if I could speak to him alone. Vinnie rose and looked at me as if I was his enemy. He made it very clear that he would attack me without question if I rose to attack George. George looked at Vinnie and placed a hand onto Vinnie's arm and assured him that everything would be fine. Everyone in the room just looked at Vinnie and me as if we would attack each other in a second. I felt as if they really wanted to see the outcome of such a battle. George rose and walked in the bedroom. I gestured for Elizabeth to stay with the others and I joined George. As I shut the door behind me, I felt his eyes on my back. I turned to look at him and asked him to be quiet as I spoke and not to respond until I was finished. He nodded his head and just looked at me. A part of me wanted to remain strong, but feared that he wouldn't understand. I looked at him and walked over to him. I stood over him for a moment and then looked down at him. He did not seem alarmed by my behavior, just confused. I started with saying, "George, I am leaving you and the others. I know you want me to help you guys to defeat the master, but the truth is that I can't defeat anyone. I can't kill; it's just not in me. I have given this great thought and decided I just can't. I think I saw him last night, but I was not sure and then this madman attacked me. I blacked out and awoke at the fountain in Love Park. I know this sounds crazy, but the truth is that I went back to the spot that he attacked me and the police was there. It seemed there was a murder or something. I got scared and came back here. Please do not hate me; I am just not ready for all of this. (He tried to rise, but I put my hands on his shoulders and held him there, sitting under my grip.) No, do not try to comfort me, I am death and I have to deal with this, but I have to do it on my own. I want to take Elizabeth with me because I love her. I can't help but to love her and I think you knew that from the beginning. I will tell the others. I just wanted to tell you first."

He looked at me for some time and then spoke. He placed his hand on my chest and looked up at me. George said, "It is your right to leave just as it is ours, but that doesn't change the fact that you brought us all into this. You are the one who have taken our joy from us. Our lives! Vinnie hates you more every day and you know why? Because you stole his love from him; He will never be able to ask Raya to marry him. Nor will any of the others you have damned. And now, you want to run off with that girl. Why!? Because! You no longer wish to share Elizabeth with the rest of the group? She is a whore and if you think she hasn't shared herself with them, you are a fool." I lost it when he said that and I hit him across the room. George rolled off the bed and onto the floor. He looked so small and impotent; I was stunned by my actions for a moment I just stood there. My hand was still shaking as if it was not me who struck George but someone else. I ran over to him and wrapped my arms around him. I kept yelling I was so sorry. As blood ran down his face and onto my shirt, I realized I had become a monster and he was another victim of my heartless behavior... He asked me to release him and I just held him and started to kiss his forehead, repeating I was so sorry. He kept telling me it was ok, but I felt so guilty that I did not know what else to do so I bit my lip and kissed him just as I had did Elizabeth. I tried to feed him the blood that I gave my other love. (Yes, I said other love, for I really did and still do love George) He refused to drink from me and pushed away.

I released him and as tears ran across my face, he came to understand how much torment I was going through. He shook his head and said, "Xavier, (reaching to rest his hand on my face) I love you very much and if you are capable of leaving us like this, then that is your choice. Yes, it is your right to walk away as if we were nothing to you. I can't tell you how you are breaking my heart right now, but I feel you already know (As he started to cry, I was drawn into his eyes). I am so sorry… you feel we are a part of your problem and not the solution." To see him so weak and so beautiful, I was drawn into his gaze and knew I had to have him. I had to make him mine. I leaned in to kiss him once more. I felt his hands on my chest, as he said no. I paid him no attention and continued to kiss him. I could feel him trying to pull free, but the scent of blood that released itself from him was more than enough to make me want him. As I kissed his face and worked my way down his long soft neck, lust filled my mind and I wanted him as much as I wanted my sweet Elizabeth. I lost complete control, but knew I would feel peace once more after I tasted the blood of the one who lay before me. As I kissed and licked his neck, I felt my teeth grow in sweet anticipation. George grew quiet and I started to bite his long sweet, soft beautiful neck. Then I felt an arm grab me and throw me across the room. It was Garrett. Before I knew what was happening to me. I was flying across the room into Casper's arms. Vinnie appeared out of nowhere and I saw my death in his eyes. He raised his hand passed his chest and drew back. I watched as his fingers became sharp claws and then Garrett yell, "No, Vinnie... he is one of us." Garrett turned back towards George and helped him up. They seemed to have passed words in their minds. Then Garrett demanded that everyone leave him and me in the room alone. George looked at me as if he was truly disappointed in me, but there was not anything I could say. A part of me did not even know why I would attack him. I tried to explain myself to Garrett before I could Garrett demanded silence as everyone left the room. Once the door was shut, I watched as he just held onto the doorknob. I few moments past and I heard him speak, "What the hell just happened here? Xavier! Why would you attack George?" I told Garrett I was not attacking George. I was not sure what I was doing. I was sure that I was losing a part of myself every day. I cannot explain how I love and hate George all at the same time. The never ending ridicule George had towards me. Then a moment later he showed an overbearing protection for me. I struck him before I knew it. Watching him on the floor so vulnerable so weak… watching the blood slowly pour from his lips, watching it run down his long slender neck slowly embrace every crevice of his throat. Somewhere deep inside of me I lost it. I had to have him, own him. At that moment I needed George's blood inside of me just as desperately as I needed Elizabeth's blood. He looked at me with such cold stern eyes. As if he wasn't sure if he believed me. I told him of how I attacked the guy the night before and that I believed I killed him. Garrett looked at me for a moment and then said, "You know, you almost fed on George and if it was not for me, Vinnie would have killed you." I snapped back, "This is what I am talking about! We all have changed. We can't and do not trust each other, fuck how could we?? I do not know what I want or what I need and neither do any of you guys. We're just making things up and avoiding what we need to do.... I think that we are avoiding them, because deep down we know we're wrong and if we kill the master, then we'll be no better than him." Garrett remained quiet and walked over to the window, as if to suggest that he was thinking about what I said. He usually took his time in answering questions I would ask, but this was different. He bent one arm across his chest and the other he took to his chin. The way he stood there was as if he was a statue. I became nervous after a few moments and then he spoke, "Xavier… We're just learning to use our new gifts in these last few weeks, in order to defeat this Joseph person who you believe did this to us. So… you and Elizabeth are leaving. Ok, you have a plan, Xavier? What, you think no one's going to come after you?

"Who… George? Vinnie? ", I asked.

I paused before speaking again because Garrett gave this look like, 'Do not go there'. But then again, I was not sure. I mean, Garrett was never the judgmental type... not like George. "Xavier. What do you intend to do... after... you... leave!?" he asked.

"I do not know Garrett! I just don't... Ugh, I just do not know."

"Well fine, I guess you will figure it all out later."

I was not sure if he meant that to be sarcastic or not, but I decided to leave it at that and walked out the room. He did nothing to stop me. He remained there looking out the window. Landis stopped me in the middle of the outer room. He asked me to wait for him. He wanted to talk with me as well. I was not sure if I was ready for him or not, but I knew I opened this can of worms. So I told him I would wait for him in the lobby, but not to take too long. With that, I walked out of the apartment. I waited for about ten minutes then the elevator opened and Landis walked out. He was wearing all black. It was odd to see him dressed that way, but I had to admit to myself that he looked very attractive. The way his T-shirt wrapped around his chest and arms. Even the way his straight leg pants fell around his waist. I mean, Landis always had a nice small body, but I never really paid attention to how fit his body was. He walked up to me and said, "Let's go!!" I looked at him as he passed me and did not look back. He truly was a Mack-daddy. I started walking behind him smiling while shaking my head in disbelief towards his behavior. Once outside, we started to walk towards Twentieth St. Landis was quiet for a moment and asked, "So are you going to tell me or are we going to play as if nothing is going on?"

I wanted to ignore him, but I knew he had a right to know just as much as George and Garrett did. So I started with the events of the past evening up to the point I seen my reflection. I told him I really did not mean to attack George. He smiled and said, "Yeah, but sometimes George asks for it. He seems to like making it easy, for himself to be the victim. It's more of his way of controlling us. He knows we look more powerful than him, but the truth is that he is just as strong as us." I looked at him and smiled, even though I did not agree. I continued to tell him my feelings and then I repeated what Garrett said to me. He just listened and did not interrupt. Before I knew it, we were at Rittenhouse Park. I walked over to the fountain and sat down. He stood beside me, looking at the few people that remained there talking to each other as if it was eleven in the morning when it really was eleven at night. We started sharing our new senses and how much we missed some of our old ways. I told him about how I always feel cold. He laughed and told me he did too. He told me how sometimes he had to remind himself that he doesn't need food. I agreed. This went on for a long time and then we were asked to leave the park because it was closing. We started to walk and Landis asked me to follow him. I was not sure where he was taking me but since the night was going good so far I did not find anything wrong with it. Well in no time, we were at the Unknown Soldier's Park. Yes, the park were my old life ended and my new one was born.

He looked at me and said, "Xavier, I want you to fight me."

"What?" I said.

"You heard me right. You want to leave us, and then fight me."

"No, are you crazy!? We're friends!"

"Exactly..."

"Look, dude! You brought me here for this."

"Xavier, just because you want out doesn't mean you ready for it. The master is still looking for us. We are learning to fight together, so we can defeat him. And now you want to roll! Cool! Fine then! Fight me and show me you can handle yourself."

"Look man! Elizabeth thought she and I could have defeated him before and I do not see how this has changed."

"Well, Xavier. If you took the time to look around you would see that it has changed. Boy has it changed! Xavier! We are all vampires now. So I do not have faith in the fact that you know what you're doing."

"Please, Landis…"

"Then fight me, Xavier. If what you are saying is true, then you should be able to defeat me easily and if not, then you are no match for the master because I am sure he has defeated beings older than both of us."

With that, I struck Landis with a blow from my right hand. He blocked and took two steps back and told me to go again. I charged him and we exchanged hand blows and blocks for about four minutes. Until he made contact with my chest and I went back. Then I leaped in the air and threw a kick at his head. He went into a handstand and kicked me out of the air… I fell to the ground and he stood back up. Landis then tried to step on my chest, so I used my powers to slow time and rolled out of the way. I kind of got pissed with using my power and I kicked him in the chest. He flew back and hit the ground. He took a few seconds to get himself together, but then he smiled and said, "OK, so you're through holding back! Good, let's play!" He jumped up, ran towards me and I slowed time again, but this time he was ready. He used his powers to 'phase out'. He ran straight through my punch and me. Before I realized it, he was behind me and struck me across the back of my head. As I flew back and started to run, he chased. We ran for a good second and I turned with a kick to his chest and made contact… He flipped back and landed on his stomach and as I charged him, he showed me another trick he had. He opened his mouth and released a spray. Some of the venom hit my eyes and caused me to go blind for a few seconds. I backed up quickly and tried to get myself together. I heard him come up on me, but was not sure where he was at, so I started using my powers to run backwards. A trick I was glad that Elizabeth showed me. This was all I could think of to keep him from hitting me. As I backed up, I started to get my sight back. He was charging towards me. I reached a tree and decided to take to the air. I leaped up and grabbed hold of one of the branches. He stopped and looked up at me. I just smiled at him as if to say, 'you're not the only one with tricks'. He leaped up to do the same, but I jumped on to the branch he was going for and broke it. I used my hands to grab a branch above me. I dropped down to find Landis under the branch I broke. I pulled the branch off of him and he laughed saying, "That a good move! Now let's finish!"

I could not believe he wanted to continue. This time he attacked me with brute strength. I tried to hold my own, but could not keep up. He struck me several times before I had to give up. We stopped and sat down to rest. I looked over at him breathing so heavy. His face was so defined and so handsome. For the most part, I was becoming lost in his beauty. As I sat there watching Landis, we heard clapping. We both turned around to see the strange guy that attacked me, the one who told me his name was Darvis. He walked towards us saying, "Nice fight." He walked towards us wearing all black. He wore this black shirt that looked as if it was silk. His pants were black straight leg jeans and he wore some black shoes. "I was hoping one of you would have killed the other. That would have made it easier on me. Now I am going to have to kill both of you." he said with a smile.

Landis said, "You're a fool to even try to attack both of us together."

"Well, I guess we will both find out."

"Yeah, dude, you will."

Darvis waved his hand and Landis flew back. It was as if the wind picked Landis up and He then turned to me and attacked with speed I never seen before. He struck me so hard that I heard my neck break as I flew over to a nearby tree. I could not move, but felt my neck healing as he walked over and stood above me. He did the same thing the master did. He allowed me to see his teeth, his power. I felt I was going to die and the truth was it was a death I looked forward to. Then it happened. He bent down to feed on me, but I felt something grab me and pull me through him. Landis used his gift to pass through Darvis and save me from my fate once more. I looked at him and we both looked back at Darvis. Landis told me to hold his hand. He said, "Darvis's powers can affect matter and as long as we stay like this, he can't touch us." We watched as Darvis tried to sense us. We decided to leave before he figured out how to get us even this way.

We released hands around Twelfth St. and started heading back to the hotel. I asked Landis not to tell the guys what happened. I wanted to deal with this guy once and for all. Landis refused and told me to face the fact that this guy is older and more powerful than both of us. "Then what the hell are the other guys going to do?" I said. Landis looked at me and said, "It was George who hurt him the first time. So maybe we need to tell them so we can handle this guy before he kills us all. Once inside the hotel, we went straight to the room. Everyone was there and we told them what happened. Garrett got pissed and was rampaging about one thing or another, but George sat there completely quiet. As Garrett started to explain what he felt we needed to be prepared for, George spoke to me in my mind saying, "Xavier, we both know this will not stop until you become a man and stop it. I will help you tomorrow night. We will set out to find and kill Darvis. Then if you still want to leave, then go... But remember, you owe us at least this much." Then he left my mind and I looked at him. My eyes must have looked as if I seen a ghost. The others decided that tomorrow they would set out to find Darvis and destroy him. I agreed. George stood up and turned from us. He started to walk in the bedroom saying, "It isn't our fight... It is Xavier's and Xavier is the one who needs to end it. If you help him now, then he will need you all the time." Landis tried to disagree, but George just shut the door. I could not get mad because deep inside of me, I knew he was right I was the cause and I needed to end this. I started too many fights and had not finished any of them. I told them he was right that I needed them to stay out of it. This person wants me and me alone. I just could not risk all of them getting hurt. Landis called me a fool to think I could defeat that guy, but I had my mind made up. The next night, I went out in search of him. I walked around the city for about four hour with no luck. Then I decided to walk up Walnut St. to the bridge where the steps lead down to the train tracks. I went down and sat down by the edge of the river that ran along side of the tracks. I sat there for about another three hours and then he spoke to me. Darvis said, "So, this is where you have chosen to die. Well, I myself would have chosen something more homely, But to each its own." I turned around to find him sitting up on top on the support beams of the bridge. I smiled and said, "No... Actually, I chose this to be your grave. See, it took some time for me to get to understand. The older one is when they are crossed over, the better his body adapts to the blood. And since you look younger than me, I think you have a few weaknesses I just need to find. So I figure tonight is as good as any other night to kill you so come."

"You are too insane to live a day longer. I watched you through your own eyes, so, I know you're alone and without your friends, your dead meat."

He flew down at me, but I moved and he almost went off the ledge. I started to run into the open field that was only about ten feet away. He followed and there we stood. I watched him as he just stared at me for a few seconds; I mean really focusing on me. Then I saw his teeth grow, but this time I saw his body become more defined as if he was pulling something out of him. He seemed to lift up in the air and float towards me. I used my time shift powers to move behind him. But it did not do much good because he followed me as I ran around him. His fingertips grew longer and started to glow. I was not sure what he was or what he had planned, but I knew this was going to be it. I was going to die. I was never surer of anything in my life. He started to fly towards me, and then I heard four shots from behind him. They all hit the back of his head. He dropped to the ground and I heard Quincy yell, "Drain him, you fucking idiot! Hurry up before he heals!" I ran over to him; fell to my knees and started feed on his neck as Quincy ran over to me. I was confused but continued to drink as Quincy bent over and pushed a small bottle next to his neck where I was feeding. After filling the vial he ran over to the River. Quincy always seemed to be a little thrown, but he threw the gun in the river and started up the step that led to Walnut St. Now as if this was not bad enough I knew that Quincy was also one of George's children. I never feared the power George had until that moment. As I said before George collected children for many years. Quincy was one of his children from a few years prior to us. I mean we met him but never really had a close connection. I realized that if he wanted to destroy any of us then he could at any time, for he had more children than any of us have known. I continued to feed on him until his blood hit me. I fell back for a few minutes and soon I heard the police and I decided to take his body from the tracks to a more private spot. As I carried him to the spot that Elizabeth took me to the first night we came here, I started to fed on him when I heard voices, I turned around to find my friends laughing at me. They soon fed on him as well. I asked where Elizabeth was since she was not with them. George said he felt it was best that Elizabeth stay behind since this was one of her lovers.

I looked at him and was so pissed that he had me kill this guy knowing who he was and what I would had felt towards this guy's death. He looked at me and then reminded me that it would have been him drinking me if he had told me. I wanted so much to hate him, but his love for me was outside of any normal realm. He would do anything for me even knowing how pissed I would get about it. He was the last to feed on Darvis, but he did something I never thought about before. He ripped out Darvis's heart and drank the blood that remained in it. Some of us vomited when he did that, but he did not stop until the heart was empty. He carried the heart out onto the tracks and demanded that we do the same with the body. He said that when the sun rose in the morning, the body would burn to ash and that would be that. We quickly did as George said. Garrett led us back to the hotel that he chose for us to stay at for the day. Shaken by what had happened that night, I walked beside my friends in silence. I wanted to talk with my friends about what happened, but feared sharing my thoughts.

After we entered our hotel suite, Elizabeth rose from the sofa to greet us. Her face had a look as if she seen death. She ran across the room and slapped George. George smiled and slowly raised his hand to his face. We were all confused but said nothing. Then Elizabeth turned towards me and asked if I realized what George did. I was not really certain what she was talking about, but George kept smiling and walked over to Garrett, who also looked puzzled. George walked over to Garrett as if to flirt with everyone in the room. "He killed Darvis tonight and the bastard had the nerve to leave me a note that he was doing It.", Elizabeth said. Everyone looked puzzled at George actions, but said nothing.

"Of course I killed him! I was not going to let him kill any of my children." George said.

"If he wanted to kill any of them, then he would have!"

"Oh! Really and you know this how?"

"You know how I know this, you asshole."

"Yes, I do, but everyone else doesn't! So, share with them some of this ~um-mm. Oh, yes! Truth…!"

"He was my lover... of years ago."

"Yes. See how good being honest feels? Now everyone is on the same page."

The look on everyone's face told a story in itself. They no longer trusted Elizabeth or anything she would tell them. Her hiding her connection to Darvis from us was too big of a lie to overlook. I knew we really had to leave now. Elizabeth was in Danger and I had to do something if she was to stay alive. I know there was no way I was going to change anyone's mind. I had only one choice and that was to get Elizabeth out of there before morning. I know I would have only one chance to escape. It was around four in the morning when everyone retired for the dawn. Therefore, I waited for about a half an hour to pass before I awoke Elizabeth.

Elizabeth awoke, shaken at first, but then realized what I was going to do. She got up and quickly grabbed her clothes as I did the same. We slowly walked out of the apartment and hoped that George did not sense our departure. George's power seemed too have grown stronger by the hour, so I was not too sure if he would be strong enough to find us even after we left the hotel. So I wanted to move as quickly as we could. As we walked through the lobby of the hotel, I felt something enter my mind, but was not sure what. It felt as if someone was trying to get in my head, but then the feeling passed. I did not tell dear Elizabeth out of fear she would grow scared and want to return to them in order to protect me. As we ran out the front doors of the hotel and down the street, I grew more confident. I knew I would have to find us somewhere to stay before the sun rose. When we reached the corner, Elizabeth pulled her hand back. Then Elizabeth told me to stop and follow her.

She walked over to the curb and waved down a cab. She told the driver that we were going to second and Market Street. I was not sure what she was doing, but felt I needed to follow her lead. Once we got in the cab, I turned to her and kissed her. She smiled and asked if I was ok with what I was doing. I smiled and told her this was the best for us all. I believed that if we found the master and destroyed him, then the two of us could live together forever. She seemed to like that, so we hugged until we were there. We got out of the cab and she turned to the driver with a smile, she looked into his eyes for a short time and then he pulled off. I thought that was cool. As I stood there smiling she grabbed my hand. We walked for a few blocks and then turned onto Cherry Street. We walked up to a beautiful small house and she rang the bell. A young Asian girl answered the door. She was a very beautiful woman and allowed us entry. It was not clear to me who she was or what was going on. Elizabeth introduced us. She told me her name was Lady Ling and that she was one of her servants.

I finally realized that this was Elizabeth's home. I walked around the house and listened to them talk. She spoke to Lady Ling in her native tongue.

I could only guess that Lady Ling did not speak English. She stood with a great deal of self-control. I thought she might had been a dancer. They spoke for some time as I walked around the house and looked at all the paintings she had hanging around the house. It was really a very beautiful home. Because my hearing improved so greatly, I never realized that I left the room and was upstairs. Then it grew quiet and Elizabeth appeared behind me. "So, here you are, my love. (She wrapped her arms around my chest so lightly.) Everything will be fine, my Xavier. " Elizabeth said. I looked back at her and smile. As much as I was afraid, I knew I could not let her know it. She told me that she did not blame me for Darvis's death. That she knew George tricked me into doing it. She knew that he had every intention to destroy any chance of her and me having happiness. She told me to take her hand and follow her to her room. As we entered the room, I was amazed at her beautiful king size bed in the middle of the room. Made of old wood with Viking like gold spikes all around it. It had so many carvings in it that I was amazed. It was as if it was telling a story. She told me to go and take a bath; Lady Ling would assist me. Then we kissed. I walked towards the bathroom, wondering what she meant by Lady, Ling would assist me… When I got there Lady Ling had ran my water and turned to greet me. After I entered the bathroom, she walked up on me. As she stood in front of me and reached for my shirt I slapped her hands away. She looked puzzled. She reached for me again, but this time I allowed her to unbutton my shirt. She removed my shirt from my person. She walked past me to hang my shirt on a hook behind the door. I did not move. I was waiting to see what would happen next. Then I felt her behind me as she reached around my waist and undid my pants. As they fell to the floor, I could sense her bending down and remove my feet out of the pants one at a time. She seemed very comfortable with her face so close to my nude behind. She hung my pant next to my shirt and then pointed to the tub. I looked puzzled at first then did as she asked. The water was very hot to me. Nevertheless, my body adjusted very quickly. She use a rag made of silk knots to bathe me. It felt somewhat strange at first, but then it felt good against my body. Lady Ling seemed to know what she was doing. I felt a little strange with the idea of a girl washing my body, but after a while, I got used to it. She massaged me as well as bathed me. I have to tell you that it felt a little weird; she washed my butt and penis as well. Seeming not to be bothered by my erection, Lady Ling continued to bathe me. After my bath was done, she dried me off. After wrapping a white robe around me, Lady Ling left the bathroom. The robe was very thick and heavy. I could tell it was very expensive and I felt rich wearing it. I returned to Elizabeth in the bedroom. She was already in bed waiting for my arrival. I allowed the robe to drop to the floor and climbed into the bed. I reach over and we kissed. We locked lips for some time. I lay beside her without breaking our kiss. I could feel my penis responding to our passion. Elizabeth pulled away from me. She told me that today was the first day of the rest of our lives. I smiled, but found that hard to believe. She laughed and kissed me with a deep passionate lip lock. I began to grope her as our passion grew. We made love for hours. I took from her as she took from me. There is nothing I have ever felt that I can compare to making love as a vampire.

The feel of her lips against mine, and the smell of her hair. I was lost in all that was happening. When I opened my eyes and was in a field. As I walked around looking at the trees and the flowers, I believed I was in Fairmount Park. It was not long before I realized I was dreaming. I was walking along a path that had been laid before me. The path led to a double gate. The gates stood about nine feet tall and made of iron. They were made with vines and angels molded in them. I stood there for some time until one of the gates opened. I could not believe the gate opened itself up. Then I remember it was a dream so I continued the follow the path. As I walked for some time, I began to see tombstones and flowers that marked graves. I grew a little nervous but continued to walk. I needed to know who was behind this. I feared it was the master and I was not sure what I was going to do when I saw him. After some time, I came in what looked like the middle of this graveyard. I looked around to see what brought me here, but saw no one. I spoke out and demanded that they show themselves. I then heard a sigh and turned around. There sitting on top of one of the tombstones was George. I asked him why am I here. He looked at me and told me to walk around and read some of the tombstones. I watched him for some time and then looked over to the tombstone on my left. To my surprise it read, "Death comes to all by many sources, but mine was by a friend. Here lies Marco." To see his named carved in stone caused my head to spin. I started to read all the head stones around me. All their names were on the tombstones and cause of their deaths…. Me! When I seen his tombstone I just lost it. I looked up at him and yelled, "Why are you doing this… Why must you make my life a hell? Must I suffer for all my days because of my mistake?" He just looked at me with a puzzled look upon his face. For a moment I wasn't sure if it was George or something I created in my mind. His face grew cold and hard. The winds begin to blow ripping the earth up from beneath it. I was not sure how he was doing this or what he was going to do, but I studied my step and braced myself. "I am making your life a living hell…? NO, Xavier! The death you brought upon us has made this a living hell. You fucked up our lives and then ran off with some dirty old bitch. You are a damn fool if you think that I am going to let you do this. Do you really think I am going to allow you to walk away from this as if nothing happened? You and Elizabeth will pay. You have no idea what she has released on us. Moreover, what is worst you do not even care? You cannot see what is in her heart or mind, but I can and I am telling you, she is using you. She is lying to you just as she did to us. Xavier, do not be a fool, I am the only reason the others have not destroyed you with her.

I love you, Xavier; I love them just as well. You are all my children and I am trying not to choose between you…. You must stop this behavior and return to us. You have no choice but to make peace with the group or they will turn on you as will. I now know we can destroy this master, who by the way is named Joseph. I know you are already aware of this but you just did not tell us. When I locked minds with Elizabeth, I learned a lot about this Elizabeth and you need to know she is an evil woman. She seeks power and is willing to do anything to get it. Xavier, you must return to us or else. I cannot allow you to destroy the others no more than I can allow them to destroy you. You must put an end to this and return to us. Together we will find this Joseph and destroy him. If she isn't lying, then we will return to our old human states." George said. I just looked at him and then looked to the ground. We both knew that I was refusing his request. With that, he rubbed the back of his hand down the side of my face. His touch felt so good against my skin. He then touched my face with both his hands and pulled my face towards his. He closed his eyes and kissed my forehead. As he pulled away I seen something none of the others would ever believe, George had tears running down his cheeks. Tears… He was crying for me. No, actually he was crying for what he was going to do to me. He turned and floated away from me. He slowly faded way and as he left my dream saying, "Be prepared, Xavier, for we are coming.

Once he was gone, I was left in darkness. I was not sure how long I was asleep, but when I awoke… I was alone. I awoke in a crazy haze. I looked around the room and the room was empty. I rose from the bed and ran into the bathroom, which was also empty. I froze in the doorway of the bathroom. My heart overtook me. At that moment, I feared that George did as he promised. Elizabeth was in Danger and I wasn't sure how to save her. Then, my ears picked up a soft sound of voices. Rage filled me so quickly; I could not control myself, with my vampire speed I ran downstairs. I reached the bottom step and seen someone standing in the other room with several men. I did not see Elizabeth and being still enraged, I released a growl. I am not sure where it came from, but in my frenzy, it just came out. They turned toward me and out of the corner of the room, Elizabeth came into my sight. She quickly ran over to me and placed her hand on top of mine. I held onto the rail so hard it felt as if it might have broke in my grip. She asked me to relax… She reassured me that she was fine and that these men where old friends of hers. She told me that they had come to bring her some good news. I took her hand and followed her into the living room. We walked past the men in the living room and stopped in front of a fourth gentleman I did not see earlier. She told me his name was Brander. He looked me over and then laughed. He said I was a newbie and found it to be refreshing. He told us how Philadelphia was being infested with elders. He informed us that the elders caught Joseph right outside of Philadelphia. They cornered him somewhere in Camden, as he was trying to locate his old friends and awaken them. They jumped him, and then drained him of my blood. Once he was drained, he was destroyed. He then told us that there were greater problems now. That the elder vampires were looking for all the new borne made from Joseph's blood. They believe your friends have to die. Elizabeth knows I would fear for my friend's lives and my own. I felt lost and confused. First, I took their human lives and now I was going to be the reason they were to lose their immortal lives.

I could not let my friends near Elizabeth, nor could I stay and watch the elders destroy my friends. Elizabeth wanted us to return and tell everyone it was over and that Joseph was dealt with. She was very worried about their safety, but I was concerned about hers. So I refused and told her we needed to leave the city. Brander invited us to go to New England and stay with one of his children. He reassured us we would be safe.

I looked over at Elizabeth for reassurance, then she smiled at me and I knew everything would be ok. Brander told the other two men in the room to bring the car to the front of the house. As we prepared to leave, Lady Ling brought down a few bags of Elizabeth's things. We quickly walked out to the car and got in. As the door closed, I felt as if someone was watching. I tried to sense the others, but I could not sense them. I guess that not even

George was crazy enough to attack with so many of us together. As we drove off, I finally felt at peace. I was not sure what was to happen next, but I knew that Elizabeth would stay alive. We drove for about an hour without any words being spoken. It seemed odd, but I was too busy thinking of my friends to speak on it. Soon we arrived outside of an estate somewhere in greater North Philadelphia. A beautiful garden and a very long driveway surrounded the house, which led behind the house. It was so huge and yet did not stand out at all. It was a white and gold home with large Vinnieian windows and large craved stone symbols. The front garden was just as beautiful with trees, flower beds and a few very expensive statues of three foot men in front of the house.

Once inside they discussed how we were to travel. I did not wish to be separate from Elizabeth, so I told them that. Elizabeth understood, but did not agree. She thought the time had come to explain that we were going to die once more. See, once the crate was sealed and we both used up all the air, our bodies would shut down. We would go into a coma type sleep... Time would reveal itself on our bodies until when the crates were reopened and air filled our nostrils, then we would rise again... I would rise before her because she is so much older and her body would need more time to regenerate than mine would. That made sense to me so I smile and told her not to worry for I would love her in any state. She smile but asked me to allow us to go in separate crates. I did not want too but decided to agree. I was a little nervous when I climbed into the crate. Then I realized this crate was filled with a coffin. I was climbing into a fucking coffin. I turned towards Elizabeth but before I could speak a word she placed her hand on my shoulder and told me to trust her, so I did and climbed into my new haven. It felt weird to look at the world from that perspective. We were going to Paris first and then from there, the world would be ours to do as we wish. Elizabeth looked at me and smile as they lowered the coffin's lid. I started to grow nervous after the lid closed and heard it being lock. The coffin was lined with very thick soft quilts. I seemed to sink into a very comfortable position as I took in my last few breaths. As the air left the coffin, I grow weak and could feel my body trying to take in more air. My chest expanded and retracted more and more. Regardless to what Elizabeth told me my body began to lose control. I grow paranoid, I tried to break out of my coffin but my body was too weak. My heart started to race. I chewed for air and knew there was not any air left to maintain my lungs and then it happened. Death took hold of me or if sleep is easier for you to understand… I am not sure. I drifted off into another state of being and at that point, my mind became filled with wild images I never seen before of places and beings.

Then I saw some kind of wars and so many people dying. I became so scared. The people I seen in this war like dream where more like animals than people. No matter what I tried, I was not able to wake up. At that point, George appeared standing beside me in my mind. George stood between the battle and me. This time I was very sure it was George. He started asking what was wrong with me. What did they do to me? I was not sure if I was dreaming or not, but His fear was so real that I knew he was there with me. He told me that he could not awake me for some reason, which he did not understand. George turned towards the war and raised his hand to his head and the war vanished. I appeared in Rittenhouse square. George knew that was my favorite place. I knew I was still in my coffin but he forced my mind to see what I loved to see and to feel what I would want to feel when I am in Rittenhouse Park. Suddenly I could feel my body being raised and lowered. Apparently so could George…

Chapter 10
The Eyes of the Many

He started yelling, "O' my god Xavier, where are they taking you? Tell me; please tell me… We will find you no matter what." You are in danger just as the rest of us. She is sending you to die. Something was different when he said those words. It felt as if the word die screamed out so loud that the entire world could hear him. He was growing weaker; I was finding it harder to hear him. Then, many eyes open in the darkness of my mind. I was not sure if it was my friends using George to contact me. I felt my body rise in the air. Then my mind went black again I took that to mean that I must have been on the plane. My mind went black and I was alone. I think it was hearing people talking but I could not be sure. After a while, I seen two eyes appear before me. They looked familiar, but I was not sure whose eyes they were. Then the eyes faded away as great flames appeared through them. As I looked upon the flames, I saw that those who were in the flames were my friends. I yelled for them and tried to help them, but was not able to do anything but watch. They fell to the ground. Then the scene changed and I saw many faces and places of no importance to me.

Once it all stopped, I appeared standing some distance from and in front of what looked like a very old temple of some kind. It was so old it seemed not to even have color just a set of steps between two columns, which had two large doors between them. The bricks looked very old and decayed. The steps to the tome doors where old and covered in cravings. Five trees seemed to be growing out of the doorframe. Vines grew all around the bricks of the columns. At the foot of the temple steps stood two very big statues. They seemed to be speaking to Elizabeth. It looked as if she was trying to demand something from them but they refused. I could not believe my eyes; they looked as if they were living statues. Their skin was so white and pure. Even their veins appear as if they were fine cracks in their skin. They seemed to want her to leave, but she refused and raised her hands into the air. Out of nowhere, vines grew from the ground around the two Being's legs. I wanted to tell the two men to watch out but the truth is that I really could not say anything. They tried to pull away from the vines grip but there was no way they could break free. One of them looked at her and she went flying into a tree. The two Beings started to howl and they fell to the ground and yelled as their bodies broke and twist in different direction. They rose from the ground and ripped the vine to strands. Their bodies twisted a little, the legs grew longer, and hair grew all over their bodies. They looked like two beautiful white dogs but so much bigger and stronger. By this time, Elizabeth recovered from their attack. She was charging towards them with a tree branch. They opened their mouths and Elizabeth flew back into another tree. She quickly recovered and charged again but they meant her attack. They both moved so quickly that I could not keep up with them. Even though this was a dream I felt lost within this complete vision. One struck her from behind and the other knocked her out of the air. It looked as if they were taking turns hitting her before she could ever recover to fight back. As I continued to watch I realized that somewhere throughout this others join in and their where about six of them attacking her. I was going insane because I could not help her... I had to watch my beloved die before me. I started to loss the image as Elizabeth lied there and the dogs howled over top of her. As the dream end, the doors of this ancient temple opened and a great light filled my mind. I was blinded for a second and my mind went black again. I felt lost and weak laying there in my coffin unable to help Elizabeth.

Time became irrelevant, until a light breeze filled my coffin.

My lungs sucked the air in as if this was my last supper. Even though Elizabeth told me what was to happen when I awoke, she never told me that my nerves would awake first. It felt as if spiders were crawling all over my dead body. I am sure that it was only my muscles reforming. Then my lungs released the breath it inhaled just moments before. The moment that breath left my lips, my heart opened and released my blood. It ran through my body like a raging river. I could feel my limbs excepting this great offer then my eyes opens. The coffin was not cracked open as I thought but actually was. I could not move nor see out of the coffin. I started panicking, my eyes tried to look over the edge of the coffin, but saw nothing. I tried to force my arms and legs to move, but they refused me. Then she appeared from over the side of the coffin. This angel appeared before me and I lost my soul in her eyes. She was speaking to me about what was happening to me. I tried to listen but I was too taken by her beauty to care why I was not moving.

She told me everything was ok. I became relax as she talked and my senses awoke. She smelled like a field of lilies. I rose from my coffin and I sat there looking into her eyes. I asked her name and she smiled saying," Emmy." I smiled back at her and gave her my name. She helped me out of the coffin and over to a chair in the corner of the room. I sat there a little drain but looked around my new dwellings. She smiled and told me that Elizabeth was not with me, but would join me later. I was a little confused because that was not what Elizabeth told me before I got in the coffin. I looked up at her and asked why? She smiled and responded that Elizabeth is now in the old world. She would not come until she saved your friends from the elders that seek to destroy them. I really was confused now and demanded her to explain what she was talking about. She stepped back and told me that she thought I knew already. "The ancients had awakened three days ago and we are not sure what woke them. I am sure

Elizabeth is seeking help from them to protect your friends. My mistress believes it had something to do with that dream that they all had a few days ago," she said. I must have looked at her liked a mad man because she immediately said;" you did have the dream… did you?"

"What dream", I said.

"The dream of the voice!" she said

"What voice."

"I had a dream five days ago. It awoke me. I was sleeping and out of nowhere I saw two eyes looking at me. Those eyes looked as if they were filled with such pain and sorrow that I could not look into them. The voice that followed sounded like it knew me, but I wasn't the one it was talking too. It said that it was coming for me. It was only after those words were spoken, I woke up. When I awoke, I was not sure why I had this dream or who this man in my dreams was. He must be very powerful for ones as old as us to hear him.'

I laughed to myself when she told me that. Just the ideal that George was seen as one who is very powerful to one so old amused me. I guess if I were in their shoes, I would feel the same. I told her that I was very weak from my awakening and I wish to wash and meet the Mistress. Emmy smiled and told me to follow her. We left the room where my coffin resided and walked through a cold damp and very dim hallway. I couldn't believe that there was so many spider webs everywhere as if this area had never been cleaned. It made me feel as if I was walking through a dungeon. The halls were long and dark with lit torches to lead the way through this maze. We walk for some time and came upon stairs that led up to somewhere. As I followed her up the steps I became afraid of what I was walking into after all, I did not know any of these people and they certainly did not owe me any form of loyalty. Never the less I continued up the steps that opened to a large white and green covered room. The walls had off white wallpaper with green vines painted on them. The painted vines on the wallpaper ran wild. Vines turned colors in different areas of the walls. It looked as if the vine was alive and parts of it were dying, as if that was possible. Many of the leaves were turning brownish gold and made very little sense out of where they were growing. Emmy must have felt that I stopped in the stairwell and turned towards me. She smiled and told me to come with her. Emmy placed her arm around my waist and led me through the room we were in. As we walked in and through the room, we came across a painting that drew me to it. It pulled at me as if it could speak and I needed to hear what it had to say. As I stared at this painting Emmy leaned into my ear from behind and letting her hand caress my chest, she whispered to me that the painting was called The Soul king. She said that the painting was why the room was in such chaos. The painting had a story of its own. The painting was believed to have been over fifteen hundred years old. I could not believe it… The painting looked as if it was just done. The longer I looked upon the painting the more I felt a strong desire to touch it. Seeing the half nude man with nothing but a rag wrapped around his waist and a weird knife in his hand. It looked as if he was in a forest somewhere and was trying to attack me. Emmy must had sensed my desire and told me it was forbidden to touch it, for everyone who owned this painting before the Mistress was found dead in front of it. As if, the painting had the power to take souls. She led me slowly away from the painting and down a hall, but I wasn't able to take my eyes off of it so easily. In the hall, she told me that the painting had to be older than any know civilization. The painting had a form of strange writings on the back of it and the writing suggested that the Amazonian Forest had a race of beings that existed there long before Brazilians was invaded by the Portuguese. The rune line writing reminded the Mistress of

Enchain writings that warn any who touches the painting would become lost in its possessed lines. What a strange saying to write on a painting I thought.

We finally reached my room and I bided her a good day. The room was no different from that of one you would see in an old vampire film. From the Vinnieian style bed made of all wood with carvings of leaves and vines all around it, to the matching table and chairs that sat in the corner of the room. Even the curtains that hung from the windows where thick and vibrant with embroidery, I laughed at the thought that they would go to such measures to live like an old film or era. I quickly climbed into the bed and went to sleep… and sleep I did, for sixteen hour to be exact. When I awoke, a strong smell filled the room and I noticed that someone was in my room at some point. There on the arm of one of the chair, that sat in the corner of the room was clothes. My clothes, I rose and moved through the room to discover that this person not only laid clothes out for me but unpacked my things as well.

At first I thought that it was Emmy but then I realized she would have to sleep at daybreak as well. I walked into the hall to find no one was around. The house was quite, I could not hear anything or anyone. I went back into my room and notice that there was a joining bathroom to my room. Therefore, I decided to bathe and dressed. The bathroom was cold even to me. The bathroom floor tiles where large puzzle like pieces. Their design where made of greens, reds and gold tints. The tub was a cast iron with Gothic legs holding it up. The tub stood in the middle of the room. This seemed odd to me, I guess because I was just used to American bathrooms. I smiled when I saw the toilet; it looked as if it was a toy. The toilet sat in a corner with its water bowl hanging over top of it. I turned the water on and got in.

Oh, god I could not believe how wonderful the water felt

against my dry dirty skin. My skin felt like soft leather as I rubbed soap against my chest. The more I rubbed the softer my skin felt. After a few moments, my skin felt alive again. I almost forgot I was no longer alive. I bathed for over an hour and could feel my skin, hair and attractiveness' was fully restored. I was a strong handsome creature once more. I left the bathroom and returned to my room to dress. I did not realize that she was in the room. She watched me as I walked nude across the floor. She must taken great pleasure watching me as I put on my under clothes. Then she giggled and said, "Elizabeth did not train you well young one. I should have never been able to get this close to you and you not sense me." I didn't continue to pull up my shorts and responded, with a smirk. "Who said I did not know you where there. If peeking at my black ass turns you on then so be it."

"I am the Mistress Mi-cilia." Rising from the chair that sat in the corner of the room she started to walk away, "yes, watching your nudity gave me great pleasure, for a moment."

She walked over to the door and waited for me to finish dressing. I wanted to give her a show but something told me she really -was no longer interested. She looked back at me and smiled. Once I was finished, she walked down the hall and I followed. I was not sure where we were going but something told me she was not in the mood to explain. As we walked, she began to speak. "You have no idea what is happening right now! No idea what you and Elizabeth have released on this Earth. Of course, you believe you do. The fact is that all hell has been set loose across the Earth and its all Elizabeth's fault. She should have never searched for and certainly never have released the damned one. Nor should she have allowed you to be created. In addition, as if that was not bad enough she created more of your kind. I know you wonder who and what you are! A part of you wants to believe what you where told, but the truth is! You are one of the damned races, the elders will seek you out, and your friends as well, then destroy you all. If only to avoid the ancients one from awaking to discover you all have been made.

Now, she placed me in an odd position for either I show loyalty to Elizabeth and protect you or I show respect to my peers and give you to them. Either way, will make me no difference. In fact, to be honest with you the only reason I am playing with the ideal of protecting you is to see what is to become of the dream. For, I am over seven thousand years old and have never seen one such as you. I am puzzled as to what you really are as well as the one in the dream. I know you are linked to it somehow. I also know the one who released it is more powerful than he will ever know. For he is the chosen one, the Elders seek. Now you may be able to help save him or he to save you but first you will have to return home to understand what I speak.

She walked to the front door and opened it. She never looked back and told me to go and find out the answers that I need to know or I am welcome to stay with her and trust what she has to teach me. I was so lost and confused. Moreover, I knew that Elizabeth needed me. Therefore, I decided to leave her home .I began to walk the lonely streets of this area… Not sure, where I was going or where I was. As I walked the dark lonely roads, I realized I had no idea where I was heading or where I was coming from. The roads soon ran into each other and quickly looked the same. I tried to use the tricks Elizabeth showed me but they helped me very little out here. I decided there only one thing left to do. I walked off the main road and entered a wooded area. I sat under a very big tree, which seem to have a very strong sense around it. I try to block out the feelings the tree was giving me. I closed my eyes and used my mind to reach out to Elizabeth again. After an hour or so, I started to see images. Boats, trains, fields and then it hit me I saw what I believed to be Mistress Micilia's home in flames. All the homes around hers were being consumed in flames as well.

Then I heard a voice, George's voice and it told me to run. He yelled to open my eyes and run… I awoke to see four creatures running towards me. They stood over six feet tall and were hairy like Gray wolves. Their nails and their fang's were as long as knifes. I grew scared so I jumped up turned and ran. I ran as fast as I could. They moved so quickly that I had a hard time staying in front of them. At some point, one of them grabbed me by the back of my head and pulled back. I screamed in such pain as his nails cut into my skull. He pulled me down on the ground and before I could respond, another one was on top of me and ripping at my chest. Everything was happening so quickly I could not think, so I got my hand under his neck and I threw him off me… In pain, I grabbed a branch off the ground near me and stabbed it into the one clawing my hair.

Another one told the others to get my heart. It never dawned on me that I was able to understand what they were saying to each other. They did just that! One bite into my arm that I used to stab the branch into the first Creature that held my hair and another climbed on top of me and tried to pin me to the ground. He tried to claw his way into my chest. This wolf went for the wound that his ally made in my chest. I reach up for the one on my chest and grabbed his claw that was trying to enter me. I grabbed his claw and crushed it. I could hear every bone breaking like sticks as he surrendered in pain. That forced him to release me and with all the pure rage in my being, I drove my nails into the back of the neck of the one holding my other arm down. Blood went everywhere, I mean my face and body was covered in it. I guess in my rage I forced my chest to heal itself, because when I rose my wound was healed. Out of nowhere, a claw struck me and I flew across the road. I was dazed and as I watched the four of them were regrouping. I felt a strong wave of power over take me, then I must have pass out.

When I awoke they were gone. It was shortly before dawn and I felt the sun begin to rise. As I begin to rise to my feet I notice that there were four piles of ashes before me but at the time I gave them no thought at all. I quickly began to run, as the sun tried to greet me, my fear set in deep and the only thought was to return to the Mistress Mi-cilia's home. It was my only hope. I ran with the speed of a leopard and as I reached what I thought was to be her home stood an old Victorian building I was sure that was the building I exited from the night before. I entered the front gates and quickly ran to the front door. I banged on the door as if my life depended on it, for it did. When the door was opened I ran passed my greeter and searched for the room that I was given earlier. I prayed my coffin was still there. Then I found it and entered the room for cover and rest from the rays of death that searched for me. The sun light entered the room through window curtains as if it was searching for me and as if god was still with me it showed me my coffin. I entered it with great relief! I am not sure how long I slept but I awoke fully charged but hungry. My wounds from the battle and the sun were gone. I was at my full health again. I walked over to the window and pulled the curtains open. The moon light filled the sky like a beam of hope. I came to realize that the window was really doors to a balcony. I walked out onto the balcony and followed the moon as if in a trance I must have stared for over an hour before I saw something or should I say some one.

I turned to see Mistress Mi-cilia standing in the doorway. She walked over to me and proceeded to sit next to me. She smiled at me and then said, "Hello Xavier, My servant told me you had returned. I guess you had no luck in finding Elizabeth. I am not surprised! You seem so young and sweet and after you left last night… I thought to myself, maybe! I should have told you everything. Even thou I realized Elizabeth has her own agenda. See, Elizabeth is one of my oldest friends. So, protecting her means a lot but something is telling me that in light of the past events this is greater than even our friendship. See, I smelled those wolfs that came here several days ago which meant that they were looking for someone and now I know who. The Werewolves that attacked you last night were meant to destroy you and by all means they should have done it. The fact that they couldn't! Is telling you're made of something much more than what Elizabeth told me." Even after hearing her I had to ask her about my dreams and Elizabeth. She smiled and asked me to tell her everything Elizabeth told me, so I did. When I finished Elizabeth's tale she just smiled at me and gracefully shook her head no.

She said, "I never realized how confusing being turned could be even in the new age. Even as time changes life remains the same boy wants girl and girl wants boy... See,"

She laughed as she spoke those words but I told her that it was not that simply for Elizabeth saved me from a true death and a living hell. I know she loves me, for I feel it in my heart as well as my soul.

She said, "Elizabeth may love you but she loves something more. A dream… a legend… a ghost! Lady Constance is not Elizabeth's Aunt. She is a Story we vampires believe once lived. She is no more real than Elizabeth's story. See, it is believed the lady Constance is the mother of us all. In a time long ago one of her children betrayed her and was punished. He was sentenced to something worse than death. He was cut off from the world and all his dreams. His quest for power became his down fall and is what caused him to be stripped from all that he could be. It is written that he desired to be the first king of our species. He desired to be Lady Constance predecessor and when it did not come to pass. A revolution began amongst our species. Joseph and those that choose to follow were ostracized. It is written that they were buried in unmarked tombs and scattered around the globe. It is believed that the oldest known vampire is Joseph and there are many different tales of how he came to be. Joseph was believed to once be the Great Lord Draco... He was to give us hope of a better life. It meant that we were the oldest creatures on this planet. Everything came after us and who ever drank of his blood then they would be able to walk in the light. Imagine walking as a human, talking with them, sitting around them just as any normal being."

At this point one of her servants brought me a glass of warm blood and handed it to me. Then he turned towards Mistress Micilia before leaving us once more. She waited until he left the balcony and closed the door before continuing.

She said, "It is believed that if any drank his blood they would become truly immortal. Now Elizabeth did read the book of Zarasgale. So did many of us; it's our bible. Legend tells mankind that it seems we have no rules but the truth is we have many of them. Unfortunately, Elizabeth broke many and now all hell is running free. You were never meant to be made nor should you be as strong as you are and if you did have a dream from Joseph's blood then you should have came to understand how wrong Elizabeth's beliefs are. It is unclear why Joseph was placed in this unmarked grave. But what is clear is that he was placed there for many centuries."

Xavier said, "Then maybe he just wished to be free, so he could return to his people."

She laughed and said, "No my Xavier…Thou it is believed that he was our maker. There is no proof that this is so. The question is how and why she awoke him. Did she hope to gain power from this action? She could never have hoped to control him nor use one as old as him for her own agenda."

"Why does everyone believes Elizabeth must have had a plan and isn't a victim herself."

"O Xavier! Do you not understand? Now, Knowing that this one called Joseph is real it leaves me to believe what else in the great Book of Zarasgale is also real. It is even possible that the ones who imprisoned him in the first place may be real as well. For the sake of all mankind let's hope not and if so… Let's pray that they all have faced the true Death. For if they too are only asleep then this new world is in much Danger. Xavier, please try to picture a world where there are creatures far greater than you and I. Creatures with supernatural gifts. Imagine if there are many things that exist outside of vampires, werewolves and Hell; for that matter even witches. She has opened Pandora's Box."

She walked around the balcony as if on stage. I was beginning to understand that my friends were right and I may have really fucked up again. I asked her if there was any way to help my friends… She smiled and picked a rose from one of the many she had around the balcony.

"I want to really train you to hone your strength so you can try to aid your friends and… if there is still time. I will return you to Philadelphia where you can try to help them. But know this Xavier not even I can tell you what you truly are for I have never seen anything like you in all my thousands of years. Starting tomorrow you shall study from the book of Zarasgale and when you have learned all there is too known from it, I shall train you in battle." With that another servant came out with two glasses of warm blood and we drank. The Evening began to seem normal after that, as if that was possible. I told her all about my life and my friends… Even what we all meant to each other.

Chapter 11
Return of the Prodigal Son

When the next evening came Mistress Mi-cilia took me to a room in her basement. It was very large and held many old things like books, statues, chairs and tables. As I walked through the room I was amazed at all the beautiful art work that hung on the walls. Some of the things were as weird as the painting I had seen earlier but I loved looking at them never the less. In the center of the room was a very old and beautiful table with thick long craved legs and embroidering all over them and in the center of the table sat only one book. It was the book of Zarasgale. Now, unlike the rest of the house it was lit by torches and reminded me of something from an old movie, I thought it was very cool. She left me there and told me to read… Learn all that I can, for these books have not been seen by many eyes. As I looked around the room I couldn't believe how many books it held.

I did as I was told and read the book for myself and was taken to a time older than anything I have ever known. I read the book of Zarasgale and many others. Much of what I read I didn't understand but I read it any way. I went from book to book... There were things written in the book of Zarasgale that made no sense to me, so I had to look up things in other books. I know you may want to know about the Books I read but that is forbidden. I learned that Elizabeth was lying to me. If my friends were still alive, then I would have to be the one to save them. These creatures that would hunt them were like nothing I have ever seen or heard of. Well, I can say that I have heard of Werewolves but these were not like the ones in Hollywood movies. These Creatures where powerful and did not fear Vampires. In fact they were as strong as or even stronger than them. The book did speak of one called the Alter King. The first Spirit wolf and he created the race of Legions. I was not sure what that meant but I was sure that I did not want to meet them. The Book spoke of many different types of creatures and vampires where not the top of the list of beings that lived before man. There were many drawings in the book and some of the creatures looked so weird to me that I grew concerned and I now know I wanted to return home. I was afraid for my friends and even George's safety. Even though we did not agree on much I didn't want anything to happen to him because of me. After what seemed like a month or so, she introduced me to Ryman one of her children. Ryman trained me for two weeks. I feared my friends where dead and now without them nor Elizabeth I was not sure what was to become of me.

Then the day came that I saw the one I was searching for. Elizabeth stood before me. She must have been about hundred feet ahead of me. Without thought I leaped from the balcony I began to run towards her but she kept moving away from me as if leading me somewhere. I followed as best I could but she was moving so quickly. I wasn't sure where I was going but knew she must have needed me or why else would she have come here. I tried to call her through my mind, like she showed me but it didn't work. She continued to move away from me. Stressed, hungry and confused I yelled out, "why have you abandoned me, my love! Why?" She stopped and turned back towards me as I fell to my knees. Lost and confused over all that was happening to me, my heart beat like a mad man and tears filled my eyes as she approached me. She bent down to look into my eyes and as I looked back, she was not my Elizabeth.

She smiled as she raised the back of her hand up to my face and said, "you gave up so much for love yet ye no not what you love. I am no more important to you than she is. You are so weak and so tired, yet you still seek to find her. Elizabeth used you to become something more than what she is. Since that has failed she seeks another route. Here feed from my wrist and let me return you to your friends. They shall need you… they shall! Now feed and come." I was confused but so hungry so I fed and fed. When I was finished I looked at her and asked of her name but she wouldn't tell me. She just kept smiling and led me down this road. I asked where we were going but she said nothing. Then everything around me went black, I awoke in a bloody sweat. I rose from my bed and worked my way into the hall. Half delirious I started calling for Ryman. By the time he got to me I was on bended knees. Drained and confused he helped my half naked body back into my room. He called for the servant to bring me blood and tried to make me lay back in bed. I just kept repeating I saw her, I saw her. He kept repeating to me it was only a dream for me to calm down. I told him it was more than a dream somehow she was communicating with me. She was telling me my friends needed me. I had to get back to Philadelphia; I had to get back to them. He told me if that is what I wish than he would make arrangements.

About two days later I was back in Philadelphia. I went to the Rittenhouse Park in hopes to find somebody. I even tried to seek George out through my mind, but had no luck. I went to Old city the see if Lady Ling had news of Elizabeth but no one answered the door. I found that odd but decided that it was probably for the best. So I went to my family home to check on them. My sister was not pleased to see me but my parents seemed understanding. After talking for some time I went to my old room and fell asleep. I tried to reach George in my dream but without any luck. I mean, I was able to create the image of George but after talking with it I quickly realized it wasn't George. The next day I thought about all the lessons George tried to teach us when we were alive and then it came to me. If I was to find them then I needed to stop thinking like myself and start thinking like them. So I knew Landis would never be found because of his nature. He would make a point to cover his tracks and leave signs that I completely missed. So without at least one of our friends helping me, finding him was out of the question. Zack was too Dangerous to seek out, because without the others he would most likely try to kill me. Then Marco and Drew came to mind but they would not be so easy to figure out. They may forgive me, let me talk or simple destroy me straight out. Then just wait for what would come next. I sat in front of my parent's home for over an hour thinking then it came to me… Vinnie!

See, Vinnie was just like Peter. He would make a point of allowing me to find him, but unlike Peter, killing me would not be his first response. He would thrive in my trying to dig myself out of this pit I created before doing anything. So, I thought if I was Vinnie where would I be. Then it came to me Arco Park. Arco Park was the most logical place becuase Vinnie would not get me the credit of being any smarter than basic logic. That is the only place we guys hungout at after meeting with George. The only park on our old college campus… I went in the house and changed into more comfortable clothes. When I returned to Philadelphia's center city area and went to the park it was empty. I looked around for signs left by at least one of my friends, and then I saw it. Around the park was a half wall of red bricks and cement tops for people to sit on. Now to most people that would be normal but a piece of the cement was replaced with a lime stone from Rittenhouse square. So I ran there as fast as I could, but no one was there; so I waited. Five hours past then a voice said to me. "Dude only you could fuck up things this bad." I turned and there stood Vinnie.

He looked at me and then spoke, "you have been gone for over a three month and now you show up. I was close to giving up on you and returning the stone." He sat beside me and we talked for a while then he suggested that we go over to the café on 19th street. When we got there we both ordered a hot tea (something about the warmth of the cup against our skin always soothes us) any way! I started to explain about everything I went through and how I met Mistress Mi-cilia and how she trained me. I also told him I lost Elizabeth and believed she might be dead. That made him laugh; Vinnie always had a weird sense of humor. Anyway I started to tell him about the Great Book and the stories in it when we both felt that someone was listening to us talk. Without moving we both prepared our self for whatever was about to happen and then someone spoke. "Now it has been a long time since I seen one of your kind." the young man said. We both looked over and their stood a very elegant young black man in a suit of all things… but what stood out to me, was the beautiful shiny fur coat he was wearing. From the look of him I could tell he was very well off from the way his long black hair fell upon his clothes and caught the moonlight or the jewelry that seemed very simple but was very reserved. It looked as if somehow he radiated his beauty. He was accompanied by four other gentlemen who had on suits as well and they all wore black shaded glasses. We both look over at him but said nothing. He smiled with the most perfectly white teeth I have ever seen and he invited himself to join us. He was so bold that he even ordered food and made a point to put it on our bill. Vinnie slightly laughed at him as if he knew him but something told me he didn't. The man introduced himself as David. He must have picked up the fact that we were both bothered by his gall. He graciously waved his hand in the air as he explained there was no reason why he should not eat just because we did not. Even immortals need nutrients he said and smiled. Now, I was puzzled. Vinnie finally spoke and asked how he knew us. David said he didn't but he knew of us and for the life of him he could not understand what all the fuss was about. Now he had our attention… He continued to act normal as if we knew what he was talking about. Then he looked at Vinnie and said, "Wait, your eyes… staring into Vinnie's eyes, by the heavens you have no idea what you are." He laughed for about three minutes. At one point it even seemed as if a tear was coming out of his eyes. "You foolish young men are both Vaingels! You may be undeveloped Vaingels but Vaingels nevertheless. Now it's puzzling to me… why so many elders are seeking your death." Taking his napkin and placing it across his lap he said, "The idea that immortals are chasing after ones such as you two seems preposterous. Those fools believe you are vampires, but of course… for they have never seen Vaingels." We weren't sure what he was talking about or what he wanted from us. It became quite clear that it was in our best interest to remain quiet and just listened. I think we both figured it was best that he only thought it was two of us. He continued to talk as if we were old friends and there was nothing that he could not share with us. One thing I had to admit the guy had style. When the server brought David's food to the table he kindly looked at it and sent it back telling them it was not rare enough. This dude really had style and I think Vinnie and I both knew that it was not going to end. He made a point to turn his head so to make eye contact with both of us while asking about the others. Then all three of us felt it, another presence. This one was very familiar for it was a vampire. Before Vinnie and I could do anything, David excused himself and moved with speed like I have never seen. Even with our vampire sight we barely were able to see his actions. I concentrated to block out the sounds around me to hear what they were saying. David's hand transformed into a claw and locked into this vampire throat; I could hear him sniffing all about the young man. Then without a second thought he crushed his neck. Somehow his nails penetrated the young vampire's throat like a knife through paper. I could hear David speak so clearly," I would know that scent anywhere; I knew your maker and I never liked Sammy either." The young vampire was turned to ash in David's grip. David returned to us as if nothing happened. He responded as if he knew what we were going to say. David said," Uh! How I hate euro trash." Taking a napkin from the table, wiping his hands... he especially wiped the one that was a kind of claw just a moment ago…

He acted as if nothing happened and started to eat his steak. Vinnie and I just looked at each other as if this dude was wilding. I could tell by Vinnie's eyes expression that he was looking around to see if anyone was even able to see what just happened but apparently not. I guess this is one of the beautiful things about Philadelphia; people tend to mind their own business. They seem to love to live in the bliss of ignorance. Then David asked about our friends. It was funny how he kept referring to them as the others. He even went so far as to suggest that we were being protected by a witch. Then looked at me and said, "Correction! Their protected by witches but you I could sense the moment you returned to Philadelphia. So how was your trip?" Then he smiled at me. Vinnie was the first to speak.

"And how do you know we were being protected by witches"

"Simple I could not sense you or your friends."

"Maybe, we left the city too and since Xavier came back I returned."

"I know you had left the city to go to New York. I believe that is where she found you. What's puzzling to me, how any of you would know a witch as powerful as her? It isn't like she reveals herself to any Tom, Dick or Harry. Nevertheless, I guess it is your secret to keep."

"Yes… If what you're saying is true it is our secret to keep. Now explain this Vaingels concept. That you believe we have become and what is the difference between a Vaingels and a vampire."

"I can sense you both are becoming uncomfortable but there's no reason. For I just now saved you and if I wished you dead! I think we all would agree you would be… Actually the only reason I'm entertaining your presence is because of curiosity;

about the one who bears the voice. Now you both can pretend you have no idea what I'm talking about but I know you do. If the one is as old as I believe him to be… Then who is he?"

"We both looked at each other not sure what to say. This guy David seemed to know more about us than we knew about ourselves. We weren't too sure if giving him George's name would be wise. He persisted constantly repeating come on, come on speak up. Vinnie just looked at him and I then said something that I was not prepared to hear. And in all truth it tore me apart inside."

Vinnie said, "Well before you interrupted me and Xavier… I brought him here so that I could tell him. We believe George is dead. Some dudes were attacking us along the train tracks and we were holding our own until it just got to be too many of them. We started making our way back to the museum at JFK and this strange man appeared. It was like scene out of a movie. Vinnie shook his slowly as if in disbelief I mean we heard thunder then a flash of light and the Dude was standing there in front of us. Dude, man… we were scared shitless. I mean dude… George fell back Garrett fell over him and Landis looked as if he was about to die… Even Marco and Drew' starting saying what the fuck and Zack's growl came out like a whimper. We stopped were we fell and he proceeded to walk past us. In some way he looked like he was Egyptian or Arabian, I mean he had on some kind of silk cloth that draped off his body, a belt made of gold and jewels. He stood over seven feet tall and looked as if he could have been a well defined dancer; all kinds of small tattoos running around one side of his bald head. They ran along his neck to his chest and shoulder. His eyes where the color of sand with black lashes that looked as if they where dipped in paint. He had gem stone embedded above his eyes as if his skin had grown around them. This dude even had a necklace plate on make of gold and some kind of black stone. What was so fucked up; the dudes that were chasing us didn't seem to know him either. Their leader stood about ten feet away from us and started threatening to destroy him along with us if he didn't stand out of their way. I mean this dude was talking shit out of his ass. He was saying that he was like 10,000 years old and if he was smart he would step away and let them do what they came here to do; but man this guy didn't seem to be bothered in the least. He tilted his head as if he was examining them then called them Vaingels parasites and then flipped his hand. In a matter of moments we watch all of them… just disintegrate. I mean he took them out as simple as someone would flick a cigarrette and then turned his eyes towards George. We all were too scared to do anything but George being George… Slowly walked up to the dude and demanded that he did not harm us. He looked at George for a little bit then looked back at us. Then he turned to George and told him the time has come. If any of us tried to follow you shall share the fate of the parasites. As scared as George was he still asked, "Dear mighty Whiska-Ra-tum please protect all my children this night and I will welcome death if that is what you seek." The Dude looked at George for a moment then agreed saying, "Even he that dwell in the other land?" and George shook his head yes. At that moment we felt an energy past through us. It wasn't long before we all tried to say our goodbyes but, as George was telling Garrett what to do, the Dude wrapped his arms around George and we think they flew away. I mean it was so quick we weren't sure, all we saw was dust."

I thought that Vinnie was wilding, but David seemed to believe him. David grabbed Vinnie's and my hand then told us that George was very brave. He also told us it was a great chance that George was still alive. If what he thinks is happening then George sacrificed himself to protect us. He told us that everything is beginning to make sense to him. Because of this dude the other immortals will watch all their actions carefully but they are not going to attack. Of course you will still have to deal with the stupid ones. There are always those who believe they must prove themselves to their master. Since we are not fully developed Vaingels we're at a disadvantage. He told us to take comfort in the fact that they cannot easily tell us apart but do not become cocky because we can still be killed. He told us that we're a part of a bigger picture, too big to even explain. He assured us that he had eyes all around the city and they will look out for us at least until he is told otherwise. With that he rose and left us to our own devices. I wanted to know more about George I just couldn't believe what Vinnie told us. I was too shocked to even try to cry. If George was dead, then he made a sacrifice that not even I was brave enough to do. As much as I despised him for always riding me, I had to respect the fact that he protected us to the very end. Something I didn't have the balls to do. I can't explain to you how bad I felt knowing that I sacrificed them all for the sake of Elizabeth. With George's death I wasn't sure how the others would take the news of what I discovered. I can't describe the pain in my heart I felt knowing that George died because of my blind love for Elizabeth. I started to explain to Vinnie about Mistress Mi-cilia and all the books she had. I told them about the war in the world of super naturals. As I kept talking he kept staring at me, then he said I looked like I was starving. The truth was I was hungry! He paid the bill and told me to come with him. He never commented on the things I told him.

We turned down an alley then he reached in his backpack and gave me a bag of blood and told me to drink. I looked at him, but I was too hungry to argue. When I finished drinking the blood I asked him were the others where. He never looked at me when he told me… That they did not want to see me! In fact, they would be enraged if they knew he was there with me. A part of me was upset and hurt but I understood. I betrayed their trust through their love and caused George's death. I asked him about the master Joseph and he told me that they heard nothing. The master has done nothing to them. In fact they have not even been able to locate him. It was as if the world had swallowed him once again. We started to walk towards 30th St. and as we crossed market Street Bridge I stopped to look over the water. He asked me what was wrong and was I regretting what happened to George. I lied and said yes but the truth was. As we crossed the bridge all I could think about was my sweet beautiful Elizabeth. Vinnie looked at me as if he didn't believe me. He always was good at reading my face. Then, he told me that everything would be fine for Garrett has taken great lengths protecting us. He even told me that Peter was still with them and when he talked to them again perhaps they will forgive. He told me how Garrett and Landis were very protective over the group since George was gone. So if I really want to see them then I would have to first talk with those two, talking to Garrett wasn't a problem because we always got along. Garrett seemed to always understand me. Landis however, is worst than George! When he put his mind to something he never backs down, and if I was going to confront him then I had to make sure I was ready. Unlike George, Landis was not going to allow his heart to rule his decisions. I asked Vinnie were they still staying in hotels; but he told me no. It was so to the point that I realized he wasn't going to talk about it. Finally we reached 30th St. station and went inside. It was pretty isolated that time of night so he wasn't too concerned about people stares. He picked the bench in the station to be where we were to meet the following night. So we shook hands and hugged. Then he went down a set of the steps as if to catch a train. A part of me wanted to follow him but I knew if I wanted to win their confidence I had to first when their trust. As I left the station I realized that I just might be able to win them over and have my friends back once again. Even though it may have cost the life of George the rest of us would be able to look after each other. I only hoped they would open up their hearts and take me back. As I walked down

JFK Boulevard the thought came to me. As sad as it was to lose George, there would be a chance for me to win back the others. I started feeling good about myself, thinking about how I'll be able to teach them the things I've learned. I was certain they were barely getting by without me. I mean I'm sure George would focus more on protecting them than teaching. I finally have the opportunity to be the master.

As I rode my train home I started practicing my gifts. Listening to the people conversations around me most of them were talking about nothing. I came to realize how blessed I was to have these gifts and my friends. When I got off the train I decided to walk home and enjoy the quietness streets. The trees seemed to be so defined, I mean how the way the wood just grown into a perfect unit. I wondered if in time we would be as lucky. Then I looked at the houses I passed, something I had not done since this all started. They seemed more vibrate than ever before. It was as if everything was talking to me. Even the sounds around me were so clear and soothing. The wind against my face felt so good that I wanted to stay outside and just take it all in. Although my emotions were not consistent, a part of me did miss George and I kept thinking about how he was trying to save me even after I left the group and went off with Elizabeth; whom I still loved and was not sure if she was alive. When I got home and went into my room. I locked my door and closed the curtains as well as pulled down the shades. I laid there for some time before sleep took me. It was the first time I actually got a good night's rest. My dream was of nothing really significant. It was a dream no different from any other. For the first time, I forgot all the madness that was going on around me. For the first time in a long time I dreamt of nothing; no friends and no Elizabeth. This went on for some time and I would wake up every night and stayed around the house or went to meet up with Vinnie.

Then the day came when he told me that the others were ready to see me. Vinnie tried to warn me that a lot had changed since George was gone. I guess I was too blinded by the fact that they wanted me back to really understand what he was telling me. The following night I met up with him at 30th St. Station thinking that we were going to catch a train. After greeting me he walked back outside towards market Street. I was a little confused but I followed. Then Garrett pulled up in a black car. Vinnie got into the passenger side so I sat in the back. Garrett smiled at me a little but seen distracted as if he was checking to make sure no one was following us. They wouldn't tell me where they were taking me but drove up to 38 streets and University Avenue and turn right on Baltimore Avenue. I looked confused because we were still in the city, which I wasn't expecting. He made a sharp right on 61st St. and parked the car. Now that didn't seem too out of the ordinary because along that street there were row homes and on the other side of the street some type of park, so I assumed they were living in one of those houses. Then they started walking across the street toward the park. I was a little reluctant but I followed. I felt that ultimately if I was going to do this then I had to follow through all the way. Once we were off the main road and more into the park area I was able to see the others. I asked them what was up and why we were meeting in the middle of the park so far out of the way. But then I decided to speak first to make it very clear that a lot of things occurred since my absence. Landis looked at me with some kind of rage. He seemed very angry with me as if he held me responsible for George's death. The anger in his eyes told a story I could not comprehend but it was very clear that whatever Vinnie was told to tell me, it was left out. I stood there, and allowed him to speak his mind while everyone else listened. After he lectured me, Peter asked him to calm down and tell me what they knew. Landis just looked at Peter and looked back at me. He flagged me and just walked away.

Garrett said, "How do we know we can trust you now. Vinnie

told us everything you told him. A part of us want to believe that you have lost faith with Elizabeth but the truth is how do we know whenever you find Elizabeth that you will not betray us again."

I started explaining about the book and all the things I read. I told them how I discovered that Elizabeth was using me and the group. I even made it clear that George is right… I was letting my heart control my mind. Blinding my eyes to the truth and putting everyone in Danger. How I so desperately wanted to believe everything she said was true. Even standing before them I felt foolish trusting her. I started to tell about the werewolves that attacked me and how I fought them all.

Then Garrett said, "We already know about the werewolves. Damn it Xavier! Sometimes you're a fuck'n idiot. It wasn't you who defeated the werewolves it was the man that….."

Before he could finish he turned away from me and I could feel the sorrow and the pain in his eyes and his heart. I knew that there was more going on than I even imagined.

Vinnie said, "It was the dude that took George……

"What…"

"You heard me…. George asked him to protect all of them even the one in New England. He answered yes as if they both knew something was happening at that moment. So whatever issues you had with George, you need to get the fuck over it… he sacrificed himself to save your sorry ass. The power that dude welded protect you as well as us that night. It didn't make sense to me until you told me about the werewolf's attacking and how they too were disintegrated. Even you felt his power pass over you when he did. George gave us a second chance so we took it. For the last month and a half we had been hunting those bastards that were hunting us. Learning everything we could to stay alive if that is what you want to call this state of being."

Marco jumped out of a tree and landed behind me telling them to back off. He reminded them that there was a lot more work we had to do. As we were talking they started sniffing the air and looking around then they backed up as if they were readying to fight. So I turned looking around to see what was going on. I saw two men coming through the bushes and was approaching us. The rest of the group knew it before I did. Landis looked at me and told me to follow his lead if I wanted to live through the night. I found it odd that these two men could sense us, especially because we were so far from the street and hidden by the bushes. Landis kept saying wait for it. I wasn't sure what he was talking about but before my eyes they turned into wolves, not like the ones I fought before they were different. They were bigger and faster, Landis turned to the others as the men started to transform and told them to move out.

They took off as if they had a plan and I simply just followed. We ran for about fifty feet and we jumped over a fence. I was so lost because we ended up in a grave yard. They all ran in different directions but stayed close to the ground. I was a little scared but turn to fight against these wolves anyway. I felt that if I could hold off four of them, then two surely would not be a problem. As the two wolves jumped the fence Vinnie and Zack ran around me using their nails to ripping open bags of dirt. As the dirt filled the air where we were I could hear other wolfs entering the graveyard. Landis was so quick I could barely see him move. The werewolves seemed lost and confused as they searched for us. I watched as Marco and Drew did the same thing with bags of dirt. The area became nothing but a smoke-covered field. Then out of nowhere one of the wolves jumped through the dust at me but before I could do anything Vinnie was on top of him and ripped the claws into the sides of the creature. Then as the wolf turned its head to try and bite at Vinnie, Zack came out of nowhere and bite into his throat whiling ripping his claws into the animal's chest. I was frozen with fear as they ripped the creature apart. Marco and Drew were jumping around the tomes as if they were playing a game of tag. Every time they struck a Werewolf it would seem to be stunned and drop. Garrett and Casper would mount the wolves that Marco or Drew tagged from the back. Take their hand and pull the wolves heads back while ripping their mouths open. It was as if they were demons or wild animals. Blood went everywhere as I listened to the creature howl in pain and fall to the ground. This sound was followed the several others. I ran to try and see what was happening. I saw Landis do something that I didn't think he would ever be able to do to another creature. He allowed the wolf to attack him and then phased out. When he reappeared he pulled the animal's insides out and they were just hanging off the creature's back as the poor thing fell to the ground crapping and crawling around in pain. I could see it was in great pain and I didn't know what to do. Landis did not even stop to see his handy work. He just ripped more dust into the air and moved on. I could hear howls from all around me but I was too scared to move. I fell to the ground and covered my ears and prayed that it would all stop. It was some time before it did. My friends jumped all round the graveyards as if they were playing a game of tag. As the dust cleared and I was able to see again Landis and the others looked like mad men. I mean their eyes was glowing as if they where flashlights and their breathings was so rapid that I thought they would attack me. Then the sky opened and rain just poured; they all walked over to each other as if they were seeing who survived. I thought they were bad when they fought Elizabeth in Landis's apartment but this was something else. These dudes were like animals; the way they were looking around the tomb stones and even the way they regrouped around Landis.

I stayed on the ground not sure what to do or say then Garrett put his hand on my shoulder and asked if I was ok. I wasn't okay but I wasn't about to let them know that. I looked at Garrett shook my head yes. Garrett looked so unbothered with everything that happened as the rain ran across his face. He looked over at Landis as if gesturing that it was now time. Landis nodded and turned to the others. They pulled the dead bodies over differing graves and Landis did something I really didn't think he could do. With the rain washing away all evidence of our battle Landis stood over each one of the creatures and used his gift to push them down into the graves. Once he was finish we all regrouped and just waited. They didn't talk much and I didn't know what to say, so we all just that there looking around to make sure everything was clear. As we left the graveyard I finally got the courage to ask Garrett why we run there. Garrett smiled and told me I wasn't the only one who learned some new tricks. He and the guys are fighting with these creatures for some time. Through most of the battles they began to learn the wolves' strengths and their weaknesses. Those wolves have a hard time separating our sent from the dead. Leading them to the graveyard worked to our advantage as well as keeping the air full of dust and debris. One of the best ways to defeat a werewolf is to force it to depend on his hearing only. As much as I didn't want to admit I was very impressed with how well the guys executed this strategy in battle. They operate like a well oiled machine.

As he walked down the street Garrett informed me that the guys were worried about where I had been and if I was still alive. He believed they all were relieved when Vinnie discovered I was safe and back in Philadelphia. He even told me what Vinnie said to him about David. Garrett being older than the rest of us had more of a leveled head. He wanted to know about the things I learned and how it could be used to help us. As I explained everything to him we all walked to their new home. It turned out they didn't live that far. They lived in a three story empty house.

From the outside it looked as if it was one of those city homes you see all around Philadelphia with the wood over the windows and doorways. Vines' growing all over it as if the city forgot it was even there. The backyard was over grown and smelled as if dogs used it for their bathroom. Even the trees in the back of the house were passed neglect, ivory growing all over them. I made a joke about them straightening up. They just walk through it all and entered their home. I asked why they just didn't find a place nicer and they told me that this was the spot they felt safer. Even if a werewolf came across them it would have little chance of sensing them over the dead animals buried in the yard. When I went into the house I was shocked; the house was nice, I mean the inside was painted and furnished. They had really nice shit all throughout the place. It made me remember that we were all artists and that we have very unique skills. It took a little bit of time before we got settled. Then once we got settled it was time for us to chill. I told him about the dream I had of Elizabeth and what I believe may have happened. I worried if she was safe. I was very surprised that something happened to George and I was not able to sense it. Maybe, because Elizabeth was in my mind throughout the entire ordeal; Then I asked them have they seen or heard anything of Janus. They didn't understand and found it very difficult to believe that Janus would allow us to continue to live as if nothing happened even if the master was out of the picture.

Garrett said, "I believe that Janus is still in the city, something is telling me it wasn't him that got rid of the master."

"Word..."

"Think about it! If Janus had the power to destroy the master then why even bother converting Peter. No, if anything happened to the master, it was not because of Janus' Doing. For all we know the strange dude that may have killed George could have taken the master. This is too many questions without answers for us to move forward. One thing for certain we cannot abandon George until we know for certain that he is dead."

"Dude, you don't believe George's dead."

"That's not what I'm saying but until we are certain we must act upon all situations as if he is still alive. George usually uses a phrase a poison cat inside of a box. The cat is dead and yet it's still alive… Until the box is open we cannot believe the cat to be either one. That is the same situation with George."

"Dude, I'm so confused I have no idea what you're talking about. Is George dead or alive."

Marco said, "Exactly, so if we act as if George is still alive. Then why he is still alive; why was Janus still looking for us."

"And where do these werewolves fit into the puzzle."

Landis said, "Look, before we even begin to discuss all of this. We have to first take Xavier through the detoxing. Xavier, we have to take you through the detoxing of the blood you drank since you been turn. And let me tell you it's not easy."

"What you're talking about… You guy stop drinking blood?"

"Yes, it occurred to us that we were listening to much to what Elizabeth told us. The hunger we were feeling was the hunger we were used to from being alive. George deciphered a lot of things Elizabeth was telling us, by how we get powers from each other's blood and human blood does nothing for us. If the power was all we gained then it was really no reason for us to feed."

Peter said, "Garrett and George were the first to stop feeding. they put themselves in some type of mental state in several days later the hunger was gone."

"Word, Elizabeth never talked about something like that. You guys sure it can work?"

Garrett said, "Remember unlike any of you George always had a deeper connection to Elizabeth since the night in Landis's apartment. We talked about it for some time and because we were sure of the outcome. I thought it was best if we did it first before allowing you guys to even try it. Now George did want to be the first to do it but I told him to allow me to go first because if anything went wrong he could shut my mind down and prevent me from harming any of you or worst a stranger on the street. That's when we found this house and because of the basement setup I know not even I could break down the metal door to the boiler room with brute strength. So, that is when we went on to reinforce the walls and sound proofing the ceilings so to make sure no one know we were here. Preparing this place wasn't easy but we pulled it off and then I went for it. I am not going to lie to you. Xavier the first few days are going to be easy but then you will hit bottom and that is when all hell is going to go wrong. You are going to want to feed like there is no tomorrow. Your gifts aren't going to help you… You're going to become an animal, willing to attack anyone that comes near you. Unlike George you will not be able to sleep through your detox as if it's a bad dream.

Peter said, "Yeah dude, we were there when Garrett went through it but George did his in one of the bedrooms upstairs, it was a while when he came out of it. We watched him for a few days as he shook and sweated like he was in an addict. I could not even reach him through his mind, but he was fine. When he awoke he looked so beautiful that I was drawn to kiss him as if I was kissing the head of an angel. His skin was so radiant and his body became more defined. Xavier, he held on to me as if I was his hope and protector. If ever I loved a man then George would surely be him."

Marco said (slightly laughing), "I think it would be fair to say that we all felt that way about him but never as strong as after he awoke. So, we all followed suit and out of all this Casper probably had it the roughest but once the hunger pass he was cool. None of us touch blood like that since. Vinnie told us you still feed and that could be a handicap. We're not sure where all of this is going to lead us but one thing we do know; if we're worried about feeding were not going to be any good to anybody. So it's up to you."

(Looking around the room at all my friends) "If you did it, then I can give it a try. I just find it hard to believe we can go on without blood."

Drew said, "Dude it's like being high at first and then it will take you somewhere else. Like I need to feed after an intense battle; I use a lot of energy in battling so the blood helps me restore that energy. It even helps me heal faster after a fight."

Landis, "Dude! That's true for all of us, it's not like using our gifts don't come with a price but we still are learning to work around those small issues. Our minds have been trained to seek food to survive every day so now we still feel the need to feed."

I wasn't sure exactly what they wanted me to do but I followed them into the basement of the building. The basement had one of those old furnaces that were big enough to burn wood or coal inside it. The room had a metal door with a small reinforced window that they fix to open only from the outside. I laughed at the level they took to make sure who ever was in the room could not just break out. They led me into the room where there were chains bolted to the floor and the walls were lined with mattresses. The floor had a rubber cover over it. I looked that them as if they were crazy but thought fuck it. The instructed me to give them my keys and everything I had in my pockets, so I did. Zack was the first to keep watch at the door and for the night everything was cool. We laughed a lot about the crazy shit that happened to them while I was gone, then I laid down on the matted floor to rest and sleep took me. I dreamt of many things but nothing that made any sense and slept the same as I usually did. When I awoke it was around seven p.m. the following eve and Marco was at the door I asked him about everyone else but he told me to focus on the next few days for they would be the hardest. I laughed as if he made a joke for I had no idea how bad things would get. We talked about George and his other children. Marco seems to be bothered by being called a Child of George but even he had to admit that he too was in love with what George became. He made it clear that in some ways they all had become very bisexual since they stop feeding. It was like they feed on something else besides blood but even he was not sure what. I listened to him for hours before sleep took me again. This time my dreams were of my family and what wonderful times we shared. About my mother and her mother cooking together in our oversized kitchen laughing at my father for something, he did years ago. I could even smell the food they were preparing. The roast beef, the chicken, and even the chitterlings smelled so good. I could see my sister setting the table with my father's mother who bought her crackling bread into the room and placed it on the table. Man, I loved her crackling bread maybe because it was something she would only make for us on Sundays. I watched as my family and I just sat there eating and joking. The food just kept coming and I couldn't get enough. At one point I even saw a turkey on the table and it was cooked so golden brown that it made your mouth water. Then the desserts started and they were just as bad. I was making a pig of myself, stuffing everything I could reach into my mouth. It was like I couldn't get full. Then at some point, I looked up and saw my Elizabeth and she was staring straight at me. I leaped for her but I awoke in a sweaty mess and leaped for the door. I forgot that I had the chains on and fell to the floor as sweat fell down my face. I looked up to see Drew standing on the other side of the door. He looked at me and pointed down to the ground. It took a few minutes for me to compose myself but after that I saw that he left me a joint and one match… (Laughing) They were not playing when they said it was going to be hard. I sat there and lit up the joint. As I smoked it, we started talking and he told me that it was around this time that he needed a joint. So while I was a sleep he came in and put them there for me. He told me that it wasn't going to get any better. I asked him about the other guys but he told me it was best that I focused on this. I told him how I saw Elizabeth and he just laughed. I knew he was thinking that all I was thinking about was my dick but the truth was I was a little scared because I leaped for her not out of love or lust but hunger.

He sat with me for most of the night then Landis came into view and I listened as he told Drew to leave him to watch the door now. Landis was nothing like the other. He looked in on me then sat down by the door. I asked him questions but he wouldn't answer. He just sat there as if I was a prisoner and not one of his friends. I started to tell him that the hunger had passed and that he could let me out but he said nothing and in fact he opened a book and started to read as if I wasn't even there. Starving and high, I rose to try to break free of the chains but failed. I started yelling that they were bugging and I wanted out but he didn't move. I started saying things that I now regret but at that moment I did not care. He just sat there and ignored me. I yelled how he wanted to take George's place and he feared that since I returned he would not be able. That struck a nerve because he looked at me through the window then responded with he wasn't the reason George was dead now is he? For some reason I got enraged and started throwing a fit. He just returned to his seat and started reading again. I raged until I passed out again. After that for the next two day I was in and out consciousness. At one point I was nothing but an animal looking around the room trying to think of how to get out. I tried to use my gifts but they did little help to aid me. I just kept passing out. Then it happened… I was standing in front of George and he was in the room with me. He was blaming me for all of this and I was telling him that it was never about me. He kept assuring me it was and I know what I was doing. I gave them their death and I wish only to rule over them that's why I did all of this. I leaped at him and ripped into his chest. I ripped him apart until nothing but his head remain and then he laughed, so I crushed his skull… I turned behind me and there he stood saying shit like did that make me feel better. Did I finally feel like the master of all masters or did I feel like the weak minded child. I have always been chasing ass all around the world in hopes that someday true love would find me. Then right before my eyes split into four different Georges and they all was laughing at me. They started circling around me, yelling at me saying they are and will always be my children, Xavier and so are you. Your nothing without me and all of us know it. He continued laughing. I was losing my mind; I started clawing at all four Georges until they were gone. Then out of nowhere smoke filled the room I was in. Then Garrett appeared behind me and walked towards me, I turned to face him but he just kept walking toward me. I leaped at him and as I made contact I tried to burry my fangs into his neck. He laughed then throws me across the room. He said, "If you're not strong enough to deal with George then how in the hell are you going to stop me." He grabbed me and sank his fangs into my neck. I could hear my bone break and feel the blood flowing from me as my body was going limp. I tried to fight back but could break his grip and know death was going to take me. Elizabeth appeared but did nothing to stop him. She stood there as he drank my life forces from my now weaken body. Then I awoke…

Everyone was standing outside the room as the door opened and I exited it. They were laughing and telling me how I was jumping around. They informed me that I was clawing at the floor and walls; at one point I tried to bite the mattress as if I was going to get blood out of it. Then I ran in circles looking as if someone was on my neck and at the end I just stopped. I stood still for about an hour then fell to the floor that was when they knew it was over. I was now free of the blood hold that life had on me. I wondered if Elizabeth knows anything about this type of act. I never read or seen it in any movie so I wondered how they came to figure it out, then made it work. I told them that was fuck'n scary as hell and never wanted to go thru that again. At least now I would only need to feed if I abuse my body or my powers. After we all celebrated me making it through the detox stage. I was puzzled by what powers I may have had so they showed me what they could do. Like Landis could faze through objects for a short period of time and Garrett's could make is body as strong as steal. So they let me go home and chill we my family for a bit while I tried to figure out what my powers was. At first I thought it was the fact that I could talk to them mentally but it turned out we could all do that.

After a week trying to figure it out what my abilities were Garrett gave me some good advice. George use to tell us that if ever we wanted to open our minds then we had to first clean it out. He called it cutting oneself with the sword of truth. You have to admit the truth about who you are and what you are. You even have to admit all the good things and fucked up things you did to people. Now the hardest part of it, has to do with owning up to it and judging yourself to be whatever you really are. This doesn't seem hard but try it and see if you still like yourself, most don't. So, I did it and grow sick from my own actions and ashamed of what I truly was. Then to have to judge myself as a _________! I think that is something I am going to kept to myself. Any way it worked because no sooner I came to terms with what I was my gifts showed them self's. As I tried to regain control of my feeling I released some form of vibration across the room but wasn't sure what it was. I contacted the other and told them so we could me up. We met in the same park we were at before and they agreed that Garrett should be the one who I used my gifts on. You know a practice run. I tried three times but couldn't get it to show itself then Landis told me to try and recreate the feeling I had the first time and like that it happened. Garrett moved back a few steps as if he was trying to regain his balance then fell to one knee. I was a little confused at what I did but wanted to know what it was. Garrett took some time to get himself together than laughed. He told me that I created some form of distortion wave and if I practice it could become a very powerful weapon. As I discovered using my new gift I also discovered great headaches from usage. I didn't do it to the point of expending my strength but I worked hard at mastering it. Then we all decided to practice and sharpen our skills. Even now, I have to admit it was fun. Vinnie and Zack seem to make a game out of disappearing in the shadows and reflecting the light. Of course Landis never showed how much you enjoy phasing through us when he attacked. Casper had a power similar to my own he could tense up so greatly that it would project energy like an invisible wall. Peter is able to evaporate like the wind and make different parts of his body solidify upon contact. Garrett never really showed with his power was, I assumed it was just great strength since he was a solid as granite. We practice for hours and when we weren't practicing we were telling each other where we made mistakes, fun was a small part of our exercise but I enjoyed it. I knew we were building up for something greater. Apparently, David was right when he said we had no idea what was going on. I was starting to wonder if we would need his help, if he was really a friend. I could tell that Peter wasn't really with us but his loyalty was unquestionable. I am not sure when he may have felt the need to return to Janus but I know he would never put us in Danger. Believe it was around that time felt it was important to talk about us and Janus. Zack ensured me that they were already preparing to meet Janus. Weather I wanted to or not I know we were going to have to face Janus sometime. Even though I knew we were training to take on Janus I couldn't get David out of my mind. I kept wondering how he knew what we were. How did he know where to find us, something told me he was more than just a werewolf and I wanted to know what. I wanted to share my thoughts with my friends but I wasn't sure how they were going to take it. Especially after the wild tangent I went on for Elizabeth. I wasn't too sure if I should share my concerns without facts. I mean even though a great deal of time passed, David was still in town. Even though he did nothing to us I wasn't sure if I could trust him. I guess since I didn't have George being my conscience. I knew I had to make better decisions and be more cautious with my actions. The rest of the guys were cool but they didn't put me on trial for everything I did. Oddly enough I came to depend on George more than I wanted to admit. So I informed the group that I was going off on my own for a bit. I certainly had no reason to alarm them about my concerns especially since David did nothing. I assured them they had no reason to worry about me since we mastered our mentally linked but I want to find this dude, I needed to know what he knew.

I returned to Philadelphia's Center City area to start my mind leaping. Trying to see if anyone seen David or knew anything about him. I came across many people that did. I discover who have actually seen him from the ones who didn't know much about him. The only thing that kept coming up in every conversation was that he was eccentric. It was clear that he was a very intelligent, young black dude. Who tend to hang in the Gayborhood! I wasn't sure if I particularly wanted to go there but I wanted to find out about this dude so I went. After checking out all the clubs I realized they were not much difference from the straight clubs. Maybe music was a little hotter and the dancers were Dudes. I found that funny since a lot of dudes in the club were hotter than the dancers. Maybe because the dancers were in very sexy underwear, showing of what god gave them. Their bodies were oiled up to show off all the details in their muscles. The customer were wearing just a little more than the dancers. I kind of wondered who was tipping who? I kept going back every night for over a week trying to spot him. I have to admit I was very attracted to the young vibrant raw energy that the dudes let off. I know I said that I had stopped drinking but I wanted to pig out in that place. Then it happened David came in with the group of guys that I originally meant him with. I guess his click was as tight as my friends. They were as diverse of races as my friends, but they all seem to dress alike as if they were in a band. They all had dark colored stretch jean and nylon colored shirts or body suits. I couldn't tell but they seem to love shades because they all had them. Either way they looked pretty cool. Not one of them was a small dude; they seem to enjoy the attention that they got when they entered the club. It was as if everyone in the club knew them. The bartender was placing drinks on the bar as if he was expecting them. As cool as the dudes looked David still stood out like a swollen thumb. He acted like a kid in a candy store; hugging on all the dudes that came near him. In truth they were kind of throwing themselves at him but whatever! David stood only about six foot and seemed to have the same type of dancer build that George had. I guessed that it was a gay thing. Even when he just stood still the guys linger around him, he was just a social butterfly. His click must have seen me around the same time because as I approached David they got up into my face, standing between us. David turned towards us, finding it funny he walked past them and stood in front of me. As we locked eyes I began to get light headed but I stood my ground. I tried to look as cool as I could. He ran his hand up my chest while locking his eyes to mine, flirting with me as if we were lovers. Part of me wanted to pull away but I didn't. I just stood there and let him have his fun. As I said before I am a hot dude.

He seemed to get a kick out of running his finger across my chest and through my long uncombed hair as he walked behind me. For a moment I thought that this dude was doing something to me but the thought soon left. I never been into dudes so, why I was allowing this struck me odd. This dude had a sex appeal that could not be denied and knew how to use it. It was very clear to me that like Elizabeth he was used to getting what he wanted and now he wanted me. Once he got behind me he slowly leaned into my ear. He told me I must be very desperate to come here looking for him.

I could feel his click found it quite humorous as if they heard what he said. The dudes that were with him did nothing but just watch us while smirking. David grabbed my hand and pulled me toward the dance floor. He told me to dance with him. I had no desire to but for some reason, I couldn't refuse him. He could tell I felt awkward, so he smiled and slowly placed his hand on my chest. We locked eyes and he said, "It's no different than dancing with the girls." As we danced, I realized he was truly playing a game with me and loving every moment of it. As he danced I could sense the men that were dancing around us seem to become drawn to him as he moved across the dance floor. I never realized how beautiful this dude was before or maybe he focused on making himself alluring. I mean I really didn't know what his gifts or powers were but the more we danced the stronger my attraction was for him. Everyone else in the club seemed to disappear to me and I was focused only on him. I was amazed at how his long black curly hair caught the different colored lights. Even the way he wore his hair pulled back by this unique metal hair comb. I quickly came to like how his body moved to the music. He seemed to release some type of hormones that I couldn't resist. I picked up his sense as he kept dancing and I was being drawn in like a bee to honey. At one point we started making out on the dance floor. There was no telling me to stop. I started caressing his body and loving it. I was loving his body as much as I did Elizabeth's. I was so into it, that my fangs responded and he must have sense it and pulled back. He smiled and told me. No, no, no, maybe later then led me off the dance floor. We partied throughout the night as if nothing was wrong. For a moment I forgot what I was even there for. I never thought I could feel so comfortable or so attracted to a dude. I became a part of his click that follows him around throughout the night.

Chapter 12

A World from New Eyes

When the night came to an end he took me back to his condominium. What was so crazy was the fact that it was right above Rittenhouse square. It looked like a rooms one would find in a palace. For a moment I thought he had the entire floor. If I had questioned rather he was rich or not after entering his condominium my questions were answered. The walls were painted with an antique white finish and very expensive molding. He had the most beautiful marble floors I could have imagined. Even the rugs in this place were so thick and elegant. He had paintings and sculptures all throughout the place. I could tell there were several rooms beyond the room we were in. The furniture was so delicate as if nothing was accidentally placed anywhere. This dude designed this room with great care. From the well sculptured chairs and tables to the fireplace that looked as if it was cut out of marble. The dudes that followed him throughout the night said their goodnights, all except two. They stood by the front door as if they were his personal security. I thought my friends were paranoid but these dudes took it to a whole new level. David walked over to one of his sofas and sat down so graceful; then patted the seat beside him as if to suggest for me to join him. I started getting a little nervous about where exactly this was going but if I wanted to lead this group then I needed to first make sure that he was someone we could trust. I walked over to him and sat beside him. I sat with my legs open and rested my elbows on my knees. I tried to look as masculine as I could but he really seem to find it funny started to laugh. As elegantly as he carried himself it was quite obvious that this was about business. He raised his hand as if he was waiting for something but never took his eyes off of me. Then a young man came into the room with a drink and placed the drink into David's raised hand. He never acknowledged the dude and slowly took a sip from his drink. He placed the glass down upon a table next to the sofa and turned back to me.

David said, "Are you going to tell me why you were looking for me? Or did you come all this way to show me how masculine and street you are."

I said, "Look, dude I need to know how you knew what we were? And why you wanted to protect us from that vampire in the Park. I have been in this city all my life and I've never seen any shit like this. I mean, after seeing what you did to the vampire; I'm not going to bullshit you by pretending we could take you. Especially since George is nolonger with us, but you have to understand we been through a lot. I place my friends in great danger from the beginning of all this. So, I need to know what's up with you."

"Well, since you are being frank. I see no reason why to play a games. You are a unique creature Xavier and though you do not understand what you are or why you were made. The reality is that you have been made. Now you must understand this. The creatures that are chasing you are acting out of fear. They do not understand what you are nor do they understand where you came from. As far as for me killing the vampire that goes without saying. I hate euro trash! If I allowed him to attack and maybe even destroy you and your friend in my presence… Well, then that would show a sign of weakness on my part. That is not something I can allow. Even in the world of supernatural's they are rules. He chose to break them so he suffered the consequences. I could lie to you and say that I wanted to protect you. But, the truth is I am interested in the one who bears the voice. A being with such a unique power can open the door to what endless possibilities."

"How do you know he's with us and not one of the vampires

that are trying to take us out?"

"Xavier, you know what I am?"

"I think a werewolf."

"That is good but I am not like the ones you read about or see in the movies. We are immortal's just as you and vampires. There are even immortal witches and many other things you have never heard about, nor would you understand. Now they are far from the ones you read about or see in your movies. Yes we all exist."

"Cool. Are they looking for us too?"

"Most witches are too busy trying to be human to interfere in the supernatural world. For some reason they long to be accepted by man. Now please don't take me to be a snob I'm far from it. I'm a realist. Everything has its time and its place. I know what you're going… through, I was once like you. I was blind to this world until I was made a part of."

"So, do you know about the book of Zara gale?"

"Yes, Xavier. All super naturals know of the great book and the veil of the mist. We all know that there was supposed to have been a race of being called Vaingels. True immortals!! Who job was to protect mankind until the day came that mankind rose up against them. That they fled into the world of the mist with so many others. like the Elfs, Druids, Nords, Shadow walkers, Giants and so on. Then they closed the veil behind them. The great witch Odessa keeps the veil between the two worlds closed until the day comes that the fourth Queen takes the throne. You must understand up to your creation this was all a myth. You're the first vampire that I have seen in over 3000 years that does not need to feed. Even your scent is different than anything I've ever smelled. Well, except for her! The one that saved me when I was first made. You and your friends are the only other beings with her scent. So to me that is a big deal. If it is because of her that you exist then I owe her a debt that through you and your friends I'm going to repay."

"You met another one like us."

"Yes I have… Centuries ago she saved me from some bigoted jackasses who sought to kill me. Being young and naïve, not aware of my abilities of talents I fled for my life. She took me in and protected me. I stayed in her care for almost 100 years then one day she was gone. She was my mother, lover and everything. So believe me, when I say I understand why you are afraid and paranoid. For if your friends are in Danger it is not from me. Sometimes Xavier you have to go where it began to understand where it will end."

"Now you talking like George"

"George! He's the one who bares the voice."

"Yeah… He loved to talk encrypted messages to us. The type of messages only him and Garrett understood."

"You seem to have a love and hate relationship with this George."

"Yeah, he always talked about light, dark and chaos. Living and working together as one. He didn't believe that anything was an accident and usually he would find a way to make it my fault."

"Really, then why didn't this Garrett protect you?"

"Garrett was more of a dark dude. If I didn't have the backbone to stand up to George, then I deserve to take whatever he chose to dish. I guess in a way he was right. No matter how much shit George would put on a plate, I would take it."

"So do you take responsibility for all of this?"

"Yeah, my friends warned me about Elizabeth but I wouldn't listen. I fell in love with her. I still feel her presence around and long to touch her once again."

He just sat there and listened to everything I had to say. He seemed to be so understanding and never interrupted with his own opinions. He made it seem so easy to talk to him. I found myself telling him everything I know in hopes that he would respond alike. When I was done telling him my story he just started laughing. He assured me that he wasn't laughing directly at me but at the situation. It appeared that his story really wasn't much different from my own situation. He commented on the fact that maybe everyone goes through this type of madness when they cross over into the life. We talked the rest of the night away and in no time Dawn approached. He invited me to stay the day at his place. As he walked out of the room he turned back towards me and smirked. He informed me that his windows were light controlled glass so I could enjoy seeing the sun if I wish. For some reason I did not think this dude would be so cool, but he was. I slept like a king and awoke to this dude names Raphael. He was David's right hand, so that meant that everything went through him before it reaches David. I chilled with him that night so he could see that I didn't mean David any harm. It didn't take him long to realize that I had a crush on David and he found that funny. We became cool or at least as cool as one could get with Raphael. He was the type of dude that took his job seriously. The eleven other dudes answered to him and reported everything that went on throughout the house. Raphael found it cool that I stopped drinking and told me so. I asked him about Janus but he said that was a story I should hear about from David. David walked around the house with very little on and even thou I tried not to stare I found myself looking. I took the opportunity by asking him about Janus. He froze for a second then led me out to the balcony. He held his beautiful silk robe that when the lights hit it correctly is show the silhouette of his body. Damn, this dude was really sexy.

David said, "Janus is no different than Christina; sorry I believe you call her Elizabeth. They both seek Joseph's blood but what neither one of them understands is that the blood is no more than just blood if they consume it. That's what makes you and your friends so much different from them. If this blood is truly the blood of the falling Vaingels they would never gain the attributes that started changing you and your friends. For beings like them, his blood is just blood and it may give them the ability to walk in daylight for some time. It may even give them new levels of strength and power but it will never cure them… They will never become true immortals. That is the true hatred between our races. If a werewolf abandons his humanity and allows the beast to take control; then like most animals he'll become a slave to his instinct as well as a slave to the moon. Vampires however it will never matter if they are true or not to their nature, the sun will destroy them all the same. They must feed until the true death claims them. True blood Werewolves are more like Vaingels because unlike vampires we can walk in the daylight. I can choose to change into an animal or will myself to remain human. Just like all vampires and some Werewolves they seek a way out; they seek true immortality. It's funny… you would think one whom has lived as long as we have, would not fear death. It breaks my heart to realize that instead of trying to help you their choosing to use you to gain their immortality as if you would know how to avoid the grand design. You would believe that one as old as they would understand you have no more control over the blood that runs through your body than they have over the blood that runs through theirs. A part of me wishes I could chased him out of Philadelphia, so you and your friends would truly be safe but like Christina; they are part of the clan that I do have a treaty with and we have free reign in each other's spectrum. As much as I would love to help you and your friends my hands are tied. As much as Janus would like to have the one who bares the voice. He must act according to protocol. For as long as the mortal race have no proof of our existence and he does nothing to directly threaten our existence I cannot stop him. Sadly my Xavier, Janus is far older than me and even if he did, I'm not sure if I could stop him. Now, there's a possibility that if he discover this George is no longer with you and he was the voice. Janus may simply leave unless he too wants the blood. By the gods! To drink the blood of one soul that is that old… He truly would be almost invincible."

"Did you know Joseph was buried here?"

"Ha, Ha, Ha… Xavier, I knew no more about Joseph than any other immortal. Let alone! His resting place because if I did I would have seen to it that no one disturbed his prison. At least not until I could give him the true death! If… it's even possible for Joseph to truly die!"

"I just can't understand why Janus will not leave us alone and let us figure things out for ourselves. Even he has to know we did not ask for this and if we're working this hard to prevent Joseph from killing us. We sure as hell are not going to bend over for Janus to do it. I think that is what Elizabeth seen in us. That we were willing to fight for our lives at any cost."

"Believe it or not that is one of the things that I admire about you and your friends. You're all fighters. One would believe that once the voice was gone and the rest of your friends are left to their own devices. You would be easy pickings but you are showing a rare strength of power if I may say. The idea that you guys can still focus and work together as a clan. Joseph may have used you to get to this George but he underestimated your groups bond. I think you guys are much more powerful than he expected or he expects to use all of you to rip through the Great Mist and return home."

"So you believe the great Mist exists. I read about it in the Book of Zarasgale. "

"There's no reason to doubt it. I have lived long enough to know even if I am not strong enough to break through the Great Mist; that doesn't mean it's not there. I realize all of this is new to you but in 1000 years you will come to understand there is a lot you will never understand."

With that David covered his face with his hands and started to cry. I realized he was talking about something greater than just Janus. I felt his helplessness so I walked up behind him. I turned him around and held him into my chest. I started to caresses his hair and comfort him. Holding so close to me, the smell of this hair lingered in the air. I lift his face up to mine and told him there was no reason to be sad and kissed him. First I gave him pecks then a full passion kiss. Then it happened… I guess the lack of blood or my hormones needing release… All I know is that one moment we were talking and the next thing I know; I was kissing him along his long smooth neck and working my hands over his soft lean body. I worked my hands across his body with such passion that you would have thought we were making a porn. I could feel my penis responding to his affection and wanted more. As I slowly carried him to his bedroom without breaking our kiss I knew I need to be inside of him. As we moved towards his room I could hear his heart beat with mine and know this was right. When we reached his bed and I achieved my goal… it was wonderful! We made love for hours and it felt so right. Sucking on his chest and working my way up to his soft sweet lips. David worked his way down to my man hood was more than I could stand and I released like never before in my life but we kept going. Knowing that we both wanted this more than anything else at that moment only heightened the experience for both of us. We continued for most of the night then sleep took us. I awoke several times just to make sure that it really happened and fell back asleep with him in my arms. David smelled so good that his scent followed me into my dreams. I dreamt of a field of flowers and a stream that was so clear that I could see straight to the bottom and could make out all the fish swimming around… it was beautiful. I didn't want to awake. Then from the stream I saw two eyes that for a moment it felt like George. I know I was bugging but I felt him and know he wasn't dead. Somehow through my peace of mind George was able to show himself to me. He just looked at me as if he was lost. Then the dream changed and in my mind I saw my love, my Elizabeth and she was in a dark room. She seemed so scared and alone. I could not make out anything that was around her but know she was in Danger. I awoke to David sitting at the foot of the bed asking me if I was ok. Of course, I played it off especially since we just made love and I didn't want him to know I had just dreamt of my Elizabeth. I told him that I was just a little worried about my friends and that I might need to go and check on them. He agreed and told me that when the time came for us to all meet, all I needed to do was let him know.

I returned to them that night and filled them in on where I been. They seemed a little bothered at first but then after thinking about it became pretty cool with it. Garrett seemed quite curious about how David's house was laid out. It puzzled him that the windows were prepared for vampires. As if he gets those types of guests often. Landis didn't trust David right from the door but knew that we needed to get answers. After I explained to him everything David told me. He seemed pretty cool with it. Surprisingly he was one of the first to be on my side about all of us meeting David. I think Garrett was reluctant only out of loyalty to George. You know in some way he felt the need to protect us the way George would have, but after some coaching he too agreed.

They told me that while I was gone Peter returned to Janus. Peter needed answers regardless if he was under Janus control or not. They also informed me that they were all going to meet Janus if only to make a truce. A part of me knew this was coming as much as I didn't like it, I had to agree. I mean after hearing Elizabeth's side of the story it would only be fair to hear Janus as well. I understood there was a possibility that Janus would lie to us. The reality is whatever they really wanted with us was their secret to keep. Zack laughed as he pointed out whatever it was they all were willing to die over it. We realize we were new players in an old game. I asked, "How do we know Janus did not help Elizabeth awaken the master. Then she double crossed him. For all we know this could have been Janus game and Elizabeth fucked it up. We start debating what could the master possibly have that would benefit Janus and Elizabeth. Elizabeth told us about how important the blood was but yet she gave it to us."

Marco said, "Let's not forget that the blood really didn't do much for us until we shared it."

Vinnie said, "But even after sharing it. The blood gave all of us different gifts and those gifts grew only after we feed off each other."

Landis said, "Don't forget Janus talked about how it was forbidden for any of us to be made, but yet he made Peter without a second thought."

I told them, "Well, that's not actually true because Janus is not a Vaingels so he fed his blood to Peter so he could control him… You know like Igor. I was the one that feed Peter before he was truly changed over. So, if anyone turned peter it was me."

Garrett Said, "Actually Elizabeth killed Peter after he feed on you. George and I went to save him. George gave Peter the choice to drink the blood of the master and he told George yes. George was not sure if you could be trusted. George asked Peter to put on a show to see where your loyalty fell… face it dude, you was kind of an ass when it came to her and us."

Casper was sitting in the corner as if he wasn't listening to anything we were saying then he said, "If the blood was so important why did not Elizabeth bargain it for a truce? Think about it she had the blood and she knew about Janus. So what's up with that?

There were so many questions that needed answers that we weren't sure who to trust. A few days passed before Peter returned and told us everything was arranged. We were to meet Janus at Penn's landing right where the bus crosses the overpass. That way we all could see if anyone was coming from any direction. Peter made it very clear that Janus didn't trust us any more than we trusted him. Especially after how many of his friends we picked off. Garrett plus Landis picked up the fact that Janus knowledge that the vampires and werewolves knew each other. We knew we had to be careful because he was very desperate at this point to get whatever it was he thought we had. When we got there Janus had six goons that we could see standing all around him. As we approached him I realized he was the dude that tried to pick me up outside of Walnut street coffee shop. He still looked like a dude out of place. He stood in the Gateway smiling as we approached. When the dude shook my hand I told him I thought he was gay the first time we met and he just laughed. He told me he was testing me to see if I could remember him or sense him especially after his mind attack but when I didn't; he realize I was not as strong as he thought.

Drew said, "You went through a lot to get us here so what's up."

Janus smiled and said, "So, you want to get right to it! I admire that."

Garrett said, "With everything that has happened. It doesn't seem that you're leaving us much choice… it's obvious that we have something you want and since you can't take it from us by force you call this little gathering."

Janus said, "That's not exactly true. I could have taken just what I wanted but that would leave me in an awkward position. See, to come and just take him would mean I would have to kill the rest of you. That wouldn't be wise especially on my part, because of your group's closeness. Plus the fact that you and your cousin are unicorns in this world. Not even I am foolish enough to touch you. That stupid bitch Christina had no idea what she released unto this earth. In seeking immortality, she awakened the devil himself. You and your friends are just his Fuck'n spawns. In killing you and your friends would open me to be vulnerable to the one I seek. I have no doubt if I killed you he would seek my death. Then the most amazing thing occurred. You all have shown great potential in your new life. So much so, that I find myself in an awkward position."

Garrett said, "Ha, ha, ha, let me fill in the blanks for you. You want George and yet you fear to kill us. Because when he gains control of his powers he will kill you. So you use those parties to do your dirty work but they fail. Now you have to get your hands dirty and risk George's wrath. Question is after George is done with you. Where will that leave you friends? So take my advice and simply walk away."

Janus said, "You're very smart for a protector but you left some things out."

Garrett got angry and said to him "No not really. Your arrogance tells me that even though you're quite old you're not very bright. In fact, I'm confident enough to tell you George is gone. He may even be dead! I am only telling you this because now I know you did not get rid of the master that turned Xavier. In fact if you had that kind of power you would not be playing these games. I think! You're a powerful vampire but we are something different. The parties you sent to test us have shown you that you don't possess the power to force us to do anything so now you wish us to compromise and work something out. Specially since you have discovered why we are unicorns. You are no different than any of the others. Your fear of my families wrath ensures that you will not raise a hand against us."

Marco started laughing and said, "Give Garrett a cigar. You figured him out… By the look in this dude's eyes I can tell you are right."

Landis said, "Marco chill out… Janus just tells us what the hell you want with us and then leave us alone. The time for games has passed. You're not going to get us to turn against each other and you're not going to kill us. One thing we know for sure, that together we're too powerful of a force to be reckoned with!"

Janus said, "Your threats may have power over Christina but they hold no will over me. Child if I wished your death then you would all be dead. What I wished was the one that bared the voice and since he is no longer with your little Group there is no reason to kept you alive."

As Janus finished speaking he froze and just stared into space. None of us was sure what was happening and as we looked at each other wondering what was the hell's going on. His men ran over to him and started calling him by name. One of them started to shake him but Janus would not respond. He stared into space as if he was somewhere else, sweat started pouring from his forehead and his body started to shake as if something was frightening him. As we slowly backed away from the dude more of his crew started coming in closer to him. We weren't sure what was going on but we knew we needed to get the hell out of there. Landis signaled us to leave and we started to back away as his men came over to him. We turned then walked away and did not look back. George once said he believed that you should never run from one that is immortal for it draws their attention. We walked straight across the over pass to Chestnut Street and did not look back. We said nothing to each other but we all knew that this was not over. For one of us bored a power they did not share with us or someone else is involved. Once we reach 10th street Garrett said, "It seems George might still be with us after all." Everyone started laughing but me. I kind of feared that if George bored that kind of power then why didn't he shows himself to us sooner. Something told me that Garrett didn't fully consider what he was saying but felt he needed to comfort us. He and Landis just looked at each other then lead our group back to the main line of center city. We stopped off at Rittenhouse square and chilled there for a while. As we sat there and checked out all the people around us I just had to ask but Marco beat me to it, "If it was George and he is still alive then that would be fucked up for him not to let us know. Special if he could simply tell us through our minds." I comment that I agreed and as we talked me felt the presence of someone and it wasn't Janus. I looked around to see if I could see anyone but there was no one there.

Garrett said, "Look there is nothing we can do tonight so let us just relax and figure out what just happened. George maybe still with us but then again it could be the women from New York that saved us or prehaps my family. "

I asked, "What women?"

Landis said, "Sorry Xavier but she asked us not to speak her name to anyone specially you. She even called you by name. She believed that your heart would endanger all of us. So we gave her our word and promised George not to tell you about his family becuase of the danger you would put us all in, if you told Elizabeth. In truth I wouldn't have made the promise if you showned any real sign of changing before he dyed."

That pissed me off so I asked them if Peter met her and knows about George and Garrett's family. Peter looked at me and said, "Yes."

I told them, "This was fucked up, Peter led us almost to our death but he knows about her and the rest of you are cool with it but fuck me. I can't be trusted. I'm the one that is the weak link."

Landis said, "Yea. You're the one that keep secrets and feed them to us as you felt we needed to know them. Unlike Peter who told us from the first night that Janus has been calling for him to return to him. If it wasn't for George's blood he would not had been able to fight it and would have already betrayed us. We know that blood bonds are real because he was honest enough to tell us that he has one with Janus. We're not sure how strong our blood bond to the master Joseph is and that maybe the only reason he is not looking for us, because he can make us come to him whenever he is ready to do what he wishes with us. Did Elizabeth tell you about that? I know for a fact that she did not tell us."

Garrett said, "Everyone calm down… Xavier, just let it go. When the time comes we will share everything we all know and so will you. We are all friends and only wish to survive this hell so, let's trust that when the time comes! We will all have sharing time?"

I said, "Cool!"

With that I left them and returned to David. I had to get away from them and think. I knew that Landis was right but it still hurt that they didn't trust me. What was meant to be a night turned out to be a few weeks! I keep thinking about what Landis was saying until I knew it was time to introduced David to the rest of the guys. He told me to bring them all by so we could get to know each other. I reminded him that they didn't need blood so it wouldn't be difficult to host for them. David seemed to hit it off right away with Zack and Vinnie of course. Landis didn't trust him and maybe because he didn't really trust me. Garrett told me to give it time and stop trying to force everything to happen on my time table. A part of me knows he was right but I just wanted to put all of this behind us. Marco and Drew seemed to like hanging with Raphael. Maybe because they could get high and Raphael had really good stuff. He would take them with him every night to practice and party. Garrett and David seemed to share a secret from the first day they met but I wasn't sure how that could be. David shared things with Garrett that he wouldn't allow us to touch. Garrett seemed to love all the old books David owned and kept saying how George would have loved to read some of David's books. I think he missed George a lot more than he let on. Even when I would talk with him, he didn't seem to be all there. The more we hung around David the more we came to realize how far apart we all were becoming. It hurt me to realize that the one I couldn't tolerate was the one that held us all together. George must have really loved the fact that we were pulling apart slowly without him.

David opened his library up to Garrett and the others so they could learn about the myths of Vaingels and the other creatures of the Mist. Then Garrett came across a place in one of the books David owned. Garrett realized that they all had been there. Garrett cross referenced that book with some others in David's mass collection and came across a Grimoire of a witch named Tulia. Garrett asked David about it but David seemed surprised that Garrett could read the pages. Garrett told him the witches name and that the book was of earth magic. He even could make out the name Odessa but a lot of the book escaped his knowledge for he told David that magical history really was George's thing. Then told David about the witch that George took them to see and how she took them into her club somewhere in New York. He told David that they had gone back looking for the club but could not find it. David looked at Garrett as if he believed everything Garrett was telling him but then told Garrett that the book he was reading was a witch's diary that he received centuries ago. That if it held any real secrets then they would be only important to another witch. He then asked was he able to read the book and Garrett ensured him that he could read some of it. That him and George use to read up on things like this for years but never found anything that was real. David asked Garrett if he would mind if they practiced some things together for a bit. David ran into another room to retrieve a book and started asking Garrett to try to do some of the spells. Of course, Garrett was able to read most of the words but nothing happened. Garrett told us that it felt like he could feel the energy but just could not pull off the spell. David seemed to be so fascinated that he spun around in his chair and clapped hands with the biggest smile on him face. We all looked at him as if he lost it. He told us that there was tales of vampires that could fly or even connect to a small part of the weather but the idea that one could do magic... true magic, that was unheard of. Garrett could be the missing link and that is what all this is really over. Garrett and George could tap into the spiritual nexus. David then told us that it was possible that our gifts were magical and not inherited from the blood itself. He said a lot of other stuff but I didn't understand. He got up and walked out of the room and went to use his phone. He called someone and they talked for sometime before David returned to us, telling us that upon the next night we were going to meet someone that could better answer our questions and no matter what; we must allow him to do all the talking. Raphael and the guys brought women in to hang with us for the night. I don't think I need to tell you what we did but it was way over do. Man I never been a part of an orgy before but this was past fun. We smoked, danced and made love all night. As I said before Raphael was a cool Dude. At some point of the night I realized that David wasn't with us so I went in search of him. I found him in his room alone lying across his bed. I climbed on top of him from behind and started to kiss his soft neck. We started making out until we ended up making love again. For some reason I found his company more satisfying than the party in the other room.

David asked if I wanted to join my friends but I told him no. For some reason I felt closer to him than I did to anyone at that moment. It must have been around 4 a.m. when I decide to join the others. They were lying asleep all around the room. Looking at them reminded me of all the college parties we used to have except without naked girls lying all around. I sat in one of the chairs cross the room and one of the girls' awoke. She crawled over to me and started to taste my manhood as I watched the other guys sleep. Raphael was the next one to awake and climbed upon her from the backside. He made love to her as she pleased me. At one point I forgot that she was there as I locked eyes with Raphael. The more he got into what he was doing I was able to see his eyes change. They glowed as if there were flashlights inside his head. I got so turned on that I was forced to join him in his ecstasy, we used her as two dogs would fight over a bite toy, pulling her towards ourselves, forgetting that she was pleasing us both. Then we both got up and walked away from her as if she was nothing. I returned to David's bed and slept the day away. When I awoke David had gone shopping for new clothes for us and had mine lying on the corner dress dummy. I smile because I never seen a mannequin carved out of wood and in someone's home but I thought it was cool. I dressed then joined the guys in the living room. Some of them just smiled as I entered the room and Landis was the first to point out if I slept well in David's ass or was he sleeping in mine. I got pissed and flared my fangs at him but Garrett laughed and told David that we were now ready to go wherever he was taking us.

I wasn't sure were David was leading all of us to but I wanted to find out as well. He took Garrett and the rest of us to old city to see someone I long forgot. I cursed my life as we approach the home of my love Elizabeth. Then Raphael and the other eleven stood outside, they howled as if it was a full moon out. At that moment there behavior puzzled me. David knocked on the door and Lady Ling answered but looked puzzled. She acknowledged David as if they knew each other and then invited us in. I could sense Landis looking at me as if he knew something. As we walked past her, she made eye contact with me as if to question why I was there. I felt a little awkward as I entered because I remember returning there when I first came back to Philadelphia but Lady Ling didn't answer the door. She led us to the sitting room. It was still as comfortable and as beautiful as ever. Like David she seemed a taste for very antique furniture. Her furniture seemed as if it came from the old country itself. You know tables and chairs with a lot of carvings in the wood. They seem to be very victorian to me but I'm not a good judge for eras of furniture. This was becoming very awkward for me quickly and I knew I needed to confront the problem. So as everyone else took a seat I stood. I introduce them to lady Ling and lady Ling to my friends.

I said, "Before we began I want you all to know this was Elizabeth's home. Lady Ling is her housekeeper and this is where we came when we left you."

Landis said, "So you and lady Ling know each other because of Elizabeth. Did she helped you leave the town too or was that all Elizabeth's doing."

Xavier said, "No, she had nothing to do with it. After discussing things with Elizabeth and her friends I felt it was the wisest thing to do. I wanted to keep her alive and safe."

Garrett said, "From whom Xavier? Us"

Xavier said, "No! I mean! Yes, I feared George was going to

kill her. I'm sorry but none of you can deny George's rage, or how vindictive his nature was... He hated Elizabeth and if he had a chance he would've killed her I know it in my heart. I know y'all all want to protect George's reputation but I know you all know it's true."

Landis said, "Xavier thanks you for your honesty. We already knew that you came that night because Drew followed you. I'm even willing to admit George was going to destroy Elizabeth if he had the chance but the fact is there is too much that Elizabeth knew that we did not know. Unlike you George would put his pride aside as well as his vindictive nature to see to it that we all survived."

The room grew quiet for a moment as everyone just stared at me. I felt so guilty about what I said. A part of me always blame George for being the way he was but the truth is we would not have survived if he was not George. I turned my back to them because I couldn't face them as I got myself back together for some reason I became very emotional. It took David to break the silence as he made a slight gesture and stated the obvious.

David said, "how touching. Now does everyone feel much better? Good! Now to the subject that brings us here. Ling darling, I have a few questions that puzzles me and I'm sure it puzzling them too. That is if they understood who and what you truly are."

Lady Ling said, "David we have never had a problem. So what brings you to my home? I have done nothing to violate the laws or your rules of our treaty. So…"

David seemed to show he was quite annoyed in a fashion that reminded me of George, I wasn't sure if it might have been a gay thing. He began to tap his fingers on the table that sat beside the sofa he was sitting in. His eyes rolled up into his head so slow that I could tell a lot more was being said from their gestures though they were using very little words.

David stated, "That is so true, but I'm not here because of a law. We are here because one of them can read one of the legendary Grimoire of Odessa. I was led to believe that only a witch could read the ancient writings of Odessa. So you understand what brings me here. I am puzzled why this Garrett can read such a book and then to make matters worse! His cousin turns out to bare the voice."

Lady Ling said, "If you are accusing us of something David, then please… State it!"

David said, "I may be confused by I was led to believe that vampires could not tap into the nexus. That is why usually most dark witches and vampires share lairs."

Lady Ling said, "Exactly what are you getting at David and why are you bringing it to me?"

Looking sarcastically David said, "I'm beginning to wonder if these children being made were truly an accident or one of you and Elizabeth's sick experiments. Because if they are! I am not happy! So, you are going to explain to me why he is able to read the legendary Grimoire and now!"

Lady Ling respond, "First of all, I have no idea what you're talking about. Besides David, you have no power here. As you just stated I'm a dark witch and you are foolish to come into my home with assumptions. Even though it is quite clear that is forbidden for me to cast spells outside of my home. We are not outside. So destroying you will not be breaking any law but before I do. Let me explain this to you, David! So you can understand our true purpose. The one that bares the voice and his cousin are believed to come from the rare bloodline of the first ones. So in them lies the potential to cross the various lines of the legend. They bear the ability to make the impossible possible."

David said smiling, "Well, thank you lady Ling. See! That was not very hard."

Lady Ling said, "No, it was not but you have now gained rare knowledge. Quite unfortunately for you none of you shall leave here alive."

David rose and began to walk to the door then stopped. He turned and looked back at Lady Ling. Raised his hand to his chest and smirked. I seen George do that enough time's to know David was about to put on a show. Gay guys seem to like the dramatics.

David said, "Since you gave me knowledge, I think it's only fitting that I return the favor. Did you know why witches celebrate all hollow Eve? Well… Let me tell you! Many, many centuries ago a day called hallows Eve was when the witches convinced man that wolves were evil wretched creature and chased them from their town. What man did not know and new age witches have forgotten is that when a pack of wolves' howls it shatters a witches connection to the nexus. Which renders her powerless for some time and that is why witches of the old world carries wands or crystals. Something to harness there power for when or if they ever ran across these wretched evil creatures. You are not that lucky. Gentlemen please leave us, so lady Ling can better learn from this mistake. "

David then ordered us to get up and wait for him outside. He made it quite clear that he and Lady Ling had a few things to straighten out. Something told me they were not going to talk and the sounds that came from her home confirmed it. David stayed in there for some time. When he came out it was Raphael that approached him. They talked for a few moments but it was quite clear that Raphael was not comfortable with David having such a confrontation alone. David Blew it off as nothing and stated once you guys howled after we went inside she was without her powers. This entire visit was nothing but an event to force her and Elizabeth to show their hands. As we all got back into the cars. I could look into David eyes and see that this was far from over. Raphael made sure that David understood that this would not end here and that she would be back. David looked into his eyes and made a comment like only in our dreams. I felt sorrow in my heart because at that moment I knew David killed her. Raphael told David that he would have the cleaners take care of everything. David made a point that he wanted Lady Ling's Grimoire and her wands. This is a side of David I wasn't comfortable with seeing, because a part of me knew that we were in the middle of some kind of war that we did not understand. I was kind of nervous watching David straighten his clothes and pull back his hair. As we drove down the street I assumed returning to his apartment. I remembered how he destroyed the vampire in Rittenhouse Square with no remorse, so killing her would have meant nothing to him.

I asked David if everything was okay and he looked at me frantically then responded, "Yes."

Garrett said, "Take your time and get yourself together. I'm a little confused with what just happened but apparently George was right. Elizabeth meant to destroy us."

David responded placing his hand on Garrett leg, "no not destroyed you but use you. Somehow she planned to use your blood rights to lift the veil. What a stupid foolish woman to believe that lady Ling would aid her in such a task."

I responded, "Elizabeth and Lady Ling were friends there is no way one would betray the other."

David turned to me and said, "Xavier, you have a lot to learn about immortals and even more to learn about dark witches. Their loyalties lie only to power. Lady Ling was willing to destroy this city if it meant that she would gain the power to rip away the veil.

There's a lot more going on than you can ever imagine. It is a good thing that Elizabeth is not here. With her out of the picture it will allow me time to find out exactly what she was planning. It was no accident that she freed to Joseph. I believe when Joseph attacked you she believed you where the bloodline that everyone was looking for. She had no idea that the essence Joseph picked up from your body belonged to George and Garrett. That is the real reason why she saved you. That is the reason why she gave you the blood. Did you not find it odd that after feeding you the blood she expected to bare great power? Power she could manipulate to her will."

Everyone in the car started laughing at me. For some reason he took great humor in the idea that Elizabeth was using me. The one I loved betrayed me for a myth. She risked my life and all of my friends because she wanted power she could never possess. Then to top it all off the only one who could give her that power she seek hated her. As ironic as it was I could not find humor in it. I betrayed Georges trust and love for her. I convinced myself that he was the enemy and I needed to protect her, she was a delicate innocent flower who saved me from a vicious heartless being. But the truth of the matter was not only did she awakened Joseph she allows him to attack me, to feed on me and then to torment me. Then when I believe death was so close she reveals herself as my great Savior. They found it funny but in that moment my heart was breaking. David looked at us with confusion, as if a joke was told that he did not understand. As tears ran down my face I truly realized how hurt and betrayed I was. Vinnie tried to comfort me by telling me the heart wants what the heart wants. As much as George was trying to warn me, I loved her and there was nothing to be ashamed of.

Garrett said, "Enough everyone! Xavier, your love for Elizabeth was real but we did try to warn you. George more than any of us told you there were things in her mind that he did not quite understand when their minds merged. He even went as far as to warn her that in time he would figure it out. I know all of you may have taken Georges overbearing personality for granted at times but I know you loved him as much as he did love you. My cousin can be very stubborn at times but he was never stupid. We've been studying the magic of the nexus for 15 years before even meeting you guys. How do you think we came to understand the three basic elements of nature? Light, darkness and chaos! I am the first to admit that George was into the mystical arts more than I. In fact that was one of the biggest reasons we always argued. I feared that something like this could someday happen to him and if he trained all of you. Then you would be in Danger too."

Landis said, "So you're telling us it was George's fault this happened!?"

Garrett responded shaking his head, "No, George never displayed any type of real power that would draw this type of attention,beyond heightened senses. Sometimes his senses were too heighten, which would force me to protect him a lot of the times. What I think is that Joseph had to find someone with George's untapped powers so he could gain whatever it is that he needs to remain free. So in looking for this power he found all of you. Xavier, George never told you what happened that night we were bitten, did he?"

With great shame I said, "No!"

David interrupted Garrett's story and suggested that we wait until we returned to the condominium. Where he could continue to tell his story and comfort me. I think we all knew this was going to be a story worth telling. Garrett agreed and road the rest of the way in silence. The fear of what Garrett was going to tell us created some kind of nervousness throughout the rest of the ride. I oddly took comfort in the fact that this was not my fault. I truly was a victim of circumstance. Circumstance created by

George out of the greed of people. As much as he always blamed me for being irresponsible and careless, it turned out to be that it was he that bought this upon us.

Chapter 13
The Bond of Bonds

Once we got to David's home and made ourselves comfortable. Garrett reluctantly continued to tell the story of how George and he were created. Apparently George had a dream that you all was in Danger. The next day he awoke and called Landis and demanded that you all come to the shcool. when you didn't show up. the next few days he asked poeple to find you so you two could talk. He even hung around the school looking for me. When he was not able to find anyone that seen me, he decided to have dinner then return to work early. Garrett thought he was just over exaggerating as usual. Something that we all knew George had a habit of doing, but this time his fear was accurate. When I ran past him when I entered the school he called Garrett. Garrett came over and relieved him so that George could go to the bathroom where he seen me in his dream. Apparently that's why he was asking me so many questions, trying to understand what happened to me and what his dream meant. As Garrett told the story I remember how much of an ass I was to him when he was trying to help me. Apparently that morning when they got off of work him and George went to the library. They stayed up all afternoon reading up on the supernatural. George was convinced that something was after all of us but Garrett didn't believe him. Apparently, when George got home he called Landis and asked him to round up all the guys to have them come over to this post that night. He explained his dream to all of them and hoped for a rational explanation. Even as all of them debated about it he knew none of them was even coming close to what he seen in his dream. Garrett told us that was when he actually started believing everything George said. Garrett pointed out he never seen George so scared. The fact that they had made an agreement to guide but never interfere with shit that happens to us he now regrets. It never crossed Garrett's mind that George would be the one in Danger.

For the next few days they argued that he was trying to control us too much and not allowing us to make choices for ourselves. Garrett pointed out the fact that George always followed his heart and trusted that we wouldn't be able to handle what was coming. I laughed at the thought that even Garrett knew George was too controlling. So George contacted some friends that was into the craft as well and told them about everything but they agreed with Garrett. It was at that meeting that George seen Landis getting attacked and we knew we were to go to help him. So after calling out of work we headed over to broad and Spruce. When they got there George told Garrett that they were supposed to walk up Bach Place to 15th Street. He asked Garrett not to go because whatever was to happen it was meant to happen to him. Garrett pointed out that he never seen George as much of a fighter or more scared then at that moment, but if it was meant to happen it was not George's place to change fate. Garrett smiled when he told us how he never back down from a good fight so he went on. He know George was too thin to hold his own in a real battle let alone something this great but if it was for his children he would never back down. As they walked up the alley they felt something move above them and just as they were nearing the end of the block something hit Garrett and knocked him across the alley. Garrett told us how he just laid there as this six foot something tall man held George by his neck. Tears ran down Garrett face as he described how George tried to break free but the Man's grip that was to strong. How George just kept begging him not to hurt his children. The way he described George's behavior wasn't that hard to believe. He told George that he went through a lot of trouble to find him and how George must had laid his essence on half the city. He seemed to enjoy George's begging him to not harm his children and how he would do anything the guy wanted. As tears ran down George's face the guy turned his attention to Garrett and gloated how helpless that Garrett must have felt not being able to protect his cousin. He told Garrett to look carefully as he showed his fangs and kissed George's throat. Garrett told us he still could hear George's screams as that maniac ripped into George's throat like meat. Watching George's blood run all across his clothes and body as if this maniac didn't know how to feed. Garrett described how he laid there while this maniac took great pleasure in causing George Pain and him watching.

How he could hear his fangs break free from George's throat as he looked back at Garrett with a smile. Oddly he took great care to lay George down onto the cold ground. Then he walked over to Garrett and called him the Great protector. He seemed to love Garrett's rage and how he fought with all his strength before he did the same thing to him. Unlike us he returned to George and feed George his blood and told George I have given you an army now use them as I shall someday use you. Then returned to Garrett and told him that his black heart deceives him. He then feed Garrett as well but unlike George he broke Garrett's neck and through Garrett over top of George where he awoke hours later.

For some reason Garrett felt guilty that he did not protect George. Garrett said that he awoke before George and that it was him who took George to Landis's apartment. When they got there that's when they discovered that Landis was attacked.

David said, "Wait, he fed George and you?"

Garrett responded, "Yes, I'm not sure if George could remember that he fed George from his wrist. He said something to George but I can't remember what it was. For some reason he had compassion with George that he showed to no one else. Then he forced me to feed. I remember him walking over to me picking me up forcing his cut wrist into my mouth. He held his wrists against my mouth with such force that I had to fight back. He kept saying to drink dark one, let your body and your rage be one."

David said, "Then that explains it. You and George drink from the source itself therefore you are hybrids. It is one thing to drink the blood of Joseph from a vial or whatever, but is something different to drink directly from the actual source. That is why you and George are much stronger than the others."

Landis said, " George told me that the one that bit him also bit me. why didn't he feed me as well? He left me to drink from George as well. We all drank from the bottle of blood."

David said, "True but you were not chosen to feed directly from your maker. Therefore you are really the children of George. Ha, ha, ha, Joseph truly gave him an army and through George's naivety he powered that army with his own spiritual energy. You all may have feed on George as much as you wish in hopes that you may grow stronger but you will grow to nothing more."

I said, "But we all have shared our blood with Elizabeth so she is George's child as well."

David said, "Sorry my Xavier, but unless she fed from George and he freely shared his soul with her. She is nothing but a vampire with Vaingels blood in her body. The master must give more than just his blood to his offspring but a part of his spirit. That is why it is called a blood bond, for a master could find his children no matter where they are, and then summoned them to him. None of you may be able to find George but trust and believe… George can always find you."

As David talked to us I came to realize that once again George won. He stole my clan from me. By all rights I should have been their master because this was all because of me. Now he's gone but we all owe him for this existence. I listen to David talk and I came to realize how the master used George to get us. Use me to find George, use Elizabeth to control me and used our friends to create a false security in this new life. He was truly an ass. He played us as if one would play chess but none of us knew why nor what was his next move. I think we all wonder if Janus knew that George and Garrett were different from us. David pointed out the fact that if they both fed upon Joseph then why the strange man did only took George. David told Garrett that he knew a few witches of the light and he try to get in contact with them. He insured us if anyone understood what was going on with them, then it would be his friends. I wasn't sure if Garrett trusted David or he was left with no choice. He seemed very interested in everything David promised him. Now Garrett always was more level headed than George so for Garrett to trust in David was not hard to believe. Garrett always gave you the benefit of the doubt until you crossed him. I told them that I needed time to think. They agree and chose to leave me in David's care.

Also they had a lot to think about and a part of me knew they were going to try and find George. If what David was saying then George had to be alive. It was written in the book of Zarasgale that no Vaingels made in the blood can destroy the flow of another so says the Queen Constance. I remember reading that and I didn't understand exactly what it meant until then. I began to wonder that if this Constance exists, then the wall of the mist existed and George would have to be on the other side. As I thought back and tried to remember what Vinnie told me about the dude that took George.

I realize one thing that the book spoke of so many names and any one of those could have been him. As Garrett and the other guys left. I could see it in his eyes that he was not going to leave it there. If there was a way to find George he was going to find it. I stayed with David to think about everything that was happening. It ripped my heart apart to think my Elizabeth used me and what made it even worst was that it was George she really wanted. I asked David if I could borrow his copy of the Book of Zarasgale to study. I know I needed to learn more about these other beings that supposed to exist on the other side of the Mist. The High Queen is the first book of Zarasgale, Apollo the Great is the second book of Zarasgale and, then there is the third book called The Wise. A Alter King was mentioned throughout all three books completely. Now the book also spoke of another name Odessa. From what I gathered; this Odessa and the high Queen Lilith gathered together with the seven councils of the sprites. For some reason they decided it was wise to separate the seven realms. Now there was more stuff with it but I didn't quite understand. I gathered that seven beings came together and through them the rift was created. They named the rift "The Great Mist". The great mist was so powerful that it not only separated man from them but separated the seven realms as well. Then it spoke of how only a few beings possessed the power to cross the rift. Reading the book I came to discover that there is supposed to have been watchers of some type. They and the Legion maintain the order over the great sleep. Then the book is Zarasgale called the man the overseer whom was to answer to the one called Asikis whom was to become queen at one time. I didn't fully understand exactly everything I was reading and the bits I pieced together were a little confusing. I wasn't sure if it was being lost in translation or a lot of the book was missing.

I read the book for hours, sometime days. I can't tell you how many times I got headaches from trying to understand what I was reading. Several nights I would go out with David to get my mind off of the book. I understood what he meant that I was pushing myself too hard but if I was to lead the group I needed to understand everything. It didn't take David long to move me to become his lover and Friend. We did everything together and went clubbing every night. Several times I even tried to drink but it never felt right. I have to admit the more I hung with David the more alive I felt. For some reason David energized me and made me feel complete. Like Elizabeth he made me feel like I could do anything. He never concerned himself with blaming me for anything but rather how he could help me figure out how we can change things to the better. He even started reading the book with me. We cross reference many of the names that were mentioned in the book of Zarasgale with the books he possessed. David was the one who came to discover that this alter King might live in the realm of man. Even David became confused with a lot of the writing and wasn't quite sure how to interpret what was written. The one word that stood out to him was Grange. We both believe that it meant some type of Temple, but was not sure of its location.

What seemed like weeks for us were actually months and then David brought to my attention that the witches of the light had been contacting him. The problem was that there were too many distinctions of power flowing throughout Philadelphia for them to reveal themselves at this time. Apparently Lady Ling's death brought many dark witches out of hiding in hopes to gain her Grimoire. It seemed as if David found it quite amusing that her death cause such a shift of power in their community. David told me that we were no longer safe, even with him and that I needed to return to my friends. I needed to warn them of all that had happened for the witches of darkness were at war. Besides battling with each other they are seeking control over the other realms. David pointed out that he and the twelve had to prepare as well for the war that was coming.

Then he told me that he had to go and see the master of the vampire that he killed. That apparently he was not alone the night he attacked us in Rittenhouse Square but ensured me not to worry. I informed him that I would like to join him and straighten this shit out but he told me no. That Sammy and him had a past so nothing would happen to Dangerous. He would return to me as soon as possible. Of course I followed him and his crew. Thanks to Elizabeth I managed to cover a lot of ground from the roof tops. It became harder when the turned onto JFK boulevard so I used my speed to keep up with them. They ended up of the other side of lemon hill drive. I had a bit of a time following them but I did it and we ended up on the other side of Lemon hill right next to West Sedgley Drive. I never been to this side of the park but it was kind of cool. David and his friends parked on the lemon hill drive side of the road right behind each other cars. Then I seen four other cars pull off of West Sedgley Drive and they parked about twenty feet away from David's Crew. The last Car was right across the street from a Ben Franklin statue. They all stayed in their cars for about ten minutes then Raphael, David's right hand dude got out of the car and walked across the street over to a square plate that's looked like a statue use to be there but was gone. Then a dude got out of the other group of cars. I could sense he was a vampire so I cloaked myself quickly. Raphael looked back at me as if he knew I followed them and smirked. He turned back and looked at the vampire that approached him. They spoke for a few minutes and it seemed as if the vampire didn't like what Raphael said to him because he postured by showing his fangs. Raphael just stood there as if he was not moved by the dude's actions. As Raphael stood with crossed arms as the vampire turned and went back to the car that was behind the one he got out of. Then he spoke to someone through the window before opening the door. I got a little nervous as another dude got out of this car and six others with him. This Dude was no joke; he looked as if he was from Greece with the hairy chest and clean shaven face. He had on an off white suit and his hair pulled back. I wasn't too sure what was happening but then David's crew got out of their cars. One of them opened David's door as he stepped out. It looked like an old mob movie but more fashionable. David had on the same nylon outfit his friends were wearing and his hair was pushed back by needles like Chinese women wear. At this point I understood why they dressed like that, so if they had to change into wolves they wouldn't be nude changing back. Anyway David walked over to the dude and I focus to hear what they were saying. David made a point to stop and speak with Raphael first and I heard Raphael tell David that they did not care that they were in his region and that they wanted vengeance for the one he killed in Rittenhouse Square. David looked at Raphael for a moment then turned to the one that was standing about ten feet away from them. David walked over to him and repeated what Raphael said but he called the dude by the name of Sammy.

David said, "Well. Sammy you're looking as sexy as ever. What has it been... A hundred years?

Sammy said, "Cut the shit David... You killed one of my offspring and I need to know why?

"Sammy why would I break our treaty and risk wars again. Your young up start choose to enter my region without provisions. I thought it was agreed that after our break-up, neither clan would enter the others region unannounced and maybe your vamp didn't know that, but lesson learned."

"David your charm will not work this time. He was a duke's son and retribution is being called for."

"Really... You're willing to risk all-out war over this foolish child that dared to attack me in the open. Let alone in front of my home. You're risking a lot... What aren't you telling me Sammy darling?"

"I've told you all need to know. From this point forwards Philadelphia will fall under my control. As for you and your dogs, you have twenty hour to leave or less."

"Sammy, your blood licking pawns is strong but we both know

you're no match for the twelve. So you tell me what really is going on. While I'm choosing to remain patience; Breaking our treaty and standing in front of me is bad enough but to threaten me over a young pup is crazy."

"David, you're not in any position to challenge me on this. You will lose!"

"Well, since you asked so nicely I will have to say…. NO! Now go to hell!"

Sammy got so pissed that he went to slap David. I panic and mentally called the guys for help. Apparently David did not need it because in a matter of minutes he avoided the attack and responded by knocking Sammy across the field with some form of martial arts move. They fought for about a few minutes before an older dude got out of one of the cars. He walked over towards them and fanned his hands apart. David and Sammy both fell back. He walked over to Sammy speaking in a language I didn't understand but apparently David did.

David stood up and said, "So it's you… Akakios! You rose to claim the voice… and you really believe I would just turn it over to you. Perhaps you believe you're dealing with a child but understand this; I am not giving anything to you or your goons so leave Philadelphia while you are still alive."

Akakios moved so quickly that I could not even see it and David was knocked in the wall of the Ben Franklin statue. I closed my eyes and started really calling my friends to hurry. Then I heard thunder and something that caused me to open my eyes. Across the field I saw Raphael and the others turn into wolves and as they attacked the vampires. The rain came pouring down out of nowhere. I mean it was now raining and they were at an all-out war; the twelve wolves were no joke they were fuck'n shit up, but the vampires were just as quick. The fact that there were more vampires than wolves I was afraid they might lose. David was almost holding his own and returned blow for blow but Akakios was just too old and powerful. He finally over powered David knocking him twenty feet across the field. He started to approach David while getting himself together. (This dude seemed to be very vain.)

Even though the twelve was holding their own against the other vampires they were not able to get away and protect David. It was as if the vampire plan to keep them separated. Akakios said something to David in a language I could not understand but it was clear that David did. I watched David struggled to get himself together while he was lying on the ground. Then the wind started picking up as if a storm came out of nowhere. I was forced to cover my ears as the thunder roared. The ground shook as if an earthquake hit the area we were in. It was so strong that I fell from the tree and as I stumble to get myself together I watched as all of them were in the same condition. Well, all of them except Akakios stood over David. He was about to kill David when something I couldn't believe happened. Out of nowhere creatures with long fangs and claws appeared. They had fur that was as long as a loin's mane but it looked kind of liked mixed Grays. Then I remembered them because they were the creatures I dreamt about fighting Elizabeth but this time it was hundreds of them. Five of them appeared out of the air from behind David and bit into Akakios. They ripped Akakios apart like paper. One bit into his face like a dog would catch a Frisbee and the others grabbed his limbs. David was on his butt and in shock. These creatures were no joke and they were three times bigger than the twelve. They bit into the vampires and tossed them to one another as if playing catch. Blood went everywhere. Their speed did not seem to matter to them because they moved as if they could see where the Vampires were going to be thrown. Once it was over, one of them looked directly at me as if they were about to attack and Raphael yelled no. One approached David and stood straight up. He and the others looked more like wolf men than wolves and the one that stood in front of David held his hand out to help David up. David looked as if he was taken back but responded. David stood up to about these dudes chest and the others walked around the wolves as if they were protecting their cubs. David asked the one in front of him what they were and he just responded, "We are Le'gionos." Then David asked his name and he tilted his head as if he didn't understand.

He responded, "We are Le'gionos."

David must had felt a little confused because he placed his hand on his chest and said, "David! And you are?"

He responded again, "No, You are Le'gionos, we are Le'gionos. We see you through the Mist, we come! We always see! You…"

With that they turned and looked at each other and then he howled like they do in the movies and they stepped into nothingness but vanished. David yelled that he wishes to join them but the one that was near him said, "No, Too young, you need to stay here. The twelve must protect you." Then he turned and followed the others. David stood there for a moment then fell to his knees and covered his face in great disappointment. I sensed his sadness so I ran to him. I stood behind him and placed my hand on his shoulder so that he could feel my presence. As we stood there waiting for David to get himself together I watched as all the vampires bodies begin to disintegrate and turned to dust. With blood all over the field I could feel my friends finally arriving. Landis asked what happened and where all the blood had come from. Raphael just laughed and he and the twelve started shaking Garrett and the Guys hands for showing up. It took Drew to pull out a bag of weed then say I thought you guys might need this. As everyone started joking Garrett and Landis join me. We sat on the ground beside David in silence and waited for him to get himself together. Even after everything that happened we could tell David was very hurt and confused. It was moments like that my heart was drawn to him because he was so vulnerable. I think I was fascinated with such a strong and prideful person that showed his vulnerability so easily.

Landis was the first to speak, he said, "David... Do you want to talk about it?"

I looked at him with disgust. It always bothers me that no matter what happened there is always someone who wants to talk about it. A part of me wished that it was I who asked the question but then again most people just want to think out what just happened to them. David looked up at Landis as if he was about to speak but said nothing. As tears ran down his face we could tell that he had a story of his own but wasn't ready to share it. I told them that we all have secrets and David has a right to keep his own. Landis assured us that was not what his intention was. I guess a part of us all wanted to be there for David but wasn't sure how. It took David some time to get himself together but then he looked up at us and smiled. We could tell that the smile was forced but we accept it. We helped him stand up, and then joined the others. Garrett commented about the cars and how were we going to get rid of them. Caspercame up with the bright idea of just parking them sporadically around Center City and let the city take care of it. Raphael agreed and that's exactly what we did. I thought it would be cool if we all went back to the club and just enjoyed the rest of the night. We partied until the club closed and made our way back to David's Condo. David seemed to be in a better mood by the end of the night. He even started making jokes about Sammy and how they dated for fifty years. He said one of the reasons they broke up was that Sammy was dead in more ways than one. Of course we all found that funny. Even though we didn't do anything to assist him he thanked us for coming to help.

Garrett asked, "was all this about George?"

David responded, "No, it was about power. Sammy and I had an old vendetta from when we broke up. He simply was looking for a reason; I think George was just a good enough reason to justify it. Now, Akakios was Sammy's maker and he always hated the fact that we became intimate. Even though it may sound very cliché but there are vampires that do not approve of our type of unions. They have convinced themselves that vampires are a far higher species than werewolves. I always thought he was a jackass but he was Sammy's maker so I respected him. I believe Elizabeth simply gave him the excuse to finally attack and eliminate me. He has always wanted to take over this region ever since the New World was discovered. You know the old saying location, location, location! Now the lines have been drawn and I would be lying if I did not say I was bothered at the fact that he actually awoke and came to eliminate me personal."

Caspersaid, "David! All these losers are so old. So, why are they so concerned about us and if this was an old war? Why couldn't they have dealt with it way before we were created?"

David said, "True all of this could've been dealt with centuries before you were created. They are operating under the illusion that if I allowed you to be created than I have lost my grip over the city and region. Just like all creatures of nature they're going to take advantage of the sick dog. You guys have no idea what Elizabeth has brought fourth and what I have to now do to put back in order. There was a time that lady Ling would never be brave enough to threatened to destroy me."

Xavier said, "Word... Then what changed?"

David responded, "Elizabeth… That's what changed. She is giving these fools a false hope of rebellion and the fact that you guys were made. Her foolish attempt to over throw me offers them a reward at the end of this madness."

Vinnie said, "I get it. By killing lady Ling; you have sent the message to everyone that this is still your territory and you still have the shit on lock."

David said, "Yes! But more to the point, Lady Ling was too powerful of a witch to leave unchecked and if I did not destroy her, then by some miracle she and Elizabeth would rejoined forces. They would not have stopped until they had Garrett and his power. It was wiser to allow Elizabeth to return to her home and wonder who bought lady Ling to her demise. Then to confirm her suspicions by allowing her to gathering the dark energies, meaning the witches of darkness. As long as she believed that the dark witches have finally got a hold of Lady Ling's Grimoire Elizabeth will not trust them and therefore keep your groups secret to herself. If what lady Ling said is true then Elizabeth will not simply handed over this type of power to anyone."

Garrett said, "But George is gone and I cannot tap into the Nexus myself. Without paying the price. So doesn't that make her whole plan pointless?"

David said, "Look, until I located Elizabeth's whereabouts and get a better understanding of what the hell is going on. I want you guys to stay here. Under no circumstance are you guys to make contact with anyone without my knowledge. There are many super naturals living within the city and throughout my region. I have to put their safety above all else. Even thou I like you guys, your presence have created a new level of order that I have not yet come to understand."

With that David rose and left the room. We were now his invited prisoners. I could tell the guys were not very comfortable with David's decision but realized they were not in any position to fight it. What started out as a friendship had turned into something much more? Even though none of the guys said anything to me, I could tell by their eyes they were blaming me for this particular situation as well. It had the famous marks of (Xavier does it again) all over it. David may have been protecting us or maybe his own needs, but I knew that I had to go and see Elizabeth's home for myself. If there was any way that I could find out what happened to her. I was sure it was her home that held the answer I sought. Casperwas the first to turn to me as if to say what the Fuck. Vinnie looked at Garrett but Garrett shucks his head no for them to do nothing, Vinnie and Zack through their hands up as if to say whatever. As the guys walked around the condo's living room I knew I had to go and speak with David. I excused myself and went to David's room. I knocked on his door but there was no answer. I entered his room to find him looking through Lady Ling's belongings as if there was something he was looking for. I asked him if he was ok but he just pulled back his hair as if he was a little frustrated. He told me that it wasn't anything I needed to worry about he was just over worked because of everything that happened. Part of me could understand that but I felt there was more happening than he was letting us know. I hugged him from behind and rested my head on his shoulder. I told him not to worry so much, that everything would find away to work itself out. He cut his eyes over towards me and smile then reached up to play in my hair. I always seemed to know what to say when it came to him. He apologized for his behavior and told me that he was worried about what Elizabeth and Lady Ling had been planning and to be honest so was I. I told him that I needed to return to Elizabeth's home and see if she may have left me clues of her whereabouts. He wasn't too happy to hear that but new that even he needed to know whether she was alive or dead. We made love the rest of that night and I set out the following night to return to Elizabeth's home.

When I got to Elizabeth's home it was as if nothing ever

happened. I knocked on the Door and to my surprised Elizabeth answered and invited me inside. She acted as if nothing happened. I questioned about her where about but she responded that she could not remember anything. She told me that she awoke several evening ago in her home as usual but Lady Ling was gone. I asked her if she could remember what her and Lady Ling was planning but she just looked at me. After some time past I admitted that I knew of their plan and how she and Lady Ling played me. She tried to explain that it was not as it appeared that she did care for me and that they only sought the power of immortality of Vaingels. As she tied to use her sex appeal on me to convince me that she meant neither me nor my friends any harm. I laughed, and then informed her that it was all over because we now knew what she really wanted. The more she seemed to plead the sexier she became to me. I guess a part of me still desired to be inside the warmth of her thighs. I knew that I could not trust her but I still loved her. We made love for some time before the doorbell ring. She didn't even bother to get dress; she simply put on her robe and went to answer the door. I could hear her speaking to someone downstairs and decide to join them. It was the Brander and he was not alone. As I entered the room in my boxers he smiled as if he found me humorous.

Brander said, "It seems the boy has become a man."

For some reason I took offense and said, "I have always been a man. Why are you here?"

Brander said, "Umm! I could ask you the same thing. It has come to my attention that you were the Dog's pup now…"

"Word… Well, I am no one's pup. I am Xavier and don't forget it."

Elizabeth asked us both to calm down. It was clear that we didn't like each other but both loved her. A part of me knew that they were lovers at one time and that he still had feelings for her but I was like fuck him. She was with me now and he needed to get over it. The fact that he had spies following me was proof enough of how bad he wanted to be with her but I didn't care. He informed her that it was believed that the dog's destroyed Lady Ling but they were not sure how it could have happened. Lady Ling was a very old and powerful witch. Elizabeth informed Brander that wolves could not take out Lady Ling because she was over two hundred years old. Her bond to the dark arts was too powerful for any wolves to destroy her. Brander looked at me as if to suggest not if I helped them. I didn't bother to commit I just walked over to one of the chairs and sat down making a point to throw one of my legs over the arm of the chair. I knew he could see into my underwear but I wanted him to know that I was the new man in this house. He turned his head from me in disgust and I just sat there smiling at his discomforted. I now knew that he had spies watching me and I was not sure if he knew much or was only guessing. I assured them that I had nothing to do with anything that may have happened to Lady Ling. I live it flowed freely because I knew nothing of her whereabouts. I made a point to look very nonchalant as I said it. The fact that Brander didn't like me made my story the more convincing.

Brander said, "I thought you went to New England! Why are you back?"

I responded, "I was... Until I awoke and realized Elizabeth didn't join me. In trying to contact her mentally I had a strange dream where she was being attacked by some weird creatures. I tried to reach out to her but was not able. I then tried to go to her but was attacked by four Werewolves. I barely escaped that my life. When I returned to your child's home she decided to train me. With the promise that once I was done she would return me to Philadelphia. Which she did! Not that I owe you an explanation but what the hell."

Brander said, "I'm already aware of all that but I'm also aware that you been hanging at David's since you have returned."

I looked at them very sarcastically said, "Are you expecting me to deny that. He's a cool dude and seems to be very nice. He has explained a lot to me and my friends in Elizabeth's absence, but did your spies tell you that when I returned to Philadelphia I came here to Lady Ling's first. Then no one answered the door. Nothing led me to believe anyone was even here. In fact since I've been back no one even reveal themselves to me to allow me to know her whereabouts or if she was even alive for that matter. So forgive me if I don't seem very forthcoming or caring about what you think. So to make things very clear I am only here to make sure that Elizabeth is okay. Fuck you and your cronies. If something happened to lady Ling I really don't care, never got to know her well enough. In fact maybe if your spies focus more on protecting Elizabeth's home than following me they could have told you what happened."

Brander didn't seem to like my response and immediately leapt towards me showing his fangs. After all I've been through Brander did not have the strength to intimidate me. I simply looked over at him and warned him very politely but very sternly to control himself. By this time it was quite clear that he knew I was aware of who and what I was. Elizabeth simply laughed as she tried to make us control ourselves. For some reason, I took great comfort in her referring to me as her Xavier. I begin to ask her what happened to her and where she went. It seemed the more questions I had for her only confused me about her where about. Not in the way that she was avoiding my questions but she was simply unable to answer them. It was as if for some reason she lost the memories of her where she had been or even how she got back. She couldn't tell us about the creatures I seen in my dreams, let alone the location that I seen her in. What made it so crazy was the fact that she was quite aware that she had gone somewhere but could not remember where? The more we talk the more she came to understand that parts of her memory were gone. Now just as Elizabeth had Lady Ling, Brander also had a dark witch named Lilly? As he called Lilly into Elizabeth's home to try to help retrieve her memory I grew very fascinated because up to this point I have never seen a dark witch using magic. Now course I've seen magic being displayed as illusions but actual tapping into the Nexus was something different. She entered Elizabeth home with such arrogance. Even her presence represented a great deal of power. She was a young beautiful blonde businesswoman but something told me she was far older than she appeared. I knew she was a woman not to be tried. She didn't do much talking but just listened. After Brander was finished telling her everything, she went over to Elizabeth and with a silver knife she cut Elizabeth's wrist. She retrieved Elizabeth's blood within a weird cup. The cup looked like a man holding up a seashell over his head wrapped in gold. It put me in mind of the statue of that God that was sentenced to hold up the earth, but at the end of the shell was a small hole. The shell looked like an old Viking's blow horn.

She returned to the center of the room and sat down on the floor. She caused six candles to appear around her. Waved her hand in all six candles lit. She closed her eyes and started chanting some weird language that I did not understand but I felt an essence being pulled into the room. The candle start flickering as if wind was blowing them but there was no wind the room. I found it fascinating how all the flames blew towards the candle next to it as if trying to connect to make a circle around her. Then it happened she placed her lips upon the small part of the shell and it looked as if she blew into it. The blood rose into the air like a small tornado. Then the blood started taking shapes and forms of different things in different places. It was as if the blood was making pictures from Elizabeth's memories for us to see.

This went on for some time but in the end they told us nothing. Brander asked her what all pictures meant and she explained that the blood only show the memories of what Elizabeth held. Because the blood was unable to gather the answers you seek, that meant only one thing. Mrs. Elizabeth may have lost, or somehow someone has taken her memories, for the blood cannot show what is no longer there. It was clear that all her memories didn't add up. I was not a witch and even I could tell that the images did not run continuously. The way it pretty much ended was her leaving the coffin in which we both was placed in and running around most type of jungle and ending up back at her home. Then she awoke with her clothes laid across her bed. Brander began to ask her to do other things to try and restore her memories but nothing worked. It was as if she did nothing in between us laying in our coffins and her waking up in her home. Then there were other memories of hers that was gone as well. She didn't remember Joseph or where he was buried. She even forgot about most of what brought her to Philadelphia in the first place. I grew concerned because there were too many questions that she could no longer answer. Brander then request that Lilly bring forth the energy patterning of all the beings that may have been in the house right up to Lady Ling disappearance. I was worried but I kept my composure because if Lilly could re-create the last night that lady Ling was in Elizabeth's home, then they would know I was lying.

Chapter 14
A New Secret is born

The one thing that stood out to be in my favor was the fact that Lilly did tell them that there was something very powerful going on. As she returned to the center of the room she wanted them to stand back because she was uncertain if she could protect them for whatever she released. She went to the center of the room, extended her hands and pulled them together into closed fists. As she stood there for a moment she closed her eyes and made candles appear again. She started to chant with words I didn't understand. As we looked upon her we could fill thick air being drawn into the room from nowhere. Then the candles lit themselves and a few seconds later she rose into the air. As she floated in the center of the room and the air began to dampen the room. We could see a black film like fog covering the windows. They looked as if the Windows were now painted black. At this point I deftly realized that Lilly was a very powerful witch. The flames rose from the candles and gathered themselves in front of her. They looked like stars floating in the center of the room. Like a bright flare the flames were gone and all that remained was a white shadow. If I did not know any better I would have sworn the shadow was a ghost. The white shadow appeared and whipped throw out the house. It went through every room of the house as if it was searching for something or someone. I was afraid that it would definitely identify all the energies that were in the home. Something told me that the cleaners that David spoke of were not expecting something like this. The shadow returned and entered Lilly. It looked like something one would have seen in a horror movie. She floated there completely still for several minutes. Then Lilly started to have some kind of seizure. Brander leaped to help her but was blown back across the room by some kind of energy. She used her hands to cover her face as her head continued to shake as if she was insane. She fell to the floor and landed on her knees. The white energy that had entered her began to expend from her body like a flower. As the light consumed her a black shadow was expelled from her body. It looked like what I would think an exorcism would look like. The white shadow then lifted from her body like a flower in full bloom. The light then shot into the air like octopus tentacles. The tentacles started to wrap around her as she just stood there and screamed. We could tell she was in great pain but there was nothing we could do. They wrapped around her like ropes bonding a person.

Then it was over and the room returned to normal. She was still in the center of the room on her hands and knees. Brander made it to his feet and went over to her. I believe Elizabeth was as scared as I was but we both sat there quietly. As Brander helped her to her feet, she just kept repeating "what have I done." He looked as if he wasn't sure if she was in her right mind but helped her to a chair to rest. At that moment I wasn't sure what happened but she looked very different. You could see the weakness in her eyes and even age began to creep up on her face. Without saying a word we knew her powers were bound. Whoever took Elizabeth made sure that no one was going to find out who they were or where she went. Even if they searched for clues they would only become victims of the traps left behind. As cool as it looked I was very afraid that such power existed. A part of me wanted to believe that David's cleaners may have had something to do with it. Even though I was uncertain what the cleaners were, in my heart it was obvious that all we witnessed was far beyond anything David's crew could have done. Brander and Elizabeth said nothing but just looked upon Lilly with amazement and fear. They sat there in silence for some time and then I had to ask what just happened. Brander cut his eyes over at me and showed his fangs as if daring me to ask another question. I realized that he was only trying to comfort her and make her feel safe but we needed to know what just had happened. She placed one of her hands upon his hand that rested upon her shoulder as if to say it was okay. She said that she was not sure exactly what happened but whoever cast the spell was very powerful. They bored powers she had never felt before and pray never to witness again. Whoever took Lady Ling and erased Elizabeth memories, wished not to be disturbed again. Lilly pointed out that not only were they powerful enough to erase any energy that they left in the home but they made sure not to bond her powers. They stripped her of any powers and wanted her to feel the pain the abandonment.

Now knowing that whoever did this had them at a disadvantage Brander and Elizabeth thought it best to leave the home she so loved. The fear in Elizabeth's eyes made me want to tell her everything I knew but something inside me told me that would be unwise. I stood there and watched as they decide to gather her belongings. Elizabeth told me that it was unsafe for me to return to her home. Since she was not sure exactly who or what she was involved in she could not protect me from the dangers I may be facing. She made me promise her that I would not return and that I would not search her out either. She told me until she was able to figure out how to restore the powers that were taken from Lilly and regain her memories it would not be wise for me to be around her. Even Brander seemed to have compassion for my safety as he agreed with Elizabeth decisions. Something told me he was only looking out for his own well-being but I knew they were right. It felt odd too feel such fear from ones as old as them but fear is what I felt. I kept asking would Lilly be able to get her powers back but they never answered me. They just focused on gathering a suitcase of Elizabeth belongings and quickly leaving the home. Once we were all outside she gave me a hug and a kiss. Her lips were so soft against mine that my basic instincts return and I wanted to feed on her. I wanted to drain her so that she would be with me forever but I knew I had to control my urges. In my heart I knew I had to let her go. As she got into what I believed to be Lilly's car I stood on the sidewalk watching them drive away.

As much as I fear that I would not see Elizabeth again I could not deny how fascinated I was with everything I had just witnessed. No sooner as they turned the corner I took off towards David's home. I couldn't wait to tell him everything I had seen. I was afraid and rejuvenated all at the same time. The ideal that I witness real magic, I mean magic and not illusions. The fact that someone was able to truly manipulate the elements of time and space blew my mind. I knew I needed to share it with David and the rest of the guys. They would never believe everything I had to tell but I knew I had to tell them anyway. No sooner than I entered David's condo I started yelling out all their names like a frantic child. Of course they all came to me like worry parents. They entered the room wondering why I was acting like such a frantic child. Once they got me to calm down, I told them that they all needed to take a seat, for what I had to tell them they would never believe. In fact if I had not seen it with my own eyes I wouldn't believe it either. I was right, for no sooner I told them everything I witnessed they started laughing as if I made it up. Everyone was laughing except Garrett and David who apparently believe what I was telling them. Garrett raised his hand to his chin as if he was studying my facial expressions to see if I might have been lying but I guess he was convinced it was the truth because Garrett looked over at David again. They kept eye contact for some time as if they were sharing a secret that no one else in the group understood. Then Garrett looked at me and said something I did not expect, "So, Elizabeth has returned? That must have given you great comfort to see her after so long." He smiled at me as I approached him showing the confusion upon my face. I wasn't quite sure how to take his statement. Garrett could be just as sarcastic as George and sometimes I didn't catch it.

Landis said, "So, somehow Elizabeth has lost her memories and has no idea where she has been. She can't recall why or who may have taken her. Well, I think that is bullshit!"

I looked over at him and said, "Dude, I'm telling you what I saw. She has no recollection of anything that has happened. When she couldn't locate Lady Ling, she asked the witch Lilly to try and draw back her memories. But whoever took her memories had the power to strip Lilly of her magic. Dude! They really fucked her up."

Vinnie said, "Um, so there's a new player on the board. Apparently they want us to know that they're paying attention to what we're doing or they would have simple killed her. She was definitely a sign to let us know to back off from looking for George. So, you're telling us that they took a great deal of her memories from her?"

Zack said, "That would be exactly what I would do if she actually seen George and I didn't want anyone to know where he was. I have to agree with Vinnie killing her would not send the message to us to stop looking."

I told them, "No, I don't believe that it had anything to do with George because they were trying to locate lady Ling. When Lilly cast the spell to find out all the energy patterns that was in the home she triggered something and that is was stripped her of her powers. A part of me believes that it probably was David's cleaners."

David laughed and said, "My Xavier! Cleaner's jobs are to remove any evidence of a supernatural activity taking place and any evidence that the supernatural world even exist. In all my life I have never witnessed any cleaner or otherwise that bored the powers to strip a witch of her birthright. Now if Elizabeth has truly came across a Vaingels. Not even I can tell you what the outcome would be because no one knows the full extent of a Vaingels powers. Are you sure her powers was stripped and not bound. For that is the skill that most witches use on each other, to bond a witch's powers its magic 101."

I looked at David and I said, "No Lilly made it quite clear that her powers were stripped from her body and she felt the pain of it being released from her body, if that makes sense."

David looked confused but assured us that he would check it out if that was possible and that maybe he had been over reacting by keeping everyone in his home. He allowed us to leave and focus on our own gifts until he could find out more on Elizabeth and Brander. We returned to our home and chilled. We even debated about what David might have wanted with us. He seemed too helpful and that usually meant that he was using us to serve his own agenda. All the guys seem to be coming and going for the next few days. They would hang around long enough to shoot the shit but eventually went out to do their own thing. I kind of wanted to join them but something told me that they all needed their own space. It was very hard for me to see Peter going off without asking me to join him. I could feel the separation between us growing stronger and didn't know exactly what to do. Sometimes no one was left in the house but me and Garrett, who seemed to focus a lot on meditating. I watched him for hours and tried to figure out what he was up to but it always escaped me. Maybe Garrett was interested in trying to tap into his magical nexus. Then I thought maybe he just was simply missing George and was trying to get in contact with him. We all were focusing on doing our own thing for about a week and a half before Raphael appeared at our doorstep. He told us that David was interested in seeing us. Apparently David got a hold of the white witch who was capable of helping us gain answers.

Of course the idea of seeing more magic intrigued me, so I was more than happy to join the guys as they went to meet David.

When we got there David was joined by three fairly attractive women and they never bothered to introduce themselves. They were older looking women compared to Lilly or lady Ling but I think that had to do with the fact that they weren't trying to cheat death. They looked as if they were three generations or maybe even sisters. All three were so beautiful with their long blond hair. They simply smile at us, got up and walked into the back of the condo. We knew to follow and they lead us into a room that was separated by a wall of glass and the door. They looked at David and then each other, then they walk through the glass as if it was not there. David told Garrett to follow them into the other side of the room. Of course Garrett used the door to join them and they seemed to be puzzled by his actions. Once inside the room they spoke to Garrett. I tried to listen in but one of them must have notice because she looked at me then waved her hand and I couldn't make out anything else they were saying. They walked around Garrett as if they were studying how Joseph made him, feeling his body as if it was like some form of an examination. Then they walked back over to the glass and turned their backs to us as if they were waiting for Garrett to do something. Garrett took a deep breath then raised his hands halfway up to his face as if he was lifting weights. He closed his eyes but nothing happened. One of the women shook her head in response to what he was doing as if he was doing it wrong as she approached him. She spoke to him for a few moments then Garrett was nodding his head yes but we could not make out what they were saying and then she joined the others again. At this point I looked at David as if we needed to get a better understanding of what was going on. David informed us that the women believe that Garrett could control his body. The reason Garrett's body was like marble because he believed it had to be so. They believe that magic ran through Garrett's bloodline just like George. His mind could undo with the blood created. It took some time but it turned out they were right and before our eyes we watched Garrett's body transform. He looked no different than the rest of us but it did not last long for he reverted back to himself. This must have amused them because they applaud him then turned and rejoined us on the other side of the glass. As Garrett tried to approach the door one of them turned and made it disappear. Landis looked at them as if he was ready to attack, then one commended that Garrett had to learn to tap into the Nexus. They pointed out that Garrett could walk through that glass as easy as we can walk through a room. We watched Garrett keep trying until finally he succeeded and joined us on the other side of the room. I have to admit I was very impressed to see Garrett doing real magic. If we could even considered that as real magic! After all even Landis fazed through walls.

David led us back into the living room area and we all sat down to listen to what the women had to tell us. The first thing I noticed is that the women finished each other sentence as if they all spoke as one. They told us that David informed them of what happened to Elizabeth and that they have never witnessed anyone being able to emulate that kind of power. Never have they heard of anyone being capable of taking away one's memories. They made sure we understood that most witches would never attempt to intervene in the world of the supernatural. They pointed out that they were very surprised to discover that Elizabeth and Lady Ling work together in our creation. Even though Lady Ling was a very powerful dark witch, it would be suicide to play with such elements. They even made a point to tell us that they have never witnessed any witch being stripped of their powers and were quite surprised to discover that was even possible. I assured them that it was exactly what Lilly told me and how Brander had to help her get herself together before they left. The more they spoke, the more concerned I became for Elizabeth safety. Even though I could not deny that Elizabeth set out to betray us, I still wished her no harm. I should've been able to see the concern on all the other guys' faces. Since George was really the only outspoken one, the rest of the guys never pointed out when I was fucking up, not until it was too late! They never warned me that I was showing signs of betraying them. I was so focus on listening to the women talking about the harm that Elizabeth may have become victim too. That it never occurred to me that the guys would take my intentions as an act of treason.

They knew me well enough to know that I was going to seek her out. Even though they said nothing, my eyes told them that my priority was to find my Elizabeth. As the women kept talking all I could imagine was that there were other forces out there hunting her. Another type of parasite that I had no idea existed. I would be lying if I said that I wasn't concerned about the Danger that I may have been putting my friends in at that moment. In truth my only concern was protecting Elizabeth. Regardless of all the things she may have done I still loved her. It could have been my dislike for Brander or simply just my pride but I did not believe he had the ability to protect her. Without Lilly or Lady Ling's powers I feared that someone would find and surely kill her. I believe David knew how much I cared for him but even he could not deny how much in love I was with Elizabeth. The way the three women replayed the events of the last night I spent with Elizabeth told me she was in great Danger. They pointed out that since the two witches were missing the power has now been shifted in the city. Many of the supernaturals would try to take over in Elizabeth's station. Maybe Lady Ling was a very powerful dark witch that a lot of the other dark witches would never dare to cross. So with her absence there would definitely be a shift in the hierarchy of power. Even though Elizabeth was quite old and powerful in her own right with so much happening around her she was quite vulnerable. Many others would seek her out to take advantage of this handicap. Not even David could openly get involved with the situation because of his position. It was believe that most super naturals had to keep to their own kind. It was agreed as long as no one left evidence of the super naturals in the city David had to stay out of their affairs. (A rule I never cared to obey.)

The women seemed to reflect some form of allure that drew the guys into them the more they told their story. Perhaps even I would have been drawn into them if it was not for my love for Elizabeth. The youngest of them told us that if there was ever a time for us to choose sides, the time was now. With Elizabeth's memories gone there was no doubt that she had to have made some kind of contingency plan so all her work would not go for not. They made it quite clear; unlike David they wish to push the dark influences out of the city of Philadelphia. They made it quite clear that a war was brewing between the dark and light witches of this region. And the winner it would take all! Even though Elizabeth was a powerful player on the board she was not the only one. For there were other vampires as well as werewolves and light witches that sought to stop or even destroying Elizabeth if necessary! They believe that the veil between the two realms should never be lifted or crossed. The way they spoke they made it quite clear that they believed in the lost books of Gores Blocs. These books taught that for some reason these dimensions were made by elders far older than even the ancients. No one really knew how or why it was done but felt it was wise to never attempt to remove the Great Mist. The three women spoke of many times where witches and vampires a like tried to break through the Great Mist; they spoke of one of the clearest occurrences of someone trying to cross the Great Mist. How sixteen clerics tried to break through the Great Mist and they brought over a spirit called Dulachan. The consequence was that though they did succeed in bringing a fairy onto this side of the Great Mist, he appeared headless and then before the Great Mist closed once again his head appeared under his arm with his spine attached to it. The transition from his realm to ours altered the Fairies' mind. It was written that he did not return back to his own dimension until he killed all sixteen clerics severing his ties to this side of the Great Mist. Thus, starting the tales of the headless horseman throughout history; they said that many other supernaturals throughout time had also tried it and shared the same fate. Though the spirit or being that they would bring across the great mist was always a little different from the last one; the end result was usually the same; death! If Elizabeth was capable of crossing the Great Mist, then she somehow located one of the few mirrors of dimensions. That means the creatures on that side of the great mist can cross over here. I wasn't really sure how all of this had to do with George. So I asked!

She said, "We've been watching George for quite some time. We felt the power of his bloodline runs through all of his siblings. George was the only one of his siblings that sought outside witches to aid him in unlocking the mystical arts. Even his own cousin loved him but did not truly believe in the power that lives in their bloodline. This power is what Joseph sought out."

Garrett said, "But George has never shown any signs of true power. So I am confused with why so many people were able to sense it."

One of the other women said, "True power, is like a ripple in water, though it is not as powerful from the initial point of contact but its vibrations can be picked up by many and may even be amplified by others. Is that not how all of you became friends? Though he is no longer with you, his essence still radiates from your bodies. Like a sheep that strayed away from its flock, George made himself vulnerable. That is how Joseph and the other located him and you. Something is telling me that George was stronger than he let on or even showed, for never have I seen vampires with the powers you all posses. Most witches that have been made vampires lose their connection to the mystical arts but you and your friends somehow became more connected to it. I am sure this is something that Lady Ling despise, and seeing it radiate from George must have infuriated her. There's a reason why witches would not be transformed into vampires even though vampires are immortal, they would never want to exchange their connection to the Nexus for that mortality."

They began to speak of Elizabeth and George's interaction as if George was still alive and may have had a hand in what happened to Elizabeth. They feared that if George was alive and Elizabeth was able to cross the great veil then she must have found one of the legendary mirrors. I had no idea what mirrors they were talking about but they spoke as if I did. Even the rest of the guys responded as if they knew exactly what the three women were speaking of. I felt like I was being left out of something once again but thought it was wiser to say nothing. The guys begin to ask questions about how Elizabeth expected to return to the other side if she had lost her memories. That was something they could not answer especially since lady Ling was no longer alive. They believe that she would have made some type of contingency plan in case things went terribly wrong. There would have to be someone she trusted with her plans just in case something happened to her or Lady Ling. They did not believe that Elizabeth would be so foolish to challenge a power so great without preparing for the unexpected.

I told them that lady Ling informed us that Elizabeth believed I was the one who bored the power they needed. That was why Elizabeth saved and befriended me.

The young one said, "Yes, that is possible but the reality is that the power they sought live within George. That is why we stayed in Philadelphia to pay close attention to the activities that followed him and your other friends. When you were separated from your friends and they escaped to New York. It was there that George did something we would have never expected. He allows our grandmother to draw blood from him. Though a lot of his visions were clouded by Elizabeth memories, he knew the truth lies within the blood. Did your friends not tell you that they spent some time with my grandmother and discovered Elizabeth's true plans? Grams agreed with George that there was someone hidden in the shadows pulling the strings of all of this. Whoever this person was they wish not to be known. George knew that none of this was by accident. Someone sought him out and used Elizabeth to do it. The fact that Elizabeth believe that she was acting on her own free will is what makes her dangerous. That is why we feel you all must stop her. There was no doubt that Elizabeth would seek George out and killed him. He would be the only witness to what she had seen and what she truly seeks."

I said, "Is that why Elizabeth and George dislikes each other?"

The older sister said, "No, They were born natural enemies. George is a mystic of the light, so he naturally would dislike the deception that he sensed from Elizabeth. We don't agree with Garrett because David informed us that George had visions of everything that was to come. Insight is a very powerful gift for any mystic to bore. In the mystical community it is considered one of the strongest of powers any young mystic can possess. The fact that he tried to give Garrett the freedom of choice to alter his destiny shows you how powerful this gift can be. We cannot stress to you the kind of Danger this world is in. No one should possess the voice and especially no one should control anyone who does. You gentlemen have no idea of the type of war you're in the middle of. But you have the opportunity to stop it by destroying Elizabeth. She must be destroyed before she is capable of connecting her loss memories and joining her friends against George. For if they have the power to defeat the one who has taken him. There is no end to what they would be capable of and even if they are not strong enough to remove the great mist, they may be able to cause it to drop. Mankind is not strong enough to defend itself from the age of the magic that will enter this realm. Fairies, imps and creatures of the shadows are nothing like the fairytales one reads in books."

Somehow I knew the guys would agree with them and that was going to be the new mission if only to protect George. As much as I wish no harm to come to George I didn't want Elizabeth to be destroyed. Before the guys could speak I told the three women that we needed time to talk this over amongst ourselves. They seemed to have understood and told us and David their goodbyes. After the women left David looked at us and told us that he would hope we make the right decision. He made it quite clear that he would not intervene in our decision. In fact, he was not even going to remain in the city too witness outcome. The only thing he did was leave Raphael with us while we stayed in his home to talked. Raphael explained his position more or less then left us alone. It was becoming quite clear to me very quickly that there would be no one to help me if the guys chose to destroy my Elizabeth. I feared she was in Danger and she could not even remember from whom. I had to admit to myself that I was very disturbed that the women played her to be a villain. When all Elizabeth truly wished was to live again. Even if it was only as a true immortal, it would be better than feeding on the blood of mankind. I wanted to understand their point of view but I couldn't accept that it was okay to leave Elizabeth to such a fate. I did not find it to be evil that she wished to be free. That she no longer wished to feed on the endless line of victim's blood that sustained her will for all these years. I remembered how I felt when I had to consider hunting human beings for my own survival.

Chapter 15
Unchained

We all started debating on everything the three women told us. Of course we all took different perspectives. I understood that it was forbidden to remove this Great Mist, but I had to ask then why where they allowed the knowledge of its existence. A part of me believed that someone wanted the veil to be removed and therefore Elizabeth was doing nothing wrong. I did not agree with her attempting to destroy George but we had no proof that she wanted too. Landis and Casperdidn't care they just wanted Elizabeth dead. Mark and Drewfelt that if she was able to travel through the veil then maybe we needed to find out how she did it. They pointed out that if a war was brewing that Elizabeth would be killed anyway and therefore she would not be our problem. They pointed out that it may have been more answers on the other side of the veil to whom and what we were. As I looked around the room and listen to the debates I came to one realization. No matter what they decided Peter was going to attempt to kill Elizabeth. He said nothing but his body language told me everything. I knew Peter far better than the rest of the group so it was very easy for me to determine what he would do. I knew out of the act of pure chaos, Vinnie and Zack would aid Peter in his endeavor. They would not care what anyone else thought besides George. But Since George wasn't here there would be nothing to sway them from acting independently from the group. Garrett however was the only one I could not read. I wasn't sure exactly what he wanted to do. I knew Garrett was quite interested in finding George and if Elizabeth knew of his whereabouts then there was a chance that Garrett would aid me in protecting her. No, Garrett definitely would help me if only to find out where and how he could reach George. As we all talked I could tell that we drawing sides. I perceived by body gestures that alliances were being drawn. I believe even if my friends and I didn't agree with one another they would do nothing to harm me.

We must have debated for about an hour before coming to the conclusion that we weren't going to agree. I believe when we left David's apartment that night it was to do what we felt was best. Unlike the others I returned to my parent's home that evening. They seemed very pleased to see me I guess they miss me after such a long period of time. We talked, laughed and reminisced about things that happened in our past. Even my younger sister seemed to enjoy my presence as she joked about my appearance. I rested the next day with the comfort and what I had to do but I wasn't sure exactly where I was to start. I mean I knew I had to find Brander but wasn't sure exactly how. I knew he had to be somewhat like Elizabeth and own several homes in the area. He could travel anywhere, but I knew that Elizabeth wouldn't want to leave the area so that was a start. I returned to center city and find climbed to the roof tops to see if I could sense Elizabeth. I ran along the roof tops as if it would remind me of the time Elizabeth and I trained together. I hoped it would trigger some kind of memory so I could find her. Then it came to me to go and visit the guys, in hopes that Garrett might be there with them. When I got there the guys where already gone except for Garrett, he was still there so I asked him for help. He told me that the guys were out looking for me and Elizabeth. That after some great debates! They decided that it would be best to destroy her before she was able to regain her memories. I told him that I feared that would be their outcome and that I needed him to help me find her before the guys did. Garrett being who he was had no interest in getting involved. This was something him and George never agreed on. Garrett always believed that what we decided to do or not do was something he and George needed to respect. In doing so they must never get involved. Garrett always felt that George was playing with fire when it came to trying to control us. He did understand why George picked us out of all his children but never felt it was his right to train us in playing this game. I didn't understand everything that was between George and Him but it was clear that he did love George. That Love was all I needed to control the events that were to come. He refused to help me until I pointed out that this was his only chance to locate George and put whatever was between them to rest. I used the fact that Elizabeth was the only one who knew where George was at. I pointed out that I knew Garrett could sense us just like George did.

I pleaded with him to try to connect with George's energy, the way they use to sense each other. I knew if he could sense George then he would find Elizabeth. What was odd was the fact that he warned me that I needed to be prepared for where ever this mad road would lead me. Then he told me that in the end he would not intervene. That unlike George he would not choose sides and would allow whatever happens, to just happen. I knew that I was playing a Dangerous game but I was desperate to find Elizabeth and Brander, Garrett was the only one who knew how to do it. Even though I knew Garrett didn't give a shit whether I found Elizabeth or not, all he wanted was George back. I knew I could use his twisted loyalty to George to help aid me in my quest. Garrett told me to follow him to the roof of the House. I thought his request was odd but I obeyed him. When we got to the roof of the house he began to rise in the air as if to fly away. Then he looked back at me as if to say come on but I couldn't because I didn't know how to fly. He looked back at me for a minute then started to laugh. It was at that moment I realized that they all may have surpassed me. I was so busy being proud of the powers I possessed it never dawned on me that they too bore powers that may have been even greater than my own. I looked down at the rooftop like a pouting child when I told him I couldn't fly. He stared at me for a moment and then seemed to be okay with it. I knew that if it was George he would have demanded that I tried until I succeeded but not Garrett he simply implies this will make it be a little bit more difficult. He smiled at me as he told me let's make a game of it. We returned to the house and got dressed in all black. Then we went into the alley and took off like the wind. I was somewhat surprised that Garrett could move so quickly and with such ease. He moved through the streets as easily as a bird takes flight. Every so often he would stop and look around as if he was trying to pick up George's scent. Then we were off again! We must have run for about two hours before I began to doubt that Garrett would be able to find anything. Then he stopped in front of a beautiful old home. It was one of those types of homes that just did not look like it would be found in Philadelphia. The home set on the side of a hill that was hidden by bushes. As we approached the home Peter came out to greet us.

I asked Peter what was he doing here and he responded that this was the home of Janus. He tried to talk us into turning around and returning home but Garrett began to act strange. He walked past Peter and approached the front gate of the home. Peter tried to stop him but Garrett looked at him and Peter went flying back across the road. I ran over to him and yelled to Garrett what the hell are you doing but Garrett just raised his hand and the Gates flew open. He started to walk up the drive way and caused the guards that tried to stop him to fall to their knees and bleed from their eyes. I was scared shitless but I could see that Peter was just unconscious so I ran after Garrett. He did not seem to care that I was there. He walked up onto Janus' front poach and the Front doors flew open. Garrett seemed to have been possessed because he would not respond to me calling his name. As he reached the doorway he stopped. It was as if he could not pass, then he placed his hands onto the open doorway as if he was touching glass and I felt energy fly around me. Garrett then entered the main vestal view to be greeted by three guys that came out of the side rooms. They tried to throw bowls of a substance that looked like blood on Garrett. They and the blood froze in the air about six inches away from Garrett, and then I saw a black woman appeared from around the corner from upstairs. She was being pulled backwards down the steps. She was lifted up into the air and then dropped before Garrett. Then women voices came out from Garrett.

They said, "Where is our Brother. Witch..!"

Something caused the Guys to fly up to the ceiling like flies stuck to a flytrap. Then six female spirits appeared from Garrett and wrap half way around the one Black woman on the floor. Then one stood in the same space where Garrett stood. I was too afraid to speak but I looked as they continued to question the witch before them.

Then together they said, "Blood from the Demons vein, return to the witch who we have now claimed. Complete the task that ye were cursed, but increased your power seven times worst!"

Then the frozen blood that was in the air circled the black woman and landed on her body. It looked like she was hit with boiling hot oil, from the way her body responded to the blood. Then it ate through her skin until only bones remained. The blood then ate away at her bones like acid until there was nothing left. I wanted to turn away but couldn't move, as the one who seemed to lead the others stood in the middle of the other six raised her hand and then Janus appeared from nowhere. He tried to greet them as if they were old friends, but they wanted nothing to do with him.

Janus said, "Welcome ladies of the holy order of light. My home is y…"

Then She cut him off in mid sentence saying, "Where is our kin?"

Janus said, "What?"

One of the other women twisted her hand and said, "Stiffen his bones and then get the neck."

Janus eyes opened wide as if he was in great pain but could not move. I could hear Peter scream from the street as if he too was in pain. As much as I wanted to go to him I wanted more to see what was going to happen next.

She said again, "Where is our kin?"

Janus wouldn't or couldn't say nothing so then another one of them said, "Drain the blood from the back!"

Then she said again, "Where is our kin?"

Janus response was still the same so another woman said "Melt his hair like boiled wax!"

His hair melted away and as it fell onto his body it took skin with it. I knew these women was not playing and cursed myself for getting Garrett involved. As Janus stood there helpless and holding onto what little life he had left. I yelled that he knew nothing but they didn't seem to care or maybe they couldn't hear me. Anyway, she asked again "Where is our kin?" This time Janus mouth moved but I could not make out what he said.

Then another one said, "Cracked his skin to define thy veins."

Then another said, "Attack his mind until he goes insane."

Then another one said, "Disintegrate the body so he won't rise again."

Then all together they said, "Now releases his spirit onto the wind."

Before I was able to say anything Janus was gone. This was spiritual magic like I have never imagined. The spirits of the women traveled throughout the house as if they were in search of something or someone, I assumed it was George. Garrett just stood there as if he was paralyzed a part of me was really worried for his safety. I knew who ever they were, they were very powerful and I began to understand what the three women at David's condo were talking about. Janus was a very powerful vampire and yet they destroyed him as if he was nothing. I slowly backed out the house to make sure that Peter was okay. As I approached him he was slowly struggling to stand up. He asked me what happened because he knew Janus was dead, he felt his death. I told him I would explain later but we had to return to the house because Garrett was still inside. When we reached the house the women were gone and Garrett was lying unconscious on the floor. As we approach Garrett he was coming too. He asked were we okay and of course we were. The interior of the house seemed to be covered with dust. I remembered the three guys that was stuck to the ceiling and when I looked up they were gone, apparently they too had been disintegrated. Garrett asked us to give him a minute to get himself together because whatever happened took a lot of energy out of them. As I described the events that took place to him and Peter, Garrett just shook his head in disbelief. He told me now he understood why George never wanted to tap into their family's nexus. Once connected, however everyone is connected and Garrett had no control over anything they chose to do. I wanted to believe him but something told me Garrett knew this would happen. Maybe he did it out of curiosity or simply to see if he had the power to tap into their family Nexus. Peters told us that Janus and all of his bloodline were destroyed. He felt their deaths, those innocent vampires dying not knowing why or by whom.

This game that Elizabeth has chosen to play was too Dangerous for everyone. How many innocents must die before I got it through my head? Elizabeth needed to be stopped and at any cost. He then posed a question, was I really in love with her or simply fighting the fact that George was right? This question was something I had to deal with for some time. A decision I had to make for them and for myself. I was in love with Elizabeth and there was nothing I could do about it. Garrett told me that he knew where Elizabeth was located. It seemed that Janus did not know anything about George but he did know about Elizabeth and her whereabouts. His cousins pulled the information from Janus's mind before they destroyed him. Though Garrett didn't believe his family cared about Elizabeth, they would care enough to analyze all the thoughts that they gather and see if they could find clues of George's whereabouts. I asked him what we to do now. He said nothing but rest there thru the day and look for whatever clues Janus may have collected on us. So that when his death was discovered no one would know of our involvement. It was odd to walk through his home the rooms where so beautiful and full of ancient items. Even the furniture looked to be expensive. I located a safe in one of the bedrooms but could not open it. I called to Garrett and Peter for help. Peter came to my side before Garrett and laughed at me when I pointed to the safe because he just walked over to it. It had one of those touch key boards locked that Peter seemed to in enjoy playing with the buttons because with great speed he kept pushing buttons after buttons. I was afraid that it might set off alarms and bring the police. The more he did it the scared I became but Peter didn't seem to care and when I asked him to stop he asked me, "why?" Garrett entered the room and told Peter to stop fuck'n with me. Garrett placed a hand on my shoulder as he entered the room smiling. Garrett knew that Peter had already unarmed it and was just playing with me. After Garrett informed me of this fact Peter decided to open the safe. It was full of currency, gold and jewels that must have belonged to Janus. Peter though it was best to take it. We quickly located some suit cases and return to the room. We filled the bags up and made our way thru the other room and did the same. We took everything that was of value and Peter seemed not to be bothered at the fact that Janus, his maker was dead. It bothered me more that Peter was able to move on so quickly as if Janus meant nothing to him. That their bond was so insignificant that he was able to move past it like a whim. I believed that his bond would have been just as deep to him, as mine was to Elizabeth. Yet I was wrong. He helped us loot Janus' home like common thieves. We took everything that we could carry within reason. I asked them did they believe this was wise. I didn't like the ideal of robbing Janus. I told them that I thought we needed to call David so the Cleaners could do what they do.

Peter turned to me and said, "What the hell do you think cleaners do. You think they look for next of kin? No, dude! They fuck'n clean the house out and take everything the fuck back to David. Fuck that! We need this money, these jewels… every fuck'n thing that we can carry. There is no longer any right or wrong it's only our survival. The sooner you accept this shit the easier our lives are going to become. (Xavier!) George is no longer here to protect you. Hell, look around dude he can't protect us. Whether George is dead or alive has no bearing right now. Stop being such a righteous dick that believes somehow you will make a moral stand and through that everything's going to be okay."

I was offended by everything Peter said, but I knew he was correct. I had to stop living in this fantasy world. I knew I had to deal with everything that was happening around us. Either I was going to help them or sabotage them. It didn't make much sense to us to bother with taking the paintings, drawing or pictures that was hung around the house. We knew the only things we needed was the jewelry and money at least that's what we thought. Until we came across the witch's chamber. I'm not sure exactly who uncovered it, Peter or Garrett, since they both was touching and pulling on everything in her bed room. A hidden door opened that led to the attic and man was that place wild. It had a glass roof dome that was right of a fire pit in the center of the room. Standing in front of the Fire pit was a beautiful wooden bookstand, it looked as if four tree branches were wrapped around each other all the way up to the top and then opened to two hands holding open a book. Garrett knew that it was her Grimoire. We were reluctant to walk around the room. The room had books, crystals, herbs on the shelves and a floor chest in the corner. As we looked around the room we had seen many different types of Wands on one of the walls. Garrett laughed as he commented that George would love this. As we walked around the room there were so many things in there that I couldn't read, but Garrett seemed to know what some of those things were because he opened up a chest that was in the Corner of the room. Before I could ask him what he was doing he read the writing inside the chest. No sooner he was done reading we felt wind whip throughout the room. Soon we watch all the Grimoire disappear, then the crystals and then the bottles of different things. We got scared and grabbed hold of each other. Not sure what was coming next the room emptied itself in the chest and then closed. Peter made a joke of how easy that made packing. When we realize that all the shelves and tables were empty, Garrett started checking the drawers. All the drawers were empty except one. In the draw was a wooden box with gold handles and a golden latch. It bothered me that Peter knew so much about this house but knew nothing about this room. He didn't seem to care what Garrett was doing or if there was going to be some kind of repercussion for what we were doing. Peter asked Garrett could he open the box that he found but Garrett couldn't. Then Peter came up with an idea. He asked Garrett if they could take the chest to each room and do the same thing. Garrett said he didn't see any reason why not. So that's exactly what they did. After they had emptied each room Garrett read that incantation again and everything vanished except that which was a part of the house and the wooden box. When we finished Peter and Garrett decided to fly the box back to our house. Because I couldn't fly I ran around the area until I came across a cab. Now the one thing I did agree with George about was that we should never draw more attention to ourselves then necessary. I asked the cab driver to take me to the 30th St. station and paid him in advance. I read his mind to see what he thought of me but the only thing he cared about was the amount of money I gave him… Apparently I made his night.

Once I got back to the house everyone was there and was going through the stuff that Garrett got out of Janus' house. I was a little bothered that I didn't see how he got the stuff out of the chest. I asked him about emptying the chest. He told me usually spells like magic chest where the same as any door. The same way you get in is how you get out. So I was cool with that answer but I still would have loved to see it happen. Everyone was asking for painting and other trinkets for their rooms and I was no different. Peter seemed to be fine with the fact that Janus was dead. I could not understand how he had no bond to Janus, his maker nor did I understand that if all of Janus bloodline was destroyed then why was he still alive. I told everyone about the event that took place at Janus's home and how Garrett became possessed by his family. I repeated to them what I have now told you but they didn't seem to care. As they kept gathering the things they wanted, Landis seemed to sense my discomforted and told me that it would be fine once we located George. He pointed out that George's family must be just as worried about him as our families would have been if it was one of us. I guess I was so distracted about Elizabeth that it never occurred to me that his family would be worried too.

Garrett made a point that we could not have any thing that belonged to the witch. No one but me seemed to be bothered by that fact. I wanted to know what Garrett planned on doing with the witches' belongings but kept it to myself. After everyone was finish dividing the loot Garrett told us to do the same with the money. It was a lot of gold bars and currency; enough that I knew that we could separate at any time. We all joked for a while after divided what we took from Janus. Then there was a knock on the front door. We all looked at each other as if not sure what to do. Garrett smile and told us that it was for him. Garrett took the chest out with him as he answered the door. An older gentleman that resembled George walked in with Keith, George's brother. Garrett led them into the living room. I tried to hear what they was talking about but for some unknown reason I couldn't. After about two hours had past they left and took the chest with them. They both shook Garrett's hand and gave him a hug. Then the older man said that the house would be protected from outsiders from now on. I found that to be an odd statement since our home was in the city. I mean it was not like the house would vanish from seeing eyes. After the two guys left, Garrett turned to me while I was just standing in the hall. I asked him what the guys meant. Garrett just smile and walked pass me to go and joined the others.

I wanted to ask Garrett what right did he have to give our magic chest to them but something told me that was a fight best to save for later. I knew I would still need his help in finding Elizabeth. So, making him my enemy would not be a good idea. Garrett returned to the group and told us that his cousins opened the wooden box that we located amongst the witches' belongings. Then with a smile Garrett informed us that the wooden box with the golden latch had two dozen tungsten spheres inside of it and the spheres would allow us to walk in day light. I cannot describe to you how happy we all were at the idea that something would allow us to walk in the daylight. Garrett told us to be careful because once we touched the sphere it would bind with us. He made sure that we understood that although the spheres would allow us to walk in daylight, it did not make us invincible. Something Janus came to discover through his death. We all took one, then Garrett told us to think of how we wanted to bind with it and the spheres vanished, mine became a solid anklet. The others did different things with theirs but I don't feel I have the right to tell you what. Anyway, I decided to rest before I headed out to find Elizabeth again. The fact that I could now walk in day light was a blessing in itself. I wonder how many others walked in day light behind this kind of magic. It was easier to understand what being a vampire was, when I looked at it as a creature of the night. Hiding in the shadows and dark alleys in order to stay alive, but now I was becoming something more of myself. I was becoming a human that needed nothing to survive. I felt truly immortal for the first time. I wanted to get to Elizabeth and know that the time was running out.

Before heading out I entered Garrett's room and took two of the spheres so I could give them to my love and Brander. I knew that it was wrong to take them without asking the group but the truth was that I had just as much right to them as Garrett did because I was there when we took them. At less that is how I felt. Then with Garrett giving the other magical things to his family I was no longer sure if he could be trusted. Garrett would see Elizabeth dead if that would ensure Georges return. This was my last chance, I couldn't past it up. With so much going on around me, I know that if Elizabeth had any idea of what was happening she would run and I would never find her again. I awoke early the next day to head out to the location that Garrett told me where I would find my Elizabeth. Before heading there I had to make one stop and if everything worked out my Elizabeth would be fine. I got George's friend Quincy to agree to help me in controlling my friends by telling him that protecting Elizabeth may have been the only way to get George back. He drove me over to her home. I told him I would contact him when the time came for his help, so to reason with the others. If anyone could get through to the guys besides George it would have to be him. The home that she was staying at was very nice for a place in the Northeast. A part of me wanted it to be like the homes one sees in the movies, big and old with over grown vines all around it but the fact is; it was a beautiful house. No different than any of the other in that area. I waited for night to approach and to my surprise they were expecting me. When I reached the front door and knocked a guy opened it. He invited me in and told me to take a seat. It wasn't long before Elizabeth and Brander entered the room. They entered the room as if they were lovers; arm in arm as they reach the sofa. I stood up but before I could speak they told me that the already knew that Janus was dead. Elizabeth told me she watched as two of Janus' children die and could do nothing to help them. They took it as a sign that something was coming and if she was in Danger then I would seek her out to aid her. I assured her that she was right and that I was there to aid them to get out of town safely but needed to know if she remembered anything about where she had gone.

For the ones that destroyed Janus was George's family and they weren't going to rest until they found him. She told me she knew nothing and even if they did attack her it would do them no good for she could not remember where she went or what she may have seen. I believed her and asked her to leave this town that night so I could have comfort in knowing she was fine. Brander again ensured me that they were going to do just that but just as I feared my friends were not going to allow that to happen so easily for they circled the area and were waiting for her to show herself. They didn't seem to care if I sensed them or not, they wanted her to know they where there and waiting. Brander told me that there was nothing to worry about because unlike Janus' home his belongs to a mortal and my friends could not enter without being invited in. Even thou he assured me of this, he decided to still contact some of his mortal friends and directed them to come visit him. He asked if I would feel better if I walked through the main floor. Now, as I already stated it was a beautiful home. The first floor seemed to wrap around the steps with a hallway that separated the rooms from the steps. I laughed to myself because I thought that was genius. We knew the rules of not allowing normal beings to know of our existence, so they would never attack us so openly.

As his friends began to arrive and entered the home, it became a party in no time. Everyone seemed to have bought food or drinks. It was turning out to be a real cool affair. Even I was enjoying the way they all interacted with each other and me. Joking and Zackcing dancing to music that my era so loved. People started introducing themselves to me and telling me what they did for a living. I found it odd how people desired the approval of another person that they would most likely never meet again. Opening their lives to one another as if we where long lost friends. It was cool to talk with norms as if I was still alive, pretending to care about their career choices and how the child took his/ her first steps. We partied for hours as everyone began to get drunk and break off into groups. I started admiring the painting that was hung in the living room and the style of the piano that sat in the corner in front of the side yard window. This home was built with a unique style, so many windows and Glass Doors. I wanted to go out into the yard but I knew it wrapped around to the front of the house so I wouldn't be able to hide myself if the guys where to attack. There was a brown stone fireplace that stood about six feet high in the middle of the wall that separated the yard's Glass doors and the Dining room which seemed to have large windows in them as well. I never pictured a vampire being as open to the world as Brander was. He didn't seem to care if his neighbors saw anything he did or was it to ensure no one would attack him in such plain sight. Up until then I never gave it much thought about what one must have to do to survive for so many years. I always seen movies about vampires attacking their victims and fighting other vampire to stay alive but I never gave much thought about the ones that didn't do any of those things and tried to live as normal as possible. Brander seemed to be that type of guy. He just wanted to be left alone to live his life. I started feeling bad about the hell I was bring into his life. As I came out of my trance, my eyes locked on the most beautiful women I ever saw. She looked as if she could have been from India or some kind of Asian country but her skin was darker that mine and maybe a little lighter than Vinnie.

I seen this beautiful woman with a body that most women would die for, talking with Elizabeth. The fact that she seemed to pay very little attention to the rest of the group peeked my interest. As I tried to get close to them it felt like everyone wanted to talk with me. For some reason they would not leave me alone long enough to get close to this woman and Elizabeth. Then they went into another room, I assume to be alone. I am not sure if I was afraid or jealous but I knew I need to get over there and quickly without alarming the other people. So, I began to excuse myself with the excuse of having to use the bathroom. As I reached hallway that went towards the kitchen I lost them. I tried to sense Elizabeth but something was blocking me out. I make my way into the kitchen but they were not then I followed the same hallway until I checked the bathroom, Den and even Branders office but found nothing. As fears begin to take me I felt her. She was in the library which was in the next room. It must have taken me fifteen minute to locate them in the library but everything seemed to be fine as I entered the room. They didn't seem to notice me as I entered the room. Their attention was on a large painting that hung over the fireplace. The painting was of Elizabeth, man was it beautiful. It was so life like and she had on the same dress that she was wearing at that moment. I found it odd but just walked over to them. I thought maybe Elizabeth really liked that dress because everything else in the painting was of an age long ago. As I approached them I could feel a strange energy over take me. My head was slowly spinning and my heart began to race. It was the kind of feeling you never forget. It kind of reminded me of the feeling I got in New England, when I was at Mistress Mi-cilia home and I stood in front of the Soul King painting. I kept my eyes locked towards the painting as I approached them. Elizabeth was showing her a painting of herself to the young lady and they seemed not to be bothered by the Painting power. It was so amazing and life like that I wanted it for myself. They however acted as if it was just a normal painting and nothing more. When I approached them the woman looked back and looked more like a young girl than a woman of Elizabeth's age. She had long black hair that waved near the tips and green tint eyes. With thick lashes that made her look more like an Egyptian. Her lips were so full but yet did not pull attention to them. Elizabeth introduced me to her and she smiled as we shook hands. Her skin was so soft and yet the hand had strength to it.

I will never forget her because she had the oddest name I ever heard and to top things off it was also the name of one of the first queens in the book of Zarasgale. Elizabeth pointed it out with such tack so the young woman would not be aware. I believe she stated that she has a name that is as old as Africa and then they both smiled saying, "Akashi!" I told her that her name was beautiful and wanted to know where it came from. She just smile and said, "It came from my mother. She is very attached to old cultures." Even the way she moved her head when she said it told me there was another story in itself. I smiled because I could not help but notice how she seemed to flirt with her eyes as she spoke. I hugged my Elizabeth to show that we were together as she just looked at us. I wasn't able to make out what she was thinking at that moment, but she shook head and then turned back towards the painting. I asked her was she an artist too. She smile and responded, "Something like that." She pointed out that she loved rare works of art and could not past up an opportunity see one being made. If only for the timeless style the artist used or maybe it's the way the artist seems to capture person's soul. I asked her how old did she believe it was and she said it was timeless. Does it not look like it was just done and with that she excused herself to rejoin the party. As I kissed Elizabeth's neck I asked her not to leave my site again. She turned to me and smile then gave me a kiss. As we made our way back to the living room area I realized that the energy changed once we left the room. I asked Elizabeth about it but she didn't know what I was talking about. I knew I would have to go back later and check it out but at that moment Elizabeth was my objective. We walked back into the living room just as the people began to smoke weed. It was surprising how everyone seem to just go with the flow. No one seemed to care that anyone was smoking weed. The ones that didn't smoke just kept talking as if nothing was happening.

Then it happened, I believed I saw Vinnie from the corner of my eye moving through the room as everyone just kept talking. I knew no one could have invited him into the house or at less I didn't think anyone did. I went after him; I followed him into the hallway then down the hall to the kitchen. When I got there he was gone. I double back to the living room and looked around but found nothing. Then I walked back pass the kitchen towards the bathroom. I was losing my mind with the thought that he might have gotten in and I could not locate him. I pulled open the bathroom door and saw two women making out. Even thou I thought that their behavior was odd I quickly walked to the end of the hallway where the den and Library resided, feeling as if I was losing my mind for he was nowhere to be found, so I quickly made my way back to Elizabeth but when I got to the living room. Everyone was gone, the room was empty. As my heart started rapidly beating I knew something was wrong. I used the door way to hold onto as I tried to get myself together. I had no idea what my friends were doing but I knew they was making their move. Then I heard laughter in the front yard and as I moved towards the glass doors I could see Brander's friends walking around in a haze. They soon felt the need to sleep or just leave.

Chapter 16
When lessons are forgotten

Brander and I both knew that it wouldn't be long before day light and the sun would rise to take us to safety, but unknown to Brander I knew day light would give them no safety. Even though I was not sure why my head was spinning, I pulled myself together and told him that he had to quickly get him and Elizabeth out of the house because my friends had learned to avoid the Sun light. Brander looked at me as if I was insane but when I revealed to him the spheres and told him how to use them. He knew I was not lying and to avoid their death he chose to listen. He quickly got Elizabeth and they used the spheres. They went out of the house through the back and jumped into a car. As the car started to take off I saw Casper come out of nowhere and ram his body into the back of the car turning it over on its side and ramming it into the side wall. Then Landis ran through the car and grabbed Elizabeth. She was too dazed to protect herself. He mastered fazing through objects very well because it was in seconds he had her and was gone. I ran out to help but was knocked across the yard by someone and they took off before I could even see who it was. With my head still cloudy I had a hard time focusing on them but I knew I had to keep up with them if I wanted to save her. As I ran after Landis I saw Vinnie and Zack moving on top of the turned over car, but knew I couldn't stop if I wanted to help my love. Since I couldn't fly I knew keeping up was going to be harder for me since they were flying through the empty streets. As I chased behind them I realized that Landis was flying very low to the ground. He was almost dragging Elizabeth on the ground. He led me to a neighborhood park or field by that point, I feared losing him. So I grabbed a trash can that was sitting on the street and hurled it at him like a bullet. He dropped Elizabeth on the field when it knocked them out of the air. By the time he hit the ground and stopped rolling, I was on top of him with my fangs out ready for battle. Landis was a short man but very muscle bound, he use to work out a lot when we where a live so of course in death his body took on even a greater tone. He stopped rolling and landed on one foot with both hands gripping the dirt.

I said, "It did not have to come to this… Landis, we are all friends! Why is it so difficult for you guys to understand that I love her?"

Landis said, "Oh please. Xavier! There was no other way for this to end. Did you really think we would allow her to get away with this? After all the hell she released into our lives?"

I tried to remain calm as I reminded Him, "She was not the one that killed George!"

Landis flared his fangs at me and responded, "No… she wasn't, but she was the one that attacked Casper! She was the one that choose to invade my home. She was the one that turned you against us and rather you're willing to accept it or not, she was also the one who orchestrated all of this madness. The only problem was! That she underestimated our reaction after bringing us into her sick fuck up game."

As I stood there preparing myself for whatever he was planning to do next. I said, "Now, you're sounding like George."

As Marco and Drewjoined us on the field Landis said, "Damn, you are so fucking stupid. It was never George you needed to worry about; it was us. Are you really that blind that you can't see George was the one protecting you. He was trying to warn your Dumb ass about us and our feelings. That bitch was walking with death and we were her grim reaper. The very moment she brought us into this new world."

At that point he charged at me and landed a punch on my chin. I went back a few steps and returned with a blow into his mid-section, while he landed another blow with his elbow into my chin again. I knew we were continuing the battle that was interrupted so long ago. But this time it was for real. Landis was willing to kill me if that was what it took to get Elizabeth. At one point he charged me I released some kind of energy that blocked out his fazing ability. Even to this Day I cannot tell you how I did it. I could see the confusion in his eyes but that did not stop him, from striking me. His open palm strike hit me head on. He hit me with such force and used such skill, it was no doubts to me that he had already foreseen this battled and was prepared. I knew Landis had a martial arts back ground but what he didn't know was that I was trained in fighting as well. We started exchanging swings and blocks for several minute without either making contact. Then he struck me in the chest, knocking me back about four feet. I underestimated his skill but he also underestimated mine, because no sooner he struck me I recovered and I retaliated by hitting him with a high kick that he tried to block by putting up his arms in front of his face. As he fell back he turned it into a back flip and it seemed like before Landis's feet could even hit the ground he was charging at me again. He was countering my attacks and was doing it while matching my speed. I thought if I continued to move fast he would show an opening but it just wasn't happening. We went from marital art fighting to street fighting. At one point he was on my back and wasted no time in biting into my neck. His fangs pierced my shin and blood went everywhere as my legs tried to give way. I tried to shake him off but couldn't. As he tried to drain me I felt my body starting to betray me, so I quickly took my nails and clawed into his eyes. In that moment his fangs loosen their grip, so I took the moment to reach over my shoulder and into the back of his shirt. I clawed as deep into his skin as I could. As I felt his skin break and blood run from his back. I held onto him as best as I could and flipped him onto the ground. Believing I now had the upper hand I made a big mistake, in trying to return the favor of his attack. I went to bite him back while he was on the ground. I was so focused on winning that I didn't see that when he landed on his back and his legs where bent. So as I went down to bite his face, he took his hands and ripped into my ankles while he pulled himself in between my legs. He did something I didn't think of at the time, he bite into the back of my thighs right below my butt. With each bite he shook his head as if trying to rip the muscle free. As I fell to the ground my face went into his groan area but before I could bite him in the balls he fazed through me rolling backwards and back onto his feet. There was so much bloods everywhere that both of us had to be in great pain. I could not see how he still bore the strength to continue fighting. With me lying there face down in the dirt he leaped onto my back and started ripping my clothes off as well as clawing into my back like a wild animal. I was too weak to fight back so I just laid there helplessly watching as Marco and Drewwalked into view and sat on a fallen tree not that far away. They covered their mouths as if to say DAMN! As they sat their looking upon us I could feel him getting ready to go in for the kill. At that moment I wasn't sure if the true death was finally going to take me. As I closed my eyes and welcomed whatever was to come, I heard a scream and Landis was knocked off me.

It was Elizabeth who attacked Landis knocking him off of me and apparently started fucking him up. The guys charged in their direction and all I could see is them flying over my head. I was too tired to turn my head and see what was happening. I knew if I could heal myself like I did in New England, then I could save her. As I laid there I tried thinking of things that could have been happening. The more I thought the more upset I got. It didn't take long for my body to respond. I started feeling my body forcing itself to heal. When it healed itself enough that I could turn my head to see what was happening. All three of them were fighting Elizabeth. The guys were not showing any type of remorse for Elizabeth being a woman. They attacked her as if they were all animals. As I lay there, I was unable to see Elizabeth's face, but I could see her body as she was moving so graceful like a Zackcer dancer. I was proud to see that she was able to handle herself against the guys that were there. As they circled her like a pack of wolves, they attacked her one by one. No sooner one jumped on her back another attacked her front. This time they were prepared for her and it seemed that they weren't going to stop until she was dead. Drewattacked her mind as Landis attacked her body. She seemed too have been holding her own up until then. Marco did something that drove her insane because she started swing at the air like a wild woman. She even tried to fly off but Landis grabbed her legs and slammed her into the side of a tree. No sooner than Elizabeth hit the ground Drewleaped at her body. She threw dirt into his face, trying to get away. I was so focused on my Elizabeth that I did not pay attention to Landis who appeared out of nowhere running past the front of her and clawing his nails across her face. I watched as Marco landed on her back, taking her to the ground. As he held her there Drew ran over to her and lay beside her. He kept demanding that she tell them who she was. I was recovering faster than usual but still not fast enough. As I struggled to get up! I kept wondering why Drew was asking such a question. When it was very obvious to all to see that she was Elizabeth. I watched as she struggled to shake Mark off her back.

Then Landis said, "It shall not matter… For she will taste the kiss of death just like that bitch when we find her."

Then I saw it. It was in her eyes. The way she looked at Drew, I knew she was someone else. She was not my Elizabeth. I did not know how she pulled it off, but this woman was not my angel. As she locked eyes with me something told me that she was playing with them. Confusing as everything was I knew I needed to save her as well as stop her from whatever she was planning. I focused all my strength so to freeze time like I did once before in Landis's apartment. I know doing it wasn't going to last too long and would take a lot of my energy, but I needed answers. If there were more players on the board then I need to know who and why. But before I could do anything, she looked at and smiled then she moved almost too fast for my eyes to see. She flipped Marco onto the ground and was standing up as if nothing happened. Then she took out Drew and Landis as if she already knew what they were going to do. As I stood up I realized that she was playing with them all along.

She started flipping through the air as they tried to attack her and she was knocking them around as if they were toys. At one point she did a flip and kicked Drew in the face. She then landed into a full split, while throwing an overhead punch into Landis's midsection who tried to attack her from behind. She rolled to the side bring her legs back together. Like a gymnast stood back up and quickly went into a side flip striking Marked as she landed. This chick really knew how to fight and she moved so graceful. It looked like something that was choreographed. As Landis, Mark and Drew tried to get themselves back on their feet. She said something that surprised us all.

She said," George would not be impressed with your behavior. Fighting each other like rabid dogs. Even I have to admit, I am ashamed to call you siblings. Look at all of you attacking each other as if you have no loyalty whatsoever. We are all bound by George… Don't disgrace his name, or his memories. Now, as for this Elizabeth! She has been taking care of… Just like all the other messes you boys have left throughout the city."

Landis being the first to speak responded with, "I guess you are the one of George children that he refuses to talk about. She responded yes; do not tell me you believe you are the only ones. Perhaps you are the loudest group out of us, but you are not alone. We knew of you. Even before you were bitten…"

I said, "In that case, why is it that we didn't know of you and how many are there in your group?"

She said, "Unlike all of you. George stopped protecting us long ago and focused his attention onto your weak minds. Though, I have to admit I like how Landis beat you to the point of death to ensure you didn't aid this Elizabeth, but in truth I believe it was a waste of time and energy because you don't even know when you're standing in front of her."

I grow angry at what she was saying and my body responded by healing itself. I demanded that she tell me what she did to her. She laughed as she walked in a circle and said, "I did nothing to her, but the one that did has ordered me to return you to her… Alone! I would have rather led you there thinking I was Elizabeth but since your buddies seen through my illusion…. Well! That's what I get when I think that everyone is as dumb as you."

Then out of the sky Garrett showed up. He landed beside Landis telling Crystal that she was done and she needed to leave. He landed as if he was flying for year and had it down to a science. He looked at her with such stern eyes that I could tell they had a past. He knew who she was even before she dropped the illusion. They locked eyes for some time as Landis and Drewstood up. Then with great speed she charged at him but before she could make her move to hit him. Garrett grabbed her by the neck, picked her up by one arm and throws her into a tree. Garrett didn't seem to have any fear of hurting her; I mean if she was one of George's children too then wasn't Garrett breaking the rules between him and George. Garrett walked over to her and demanded that she show her true face. She stood up barely but changed into a beautiful black woman around our age or maybe just a few years older. She stood to be about 5"6 inches and had a very thick frame. She had long brown and black wavy hair. I could not tell if it was dyed that way or if it was her natural colors because she was already turned over, and of course once this new life takes us everything becomes natural. She had the type of breast that most dudes would love to bury their face in for hours. The fact that she felt very comfortable in Elizabeth's attire made me feel that she too liked manipulating men. I knew from past experience that Garrett always was attracted to thick women, so that led me to believe that maybe the tension I sensed was from their past. After she transformed back into her natural form I was sensing a stronger level of rage and resentment. I now knew she was one of George's children but wasn't sure from how many years ago. See, George started working at the college when he was 24 years old and been there for about ten years so that was a lot of children he educated with his beliefs and shared his knowledge with. So I was not sure if she was pissed because Garrett interfered or because of their past relationship, but I wanted to know. You must understand George never hid the fact that he had other children before us and that there will come a time when he would have children after us. George always preached about this balance in nature that every human being falls under.

George use to say, "There are three major natures; light, darkness and chaos. Now, under those three major natures fall three sub natures; lawful, unlawful and destructive. It is always easy to see the major nature of every human being because that is what defines their main behavior, but the sub nature does something different because that is a part of them that they do not control as much as they might want too. They may act one way but will eventually revert back to who they truly are. He always warned us to be careful because though someone may seem to be of a different alignment, it is only a matter of time before they will revert back to being who they truly are. They are no more in control of their nature than, the sun light that lights the sky."

As she got herself up and back together dusting her clothes off, straightening out her hair and slowly walking across the field towards us. This chick knew how to work her sex appeal for even I wanted her and I didn't even know her. She smiled at Garrett like the cat that swallowed the canary.

She said, "Well, I guess with George gone the rules have changed and you're choosing sides."

Garrett responded, "No. Just making sure none of George's children kill each other. At least without them knowing who each other are and while he is gone.

She said, "So, you're admitting he is still alive my love!"

Garrett said, "Of course, don't talk stupid. You're not speaking with Landis and the others. We both know he is alive and we both know why Quincy choose to help Xavier so freely. Now it has become obvious you cannot have Xavier without tricks, so I am going to let you take him and leave before I do choose a side; By placing your head on my mantel piece, if only to show why George shouldn't have given any of you the knowledge he wasted... And before you decide to say something you won't live to regret, take this as me being kind. We both know what is in my nature. Now, Xavier! You do have a choice as well and that is to refuse her and I will see to it that she leaves you alone."

As tempting as Garrett's offer was, I knew in my heart that I had to find out what happened to my Elizabeth and she had the answer. So I decide to go with her, but with some regret. Somehow I knew I was betraying my group of friends for another one of George's group of children. I had no idea what this woman had intended for me, nor did she truly have the answers of Elizabeth's whereabouts, but I could not risk losing her again.

I had to know, that my beloved was safe and out of harm's way and then if George was really still alive. Obviously she knew things about George that Garrett was not willing to share with us and I wanted to know these things as well. As we walked away I kept looking back as if Garrett might change his mind and stop us but he didn't. In fact when Landis tried to say something Garrett just raised his hand as if to tell him to let us go. I could see that Landis wasn't happy with Garrett's decision as he turned his back to me and kicked the dirt. Landis always had a temper so it was always easy to see when thing didn't go his way. Crystal just smiled at me and told me to continue to walk. As I followed her out of the park, Quincy's car pulled up. We said nothing but got in and took off. I kind of hoped that the Guys would come after me out of some kind of loyalty but they didn't. As we drove off, I just sat back and looked at her. Only God knows where we were going but I thought this was the perfect time to talk to her. As I turned my head to say something, she cut me off. She never bothered to even look at me. She just sat there like a perfect statue. The way she spoke reminded me a lot of George, even her mannerisms and how she carried herself. Everything seemed to tell a story to anyone who was willing to read it.

She said, "Worry not! For your friends do care greatly for you. If not, they would never attempt to destroy Elizabeth, so recklessly and so openly. But something tells me that is not the question that has you presently baffled. So let me answer the question that seems to actually puzzle you. I was once one of George's children as well. I was a graphic designer and he took to me just as he took to the rest of you but over a year we debated about the three levels of nature. It was not long before I started meeting my peers just as you did. We were meant to met before the year's ended, we started having great debates, the one thing that none of us knew, was the golden rule that lie between George and Garrett. George believed it was his job to teach us our nature and his responsibility to teach us about our alignment in that nature. Then how we must carry ourselves once the time came that we were aware of who and what we were. Garrett did not agree, in fact he believed it was something that everyone must come to terms with, in their own time, even if some of us would never wake up to this reality. He believed that tampering with one's nature could change their alignment and that they would fall under a different nature and guidelines. The outcome could cause such chaos throughout the group. This debate meant nothing, not unless one of them broke the rule by sleeping with one of the children. Then the unspoken rule would take effect and George would be forbidden to intervene for that child would no longer be conceded one of his children but now one of their peers. It would be a simple matter of time before they would announced own awareness and that they no longer needed, George & his twisted teaching. This chaos could shatter the strongest alliances and it did. What started out as nothing more than Garrett and myself sharing debate concepts and beliefs eventually turned into a relationship that lasted for 2 ½ year. I never meant to challenge George's teachings nor insult his insight, but in the end, that is exactly what I did. In crossing the line by sneaking around with Garrett I slowly forced myself out of my true nature. I went from the elements of light into an element of the darkness. It was six months into our relationship that I decided to confront George but before I could even say a word. He told me that he hopes Garrett and I enjoy what was to follow, for the person that Garrett has chosen to pursue would become the person of his destruction. He insured me that he could no longer teach me anything and that if I chose to speak to him he would only listen… That arrogant bastard! Though he refused to accept me on as his child, but he could not deny who and what I was no more than I could deny what he said, that came to be true. For me and Garrett's love slowly became hatred and we became bitter enemies. One which had truly became a love-hate relationship. Somehow we both blamed each other for the wall that came between George and me. Though, George never openly showed hatred towards me, I never could fully forgive myself for the pain I caused him. We are a lot alike Xavier! For as much as we despise George. We love him, because we know, his love for us is unconditional. It is too bad that neither one of us can say ours is the same."

As she finished speaking, I realized despised George because he had more honor than me. I was not sure why, but a part of me was quite insulted at the idea that she thought George was better than both of us. I pointed out that if George was so much better than us. Why he would have turned my friends against me? Why would he use us to try to kill my Elizabeth? Why would he do all of this to us? Why would he have allowed even your group to go through this and not warn you of what was happening? Even after you all were bitten, why he did not tell us about you guys? Are these actions of an honorable man? I made it clear to her whether she wanted to accept it or not, George was a coward who hid behind his ideals. His ideals that set our live in this stage, while he himself acted on what he believed in and he used those concepts as a shield to not take responsibility for his own actions, but yet he preached to all of us that we must always take responsibility for everything we allow to happen to ourselves and those around us. I made a point to mention why we should allow him this freedom of irresponsibility and allow him and Garrett immunity. Everyone is nothing but pawns in their pathetic game. So, What! Now that we are all immortals, their game has a right to continue but on a higher level. When will there be an end to this chaos before they both realized the hell they have released, this is not Elizabeth's fault? No sooner the words left my lips. I felt sorrow, but the truth was, there was an enemy amongst us and we called him a friend.

Quincy stopped the car and turned towards me. Unlike Crystal, he did not see any reason to pretend to care about my feeling and pointed out that if I kept disrespecting George, he would end my sorry existence. Yet he never had a problem with the fact that all of us were upset because we were transformed into these new creatures, against our will. But the reality remains the same that George wasn't in no better situation than we were and Quincy definitely was not going to allow us to use this situation as an excuse to justify our behavior before we were turned, he made it quite clear that if I wanted to say something about George, it better be out of the truth, not out spite. He pointed out that the reason Crystal lost face in George's eyes was not because of some fucking disagreement, it was because she chose to spread her legs and let her emotions glide her from the true intentions that Garrett held. It was not George that turned away from Crystal, but the reverse because she loved Garrett. So much that she cannot possibly imagine him to be exactly whom and what George said he was. Then he pointed out that my only problem with George was the fact that he had no sympathy for me, allowing me to be led around by my dick and ignoring my head. So if I wanted to pretend, by playing it was my heart that knock myself the fuck out, but he is not going to sit here and allow us to blame George for the shit that we were doing to ourselves. No more than he would allow Crystal to do it! The madman that attacked us had his own agenda and there was nothing any of us could do, including George. Yet he did point out that if his friends had listened to George and kept their fuck'n dumb as shit asses inside like George suggested that night, Then maybe, they too wouldn't have been changed either, just like he wasn't. He pointed out that George may have been an intelligent dude, but the realities are he was just a human being like the rest of us and whatever that creature was that attacked everyone was obviously something much more.

After verbally attacking both of us he turned around in his seat, adjusted his clothes and started the car, once again. We sat silently for some time before Crystal pointed out, "Did I really believe it was wise to give Elizabeth something that would allow her to walk in daylight? Even if I did give Elizabeth the sphere out of love, I had to understand the consequences of my actions and the Danger that it would put the rest of the realms in. She made a point to mention that there were reasons why super naturals had such handicaps at kept the balance in nature. I thought for a moment and took the opportunity to ask her about my Elizabeth. I wanted to know what did she do to my Elizabeth, but I remember that she said it was not her and that it was someone else, so I questioned who. She smiled at me and said in truth she could not even tell me. The fact of the matter was that she was sent only to ensure that I did not give the sphere to Elizabeth, and she was to stop my friends from killing Elizabeth, because there were questions that she needed to answers. Her intention was only to take Elizabeth's place and in tricking me into giving her the daylight sphere. She informed me that she had no idea why she transformed into that women called Asikis because she never seen her before, nor did she understand why she led Elizabeth into the library where the real Asikis was at. In fact the only thing she did remember was that she turned into Elizabeth at some point but didn't know where the real Elizabeth went too. From that point all she did know was that she and Asikis were to greet me as if nothing was wrong. She knew for some reason that she was to lead me out of the library once I started asking her about the strange energy I was feeling inside the room. She point out that her head didn't seem to clear up until after the car incident, and by that time, she is watching Landis attacking me. It did not take her long to realize what his intentions were and that she knew she had to stop him. She made it quite clear that if she could not return with Elizabeth then she needed to return with me.

We drove for about 20 to 30 more minutes before pulling into a home that was off the beaten path. The home was hidden in some type of wooden area. From what I could tell, the only way in or out was by a dirt road that turned in several different directions. I myself was not even sure if we were still in Philadelphia but something told me it would not be wise to ask. As the car pulled into this underground garage, I felt as if I was in a scary movie. After parking the car, it was Quincy who was the first to get out and he opened Crystal's door so I decided to follow their lead. Once we got out of the car we walked across the garage into a side passage that did not look much like a doorway. After entering it I could see light coming from a room at the end of the hall. I was a little nervous about following them but knew I needed to find answers. As I walked into what I would assume to be their living room I realized it was really in their basement. I took a seat and as I watch the people walked past me as if I was no body. One guy walked up and offered his wrist to me as if to offer me to drink but I kindly shook my head no. Then a door opened and out came a guy I did know, his name was James. I meant him a while back when George first started talking to us about natures. He was one of George's children but what was so odd was that he seemed to be more like Georges lover that child. The way they interacted was so amazing that I was jealous. They seem to finish each other sentences when they spoke and even seem to catch each other jokes as if they shared them before. It was weird and yet amazing to watch. He stood about six feet tall and was clearly Caucasian but mixed with some other nationality. With Long black hair that fell to his waist. He was truly a beautiful man. The way his hair ran down his back, even how the front fell upon shoulders and then continued to fall to his waist line, being turned seem to add to his attractiveness. As he entered the room it was quite clear that he definitely controls the group and for some reason Crystal seemed to be very loyal to him. As she walked beside him and whispering into his ear. I had no doubt she was telling him of the events that unfolded. He looked at me and then proceeded to laugh, he commented on how one must love Garrett. Just the way he said it made me think of George. He seemed to mimic George so much that it annoyed me. He annoyed me to the point that I demanded answers. Apparently, he did not find that quite amusing because he raised one hand, extended one finger which sent waves of pain through my mind to make it quite clear he was not George and he didn't have the restraints that George showed towards George's children. He did not believe it was always in the best interest to favor one over all the other children. And besides he will never put one spoiled, ungrateful, wretched, narcissistic brats above all the other children. Be it one in his group or one from George's many other selections of children. He wanted to make it quite clear that he understood George's favoritism at times and that even he himself was guilty of such actions. Like when he sent Quincy to shoot Elizabeth's lover in the field so that I was to survive. He seemed to get great joy out of the fact that George was forbidden to tell me it was not him who was responsible for my survival or for Elizabeth's lover's death. He laughed as he explained to me about that time I blacked out. When the guy tried to Rob me and how he was left to fuck the dude up for me. That he was the one to cause it and that when the guy grabbed me, he made the guy shoot me in the chest and when the bullet went through me and ended up in the guys arm… well it was time to eat. There was no reason to let all that good blood go to waste and after all, I ran off like a bitch. As he continued to tell the story I remember that George told us that there was no bite marks on the guy when he and Landis went to investigate. Like the smart ass that James was he pointed out why I would need to bite someone bleeding freely, and then proceeded to call me very stupid and how George really wasted his time on teaching me anything.

He could clearly see in my eyes, that I was getting very irate with his sarcastic comments, but he didn't seem to care. He commented that I need to be ashamed of myself. With all the things that were happening around us and the only thing I was worried about was pussy. Here George broke one of his first rules by interfering. At this point, James moved across the floor so quickly I barely was able to see him. Out of nowhere, he was in front of my face with such anger in his eyes. If I didn't know that he was straight before he was bitten then I would believe that this new life had open new levels of aggression in him. He reminded me of a cross between Landis and George.

He said, "What in the hell makes you so important that George would interfere and jeopardize all of our lives. You are a selfish ignorant, narcissistic piece of shit; that cares about nothing… Nothing! Here we are fighting for our lives and the only thing you seem to care about is this Elizabeth. Has it ever occurred to you, that with George's absence, we are left vulnerable? Whatever the reason was that George never intervened with our actions; might have had to do with our own safety. That once he intervened! It changed the arena of the game."

I told him, "Look. I don't know what you're talking about I came to find out what happened to my Elizabeth. Besides, Garrett already told us that George was not dead so whatever he is doing I think it's his own business."

We locked eyes for a moment and then he turned from me and said, "Everyone, Garrett was almost right. He is afraid that George's death was his fault. He is afraid of why George gave up so much just for him. Why, why, why! Xavier, the great victim, so lost in his own world and so oblivious to all the things that are happening around him! He has convinced himself that if he could save the girl, everything will turn out fine, but things are not fine.

His friends have abandoned him. George has abandoned all of us. For all we know George could even be dead, but those of you who have hope; believe that George is still alive on a magical isle. Look around you, Xavier and see the legacy that George has left behind; and all the victims of the master who searched for him. While you run after your one true love; the woman of your heart… but wait a minute! Did you not end up in David's bed? O' but then I guess he would be the man of your heart. Tell me, Xavier has Crystal now taking your heart since you have lost your true love? In case, he is not bright enough to figure this out, Should I tell him, everyone? That I, like George can read minds and his thoughts are telling us everything we need to know."

I tried to comment, but before I could say anything. He turned towards me and started charging towards me, forcing me to back up until I fell into a chair, that someone must place their because it was not there when we entered the room earlier. I knew he was playing a game with me; a very Dangerous game. I realize rather quickly that all of George's children were not aligned like him or my friends. James would kill me and not have a second thought. As much as I hated to admit it, this was one time I longed for George's companionship, his protection, his wisdom. If ever there was a time that I was in over my head, this was it. These guys did not care one way or the other, nor did they seek for me to learn a lesson, whatever Crystal was to obtained from Elizabeth, he decided to obtain it from me. I realize I was foolish to go with Crystal even after Garrett warned me to think before deciding to leave with her.

He was screaming at me and saying things that made no sense but perhaps they weren't supposed too. While he was doing that I felt him probe my mind for all of the details and all of the places I have been, things I have seen, the books I have read. He wanted to know everything about me and he left me no option to deny him. At one point, he seemed to levitate around the chair that I was sitting in and he continued to drain me of my knowledge screaming and screaming and screaming. There was no secret in my mind I bore that was safe. I was able to feel the link between him and the others. It was as if they were one great interlink. No sooner he pulled things from my mind. He dispersed it amongst the group. It became quite clear to me immediately, their group held no secret because their community kept their minds linked to one another, something me and my friends would have never done. To be honest it was something that not even George would have ever suggested we do. As he drained me of my knowledge I understood why Elizabeth would have never opened herself up to this group, they were too Dangerous… too reckless even more reckless than I. As James probed deeply throughout my mind causing me to relive all my memories, from the first moment I encountered Joseph. I was forced to regret a lot of things as I watched the interaction between George and myself, in my mind. I realize how much he cared about me and looked out for me. I begin to understand why everyone was enraged with me. I realize how afraid I was when Elizabeth's lover tried to kill me and how much at peace I felt when George reached out to me when I went to New England. I watched as the wolves attacked me and the energy that passed through me to destroy them... My emotions were betraying me as James dug deeper into my mind. For it was not my Elizabeth that heart was bleeding for but George. He meant more to me than I wanted to believe and he was protecting me over all the others. As James went through my mind and peeled away the false rage I held towards George I began to see everything differently. He went through every aspect of my mind not allowing me to hide anything from him and the others or even myself. In the end I was forced to see things I did not see before. Even at Brander's house some things were different when I was at the so call party. It was Elizabeth and Asikis that I followed out of the living room but in my mind

I came to understand that it was really Elizabeth and Crystal that I followed out of the living room. Even when I relocated them it was not my Elizabeth that I was hugging but it was Crystal. So, I now know that Crystal must have turned into Elizabeth after Asikis got rid of her.

Then James tried something I never thought was possible. When I locked eyes with Asikis in the library, he froze that thought and tried to enter her mind. Who would have ever thought that a telepath could do something like that, but as he used my eyes to enter her thoughts something happen Asikis changed and we were no longer in Brander's home but was somewhere else. Even Asikis changed and she had her back to us. She turned towards us as if she knew we were there and smiled. Her fangs were twice as long as any of our and she just slowly shook her head as to tell us big mistake, then her eyes lit up like lights bulbs and I felt all of their memories past through me like water being sucked through a funnel. She was not only reading James thoughts but the thoughts of everyone in the building. She feed on our memories as if she was a giant computer reading the data of a hundred lesser models. She was going through our mind like it was child's play. Her grip on my mind was so great that I dug my nails into the arms of the wooden chair I was sitting in as if I too was going to be sucked into my own head. I could feel my body begin to shake and as the images flooded my head. So many images of places and things, that I could not make complete sense out of most of them. I got to see so many images of Garrett and even more of George that I thought I might lose my mind at one point; I was not even sure who I really was. I finally got to understand what George felt like when he locked minds with Elizabeth. How it was so easy to lose your own identity when you're seeing and feeling the thoughts of someone else. I came to realize that James loved George more than I ever could and so did the others that were there. I felt that our group were spoiled brats and took George's love for granted. I began to dislike my friends just like James did. I got to understand their hatred towards us. We were the reason George showed his powers and opened all of us up to this new life and we had no remorse for what happened to him. What he sacrificed to ensure that the last of his children were safe. I felt the abandonment that James and the others share because of George's love for us. Asikis took control over parts of my mind that I might never have been able to access. Even I wasn't aware of the level of her abilities, as I sat there in the chair, helplessly struggling to maintain focus and control of my body. As James and the others fell to their knees gasping for air and their sanity, then it was over. The images stop and she was gone. My heart was beating as if I ran a marathon. I saw that James and the others were in no better condition than those that were human. The few humans that was amongst us simply passed out.

I tried to gather myself since it was clear to me that Crystal and her friends were not going to aid me and if James pieced together that I believed that Elizabeth was in the painting at Brander's library, and then I had placed her in danger as well as myself. James hatred towards me and my friend seemed to be so great that destroying me to get to her would not be a problem for these guys. While they tried to gather themselves I made my way to the entrance that we used earlier when I got there. I really believed that I was going to get away but out of nowhere I felt some one jump on my back and bit me in the neck. He wrapped his legs around my waist and gripped the door way to pull me back inside. As we fell backwards he released my waist and I landed on the ground alone. Then the rest of them attacked, I tried to fight them off but they were not going to allow me to leave. It was clear that this was going to be my burial grounds. They bit into me at ever opening they could find. They feed as if I was their last supper. As the blood escaped my body I heard him, George! Go to sleep my Xavier everything will be fine. Just close your eyes my young little angel and wait for my return. I shall never allow any to destroy you. Go to sleep my baby boy and dream the dream that has always made you feel peace. So, I did just that and soon I was in Rittenhouse square and watching the people walking around me. The business men were rushing off into the distance and the bums where talking to each other as the young people on skate boarders were skating around me. Girls were walking past me in their jeans and short shirts. Then I saw him, he walked out of the crowd and walked over to me. He didn't speak; he just pressed his lips to mine and kissed me. It was so passionate and yet it was something different. It turned from a French kiss into him sucking the air from my body and then I began to feel the blood in my body began to retract into my heart. I felt my body shake as if others were trying to get more blood from a body that held nothing more to give them. Then he released his embrace and smiled at me. A smile that told me I was safe and he was with me. He started to walk away but I ran after him. He never stop looking back at me as I walked towards him then he was gone. The last thing I felt was my heart close its veins and lock what blood I held within it. I knew this was to be my new fate until the day that he returned to free me

I slept for many years it seemed and the world has changed around me. I dreamt so many dreams; Even as I laid there a part of me knew that time had forgotten me. I feared that even my friends may have forgotten of my existence. Then, just as I was about to give up all hope fate smiled upon me. I felt the liquid that was more precious than gold released itself from my heart, as it ran its course working its way through my veins restoring my old decrepit body with life. Removing the decay that was cursed upon my body by father Time and his mate Mother Nature. As I slowly felt my body returning to its former glory, my mind become aware of my surroundings. My senses no longer betrayed me as I took my first breath and inhaled the scent of the decay box that was meant to be my prison. The box, time showed no favor too as it fell apart around me. Then my eyes finally gather the will they needed to open and my hands gather the strength they needed to move. Though I was lost and confused about my whereabouts. I was amazed to find that I was alive once again. It took me some time to gather myself, but I stood and looked around my tomb. As my eyes adjusted to the darkness that embraced me, I came to realize what awoke me. The dozen or so dried out rats arranged around my tomb told me my story. For as they must have fed upon me for years, unaware that their death would bare me life once again. I was weak, but yet I was alive. I was unsure where I was or of how much time that had actually passed. It did not take me long to realize I was in somebody's basement as I walked towards the stairs of my prison. I tried to heighten my senses to sense who else was in this home, but I heard nothing. Nor did I smell anything I felt it would be wise for me to take the stairs slowly and that is what I did. As I exited the basement and looked around the room I had just entered, a peace came over me. Through the room was old I was able to identify exactly where I was. I was inside Elizabeth's home. I was a little confused as of how my body got there but I knew there was no way that my Elizabeth could have possibly saved me because I was aware of her fate.

Then I thought perhaps it was George who returned and rescued me. As I walked throughout her home the memories of how beautiful her house was keep entering my mind. As I walked throughout the house I looked over the furniture that was covered with white sheets. I thought that it was odd that someone went through so much trouble to her furniture. Then I entered the living room and was greeted by my Elizabeth's painting. It was hung over her mantel and I felt that stranger energy coming from it. I wanted to touch it but remembered what happens to people that touch these type of painting. I stood there for a minute as fear took my heart. I just couldn't understand how I or it got there. The fact that I knew no one could touch the painting but yet it stood in front of me. Who know I was here and why did they cover the furniture. As if they were closing the house up until they returned. I walked upstairs and admired the rest of the house until I got to her bedroom and discovered that everything was still the same. As if no one has been inside of it for years. I decided to change my rags for what I believe were Brander's clothes that were hanging in one of her closets. As I changed my clothes I could not help but look at my ankle bracelet and see how new it looked. It still looked as good as it did when it first bonded with me. I finished dressing and left the house to find my friends. I decided that Landis's apartment would be my first stop. Since everyone hung out there and I knew that I had a better chance of finding them there if they were still in town or for that matter even alive. I didn't forget how powerful James was and I knew that he hated them just as much as he hated me. What I wasn't sure of was if George would be able to save them too.

As I walked up Second Street and over towards market I was amazed at how the city seemed to have changed. Guys walking around with their pants hanging off their hips and not too many women were wearing dresses. I guess I sleep through the social change of my era. Even the buses seemed different with pictures wrapped completely around them as they road up and down the street. I made my way to the street called Strawberry and decided it would be wiser to go to an area that I was more for familiar with, so I walked through the small alley. I was amazed how well the buildings were maintained and even how clean the parking lots were. I came out onto Chestnut Street near Pete's Pizza and laughed to myself. It was as if time was playing a game with me, because even though most of the businesses where the same as I remembered there were still a few things that changed. I watched as people feed money into the green boxes that seemed to have replaced parking meters. I could not help but sit across the street from the best Western Hotel and take in all the sites of the buildings. For some reason I was quite fascinated with how the new and the old merge so well together. People seem to be so oblivious of how so many eras of this city seemed to exist in such a small scope of space. After about a half of an hour of watching the people I decided to venture forth to Landis's apartment. Once I put my mind to it. I was at his apartment in fifteen minutes or so, I stood outside his apartment for some time, in hopes that I would see him, but to no avail. It seems that as I slept the city rebuilt itself up around his apartment building. I still was unsure how many years I slept and a part of me feared to know the answer. I sat inside a Star bucks for several minutes, mustering the strength to ring his doorbell. When I finally gathered the nerve to do it I was shocked to find out that he no longer lived there. A young white woman answered the door; I only could assume she was a college student. She informed me that I made a mistake and that she has lived in that apartment since she started school, so my friend must have moved over three years ago. I gave her my apologies and informed her that it was quite some time since I have been in the United States. A story she seemed to accept very easily. Then she gave me an idea that perhaps I should try the University for that was where we all met and perhaps they would have a lead to where he now was residing. I knew she was right but I wanted to first check and see what became of our home on Carpenter Street. So I ran down walnut to 11th street and headed to what once was home. The neighborhood had changed a lot but I know my home or should I say what was my home. For not only did Marco and Drew move on, it became clear that it was time I did as well. Then I thought of Vinnie who always hung around Rittenhouse square. I believed if anyone was still here then it had to be him. For he would never abandon the city he so loved. I retraced my footsteps and went to Rittenhouse square. I hung there for a while until I accepted that either they were avoiding me or they were dead. I was so desperate that I ran down Locust Street until I hit 15th and turn south to head over to the university's Arco Park in hopes that there would be someone there that I would recognize. Then they would be able to assist me in locating my friends. I was confident that there would be a familiar face that knew the where about of perhaps one of the guys if not all of them. I was really hoping that maybe one of the guards even knew of Garrett's location. As I reached the corner of 15th and spruce my heart felt as if it sank to the sole of my feet. I cannot describe to you the shock I felt when I reached that corner and I notice that Arco Park was no more. The place where we spent countless hours conjugating was no more and standing in its place now was the Kimmel Center. The building was so magnificent even I had to stop and stare at its beauty, studying its simple lines of erotic curves over the glass windows to the intense way how it hugged the entrances on 15th St. side of the building. Then as I walked around the corner to its main entrance I was blown away with how massive it looked inside. As much as I hated the idea that Arco Park was gone, I had to admit this building was cool as hell. I walked to the corner of Broad and Pine to sit on the steps of my alma mater, so I could figure out what to do next. Because it was clear to me that there wasn't anyone left around that I would know or would know the ones I seek.

As I sat there and took in the changes that had unfolded as I slept. From the once 309 building that held our dance school too 313 that held our drama department. One was now vacated and the other was now a garden to structures that I could only assume was from the Industrial design department. A part of me wanted to return home and see if Drew and Marco was still there but I knew that was just as crazy as returning to Landis's old apartment. Then I thought perhaps they took refuge in the home they had in south Philadelphia. As I stood to leave I heard a voice as I turned around and there stood Kenny one of Garrett's old security partners. I was a little surprised to see he remembered me because even he commented that it has been over twenty years. We exchanged our love, with what's up and I proceeded to ask him about Garrett's whereabouts. Rubbing the top of his nose, a habit that Kenny seemed to always have before speaking and twenty years did not break. He informed me that he had not seen Garrett since George's funeral. It seemed. His family buried him even though his body was never found. They thought it was the best thing to do. He believed that in some way it gave them closure. He pointed out that everyone was there and that it was a beautiful ceremony, but after that he did not really get to see anybody. He assumed that most of them moved away or got jobs in another part of town. I just laughed to myself at the thought that he had no clue. After talking with him for awhile I decided that it would probably be best for me to head over to their house in southwest Philly.

What I discovered when I got there was a little surprising because not only was they gone, but apparently a family had moved in. When I knocked on the door, I was greeted by a fairly young lady and from our conversation. She informed me that she brought the home over ten years ago. At this point, I was totally lost. Fear stopped me from seeking out my family, no idea where my friends were located and uncertain how to free my Elizabeth from that accursed painting hanging in her living room. I realize that I was running out of options, so I decided to seek out my David and if anyone knew where they; then it would have to be my David. As much as I hated to admit it, a part of me desired to touch his smooth skin and to smell the beautiful aroma that his body released when he stood near me. He was probably the only man that ever smelled more intoxicating that any woman I ever met. It seemed the more I thought of David, the faster I move until in a matter of minutes I stood in Rittenhouse square right in front of his condo. As I looked around the Street, I had to laugh because so much changed throughout the city and yet this area still looked the same. For once I took comfort in the familiar surroundings as I entered David's condo lobby. The Door man was different from the one I remembered so I informed him who I was looking for and what floor he was located on. After laughing at me for some time he informed me that one, David have not been home for some time so he couldn't have been expecting me and two he pointed out the fact that all expected guest was on his list. As annoyed as I was with that jackass's behavior I knew he was right. I knew I had to do something then I thought about George's brother. I knew if anyone would know how to find them then it would be him. After all Garrett was his cousin and they would have kept in touch.

It was getting late and I was becoming tired so I decided to return to Elizabeth's home for the rest of the night. Once I got there I was greeted by Gregory, he was one of the twelve that protected David. He informed me that it was him that Kept the house up until the day I was to awake. He told me that my running about the city was getting a lot of attention. So much attention that it got back to him. He pointed out that he was never informed that I could walk in the day and if he had he would have made a point of having someone here to greet me when I awoke.

I asked him, "Why did David have you watch over me as I slept?"

He smiled and responded, "My name is pronounced Gregorius, which was the Greek name ρηγοριος."

I looked at him and said, "Dude! What the hell does that mean?"

He walked into the house while responding, "The watchful or the alert. Even thou I never really got to know you I always thought you were an ok type of guy. So, when Garrett agreed to give your body to David after they tried to awake you for several months. I stepped in and asked to be your protector until you awoke. In truth I didn't think you were going to wake any time soon, so I continued with my every day routines as if you where dead for good. Hell, even your friend's stop coming by after a year or so. They believed you were dead but out of respect for George they did not bury you. They felt that if you where to be buried then it was only fitting that George pick where."

"So what happened to my friends? And why is Elizabeth's painting here? "

"First of all… The painting was sent to David after the Cleaners straighten out your little mess at Brander's home and he felt it was best to keep it here out of harm's way. I tried to cover it up just like the furniture but it kept causing the Sheet to decay over time. Then your friends decided it was time to move on with their lives so no to draw attention to this house. Frankly I agreed with them. It wasn't like you were going anywhere. Besides they never would tell David what really happened to you and David did not trust them to protect your body as you slept. He did not believe you were dead and none of the witches he spoke too could tell him if you were under a spell."

"So my friends have left the city or are they making a point to avoid me?"

"That's a question I can't answer. I never really understood your friendship, but is there a reason for them to avoid you?"

His question was one that I did not want to answer so I just walked pass him and started pulling the covers off the furniture. He said nothing else but decided to start helping me restore the house into a home. We worked in silence for more than an hour before he asked did I try to reach them mentally. I wanted to say of course but the truth was I didn't. The though never entered my mind. I thought that I would be able to sense them if they were near but I couldn't sense any of them. I knew that I had traveled enough around the city area that if they were near then they would have sensed me. I guess Gregory felt bad for me because he sat at the dining room table across from me and reminded me that it has been over twenty years. That it may feel like I went to sleep just yesterday but the truth was I been asleep for over twenty years. So naturally, my powers would reflect that… He made a joke about how one of the twelve slept for five years and when he awoke his senses were not as sharp as the others. He had to practice day and night to hone his skills again, of course all the guys helped him but the fact remained that when he slept he became so relax with his surroundings that it Allow him to lose that mental edge that kept his skills sharp. We helped him to hone his skills but it was funny to see how bad he had gotten.

He even offered… if I wished… to aid me in sharpening my skills. He walked over to a backpack that he had with him when he came into the house and pulled out a bag of blood. He made a joked about how they warned him that I didn't drink from the living so he thought it would be wise to bring me some plasma. I told them that they had it easy. At less they could eat like regular people and blend into society. He looked at me for some time and then commented that the grass always look better from the other side. That nothing could be perfect in an imperfect world. As much as I wanted to rip into the bag the very moment he gave it to me I felt uncomfortable eating in front of him. He must have been able to see how hungry I was because he smiled and told me to run hot water over it for a bit and it will be as good as mother's milk. He told me the address where his shop was located at and that if I need anything to come by so he would take care of it.

With that he left he put his back pack on and headed towards the front door. I walked him to the front to see him out and then I ran to the kitchen to run hot water over the bag of blood. When I bit into it tasted like sweet love. I was so hungry that I drank it dry. I drank my full and decided to go and take a shower and release the years for dirt from my tired body. The lather was thick and quickly removed more dirt from my hair than was appeared to be there. I quickly came to realize what he meant about my skills slipping because as I soaped up my body and my fingers ran over my body a familiar feeling came over me. My body started to betray me and I felt things I had not felt in a long time. As my fingers ran over my body so slowly my male member rose and without a thought released its treasure all over the shower wall. I fell to the floor of the tub and gathered my strength. I felt like a child again forgetting how to control things as simple as my body. As I rested on the tub floor I remembered the first time I was in this position. The way my legs gave out on me and me touching myself was like making love. The way I had to pull myself out the tub by holding onto the toilet. As I sat there on bended knees I was force to accept that maybe Greg was right and I had to retrain my body to gain control over my senses. It struck me funny how I watch old vampire movies and they would awake as fresh and as powerful as they were before they went to sleep. Now, I realized how unreal that is. I felt like a child learning to walk again but what was worst was that my friends were not there to aid me.

That night I slept like a baby and didn't rise until pass noon. I know I had to go visit George's brother if he was still there because that was my only lead to finding the others. I quickly went into the shower; I focus my senses to hear everything going on around the house. As the water was running over my body, I was able to block out the sound the water made as it hit my flesh and the floor of the tub. I was hearing a faint sound of cars as they drove pass, People talking as they walked in the street and even some birds scratching at the roof tops. I tried to calm myself by resting my hands on the shower wall. I was able to expand my hearing a little wider. As I begin to take in the sounds of some form of construction work being done, I was able to hear a sound I could not hone in on. It's exact location or how near the work being done was. Nevertheless, I was impressed with myself.

I continue to concentrate until the water started to feel like pins against my skin, so I lathered up my body. Working the soap over my chest and into my hair, I felt like an animal being bathed. The lather was thick and quickly removed more dirt from my hair. It was more dirt than I even realize was there. One would have believed I never bathed before or I was an animal that ran through pure mud. Once I was finished, I returned to Elizabeth's bedroom. I put on the clothes that I had on the night previous. I walked over to her dresser and decided to do something different. I combed my hair out and took a black hair wrap off her dresser. I pushed my hair back and put it on. In no time I ran down the steps and was out the front door. As I walked up the street I came to realize that getting to his home was not difficult, but I did realize that it was over twenty years and therefore George's brother may have moved on. One thing I came to understand very quickly was that most super natural beings do not like to state put in one area for too long. So for him not to be there would not surprise me but I had to try something.

I felt ambiguous as I walked down the streets of North Philly. As I walked through the streets I begin to think about what Greg told me and decide to test the limits of my abilities. I began to do some parkour on the streets that were vacant. I ran as fast as I could on the streets that had some people on them and others I simply took to the roofs. Off the roofs into trees from the trees to the payments back into the alley's back onto the roofs of trucks I made a game out of it, but I covered a lot of ground. The fun part of it all was. No one saw me and if they did; they did not act as if so. I move so quickly that I really lost track of time, but I ended up in nice town. I was lucky to see that the area did not change much. The large church still remains on the corner and the Checkers restaurant still stood there. As I walked down Butler Street I realize a lot of people were staring at me, but I knew it was in my best interest not to acknowledge their attention. I felt my only chance was to continue to walk straight until I reached Camac Street. When I reached my destination I came to realize that it was a dead end because in the window of his home was a for rent sign. I decided to sit on the curve and gather my thoughts with my hands pressed firmly against my face. I sat there for only a few seconds before I began to hear a woman's voice telling me to take my drug using ass somewhere else or she was going to call the police. Now I realize that times have changed, but there was no mistake that she could clearly see, I was not a drug addict and farther more I never feared the police when I was alive. So such a threat held no power over me. I looked into her eyes and without trying I was in her mind. Her thoughts were so clear and I was able to pull the facts from her like one would from reading a book. I came to realize that she was not well and that not only he no longer lived around there but he had made her one of his tenants. A fact I decided to use to my advantage. I planted the though in my mind to call him and tell him I was here looking for him and that I were I was staying. She stopped talking in mid sentence and walked into the house so I decided that it worked and I left.

I returned to Elizabeth's home and waited for Greg to show up. I must have waited for about two hours when there was a knock on the door. I was sure it was Greg so I went to let him in but to my surprise he was not alone. Keith was with him so I invited them both inside and led them to the living room. Before I could ask how they know each other Greg informed me that they met on the front steps. Thou they were not acquaintances' they know of each other. Keith even make a point to compliment the good work Greg did in keeping the city clear of reckless immortals and Greg did the same to him for great level of control his family had over the witches problem. Now, the fact that Greg used the word problem did stand out to me but I felt that was a conversation best left for another time. As they talked of a bit Keith pointed out the painting of Elizabeth and laughed.

He stated that the painting reminded him of the one called The Soul King. I timidly asked if he could release her but he looked at me and said, "Sadly no. The witch that cased this spell was far more powerful that me and from the looks of it. They probably were the one that created the ordinal spell. Magic this complex simple no longer exist. This is very old Magic.

I responded, "Black Magic!"

He looked at me for a second then turned his head back to the painting. He raised hand to the painting as if he was going to touch but didn't and said "Now you're sounding like George… Magic is neither Dark nor Light. What defines it is the caster. Whoever did this was very old and powerful. Hell, far more powerful than even I would like to imagine. Look at the way the paint weaves though the canvas and create a dominion of time and space. No average witch spell created this. I can safely say not even a full convent could pull magic like this off. So if this is what you wanted with me then forget it. Only the one that imprisoned her can free her… My advice to you would be to leave it alone. They are not one to mess with."

As disappointed as I was to hear that I informed him that wasn't the reason I was looking for him. I wanted him to cast a location spell and in exchange I would tell him about George. He looked at me for some time and then told me, "NO." For some reason he fused to get involved with me and my friends problems. Not even for information about George. He made it quite clear that George broke the rules by teaching us about our natures and that many in his family believed that George did more than that…. So it was in everyone's best interest to let sleeping dogs lay. I couldn't understand exactly what he was talking about. I guess it had a lot to do with the fact that I was asleep for over twenty years, but I knew I needed his help if I was going to locate my friends. I decided to tell him about my last night before I was cased into my sleep and how George saved me. He didn't seem surprised at what I was saying nor the fact that George was still alive. I told him my story and even about George's other children.

He just stood there admiring Elizabeth's painting then after some time turned to me and He said, "Look, Xavier. George played a Dangerous game by including you guys into a life that you should have never realized existed. Besides I would think one of George's children would find a more tactful way to get things done that they desire."

With that he turned to Greg and said his goodbyes. As he exited the living room and turned towards the front door. I tried to stop him but Greg grabbed me by my arm and told me it would be best to let him go. I looked at him then pulled away and ran after Keith but he was gone. He didn't use the front door because it was still closed. I looked back at Greg and he told me not to worry because everything will work itself out in time. An answer that never worked for me, so I asked him to excuse me for not wanting to practice my skills that night and just wanted to be alone. He seemed to understand but the truth was that I was one of George's children and there for I would find a way to find my friends with or without any of their help. After he left me I wondered the city streets with no real direction and ended up in my favorite place, out of all places. In fact I was sitting in Rittenhouse Square when I read your mind and came to realize that you were my answer. A skilled writer! Who could share my story to the world and not taint it as some kind of dark endless nightmare. The kind of nightmares that many people would read with the hope that our deaths were its ending. So here we are.